THE CRYING HEART TATTOO

Also by David Martin

TETHERED

THE CRYING HEART TATTOO

A NOVEL BY

DAVID MARTIN

Holt, Rinehart and Winston
New York

Copyright © 1982 by David Lozell Martin
All rights reserved, including the right to reproduce this
book or portions thereof in any form.
Published by Holt, Rinehart and Winston,
383 Madison Avenue, New York, New York 10017.
Published simultaneously in Canada by Holt, Rinehart and
Winston of Canada, Limited.

Library of Congress Cataloging in Publication Data
Martin, David Lozell, 1946-
The crying heart tattoo.
I. Title.
PS3563.A72329C7   813'.54   81-6956
ISBN 0-03-060488-5   AACR2

First Edition

Designer: Joy Chu
Illustrations by Rita Grasso

Printed in the United States of America
10 9 8 7 6 5 4 3 2 1

"You Made Me Love You (I Didn't Want To Do It)." Words
by Joe McCarthy, music by James V. Monaco. © 1913
Broadway Music Corp. © Renewed 1941 Edwin H. Morris &
Company, a Division of MPL Communications, Inc., and
Broadway Music Corp. International copyright secured. All
rights reserved. Used by Permission.

FOR MATT
AND JOSH
AND G.

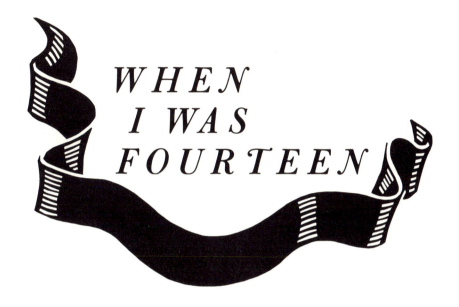

WHEN
I WAS
FOURTEEN

*W*hen I was fourteen, I began what turned out to be a lifelong love affair with Felicity Annabel Arlington Jones. For a year before I met her, she was only a name to me—that strange and florid signature written across the entire width of the page, at the bottom of letters she sent from New York City to my father. Then she moved to the prairie, into a little square house that was half a mile down a flat, straight road from where I lived. She was thirty-four when our affair began, an affair that survived four marriages (three of 'em mine) and thirty-six years. My sister called from Illinois yesterday morning at seven to tell me it was over. I was sitting at the kitchen table, drinking grapefruit juice and looking out the window. The sky promised snow.

"Sonny?"

"Yes. Sis? Is that you, Sis? This is a terrible connection; sounds like you're a thousand miles away."

"I'll get the operator and call right back."

When I picked up the telephone the second time, Sis said, "But I *am* a thousand miles away, Sonny."

"I know. It's just a joke."

"I don't get it."

"Never mind."

I now live in New York City, where Felicity once lived. Whenever I was back in Illinois and visited her, I'd whisper in her ear: "When I'm with you, darling, my other life seems a thousand miles away." And, of course, it was. She'd laugh—laugh every time I said it to her. But I didn't tell any of this to my sister, didn't try to explain to her that the joke was as important, or unimportant, to Felicity and me as is a single brushstroke important, or unimportant, to a painting that contains ten thousand of them.

"I have some bad news," Sis said.

I knew that. I'd received these notifications from her before: our father's death, our mother's death. I knew who it was this time. "Felicity's dead."

"How'd you know?" She seemed disappointed.

"Psychic."

"Between you two, I'd believe it."

The news of Felicity's death gave me a jolt of excitement, but it didn't make me feel like crying. My voice was even: "When?"

"An hour or so ago, I guess. The nurse who was staying with her just called me. She waited until the doctor got over there and made it official."

"So now it's official?" I asked sarcastically.

"What?"

"Nothing. Had she been sick again?"

"Well, yes. Don't you two talk to each other?"

I shook my head.

"Sonny?"

"Uh, no—we don't."

"Well, for the last few months she's been bad off. And then a couple weeks ago she had to hire a nurse to stay with her. But I was with her last night. At her deathbed."

Deathbed? People still use that word? "Why were you there?"

"You can hardly refuse a deathbed request."

I realized then that Sis was going to play with the news, perhaps to get back at me for having guessed the headline. "What do you mean?"

"I mean she called last night and asked me to come over to her house."

"Really?"

"Yes. And do you know what she said while I was standing there by her bed?"

"I haven't the slightest idea."

"She took my hand and said, 'This, Honey, is what they call in the trade: *her last words.*' At first, I didn't know what she was

4

getting at. You know. I was trying to be polite, reverent and all that, but Felicity seemed to think it was all a big joke."

I laughed.

"What?"

"Nothing. Did she do it, tell you her last words?"

"Yes."

"Well? What were they?" My sister started to say something, but I interrupted her. "Wait a second. If she didn't die until this morning, how could she have told you her last words last night? I mean, she might have said something to the nurse after you left. What she told you weren't *literally* her last words."

"Yes they were. When I talked to the nurse this morning, she said that Felicity didn't say another word after I left her house last night."

I laughed again. "That's marvelous. The way she worked it out like that. Always a stickler for authenticity. I mean, if she wanted to plan out her last words, then by God, they were going to be her *last words*. That's great. That's . . ." Suddenly distracted, I forgot what I was going to say next.

"Sonny?" Sis's voice had a worried edge. "Sonny? Are you okay, Sonny?"

"Yeah. Yeah. I was just thinking how careful you have to be, or should be. Usually, you have no control over what'll be your last words. If you die in your sleep or have a heart attack on the street—"

"Have you been having trouble?"

"What? With my heart? Naw."

"You know what the doctor always said. When did you have your last checkup?"

"Forget that. I'm trying to tell you something important here. Let's say some guy gets up in the middle of the night and his wife asks if everything's okay and he says, 'I gotta take a leak.' Then he comes back to bed and dies in his sleep. His last words would be: 'I gotta take a leak.' See what I mean?"

"No."

"Come on, Sis. Think about it. We leave it up to chance, something as important as dying words. People used to write last words on tombstones, as epitaphs. 'I gotta take a leak.' How'd you like something like that chiseled in granite over your grave?"

"Have you been drinking?"

"It's seven o'clock in the morning, for chrissake." But what an excellent idea. Not by accident does my telephone cord reach to the liquor cabinet. As I continued talking with my sister, I grabbed a bottle of tequila and poured some in the grapefruit juice I'd been drinking. Not bad, not bad at all. "I have to think something out," I told her. "I was home alone last night, didn't get any calls or anything. Watched the tube awhile. Read."

"What're you doing?"

"Trying to figure out what my last words would've been if I had died in my sleep last night."

"Morbid."

"I guess the last thing I said to anybody was when I told my secretary good-night at the office. I said . . . uh . . . let's see. I said, 'Good night, Love.' Hey, that's not bad, huh? That's not bad for a man's last words. 'Good night, Love.' "

"*Love?* Is she going to be number four?"

"No. Goodness, no. I just use a lot of endearments." A pause. Then I shouted: "Wait, wait! I spoke to the guy at the parking lot. He was talking about the weather."

"Sonny."

"And I said, I said, 'It'll snow before morning.' That's not bad either, you know? Kind of mysterious, but it'd look good on a tombstone. 'It'll snow before morning.' That'd spook people, wouldn't it? Somebody walking through the cemetery and see that, wondering what the hell it means."

"Sonny, do you want to hear about Felicity, or are you going to keep joking around all morning?"

"Sorry, Sis."

"Okay. Like I was saying, she was holding my hand. She was having trouble breathing, and she had to speak in a whisper. All those cigarettes she smoked. Had one in her mouth every time—"

"Wait! I'm sorry, Sis, but I just remembered something. I went out, late, to get a pack of cigarettes and . . . and this couple stopped to ask directions. They wanted . . . uh . . . they wanted to know where the nearest drugstore was, and I said, I said . . . oh, no!" I was laughing. "I told 'em, 'Four blocks straight up this street. You can't miss it.' Can you believe that? Sis?"

"Yes," she said icily.

"If I had died in my sleep last night, my last words would've been: 'Four blocks straight up this street. You can't miss it.' Wow. See what I mean? It takes someone like Felicity to control her last words. Me, I would've had people sitting around at my wake and telling each other: 'Well, from what I hear, his last words were, "Four blocks straight up this street. You can't miss it." Don't have the slightest idea what he was getting at.' Wouldn't that be a crock? Lord, when you think of the opportunities you let slip by. Damn! *Sis?*"

"Well, Sonny, if it had happened the way you just explained it, no one would've known that those were your last words anyway."

I was angry with her refusal to play along with me, to play Felicity for me. "Yeah, well that's not the point. The point is that something as important as your last words shouldn't be left to chance. Felicity had the right idea."

"And do you want to hear what her last words were or not?"

"Of course I do."

"All right then. She held my hand, looked me right in the eye, and said—"

But I *wasn't* ready to hear it yet. "Why do people always say, 'You can't miss it'?"

"Sonny!"

"Okay, okay. This is the last interruption, I swear it. But have you ever wondered why people always say, 'You can't miss it'? I mean, you can give some guy the most convoluted directions in the world and you know, you absolutely know, that the poor slob doesn't have a prayer of finding the place and *still* you'll say to him, 'You can't miss it.' Your mind gets so damn cluttered with clichés, with things that just come out automatically. I was in a meeting the other day, and this guy, this real asshole, he started in on me. Not only blasting the way I was handling one of our new accounts but making personal attacks on me. When he got done, everybody kind of looked at me. And you know what I said? I drew myself up and said, 'I'll not dignify that with a response.' Do you believe it? Can you imagine a more pompous, idiotic thing to say? I mean, I should have walked over and punched him right in the mouth. The asshole. Instead, I come out with, 'I'll not dignify that with a response.' Jesus Christ! When it gets right down to it, I mean, when push comes to shove, my response is some . . . *Did you hear what I just said?* Did you . . ."

I suddenly sobbed. It came without warning, and although I performed a short fit of coughing to cover the sob, Sis was not fooled. When she next spoke, she did so softly.

"Felicity's last words were: 'Your brother broke my heart.' "

I didn't try to speak, didn't dare to.

"And then you know what she did?"

Yeah. And then she laughed like a fool. But I didn't tell this to my sister; I didn't want to spoil any more of her surprises.

"Sonny? After she said that, she laughed."

I still didn't speak.

"She *laughed*. Like it was all a joke or something. Can you believe that?"

Of course. The last time I saw Felicity—five years ago—I did indeed break her heart, one she'd made out of glass. And I suppose that over the years, I'd broken the other heart, too. That's what's so wonderful about Felicity's last words: They are true, literally and figuratively *true*.

· · ·

When I was fourteen and found out that Felicity was going to be a neighbor of ours, I waited for her as I had waited for the circus to come to town the previous summer. Her letters to my father were so full of advance publicity on such a variety of oddities and eccentricities that I half expected to see her arrive on the back of an elephant, as had Rhonda The Magnificent.

8

My father, who owned a real-estate and insurance business, first heard about Felicity from a friend of his who worked at a nearby veterans' hospital. Felicity's husband, a naval officer who'd grown up in southern Illinois, recently had been transferred to the hospital's psychiatric unit, and Felicity wanted to move out from New York to be near him. She was looking for a house to buy. Dad sent her a list of properties then on the market.

In the first letter she wrote directly to my father, Felicity said she wasn't interested in seeing listings but would describe the kind of house she wanted and then leave it up to him to notify her if such a place ever came up for sale. In the letters that followed, she added flowery detail to what she called "my little house on the prairie": a small, neat place with few if any trees on the property, situated on a flat piece of land, and possessing an unobstructed panorama. My father answered each letter, saying that no such house was on the market but that he'd keep looking.

Felicity's subsequent letters became more personal. She asked my father to describe himself, to tell her about his family. "I have in mind an image of you," she wrote, "and can only hope that you meet my expectations." She told about herself, how she'd grown up in Louisiana and had lived in San Francisco while her husband was off to war and then had moved to New York City but was coming to Illinois because she thought it was best for her husband to recuperate "in the land that nurtured him as a boy." She enclosed poems she'd written.

The letters upset Mom, especially when she read things like: "You're a darling for going to all this trouble for me." My father's responses continued to be strictly businesslike; he showed the carbons to Mom. Sis and I, meanwhile, kept current on the correspondence by looking up the file whenever we were alone in Dad's office.

It was shortly after Felicity's letters began that the circus came to town. I was disappointed in its raggedness, in how the muzzled bears and big cats were nowhere near as ferocious as the posters that preceded them. All the circus animals seemed old;

they walked gingerly, as if on tender feet; they went through their routines with bored obedience.

The ringmaster was not young and handsome, and he did not have a full head of blue-black hair. Perhaps the ringmaster in the poster had gone off to war, and maybe it was his father, old and fat and bald, who took his place. Even from the stands, I could see that his red cutaway was frayed.

I also noticed that the performers played multiple roles: The tightrope artist was the lion tamer, and after the tumblers finished tumbling, they covered their tights with overalls and cleaned up behind the thick-backed horses.

The big top was patched.

But Rhonda The Magnificent was more, so much more, than her poster could possibly show. She entered on an elephant, *standing* on the elephant's back and balancing herself with one hand casually holding a rhinestoned scepter that somehow was attached to the elephant's neck. Rhonda was wrapped, from her neck down, in a huge embroidered cape that covered the sides of the elephant and went off its back to drag imperiously on the ground behind. As she approached the center ring, Rhonda loosed a knotted ribbon at her neck, and the cape dropped away, down the elephant's back and then to the floor. She rode as a queen would, as a warrior would. In the middle of the darkened big top, held by three spotlights, Rhonda extended one foot. A rope was lowered to her; she put that slippered foot in a loop and ascended to her trapeze, pulled up and away by unseen roustabouts who perhaps themselves recently had been in the spotlight facing great heights—or lions and tigers and bears.

Reading Felicity's strange letters and trying to picture what she might look like, I used—for purposes of daydreams—the image of Rhonda The Magnificent. And now when I try to recall Rhonda's entrance, it is Felicity who rides the elephant's back.

In the spring of 1944, one of our neighbors died. He was a widower who owned the farm that lay between our house and town, and his property included two houses: the main farmhouse and a much smaller place on an acre of land at the edge of a large, flat field. Dad immediately bought the small house and wrote to Felicity about it.

Mom was angry. "That crazy woman will probably never show up and then you'll be stuck with that place."

Dad insisted he had just pulled off a shrewd deal and, at the time, I was rooting for him. But after I fell in love with Felicity, I tended to agree with my mother: Dad was acting like a damn fool, providing Felicity with much more customer service than was called for.

Felicity wrote that the house seemed perfect and that Dad should have the papers ready, because she was willing to buy the property the very day she arrived in town. "Now there's a woman who knows her own mind," Pop declared.

"I bet she's dying of a broken heart because of her husband being in the insane asylum," my sister, who was sixteen at the time, speculated. "I can't wait to meet her."

"I think the whole thing is pathetic," my mother said. "We'd better just keep to ourselves." Which is exactly what she told me when the circus came to town.

On the day of Felicity's arrival, I went directly from school to Dad's office and spread out my books and papers on a table in the back room. "Doing homework before supper, huh, Sport?" he asked.

I mumbled something about a big test.

"Catch you later," he said. "I got to go to the train station."

I nodded, not looking up from my books and pretending I'd forgotten who was arriving that day. Dad was wearing his best suit.

Two hours later, I was filling in all the o's on the table of contents of my history book. Where were Dad and Felicity? Even if they'd gone directly to the house, they should've been back by now.

From the back room, I couldn't see into the main part of the office, but I heard them laughing even before they opened the door. I sat up and listened closely, becoming embarrassed at the way the two of them were carrying on—like a couple of gay old friends. *And they had just met.* The woman seemed enchanted by my father's usual salesman patter, and each time I heard her masculinely robust laughter, I adjusted my mental image of her. Maybe she was like those gum-cracking waitresses I'd seen during our family's annual trips to the Ozarks—the ones who always were joking with truckers. That's not exactly what I'd had in mind when I read her letters and studied that signature. Rhonda's laughter wouldn't have been so indelicate.

"The house is perfect, just perfect," Felicity was telling Dad. "And I know the local legend about the place, too—what prompted the original owner to mark off a lot and build a house in the middle of nowhere, at the edge of a huge field like that."

"You do, huh?" my father said.

"But of course." Then she started telling him the legend and, ignorant of any such story, I put down my pencil and listened even more closely than before.

Generations and generations ago, Felicity said, a man owned a thousand acres of this prime prairie land. He lived in a huge house with his widowed mother. They got along fine until the man married, married quite late in life and to a woman who didn't get along at all with the man's mother. So the wife asked her husband to take an acre of land from the thousand he owned and build a little house for his mother. The farmer argued against doing any such thing, because it was so impractical: The house they were living in was plenty big for three people and, besides, it would be a crying shame to mess up a perfectly square field by marking off an acre lot. But the woman eventually persuaded her husband to do exactly that.

"I would suppose," Felicity said, "that requests made in bed are mightily persuasive to a man accustomed all his life to sleeping alone." I was shocked. *Requests made in bed.* But Dad just laughed; I wondered if he'd forgotten I was in the back room.

The old farmer walked off an acre at the edge of one of his huge fields, Felicity continued, and built a tiny square house in the middle of the lot. He laid sod and planted a tree in front. When he showed the house to his mother, she said it was a crying shame to mess up a perfectly square field with a house that looked too small for two people but that if her son and his wife wanted to move into such a house, that was their business.

The farmer had to explain that the tiny house was for her, his mother, and not for the wife and him. If you move me out of the home your father built for me when I was a seventeen-year-old bride, the old woman warned, I'll never speak to you again. But that's exactly what the man did, and his mother kept her word—never speaking to her son for the rest of her life. "And rumor has it," Felicity said, concluding the story, "that the farmer wept whenever he walked by that tiny house. One can only hope he was crying over Mother and not the loss of an acre's corn."

I heard Dad slap his leg. "That's a good one. I don't know how you found out about it, but that's the legend all right." Then they both laughed again.

"Someone I want you to meet," Dad told her.

When I realized that the someone was me and that I was about to lose my comfortable role as eavesdropper *and* that I was going to see Felicity, I went stiff. My ears rang, and spit at the sides of my mouth dried instantly. Before I could do anything more than grab a pencil, they were in the room with me.

My God, she was beautiful—the most exotically beautiful creature I'd seen since Rhonda. Her facial features were startling in their boldness: the bridge of her nose perfectly straight up and down, heavy cheekbones that jutted ledge-like under the outside corners of her eyes, and those eyes so blue that had you seen them in a photograph you would have assumed they'd been painted in. She had what seemed to be a bushel of dark hair, styled in a fashion that reminded me of the Egyptian princesses depicted in my history book. Big tits, too—made all the more prominent by her shoulders-back posture. She was thirty-four years old but had the nervous energy of a teen-ager. Her expression was so vibrant as to be unstable, a wide-open grinning that made me anxious—as does a firecracker with a fast-burning wick. I just knew it was going to go off at any second, booming out in laughter or some loud comment.

But Dad spoke first. "Cat got your tongue, boy?"

Had I been armed, my father would have died for saying that. I tried to smile, but I'm sure it came across as a wince.

"He's a vision!" Felicity's voice exploded.

I was trying to think of something terribly witty to say when Dad tousled my hair and the two of them left. She was wearing a knit dress that moved enthusiastically with her hips. I felt like beating my head against the table. But with all that, I still didn't fall in love with Felicity. Intrigued and excited by her, yes—but not in love. Not yet.

The house Felicity bought was exactly halfway between my family's house and town: a total distance of one mile, even. Everything on the prairie seemed even and exact. Felicity's lot was precisely one acre, laid out in a perfect rectangle with a square house in the middle, making the backyard the same size as the front. My family's house was a roofed cube sitting at the edge of a large and rectangular reservoir. The road into town, past Felicity's place, ran as true as taut string. as did the railroad tracks that went through the middle of town and proceeded without curves or bends across the prairie—hundreds and hundreds of miles of straight steel. That was the way you subdued the vast flatness: with the awesome power of straight-line geometry.

On the way home for dinner that evening, after Dad had helped Felicity move her things into the little house, I told him I'd never heard that story about the farmer who built the house Felicity had just bought.

"Neither did I," he said, reaching across and pointing to a place on my shirt near the top button. When I looked down, he flipped up his finger and hit me on the nose. It was a joke he'd been able to pull on me ever since I was a toddler; he'd do it only once every few months or so and I'd forget about it from one time to the next. "Not until today did I hear that story," he said, laughing and puffing on his cigar FDR-style. He always was the king after making a sale. When we got home, he threw the butt at the edge of the porch; Mom allowed no cigar-smoking in the house.

About once a month, I had to go around and pick up all the accumulated butts; he dropped them by the steps when he came home from work and tossed them over the railing after his evening smoke on the porch. I hated the job. It was demeaning, and you could never be sure that what looked like an old butt wasn't really a dried-up dog turd. I offered to get a bucket of sand he could use as an ashtray but he refused, saying, "It makes me feel so grand to be able to toss them butts out in the yard the way I do." I thought: Pick up a few crumbly dog turds and see how grand that makes you feel; but I said nothing to him. I just made petulant faces and sighing sounds, which he always ignored.

Within a few weeks of moving into her little house, Felicity took down the fence around her property and, in its place, planted irregular paths of flowers. She had her perfectly straight driveway reshaped, making it curve unnecessarily. She filled her front yard with an odd assortment of cast-concrete figures (frogs sitting on mushrooms and seemingly pining for lost love), half-buried wagon wheels, park benches—"junk," according to my mother's friends. And Mom agreed. A lot of people, as it turned out, were upset with Felicity's doodling on the rectilinear landscape.

Then she committed a crime. ("Did you see what that woman did?" "Yes!" "It's a crime, ain't it—just a crime.") Felicity commissioned the felling of the large Norway maple that dominated her front yard, an act that even my father and I, who were intrigued with the woman, thought was wrong.

The only major trees on the prairie are those planted by people, trees that are clustered only where people live. Trees that stand as an oath against the land: We intend to stay here. And with each passing year, as the trees become bigger and more firmly rooted, the oath becomes stronger: By God!, we intend to stay here. Felicity's tree, four feet in diameter, had provided an oath against the land for generations.

The workmen who cut the tree said that Felicity had instructed them to leave a six-foot-high stump, and even after they told her that it would involve a lot of work and cost her more to do it that way, she insisted. People were starting to say that maybe Felicity should trade places with her husband.

A week after the tree was hauled away, we were driving toward Felicity's house and saw her working in the yard, near the road. Mom told Dad to stop the car. "Ask her why she left that stump so high," I urged Mom, who told me to shush and then called out the car window: "We were so surprised to see that you got rid of your tree." In a small town, where one does not criticize one's neighbors in even the most oblique ways, this was a rash statement for my mother to make.

Felicity walked to the car and looked in. She was unhurried and spoke with a noncommittal flatness: "I do not like trees, and that one was stealing sunlight that by rights belongs to me."

No one in my family knew what to say. We were plain and decorous people, and this beautiful stranger, so aggressively sure of herself, was talking crazy.

"But that tree took a lifetime to get as big as it was," my mother finally said.

Felicity looked at each of us. "I believe my surroundings should accommodate themselves to me, not the other way around," she said, smiling. Then she winked at me. I was electrified—but not yet in love.

"Still, it seems a shame," my mother replied, jabbing Dad in the thigh. He got the signal and drove off, nodding good-bye to Felicity. "It's a crime," Mom muttered. "An absolute crime."

Then matters became even more curious. I walked past Felicity's house on my trips to town that summer and noticed that she'd begun working on the huge stump—chopping away at it with a ridiculously small hatchet. I wondered if she intended to reduce the six-foot stump to wood chips—chop by tiny chop.

One day she stopped working and looked at me, so I bravely called out: "My Dad's got a two-man crosscut! We could come over and cut that stump right off at the ground for you."

She walked to the road so quickly that I got scared, thinking she'd misunderstood what I'd said and was angry with me about something. "You know," I explained nervously when she reached me. "Get it nice and flat so you could put a pot of flowers or a birdbath there."

Holding my attention with those blue and then blue-green eyes that changed shades with the light, with the sun's progression behind and then away from clouds, she finally asked: "And what're you going to do with *your* life, Babyboy?"

What did that have to do with my offer of cutting down the trunk? I didn't know, but Felicity obviously wanted an answer to her question. She was intent, standing there hot and sweaty and close to me. I took her flush of exertion, the red face and wide eyes, as demoniac tendencies, and I was frightened. She was, after all, still holding that hatchet in her hand. So although I'd never told anyone my real plans, I dared not lie to Felicity. "A writer," I blurted out. It was the first time I'd said it.

Her expression softened momentarily, as if she'd just been shown a bucket of puppies. Then she tightened up again, all the more serious as she dropped the hatchet and put her hand to the side of my face. "Yes. I've been watching you walk into town and back. Novelists have to be walkers. Not sprinters, not even long-distance runners. *Walkers.* And you're a walker, right?"

I nodded vigorously. Actually, I wanted to be a newspaper writer, a war correspondent—not a novelist. But I didn't explain that detail to Felicity. I just kept nodding, hoping like hell she wasn't going to do anything that would hurt.

"Okay!" she shouted, making me jump. "You got it. My faith in you as a novelist. And remember this, Love Button." She put her other hand to my other cheek. "I'm a disciple of delayed gratification. Built for distance, not speed."

I had no idea what she was talking about.

"Oh, I can see it now." She stepped back as if to admire me. "Paris, Madrid, San Francisco, Havana. And New York—*of course*, New York City. Such adventures you'll have." She was clasping her hands to her bosom, and I think I still was nodding, unaware that any of this might be a performance.

"I know your fate!" she suddenly declared. "What life has in store for you. Yes! You will be *lionized*!"

1 7

And *that's* when I fell in love with Felicity. I didn't even know what "lionized" meant, not exactly, but I instantly knew that I wanted it, I had to have it, that I desperately desired and needed to be lionized. She made it sound so wonderful—and made me feel special and glamorous. Paris, novelist, New York City. Sure, my parents and teachers had complimented me for good posture and high grades, but this woman was talking lionization! How could I have *not* fallen in love with her?

"You watch what I do with that tree stump during the next months or years," she said, "and you'll learn the most important thing you need to know about writing novels."

I just kept nodding, no longer concerned that I didn't understand what she was talking about. She turned around, and I headed home to look up "lionize."

Sixteen years later, when I was living with Felicity, I told her this story—about the exact moment and reason I fell in love with her. "I was a late bloomer and hadn't even gone through puberty yet," I said. "So regardless of *your* sleazy motivations for beginning a love affair with a boy of fourteen, my reasons for falling in love with you were completely chaste."

I was saying all this while we were naked and playing Gladiator and Slave Girl. I loved telling Felicity provocative things when we were in bed together, because her reactions there always were so delightfully unpredictable. I thought the story about my chaste love, for example, might elicit from her a gush of sentimentality, perhaps even tears. But Felicity just looked down at me (I guess this was during my turn as the Slave Girl), and said in a wisecracking, side-of-the-mouth, Mae West way: "Well, Sugar, like I always say, 'Chaste makes waste.' You know what I mean?"

·   ·   ·

When I was fourteen, soon after I fell in love with Felicity, I got sick. I was suffering aches in the joints, a general feverish weakness, weight loss, and a wildly beating heart. Unimaginative doctors examined these symptoms of love and came up with the diagnosis of rheumatic fever. I was in the hospital the rest of the summer and at home, missing school, for another three months after that.

A bookish and prissy child, I seemed to have had a predisposition to a disease like rheumatic fever, which makes its victims weak and wan and given to highly emotional states. While I was hospitalized, my father brought me biographies of Teddy Roosevelt and other famous Americans who'd overcome sickly childhoods to grow into robust men, but just reading about the tremendous amount of work and will required for such a transformation made me all the more tired. I lacked gumption.

But I was pretty good with an audience. I truly was convinced I was going to die, so I gave languidly affecting performances for friends who visited me. "You can have my bike, Chops. No, no—take it now. I'll never ride again." "You don't have a rifle, do you, Pauly? Take mine. Tell Dad I said it was okay." Subdued by the surroundings—the quiet, the institutional white, the medicinal smells—my usually boisterous friends allowed me to hold court as the dying prince. At least in the beginning.

The first time Felicity visited me in the hospital, in fact, I was in the middle of a damn good and serious act about how disappointed I was to be dying in a hospital in the Midwest instead of on a battleground over there: ". . . and if you guys get over there, kill one for me. Kill one for the buddy who didn't get the chance to ship out with you."

She strode into the room, walked directly to my bed, and spoke abruptly to the three adolescent males who were in attendance, hands folded and eyes down, at my bed. "What're you boys talking about?" It was more of a demand than a question.

They looked at me as if I should be able to explain this woman's behavior or at least vouch for them so she wouldn't attack them physically. I shrugged.

"Talking about how you're all going to go kill Japs and Krauts, huh?" she continued. "Come back acting mysteriously war-weary, impressing the girls with your well-decorated uniforms? Huh? Huh? Is that what you were talking about?" It was, of course; she must have been listening at the door. "If every pipette were snipped off at birth," she said, acting as if she were angry about something, "we'd never have another war. What fragile, dangerous creatures you all are. Jesus Christ. Now get out of here."

With quick waves to me and wide, wary eyes on her, my three friends rushed from the room. The cowards. I was glad I wasn't going into battle with them.

Felicity suddenly was all sweetness and light, sitting on the edge of my bed and smiling. "Well, maybe not *every* pipette." The performance of mine that she'd interrupted was a wisp of nothing compared to the one she'd just given. She was majestic, and I begrudgingly admired her, although I had no idea what she was talking about.

"For you," Felicity said, pulling a waxed-paper package from the pocket of her dress, "I got blackberries."

"I don't like blackberries," I said petulantly. Actually, I loved blackberries, but I wanted to punish her for upstaging me.

"Every kid likes berries," she declared, holding one to my lips. "And these are the last of the summer. I didn't pick them this morning, *early* this morning so they'd still have the dew on, and then schlepp them down here for you to clam up on me."

Turning my head away from her hand, I said (with what I hoped was maddening politeness), "No, thank you."

She laughed—and then reached around and gently crushed the berry against my closed mouth. I felt juice and pulp on my lower lip and became angry. This woman was not playing the game, was not showing proper deference to the dying prince. I was determined not to eat one goddamn berry.

As she crushed a second and third one against my mouth, I stared defiantly into her face. With the next four berries, I could feel the juice trickle off my chin and down my cheeks; my neck was wet, and I knew the pillowcase was being stained. I became angrier, more humiliated, and a couple of tears joined the berry juice on my pillow. But, *still*, I didn't give in, didn't accept one berry in my mouth, and did not turn away from her. I just lay there and stared.

"Oh, here's one you'll really like," she said, holding up an especially large and dark blackberry. She crushed it gently against my lips and said, "See, I was right, wasn't I? Mmm, mmm, good!"

My resolve weakened.

She placed a berry on my cheek and then slowly leaned down, large breasts flattening against skinny trunk, and picked it up between her lips. Holding it there a second, she then pushed it into her mouth with a single finger. Her smile was odd. "Cheekberry," she said seductively.

I was astonished.

Then a berry was put right on my eye, so that I had to close it. Again she leaned on me—I was watching with my left eye—and picked the berry off with her lips. Except that this time, she seemed to rest hotly against me for several minutes, although it couldn't have been more than a second or two. I wondered if this was some form of sex play.

I felt feverish; my heart beat wildly.

She balanced two berries on my upper lip and then sort of tucked them to the edges of my nostrils. My berry-stained lips were fighting a smile. Felicity showed her teeth; the smile I was resisting became an anxious one. She was on me, using teeth and lips to get at the berries.

"Mmm, mmm—nostrilberries! Love dem nostrilberries!"

I laughed. It was the most outrageous thing that had ever been done to me, so what could I do but eat the rest of those goddamn blackberries? No one could resist her. I was convinced that had she crawled up on Lincoln's lap in his memorial and done to him what she did to me, eventually those tragic eyes would've brightened and those huge marble hands would've uncurled to accept a berry from Felicity.

After I finished the blackberries, Felicity cleaned my face with a washcloth and then pulled a chair next to the bed, sat down, and made another of her declarations: "Now I'll tell you a story."

She began reciting in a slight and somewhat staged Southern accent, saying things that surprised me, confused me, and sometimes made me laugh. The story lasted about twenty minutes that day, a half hour the next day, and fifteen or twenty minutes on each of the succeeding days she visited me. At certain intervals, she would announce the number of the chapter she was on, but I wasn't keeping track. I wasn't making a great deal of sense out of the story, either, but I always looked forward to those afternoon visits.

My mother and father and sister, good-hearted but as flat as the prairie, didn't do much to cheer me when they visited in the mornings and evenings. And although I still believed I was going to die, other people became bored with the topic. My school chums began interrupting my soliloquies whenever scatological jokes (based on various items of hospital paraphernalia) occurred to them. And because my parents had not allowed any of my possessions to be taken, I no longer could hold my friends' interest with promises of bequests.

Felicity and her strange story became the center of my day, what I waited for in the morning and thought about in the evening. She got through several chapters while I was hospitalized; the story hadn't really ended when I went home, but Felicity didn't visit me at my house. I thought a lot about her story while I was sick, recognizing that some of the characters were based on people we knew—on me and on her. The implications I was drawing, even back when I was fourteen, were rather heady.

Felicity continued that story whenever I stopped by her house to see her; she continued it while I was in high school and then on my visits back to Illinois after I'd left home. She continued it for thirty-one years: the most amazing thing that has ever happened to me in my life, to be told that story.

I always believed a lot of amazing things would happen to me, but the war ended while I was in high school and I never got a chance to play most of the scenes in which I'd imagined myself starring. I especially wanted to play one scene I'd read in a dozen books and watched in a dozen movies: I wanted to be a soldier (or a war correspondent) saying good-bye to his sweetheart, with the troopship in the background and with bumping bodies, crying babies, and general confusion all around us. I wanted to see tears in her eyes and feel the longing that her body already was anticipating and, in reaction to all that, I wanted to be brave and silent and Gary Cooperish.

But without a war, all I could do was parody the scene: at train stations and airports and next to the open doors of cabs—a businessman off on business. Hardly significant enough to warrant tears, although for years and years I've tried for tears. Tried for them by leaving woman after woman, by leaving my family repeatedly, even by leaving Felicity.

More than anyone else, she accepted my departures, celebrated our reunions, and mourned quietly the absences. She made it easy for me to be selfish: home from the wars and the woman you left behind is so happy to see you (home from the wars) that no recriminations are made about the past and no promises are extracted from the future.

Felicity finally finished the story during my last visit with her, five years ago. At that time, she asked me to begin telling her a story—something I could recite on subsequent visits. I said I would.

Felicity was sixty-five then, but I felt no urgency about arranging trips home to see her, to begin telling her my story. With Felicity, it was easy to be fooled into thinking life's an endless affair.

But apparently it's not. At least that's what Sis was telling me yesterday morning on the telephone.

After she passed along Felicity's last words, my sister kept asking me if I knew what they meant. How had I broken Felicity's heart? I told Sis it was a long story, and I didn't want to go into it then.

"What was so funny?" Sis asked.

"About my breaking her heart?"

"Yeah."

"Felicity thought everything was funny. You know her."

"No I didn't. I don't think anybody knew Felicity. Except maybe you."

"I guess you're right."

"Are you coming home?"

"For her funeral?"

"Yeah."

"I don't think so."

"Why not?"

"They going to bury her in the backyard?"

"How'd you know that?"

"You mean they are?"

"Well, that's what she wanted. Put it in her will. Gave everything she owned to the church and put in a request that she be buried in her own backyard."

"But they're not going to allow it, right?"

"No. There's laws against that sort of thing."

"Yeah. I suppose there are."

"But you'll still come home, won't you?"

"No. If I do, I might get drunk and steal her body and try to bury it in the backyard myself."

"You could come home to see *us*, you know. It's been five years. I don't feel like I even have a brother. What is it with you, Sonny?"

"I'm a disciple of delayed gratification."

"What the hell is that supposed to mean?"

"Something Felicity used to say."

There followed a long silence, the telephone company's meter ticking in the heart of some computer somewhere. Then I asked my sister: "Tell me again, will you?"

"What?"

"Her last words."

Having a natural talent in these matters, Sis waited a nickel's pause before she spoke. " 'Your brother broke my heart.' "

"And then she laughed."

"And then she laughed."

"Yeah. That's Felicity for you."

"Sonny?"

"Hmm?"

"Come home, huh?"

"Maybe."

"Sonny, Sonny, Sonny."

I hate, hate it, hate it when she calls me that. With Mom and Dad dead, Sis is the last person in the world I ever talk to who still calls me Sonny. After a lifetime, how can I ask her to stop using that name now? She's two years older than I am and although I wish her the longest and happiest of lives, I can't help thinking that with her death, so dies Sonny. I won't ever hear it again.

But it won't work out that way. She'll be at *my* deathbed, too, and she'll be sobbing and saying it over and over—calling a dying old man "Sonny, Sonny, Sonny." Until I'll have to rise up and tell her: "Don't call me Sonny!" And *those* will be my last words.

(Felicity never called me Sonny, not even when I was a boy. She didn't use my given name, either. Instead, she applied to me a large and silly variety of endearments: Honey Sac, Love Pot, Noodles, Dearheart, Sweetness, Honey Bear, Honey Bear, Honey Bear.)

My sister and I chatted for a few minutes more, about how her kids and *their* kids were doing and whether her husband still hated me, or ever hated me, for the way I've treated him over the years. Sis said he didn't, never did. By that time, I'd had three juice glasses full of tequila and grapefruit juice, so I told her I didn't really care one way or the other, and that ended the conversation.

I called my secretary at her apartment and told her I wouldn't be in the office that day, maybe not for a couple days. She asked if I was sick, if she should come over; I said no to both questions and told her about Felicity.

Then I decided to fix a Margarita, to do it the way Felicity would: squeezing limes and lemons for fresh juice, putting salt around the rim of the glass, using the blender to create heavy foam. Felicity always made drinking an event; it was she who addicted me to the process.

Drinking Margaritas at seven-thirty in the morning made

me feel like a child who was getting away with something naughty—which is not a bad feeling to have, to still be able to summon up, when you're fifty years old and have gotten away with as many naughty things as I have.

I sat and drank and thought. Then I began making telephone calls, telling friends about Felicity's death, about what she meant to me—everything I could think of during a telephone conversation. They listened politely; a few said they didn't recall my ever mentioning Felicity, and that bothered me. But it didn't bring tears. I was trying for tears, because except for that one quick and sharp sob during the conversation with my sister, I seemed emotionally unaffected by the news of Felicity's death, and *I wanted to feel something.*

By noon, after almost five hours of Margaritas, the calls became bizarre. I was calling back friends I'd talked to earlier; they asked if I was okay and I kept telling them, "No, I'm not! Aren't you listening? Felicity's dead!"

When I used up all the numbers I knew by heart, I took out my wallet and sorted through business cards, slips of paper, torn-off pieces of napkins—anything with a telephone number on it. I wanted to tell as many people as I possibly could about Felicity's death. I wanted to make sure everyone recognized the importance of what had happened; I wanted to feel something.

Alcoholic blackouts are neither gradual nor well ordered; they seem to come on suddenly but then later there'll be gaps of light in them so you can see too clearly certain things you did, embarrassing vignettes that make you anxious about what went on in the darkness.

I blacked out at some point in the afternoon, but I know I kept making telephone calls because some of them have, for some reason, been preserved in my memory. A nice lady at a cab company urged me to call an ambulance or the police. An officious man at an insurance company asked me for Felicity's policy number and wanted to know if I was sure it was a Prudential policy. I thought these people were crazy; what a time for the world to go mad, with me drunk and in deep distress. But I realize now what they must have thought when I kept repeating,

2 6

"Felicity's dead, Felicity's dead, my God do you realize what I'm saying, Felicity's dead."

I remember talking to Sy Lamont's mother. He was someone I used to work with; we were on the road together for three months. He died years ago. I knew that, of course, but I guess I was calling every number I had in my wallet and for some reason I still had his. I must have had it in two different places, because I recall his mother crying and asking me why I had called again and then finally threatening to turn me in to the police or, even worse, to the telephone company.

Of the calls I remember, the only one that made sense to me at the time (and even now) was the one to Cherry's Escort Service. The lady there (maybe it was Cherry herself) offered to send someone over to keep me company, and I said that was a grand idea, but I guess I screwed up giving her the address, because no one showed up. At least I don't remember anyone keeping me company yesterday.

When I awoke, it was dark and I was on the floor with the telephone and the contents of my wallet next to me. I saw cards belonging to business associates, and now I wonder how many of them I talked to, what I said to them, and how I should go about apologizing. But awake on the floor yesterday, all I was worried about was putting great quantities of water in my body. I took four aspirin and lurched to bed.

I got up at the regular time this morning, thus rediscovering the key advantage to starting your drinking at seven A.M.: You can get drunk, make a fool of yourself, pass out, wake up, go to bed, get a full night's sleep, and still start the next day on schedule.

I was physically ill this morning, but I wasn't heartsick. I hadn't cried and didn't feel as if I were about to. I made coffee, sat at the kitchen table, and looked out the window; finally, it had snowed.

I think about the thirty-one-year story Felicity told me: the most amazing thing ever to happen in my life and there are large chunks of it I simply can't remember. I know the story in a general, overall way, but so many of the details, the goddamn beautiful details, are lost. I wish I had listened more closely. I wish I could write it exactly the way she recited it. I wish you could understand.

I am a fifty-year-old businessman. I am successful after a fashion, treated with deference, at least by the people over whom I have corporate power. I have a fine apartment, the rent on which still shocks me. All three of my ex-wives live in big houses. Current lovers are not without talent.

Still, I am childless, motherless, and now without Felicity. I will never, for the rest of my life, ever be addressed as someone's Honey Bear. It is this realization, this thinnest of revelations, that leads me finally to weep for the loss of Felicity.

You have to understand. Whenever I wasn't with Felicity— before I met her and all the time I was away from her—life was told to me in block letters with heavy, squared-off serifs. Felicity explained things differently, in wildly curlicued calligraphy.

GRAVĒDA

The part Felicity told me when I was fourteen and hospitalized with the symptoms of love, the diagnosis of rheumatic fever.

1. Here comes Gravēda! Proceeding through the forest like a force of nature. She's been separated from her tribe for twenty years, the last ten of which she's been traveling alone on the tribe's trail, trying with some desperation to catch up so she can get herself a man who'll make her pregnant before it's too late. She's forty years old, five feet and five inches tall, top to bottom all woman. Her body is made for making one baby, which she needs to guarantee her a spot in heaven. That's the way things work in her tribe.

Today she's traveling with her sword out 'cause she's mighty hungry, and if any lizard, chipmunk, toad, snake, killdeer, bunny rabbit, or any other little creature crosses her path, she'll stick it—just reach out and jab it with her sword. Kill it first and figure out if you can eat it later, that's her motto.

It's high afternoon when she spots a woodchuck hole at the base of a tree. She falls to her knees at the hole and commences to dig like a dog, throwing up a dirt storm behind her. When roots get in her way, she hacks 'em in two with her sword. But she finds nothing. No big woodchucks, no baby woodchucks. Too bad; woodchucks are kind of greasy, but she's been known to eat 'em. Just to ruin Mr. Woodchuck's day as much as he ruined hers by not being at home when she came calling, she squats over the hole and leaves him a message. Then she resumes walking—hungry and muttering and mean.

She chops off tree limbs that hang in her way, flips a box turtle on its back and leaves it to starve, knocks down a bird's nest in hopes of finding little speckled eggs she can crush against her thumb just to smell 'em for ripeness. (She doesn't eat eggs, not since all that trouble with the ravens that still follow her.)

When it gets dark, she uproots half a dozen saplings, and three big bushes, pulls some vines loose from a tree, and digs up a yard or so of sod. Piles everything in a big heap and then sprawls on top to sleep—alone again tonight. First thing in the morning, she evacuates her bowels right smack in the middle of the trail.

You have to understand. Gravēda likes to be able to turn around and see that the land bears testimony to her passing.

2. Now, as Gravēda walks through forest and across meadows, all the little injuries she received yesterday—when briers cut her ankles and the broken roots in the woodchuck hole bruised her forearms—announce themselves with irritating stings and low-voltage jolts of pain. She's still hungry, too. But she keeps traveling and tries to shake it off—all this morning vulnerability.

As she waits for the walking to grind off the edge of the morning and numb her up for the day, her mind drifts to thoughts of rabbits. Plump and sweet and juicy good rabbits. She whispers to any rabbits in the area that, were she to kick one up, she would stick it in a real respectful manner—'cause it'd be an honor for her to kill a rabbit this morning. Honor for the rabbit, too, Gravēda points out. Its flesh going to fuel a traveler such as her, helping to sponsor today's portion of the holy journey. "Hell, I wouldn't even squish your skull to make your marble eyes pop out, like I usually do just for the fun of it. Lordy, no—not this morning. I'd say a little prayer for you this morning, Mr. Rabbit, reminding God what a right honorable thing you're doing as I cut your furry throat oh-so-ceremoniously."

But any rabbits in the area apparently are unconvinced and keep to themselves. Walking, walking, by midday Gravēda is dragging her sword along behind her. No rabbits. Oh, she knows they're around here, all right. Hiding from her. Coveting their useless little rabbit lives that by all rights belong to her. *Denying* her. For what? Just so they can run around for a few more weeks and eat grass and make little pellets that excite foxes into prancing. "Damn, selfish rabbits. Brother, I'd love to see one of them little cowards now. I'd stave in his head with my foot and rip out his guts and toss 'em aside." Rabbits got no sense of priority, Gravēda concludes.

She uses her hunger and frustration to fuel her walking. She is one hell of a walker. Conceived, born, and reared a walker. Been doing it for thirty-seven years (her Momma carried her till she was three), and now she's got rhythm in her walking. Got herself a style of walking that shows no strain, builds no debt to weariness. She can even catch a nap and keep walking 'cause it's all become automatic—muscles contracting, muscles relaxing. Put it to you this way: If there was a bridge to the stars, she wouldn't need no husband and child to get her to heaven. She could walk there.

3. It's late afternoon now, with Gravēda following the tribe's old trail and watching for any clothing, utensils, weapons, or jars that might have been discarded years before. Because her tribe is dwindling, each generation half the size of the previous one, there's always a surplus of equipment. But Gravēda finds nothing today.

She walks all the way to the end of the day, tears up some of the landscape for a bed, and tries for sleep. When sleep doesn't come, Gravēda tosses and turns and props herself up and then lies back flat and stares at the sky. She reaches up at the stars, holds her hand in the air a moment, and then lets the hand drop beside her. "Oh, hell," she sighs. Gravēda gets this way at night.

Her mind, now in sleep and now not, goes back to when she was a kid traveling with her folks and the tribe. Gravēda remembers teasing and being teased by boys, and she recalls girlish fantasies of what her future husband would be like: a handsome man with straight and white teeth. She remembers holding her hand in front of her mouth when she smiled so that the boys couldn't see that her teeth were bad.

Gravēda also recalls everything the priests told her because, in spite of her rebellious efforts, she was educated by priests who were smart enough to know that you don't have to get a child to accept or believe what you're telling him, that you just have to make sure the child learns it and remembers it. Then, years later when the child no longer has the protection and arrogance of youth, that former child will reach back for the comfort provided by that early education.

Which is what Gravēda is doing tonight: Alone and hungry and tired and still scared of the dark after all these years, she tries to comfort herself with the faith in which she was educated. God created her tribe and told it to travel toward the setting sun, each couple able to have only one child so that the tribe will reduce in number until the final sixteen will produce eight who will produce four who will produce two. And those final two travelers will have a child who is the end product of refined and pure faith. That's what Gravēda was taught: that the tribe was created by God to produce a refined and irreducibly pure faith and that by the time the tribe dwindles to the last and remaining member, the westward journey will have reached the spot where God waits for The One. That's what Gravēda believes in the night, in the dark: that her ancestors, her parents, she, and her child all will be part of the chain that leads from the original tribe created by God to The One who actually will meet God. But to be part of that chain, she has to have a child and to have a child, she has to catch up with the tribe.

The education of priests leads Gravēda to sleep, and even in her sleep she does a little walking—her leg muscles firing in a remanent rhythm.

4. At first light, Gravēda wakes, spits, pees, and walks. She doesn't hold much with elaborate morning ablutions.

The trail takes her onto the crest of a fat, rounded hill, one of a parallel series of low hills that looked from the distance like giants' thighs under a thick sod blanket with tufts of bushes and an occasional splinter tree. Easy walking now, 'cause the hills run at a gentle slope in the direction of her travel.

A sudden pain in her lower belly makes Gravēda stiffen.

Pains worry her, because without priests and their potions, Gravēda can do nothing with pain except suffer it.

A few years ago, a molar (lower right) went bad and made Gravēda crazy with pain; she screamed in the night and cried all day walking. She didn't even have any ambergrist, that syrupy substance with its ability to lift the spirits and dull the effects of hunger and fatigue and pain. What eventually saved her was the distillate she found on some travelers' graves.

The tribe always puts two items on each traveler's grave: A tall stake, sharpened at the top, is driven into the grave at an angle so that the stake points toward the setting sun as a sign to the world that the traveler died on the journey, heading toward God; the tribe also leaves a jug of distillate on the grave, as a symbol that the dead traveler, in his own way, was faith partially distilled.

In the middle of her tooth trouble, Gravēda happened upon something of a bonanza: three graves, each with a large jug of distillate leaning against the westward-pointing stake. She sat right down and started drinking, grateful for the way the distillate regulated her heartbeat, smoothed the flow of her blood, made her nerves pacific, and put her in an expansive mood.

"I see by the size of that grave that one of you was a kid," Gravēda observed when she was halfway through the first jug. "Nothing sadder than the death of a child." Parents who are childless can't be linked, through future generations, to The One and that makes their chances for heaven kind of dicey. They usually become priests.

"But these other two jugs probably are the folks," Gravēda said when she finished the first jug, "so that ends that. Probably ate something that disagreed with you and now no one's mourning but your ancestors 'cause they're all unlinked. Nobody mourning but them and me."

Then she started telling the three dead travelers about her own troubles, how she was planning to marry a man named Ismo but then her Poppa got killed and her Momma was crippled and the tribe had to continue the journey, so Ismo left and she stayed with her mother. "Ten long years with a bitter, crippled-up old woman," she said, looking at the grassy humps and starting on the second bottle of distillate. "If Momma had been killed along with Poppa, I could have gone with the tribe and married Ismo when his parents died. We even considered breaking the rule about waiting until your folks are dead before getting married—that's how much in love we were. I was twenty and he was a few years older, a big, brawling . . . Anyway, he said he'd come back for me after his parents died, said he'd mark the trail and come back for me no matter how long it took. Well, it's been twenty years and I ain't seen hide nor hair of the bastard since. *Men.* Don't get me started on that."

By the time she started on the third jug of distillate (this one was blackberry; the other two were apple; all three had been aged into potency), Gravēda was jaunty: "Been traveling alone so long now that I ain't scared of nothing. If you discount God. Ha!"

Then she began explaining about the tooth trouble, but when she reached into her mouth to show exactly which tooth had been hurting her, Gravēda discovered she could touch the tooth—wiggle it, even—and feel only a dull, distant sort of pain. She drank some more, remembering nothing after that. She woke the next morning suffering a hangover. Dried blood was caked all around her mouth and tightly grasped in her hand was a rotten tooth.

But the pain that's bothering Gravēda today isn't a tooth. She knows what today's pain is, an old familiar one. Been with her off and on ever since her mother died. Gravēda believes it to be her womb that's pestering her, chastising her for not giving it the baby it's been ready to hold for all these years. "Like it's my fault or something," she says as she walks. "Hey, womb, excuse me all to hell but I ain't seen a man in twenty years, you know? You find me a man and I'll get you a baby so quick your neck'll twist. Till then, you might as well quiet down and stop paining me so bad."

The pain is caused by her womb or by hunger; Gravēda can't always tell which.

When the hills flatten out onto a scrub plain that runs at a gradual incline, Gravēda leans forward and places her weight at the precisely correct attitude to make her walking work at peak efficiency.

Then the land stops. Here it's a grass-poor plain but on the very next step there's nothing—nothing but a fifty-foot drop down a cliff, at the bottom of which is a sandy beach about a hundred feet wide. At the edge of that beach is a world of water.

Gravēda has never seen anything like it. She looks along the beach and, to the right and to the left, it runs beyond the end of her eyesight. As does that world of water stretching out in front of her. An unnatural expanse of water.

Gravēda mutters and kicks. Then she puts her head way back so her windpipe and mouth are in direct line with her lungs, which she stretches full of air. She lets out a shriek-scream that lasts a full minute. One of her better bellows. The kind that cowers carnivores and shuts up songbirds so they have to wait till night to sing. The world of water seems unimpressed.

But from the bottom of the cliff, right under where Gravēda stands, a dozen children flee—looking back and up at her in horror.

"Well, I'll be damned," Gravēda says. "I've caught up with the tribe."

5. By the time Gravēda finds a way down to the beach, the children are gone. She walks to the edge of that world of water and puts a finger to it. Warm. Tastes it. Salty! And don't that beat all, she thinks. What's the use of a world of water if you can't even drink it?

As Gravēda follows the children's footprints, she imagines how the tribe will honor her. A big party, probably—and lots of food. She salivates with thoughts of roasting meat, trays of nuts and persimmons, cups of sassafras tea, and little bowls of honey into which she can dip her fingers at will. And the distillate will pour all night long, Gravēda thinks as she walks quickly, almost skipping along in the sand.

Then she stops. She isn't sure she's ready to meet the tribe after twenty years apart from it. Will anyone remember her? Will Ismo be there? Maybe he's married someone else. Twenty years is a lifetime, and Gravēda decides she should take an hour's more time to prepare herself for the reunion.

In a place where large boulders have created calm pools at water's edge, Gravēda strips down naked, taking off her robe and the leather bands she wears around her major muscles. She places all this and her sword on one of the rocks and then enters the water to wash herself. When she's finished, she climbs out and lies on her stomach to let her backside dry; looking down at still waters, Gravēda sees her face and concludes it is startlingly beautiful.

At least her nose is startling. It is straight and aligned in vertical perfection, arising from a point directly between her eyes and running without bumps, humps, or bulbs to just above her upper lip. If a knife blade were held flat against her forehead and brought straight down, it would not cut any portion of her nose because unlike most noses, hers is not protuberant.

The rest of her face sweeps back from this straight and narrow prow. Cheekbones set wide and so prominent that they draw the skin of her lower face. She has heavy lips that fold back in a fleshy display.

Her thick, dark hair parts down the center of her head in a straight-line perfection that accents the vertical nature of her nose, giving her entire countenance such an axisymmetric look that it would appear the vertical halves of her face are mirror images.

Years of traveling the open trail have given her the complexion of twilight, but in this dusky face are set the eyes of generations—eyes so light and clear that an observer might mistake them for originators, not simply receptors, of light. As clouds pass high over her now, she notices the sky experimenting with intensities of light upon depths of water—and occasionally this saltwater she's staring into achieves a green-blue combination that comes flatteringly close to the color of her eyes.

She concludes she indeed is as stark a beauty as she was twenty years ago. "How you say? An aggregate of qualities that give pleasure to the visual senses." Gravēda never has been coy. She wonders if beads of sweat will pop out on the upper lips of the men who will see her today. Still staring at her reflection, she sits up. "Nice jugs, too."

Then she notices another's reflection. Black, in the air, diving. The reflection grows larger with alarming speed.

Instantly knowing what it is, Gravēda plunges her hand into the water and comes up with a large stone. She turns and chucks it at the raven. A lucky throw, hitting the bird hard enough to stun it.

The raven flops on the sand and Gravēda is upon it. In a quick rage, she steps on the body and rips the wings off the still-living bird. It makes a terrible racket until Gravēda pushes its head into the sand. Then she throws everything—wings and body—into the water.

She washes the blood and feathers from her hands. Gravēda is surprised the bird didn't give the usual warning caw. "Zealot," she hisses at its three major floating parts.

Then she looks back into the calm pool and studies the reflection once again. She elevates her chin ever so slightly because to do so favors her appearance. Gravēda figures she's as ready as she'll ever be to rejoin the tribe.

6. Gravēda stands on the rock—and dresses in her leathers. Nine leather bands of varying widths go one each around the major muscles: upper and lower legs, upper and lower arms, and one wide and especially thick band around her abdomen. For protection against animals and injury. Had her Momma not been wearing heavy leathers, that old she-bear would have killed, not just crippled, the woman. Gravēda's Poppa, a runner, wore thin leathers that protected him against briers, not bears.

Not to think about all that right now, Gravēda tells herself as she ties on the leathers with the closely spaced thongs facing front so she can reach them. When she's married, the thongs will be worn in the back, and her husband will tie them on, take them off. *That's* what I should be thinking about, Gravēda concludes. Grinning.

She puts on the robe, grabs her sword, and takes off down the beach.

Walking, walking, she smells evidence of the tribe before she reaches it. A stew, she decides—something thick and spicy. Her pace quickens.

Gravēda tries to talk herself into being calm. She wants to remain dignified even as the tribe goes wild in welcoming her. She worries about reacquainting herself with the social graces and wonders if, after twenty years, anyone will remember her or if she'll recognize the people she used to know. Those kids she frightened weren't even born when the tribe left her and her mother. How much has the tribe changed in twenty years? Why were those kids wearing nothing but strips of cloth around their loins? They seemed so flighty, so *clean.*

Gravēda looks down at her hands: The tips of her fingernails are broken and split and still dirty; there are scars and scratches on the backs of her hands and along her wrists and forearms.

But when Gravēda sees a big foodpot over a fire in the middle of the beach, she forgets everything—questions and worries and dignity. She runs to the pot and touches a finger to its steaming surface, an exceedingly stupid thing to do. She yelps and jerks back her hand. Gravēda looks around but sees no one. She takes a stick from the fire, knocks off the red coals, and uses the stick to get a taste of the stew. Kind of fishy but not bad, she decides as she takes several more quick, hot bites.

"Who are you?"

The question, coming from behind her, startles Gravēda; she turns fast, in a crouch, ready to fight.

"Who are you?" the man asks again. He's skinny, has a long neck, and stares hard with big bugged-out eyes. Gravēda remembers him: a priest who was forty years old when she and the tribe parted twenty years ago; already acting like an old man back then. Gravēda even remembers his name.

"Crat," she says softly, "you haven't forgotten old Gravēda, have you?"

He looks puzzled but then the expression on his face changes. "My God," he says in a reverent whisper.

"No," Gravēda laughs, "just me. Gravēda!"

Crat stands there, not moving or speaking.

"Come on," she says. "Call the rest of the tribe together. And can you get me a bowl so I can have some of this stew? I ain't eaten in two or three days."

"We'd given up on you," Crat tells her. "No one dreamed . . . What? Twenty years?"

"Yep. Momma lived ten years and I been traveling the last ten by myself, trying to catch up with you guys."

"Lord, what a trip that must have been."

Gravēda smiles. "It had its moments. I'll be damned if it didn't have its moments." She uses the stick to get another taste of stew. "Say, can you get me a spoon or something? I'm really hungry. Where is everyone?"

"So much has changed."

"I can see that," Gravēda says, still eating from the pot. "When did you priests start wearing *those* outfits?"

Crat looks down at his dark purple robe with the wide red sash. "We wear these as evidence of our rank—as priests. Other travelers don't wear much of anything." Then he adds, absently, "Don't put that stick in there."

Gravēda, ignoring the request, says, "Yeah, I saw a bunch of half-naked kids. Hey, have someone bring me a bowl, will you?"

"Let me think this through a moment. I'm not sure what the impact of your appearance will be. We have to proceed slowly in these matters."

Now Gravēda remembers how officious and stern he was as a priest, always whacking her and the other kids when they didn't pay him proper attention during readings of the creed. "Proceed slowly my ass. I been traveling fast as I could for the last ten years and now I want a celebration. A party! Dancing! Food—I want food!" She's hollering.

Several teen-agers have gathered near the cliff; they stare at her.

"Quiet," Crat whispers urgently. "Don't make a fool of yourself. And please keep your stick out of the communal foodpot."

"What is this stuff anyway?" she asks, taking another bite.

"Fish stew. Put that stick down and I'll get you a bowl, but first I want to explain to you what's happened. We've been on the beach here for ten years—"

"Fish stew! Yuck. Still, it don't taste half bad." She puts the stick to the pot once more. "Now, what's this nonsense about being on the beach for ten years?"

Crat slumps in a gesture of exasperation. "Gravēda, *the ocean.* We can't cross the ocean."

She looks out at the world of water. "Oh, is that what you call it? Well, we'll figure out a way to get across," she says confidently, taking another taste of the fish stew.

"Don't be stupid," Crat says, roughly grabbing her hand so she can't put the stick in the pot again.

Unaccustomed to being touched and angry at the way he's been treating her, Gravēda hits the priest with her free hand. The blow, landing just above his ear, rattles Crat, who begins stretching and twisting his long neck (with its Adam's apple so prominent as to give his neck the appearance of being jointed) in an effort to clear his head.

Gravēda laughs until she sees that the teen-agers are moving close. She grips her sword, which she'd stuck in the sand near her, and says to the dozen or so kids: "I'm Gravēda. Been separated from the tribe for twenty years, half starved, and he wouldn't let me have any of this stew."

But the children, who now comfort Crat, don't speak to her. Finally, the priest says, "Gravēda, we have *regulations.*"

She shrugs and goes back to eating stew with her stick.

One girly, about fifteen, tells Gravēda she should respect priests and follow the rules like everybody else.

Keeping one hand on her sword, Gravēda continues eating stew.

The girl is persistent, squinting up her face in disgust as she tells Gravēda that she's dirty and has nasty habits and she should go back where she came from, wherever that is, and it's a few rotten apples like her that cause trouble for the whole tribe. And when it looks as if the girl is never going to shut up, Gravēda draws her sword from the sand and cracks the teenager upside the head. She drops instantly, heavily for one so slight.

The other kids become agitated; some of them scream at Gravēda. She wants to tell them that she just tapped the girl with the broad side of the sword, that the blow was well calculated: not to kill but simply to cold-cock.

They don't give her a chance to speak, however. The kids are hollering and crying and telling Gravēda she is horrid. The word "monster" is used frequently. "She *is* a monster," Crat interjects.

Gravēda finds it all terribly tiresome, and she goes back to eating with the stick.

The girl and Crat are helped to a rounded boulder that sticks out of the sand about twenty yards from Gravēda and the foodpot. Only one young man stays near her, and Gravēda stops eating to watch him.

The boy, perhaps twenty, is tall and lithe and half naked, as are the others. But this one, standing silent and seemingly unafflicted by the general agitation of the others, is willing to return Gravēda's direct gaze. Everything begins with the eyes, and his eyes are dark and serious, creating an unnatural contrast with his blond hair and light complexion.

In response to sudden and rapid contractions, Gravēda sneaks a hand to her lower abdomen. This one?, she asks silently. This *kid*? Oh, womb, don't be so impetuous. Still, he is lovely and his eyes are chocolate and . . .

Crat, who has climbed on the little rounded rock, interrupts by yelling, "Rule number one!" The kids shout back: "No violence on the beach!" Crat yells again, this time shaking his fist at

Gravēda: "Rule number two!" Everyone except the boy replies in unison: "No weapons on the beach!"

Gravēda is astonished at this sacrilege: Crat has the youngsters shouting beach rules the way he once made his students recite the holy creed.

As Gravēda walks toward him, Crat leads another chant: "Rule number three!" The kids reply: "No swimming!"

"Ha!" Gravēda snorts. The hand that holds her sword twitches.

Although Crat is shaking, he looks at her and pronounces: "I fear you not, because I stand upon the rock of regulation."

Looks like limestone to me, Gravēda thinks, but what the hell do I know? She shrugs and uses her sword to jab at Crat's foot, hitting it and causing him to squeal like a porker as he falls off his limestone rock of regulation and rolls around in the sand.

Although his pain is intense, Crat is under the impression that Gravēda has only bruised him, has merely given one of his toes a severe stubbing. It is not until he sits up and makes a quick inspection, counting four where once there were five, that he realizes Gravēda has performed upon him a little toe-ectomy. Yes. She snipped that little sucker right off.

Crat grabs his bleeding foot and cries, "She's cut off my toes! She's cut off my toes!"

Gravēda tsks at such an outrageous exaggeration. She cut off only one toe—and the little one at that.

Crat's distress puts the children into serious hysteria—moaning and crying and screaming. They wiggle little fists at her and flap their arms in helplessness.

Finally, Gravēda is forced to close her eyes and cover her ears. She can't stand it anymore. She shakes her head wildly. The racket reminds her too terribly much of the ravens.

7. Gravēda had been seven years alone on the trail when it happened. A great drought had scoured the land of edible vegetation and had made even skinny game scarce. Gravēda spent

most of her time not on the journey but looking for food. Those were days when she thought she truly might starve to death.

One afternoon—stumbling, thirsty, searching for something to eat—she saw a cathedral tree at the edge of a forest. Scraping at the skies and broadly, boldly fanned to the sides—and still reaching limbtips for more—the tree held what seemed to be a million huge nests. Ravens.

Light-headed from hunger, she rushed to the tree and shinned up, using her sword to wave away the few birds posted all around as sentries. She was in luck, or so she thought at the time: Nearly all the nests contained eggs.

Eagerly, she grabbed the first egg she could reach and tapped it against one of her canines to make a suckhole. Trembling and sighing and issuing sounds of a small and private nature, Gravēda put the suckhole to her mouth and drew out the thick and slippery insides. The relief was immediate. She quickly climbed from nest to nest, shooing away protesting ravens and sucking down their eggs as fast as she could. She'll never forget how good and warm those eggs felt in her stomach. She could have, should have, left after eating the first dozen. Her hunger was slaked and she would have been able to get away from the tree before the sentries returned with the rest of the flock.

But Gravēda always has been given to excesses. She visited and emptied nearly every nest, eating eggs until her stomach felt as sloshy full as a skinbag of water. She was, in fact, so heavy with raven yolks and raven whites that she had a hard time climbing down.

Before she got to the ground, the flock had returned and was upon her—cawing, screaming, cawing. Some of the birds actually struck her, flying into her back as her hands were occupied with the effort of getting out of the tree. Once on the ground, however, she was able to swat them away with her sword. She killed several before making her way into the forest.

They followed her throughout that day, flying short hops to take up screaming positions in trees near the path. At dark she built a great fire and kept it going all night, which was silent.

With the very first application of light, Gravēda searched the trees around her. She could see shapes, but they were indefinite—branches, clumps of leaves, maybe nothing more than those tricky dawn shadows. Then she saw *them*. They seemed to appear suddenly in the trees, although they'd been there all along and were revealed only with the full light of the morning: an entire, surrounding forest of trees full of black and silent ravens. They had kept the vigil all night, growing quiet with the cold and dark, coming awake with the day. They ruffled feathers and moved stiff legs into more comfortable positions. Then they saw Gravēda and remembered why they were there. Instantly, they began wailing in their bird-raven way, taking their case to the entire hearing world: This woman has destroyed our posterity!

Gravēda crept away, but the ravens followed. They followed for days, silent only in the dead of night, finding her with each morning's light, remembering by the sight of her what she had done—and then launching again and again their hoarse and ceaseless attack.

Eventually, Gravēda began screaming back her own arguments: "I was starving and desperate that day!" Her voice silenced them momentarily. "As soon as it rains, my stomach'll be full of flowers and berries and tubular growths and, really, I won't be the same person who sucked down your next generation."

But they listened only briefly and impatiently before breaking in with their cawing, cawing, cacophony.

How long? Weeks maybe. Deprived by Gravēda of their normal raven pursuits of family, they were free to prosecute: You have not simply stolen a few eggs as a tree weasel will do; you have invaded our home and actually destroyed our future.

"God, I'm sorry, shiny black wings, big beaks, mean eyes. But listen to reason; don't be so strident. What's past is done— now go back to your meadows and let me follow my tribe in peace."

But their response was a hatred so pure that Gravēda thought for sure it must arise from some mysterious intelligence and not simple instinct. And in truth they followed her forever. Her black and personal sins, flown from her soul to take up positions in a tree—for the entire seeing world to see.

8. To make the youngsters shut up, Gravēda clangs her sword against the foodpot. Iron on iron sets up an urgent and shrill cry that Gravēda knows from experience can be made worse by twisting the sword in her hand, rapidly changing the pitch of the sound until it is given an articulation that approaches language. To the kids, such swordtalk is frightening and terrible; they grimace and put their hands over their ears. With them staring and one-toe-less Crat writhing on the ground, Gravēda escapes up the beach.

She walks as night arrives quietly by degrees. Gravēda climbs among some huge boulders that lean in a tumble against the cliff and, finding a den, there she sits—shaking with the aftereffects of rage. She breathes deeply, hoping for quick sleep.

But Gravēda is too hungry and confused and too damn stupid to sleep. She chastises herself for the way she acted, and her mind torments itself with questions: Where was the rest of the tribe? Where is Ismo? Why weren't they happy to see me? Why didn't I grab some more stew before I left? How did things go so wrong so quickly? And then she asks the question that amuses the Old Man most of all: Why me?

She strips and, carrying only her sword, climbs down to the beach and walks to the edge of that world of water. She steps into the small and regular waves that duck their heads and somersault gently onto the sand. As she enters the saltwater, the scratches and cuts over her body sting, reminding her of morning, but she continues out until her breasts are covered.

Swells cause her to lift and sway, lift and sway with the massive peace that can be owned by an entire world of water. And when she walks onto the beach, Gravēda is disappointed to be leaving the ocean's support and returning to the harshness of air, the full effects of gravity.

Just as she steps out of the water, she hears a strange sound that seems to come from way out in the ocean: high pitches sliding to low, plaintive and suggestive of a patiently enduring wisdom and sadness. Gravēda wonders if creatures live out there in that world of water, and she wonders if they're addressing her.

Gravēda throws back her head to scream, to shut up those spooky sounds. But the prospect of yelling in this soft and quiet night makes her suddenly shy, so Gravēda listens for more of those ocean sounds and, not hearing any, she returns to the boulders.

Seeing a bonfire way down the beach reminds her of evenings during the journey, back when she and her folks were traveling with the tribe. She feels an urge to rush down there and see if they're singing songs and telling stories and laughing—but then she thinks, To hell with it.

Gravēda dresses in leathers and robe and lies down among hard rocks to sleep.

9. That part of the mind that never sleeps, that tells you someone or something is there with you in the dark, awakens Gravēda just before dawn. She peeks over a rock and sees the young man with foreboding eyes, the one who was so calm while the rest of the kiddie flock went crazy. He puts a bowl of something hot (she can see the steam, eerie in what's quickly becoming half-light) on a flat-topped rock near the base of the boulder pile in which Gravēda hides and watches. The boy moves carefully and quietly, as if making a sacrificial offering.

Gravēda climbs down and comes up behind the young man. She suddenly growls in a low-throated, menacingly breathy "*Whoof!*" that makes him whip around, stumble, and fall on the sand. She laughs, still growling.

The boy stands and points to the bowl. He does this several times and then begins to make eating gestures, jabbing his fingertips toward his open mouth.

Gravēda rolls her eyes. That boy really does think I'm some kind of monster.

He continues gesturing.

Yeah, yeah, I get it—*eat*. She's about to slap his hand when the boy gets a spoonful of stew and holds it to her mouth. His entire arm is trembling.

Throwing the spoon to the sand, Gravēda takes the bowl and uses her fingers to eat rapidly and sloppily, letting the stew run down her wrist and off her chin—eating as she thinks a monster should eat, trying her best to disgust him. She wants to see how he's going to react, but he just watches, eyes full of doom and other dark stuff.

"I know who you are, Gravēda," he says softly, his voice shaking. "I was born the year the tribe left you and your mother. My parents told me all about you. People talked about you all the time we were on the journey, saying it was terrible how they had to leave you but that the journey can't be halted for anything. I felt bad for you."

Kind words, gentle youth, will not penetrate Gravēda's rock heart. It's been toughening for twenty years.

"They said you were real brave, not crying or anything. I used to wonder if I could be that brave if the tribe had to leave me. They said you were a beautiful young woman and it was such a shame that you had to be left behind like that."

Oh, sure, now you get to her. But Gravēda is becoming teary on behalf of that beautiful, twenty-year-old girl who was left behind and who stood there watching the tribe's departure, trying her damnedest not to show how much she hurt. That's why I'm getting blubbery, Gravēda tells herself. *For me.* Not 'cause this handsome young man is offering sweet attention, which I ain't had in years and years.

"I got to go," he says. "The priests decided tonight that they don't want us talking to you. Lots of trouble around here lately. Some of us have built boats and want to try crossing the ocean again but the priests don't want us to and, well, we've all sort of agreed not to do anything as long as there still are old travelers alive. You know, the ones who are holed up in their caves and can't travel anymore."

In the increasing light, Gravēda notices that his teeth are straight and white. She stops eating the stew and wipes her hands and mouth on the robe.

"What you must have gone through to catch up with us, Gravēda. Some journey, huh?"

"It had its moments," she says hoarsely. "I'll be damned if it didn't have its moments."

He looks out at the ocean and then back to Gravēda. "I used to have dreams about you," he says shyly, bending down to brush sand from his legs, although there's no sand there.

Gravēda realizes he's embarrassed himself, but look what's happening to her: She actually has to issue orders to her hand to prevent it from reaching out and touching the downy blond hairs along his arm. Damn! Too long on the trail, she concludes—that's my problem.

"It was silly," he says, smiling thinly. "I guess it bothered me so much, the idea of you being left behind, that I used to think . . . to have dreams about you catching up with the tribe and then I'd get to meet you and . . . Well, I don't have those dreams anymore."

He faces away. "That's okay," Gravēda tells him, nudging the boy's shoulder and feeling the mammal warmth of his skin. What she doesn't say is that she still has those dreams. Dreams so real that she wakes up in the morning smiling—and wondering briefly where everyone has gone.

"Gravēda?" He pauses and then speaks quietly: "Welcome back."

Surreptitiously, she jabs a thumb in her chest in hopes of causing enough pain to stop her silly, stupid, little girl's heart from beating birdlike in her broad, old chest. *You can't have him.* And now she's playing in the sand with her gnarled toes. What next?, she wonders. Steal a kiss and run away giggling?

"Bye," he says suddenly—and then turns to walk away.

She makes a noise to stop him, to keep him near her for a moment more. "Psst." I'm an idiot. But again: "Psst."

He turns around.

"Na . . ." She clears her throat. "Name?"

Again he smiles—and again those perfect white teeth. "Genipur," he says quickly before running down the beach.

Her eyes follow him; her suddenly softened heart continues to beat rapidly. And in the following days, whenever she sees him walking back and forth in front of the rock den, her womb and the other stuff down there urge upon her all kinds of dumb advice: Call to him, Gravēda, go get him, don't let that sucker get away, *he's the one.*

WHEN I WAS
IN HIGH
SCHOOL

*W*hen I was in high school, the war ended and I lost the bulk of the material I'd been using for daydreams and what-would-I-do-if scenarios. The war was a great thing to have waiting after high school, because it saved you from having to make decisions about what you were going to do with your life (you were going to join up, of course) and it gave you a chance at being something more than ordinary. I'd seen what the war did for some of the local stumblebums, how they were considered common until they came back wearing their uniforms. Hell, one of the mechanics in town (he was slow-witted) became a bona fide hero—Silver Star and everything. I knew I could do better than that guy. So until the war ended, I daydreamed of exotic places and exciting assignments (if not a war correspondent, maybe a bombardier; I liked the sound of the word) and I imagined what I would do if I were called upon to give my life for my buddies, if I were captured and the enemy tortured me to get my secrets, if there were a suicide mission and the commander asked for volunteers. I contemplated big issues (killing, dying, heroics) and foreign places (Guadalcanal, Iwo Jima, Salerno, and the Ardennes); all of it was waiting for me after high-school graduation.

Then the war ended, and I was left with such prospects as getting an education, finding the right job, marriage. I began daydreaming about an entirely different class of what-would-I-do-if scenarios: What would I do if I had a million dollars? What would I do if my parents and sister were killed in a car accident and I suddenly was an adolescent orphan? What would I do if I had only a few hours to live? That's the only one I've continued to consider throughout my life—the one about having only a few hours to live. The answer keeps changing.

The summer after I turned sixteen, I had a lot of time for daydreaming because a second bout of rheumatic fever put me in bed for several weeks. The attack was relatively mild, so I was able to stay home. Home *alone*, as it turned out, because my folks and sister went on our usual early summer vacation to the Ozarks without me that year. (Felicity and I spent a lot of time together during the three weeks I was alone that summer, and if her prophecy of lionization was what made me lose my heart to her, what happened between us while my family was away on vacation was the cause of my losing the other, more southernly, parts of me to Felicity.)

Convincing Mom to leave me home alone was a battle. I argued that the vacation represented the last time Mom and Dad would travel with Sis, because she would be entering nursing school that next fall. (She made it halfway through her first year and then quit to marry her high-school sweetheart; seven months and one week after the wedding, she gave birth to an eight-pound, twelve-ounce premature baby girl. And life's a constant mystery.)

Continuing with the whining, nagging, arguing, pleading campaign, I reminded Mom that the doctor himself had said that bed rest was the main ingredient in my recovery, that I could rest in bed without any help from the family, and that Mom's friends from church could come to check on me every day. And three weeks alone would give me a chance to "hit the old books" so I could keep up with my classmates. (None of these arguments moved Mom, although she seemed pleased that I'd even bother to offer the academic angle.)

Dad came over to my side. I thought at the time that he was just concerned with vacation reservations and with caretaking arrangements for his business (both of which had been made months before), but I realize now that at some point in my campaign, the old man clicked—saw something, remembered something, somehow suddenly knew how important it was for a sixteen-year-old boy to be left alone for a few weeks. He started taking Mom out every other night for shrimp-cocktail-and-steak dinners, during which he pleaded my case.

But it was my sister who finally won the argument for me.

One night after a date, she came home with her blouse buttoned wrong, with all the buttons fastened one hole off. When my mother pointed this out to her, Sis said, with what I thought was a great deal of aplomb, "Goodness! I guess I left the house like that tonight. How embarrassing." Further discussion was held out of my earshot, but the next day I was told that the three of them would indeed be taking the vacation to the Ozarks.

When I finally was alone, I immediately plunged into doing what I had in mind doing all the time I was trying to convince Mom to go on that vacation without me. I was, after all, sixteen; my body was awash in a hormonal soup; I was masturbating before the dust from my parents' vacation-bound car had settled back onto the country road.

Oh, I knew—at sixteen—exactly what I'd do if I had only a few hours to live. It was so absolutely clear to me back then: I'd want to go out screwing. So obvious; I was positive that's the way everyone wanted to die. I just knew that the lava of Pompeii must have preserved hundreds of love-locked couples and that, along with great chunks of sea-green ice, screwing couples were sliding around on the slanting decks of the *Titanic*. I was sure. When I was sixteen, I was so sure.

The church women, with whom my mother had made arrangements about looking in on me, were the mothers of my friends—women who wore dark dresses with big yellow flowers printed on them, women whose hair was pulled back to display faces that looked severe even when they were smiling, women who gave the impression of wearing a lot of heavily constructed undergarments, women whose gagging perfume announced their arrival and lingered after them, women whose feet were bound into black and sensible shoes. *Still*, in the state I was in, I employed these women in sexual fantasies that even today I'd be embarrassed to describe.

Of course. When I was sixteen, I knew exactly what I'd do if I were about to die. But in my twenties, the hormonal rage abating, I wasn't at all sure what I'd do in the last moments of life. I thought I possessed truly great and profound ideas and, if

I had only a few hours to live, I guessed I'd try to write the highlights of, the bare outlines of, those great ideas so they wouldn't die with me, so they wouldn't be lost to mankind. Maybe someone would be able to do something with my ideas and I'd be celebrated posthumously.

By the time I was into my thirties, it was clear to me that *I* wasn't ever going to do anything with my great ideas and that they weren't that great after all. My early thirties were bad times, with the second divorce and trouble at work and with booze and with evil. I hated a lot of people back then and I used to think that if I had only a few hours to live, I'd try to make as much trouble as I possibly could: calling people and telling them secrets I knew about their wives and husbands and lovers and employees.

Now, however, life has become calm. I'm fifty, with neither the ambitions nor the erections that once pressured me into doing things that led to trouble. If I now had only a few hours to live, I guess I'd just sit and think. Maybe have a drink or two. Ask my third wife or some other comfortable friend to come over and keep me company. I'd want someone there to hold me tight when the actual moment of death arrived. With a rheumatically scarred heart marching unsteadily—and occasionally shuffling—in my chest, I no longer consider the few-hours-to-live scenario as a purely theoretical exercise. I've abandoned great ideas and revenge. Now I just want someone to hold me.

When I was a kid, my family and I occasionally would drive to the river for a weekend stay in a cabin on stilts. The tall, sheer rock bluffs along the river road were amazing to people like us, who lived on the prairie. My father claimed that one of those cliffs was a Lovers' Leap, where over the years star-crossed lovers had committed suicide together.

I've often thought of lovers leaping off that Lovers' Leap. Their embrace on the way down (and surely they do embrace on the way down; they wouldn't just hold hands, would they?) must be one of the most sincere acts two humans can perform. Arms squeezing tightly enough to break bones that soon will be broken, faces shielded in a neck or shoulder to avoid the sight of what already is anticipated, and spending that last blink of time hugging, hugging—with no time left for anything but hugging. The entire act would last—what? A few seconds? Two or three? I don't know. From how high do lovers usually leap? But for however long it lasted, what a hug that would be.

And that's exactly how I want to spend the last few seconds of my life: being embraced with a passion that approaches that of leaping lovers.

Felicity used to tell me that's how she wanted to go out, too. And if you can't be held tightly by your lover, she said, be held tightly by *someone*. I wonder who did that for her. Maybe the nurse. I hope so.

•   •   •

When I was in high school, sixteen years old and alone at home in bed with heart and hand beating wildly, Felicity came to visit me. She wore sundresses. She wore sundresses.

She'd never been to our house before, but I'd visited her several times. On my way into town, I'd still stop to watch her working on that six-foot tree stump, from which she had chopped and chiseled and gouged a magnificent, high-backed chair. Its base was solid tree trunk; a couple of feet from the ground was the smooth seat, flanked by thick armrests; the chair-back, curved in the shape of the moon's waxing crescent to accommodate the sitter's back, was four feet tall. I thought it was the type of chair that royalty and warriors would use—kings and queens and Vikings. The type of chair in which one could slouch, throw a leg over the armrest, allow an arm to dangle and trail, and *still* retain an air of supremacy. Even as Felicity added designs and carvings, swirls and fleurs-de-lis and such, the chair's statement of massiveness was not diminished. It looked as if it weighed a ton. And remember: The chair was held in place by a root system that once had supported a huge tree, had kept that tree upright during the worst of midwestern storms. I got the idea that Felicity's chair had geological permanence.

In my talks and visits with Felicity, before my second (and last) bout with rheumatic fever, I never mentioned that I was in love with her, of course. But she must have known the impression she was making on me. I was moony around her. She was what I thought a movie star would be like, if you ever were to meet one in person, up close: someone whose specialness was obvious, immediately apparent, undeniable.

Sometimes she'd ask me in for a glass of lemonade or ice tea and, as I sat drinking stiffly at her kitchen table, she'd tell me more of her story. But the recitations didn't begin again in earnest—in that dreamy, hypnotic way—until she visited me in my house when my family was away on vacation.

She wore sundresses. She wore . . . I mentioned that, didn't I? Such dresses. Bright, bright colors, scooped necklines, and a light, silky material that pulled and puckered over her breasts, the swell of her hips, and across that gently rounded stomach. She wore white high-heeled shoes with straps that wrapped around her ankles. I was impressed with the idea that she would dress up just to come see me.

"Ours is a sick relationship, Honey Bear." That was the opening statement she made when entering my house for the first time that summer.

"Sick?" I became anxious; what did she mean by that?

Felicity laughed. "The only time I get to visit *you* is when you're sick."

I forced a guffaw, wishing I'd been bright enough to figure out the joke on my own.

"Now, where's your bedroom?" she asked.

I became dumb, nervous, and stiff. Felicity laughed and explained that she knew I was supposed to be getting bed rest and that she didn't want her visits to interfere with my recovery, "so you stay in bed and I'll talk to you and take care of you and tell you stories. Remember when you were in the hospital?"

"Sure."

"It'll be like that. I'll tell you some of the story every time I come over. But this time I won't smear any blackberries on your face."

I laughed and showed her to my second-floor bedroom.

"Go ahead and get in," Felicity said, holding the sheet, which she tucked and arranged at my neck.

"Gee, I'm not a baby, you know."

"Ooo," she pouted, pinching my cheek. Then Felicity bent across me to fix my pillow and, in doing so, displayed cleavage and a colored bra. I knew then what was going to happen that summer.

(Where has all the cleavage gone these days? Today, a woman's chest looks so unmysteriously, realistically anatomical: two individual breasts. Open blouses or low-slung dresses reveal sternums, on each side of which are the rounded edges of breasts. But no solid bosom. No shelf of flesh. No cleavage. I don't especially miss cleavage; I never had a fetish about it or anything like that. I'm just curious about its departure. All a matter of the ever-changing style of underwear, I suppose).

Until Felicity leaned across me to fluff my pillow, I never realized that brassieres (as we called them back then) came in colors. Seeing her bosom and cleavage and color gave me a sexual rush that has never been matched for pure, heart-thumping, belly-tightening excitement. These days, of course, belly-tightening excitement is hard to come by; I'm jaded, more tired, and no longer suffering from hormones or rheumatic fever. In Houston, I once spent $200 (in 1965 dollars) for two young women of Oriental extraction to show me things I'd never seen. And they did. Curious, curious things. I was fascinated, and I was intrigued. But my belly didn't tighten and my interest remained largely cerebral—nothing at all like the physical flash that the look down Felicity's sundress set off in me.

Nothing happened that first day. On her second visit, she asked me what I thought of the Gravēda story she was telling me.

"I figured some things out," I said, grinning and blushing.

"Really?"

"Yeah. Gravēda is, well, supposed to be like you or something."

"You figured that out, huh?"

I nodded like an idiot.

"And Genipur?"

His physical description matched mine (as Gravēda's matched hers), so I pursued my articulate literary analysis: "Well, he's, you know—supposed to be like me or something, you know."

"Can't get anything past you, can I, Sweetness?"

I shook my head and grinned and grinned. Felicity couldn't help but laugh; she roared. I've never know anyone who laughed as much and as infectiously as did Felicity. I was too young then to have any depth of humor, but in later years I laughed with her—laughing until the two of us were reduced to tears and coughs and slaps of our hands as we said those damn, damn, damns.

But nothing happened that second visit—or during the third one, either. Still, I was sure that Felicity was going to seduce me. I was positive. I was counting on it. I remember lying in my bed—covers close to my neck and knees up to make a tent that would hide things—and listening for accumulated hours to that story but all the time staring at her face and body and, in the back and front of my mind, thinking, thinking, thinking that at any moment she was going to sneak a hand under my covers to find me or was going to stand and drop her sundress like a drape falling away from a voluptuous statue wearing colored underwear. I was sure of it. I was waiting for it.

On her next visit, we sat at the end of my backyard, which ran to the edge of the rectangular reservoir; we watched the sun settle at the far edge of the prairie. "If you squint just right," Felicity told me, "you can imagine that lake as a flat and calm sea." I squinted and imagined but came up with nothing; I'd never seen the sea. When I told her that, she said, "What a shame. In San Francisco, where I lived as a young woman, the ocean is magnificent. I wish you could be sitting out there and looking across the ocean instead of this hole dug in the prairie. But you will someday. Farm boys have a fascination for the sea."

"I'm not a farm boy," I told her. "And I'm not a boy, either."

She gave me a surprised look, nodded, and then recited another chapter. But nothing happened. On her next visit, I tried to get her to stay longer than she usually did—to give things a chance to happen.

"I got to get going, Moonbeam. Your mother's friends come over after supper and we wouldn't want one of them to catch me here. I think they consider me something of a renegade. People wouldn't understand about a woman like me coming to see you like I do, like I do."

"I won't tell anyone."

"Neither will I."

And so then we were conspirators, too. But nothing happened.

After she'd been visiting me for a week, I was moved to distraction by this idea I still had, this itch of an idea, that Felicity was going to seduce me. I decided to take the initiative and get her talking about herself—to see where that would lead. "Don't tell me any more of the story today," I requested.

"No?"

"No. Tell me why you came out here from New York City."

She eyed me suspiciously. "You don't want to hear that old story, Doll. It's common. Everyone knows it anyway."

"About your husband being in the hospital?"

She nodded. "I bought that little house from your dad so I'd be close enough where I could visit my husband anytime I wanted—and so I'd have a place to bring him when he got out. But God only knows if he's ever getting out of there. You would not believe the battles I have with the bureaucrats over there, even to get permission to take him on the grounds when I go see him. I guess they like to keep their war heroes tucked away." She stood, walked away from my bed, and looked out the window. "Something bad happened to him in the war, in the jungles. He can't tolerate trees, woods, tall buildings—anyplace where someone has a place to hide."

She looked at me, noticed the confusion on my face.

" 'Cause he imagines that people are spying on him. Hiding and getting ready to jump out and get him. That's why I thought that little house in the big, empty field would be perfect."

I wanted to say something that'd make her feel better but as time passed nothing came to mind.

She stood at the window, her head turned away from me so I had to listen closely to hear what she was saying. "He was quite a man. A big bruising . . . but gentle with me, like I was crystal or something. And funny? Lord, that man could make you . . . But the crazy thing . . . *Jesus*." Her voice, stumbling along, finally broke. I couldn't see her face. Tick, tick time. "I don't visit him as often as I should, but I can't bring myself to leave, to leave him here. My friends, our whole life, everything's someplace else—New York and San Francisco. My family's down in Louisiana. *Jesus Christ*."

Then she left, just waved at me and left. I was sorry I had started that conversation and resolved not to bring up the topic again.

Two more visits tensed by without anything happening, although on occasion I saw my very own right hand creeping along the bedspread toward her, as if that hand were on its own mad mission to make something happen—a mission under the command of my groin, which somehow had found a synaptic route for bypassing the higher levels of my brain to send orders directly to my dumbly obedient right hand. I countermanded the orders as soon as I saw what was happening, what was creeping toward Felicity, who sat so very close to my bed during those quiet, clock-ticking, fly-buzzing late afternoons thirty-four years ago.

And then it happened. I guess it had been happening, little by little, all along: her hand resting on my thigh or lower belly as she recited Gravēda, the story itself becoming suggestive, the sheet slipping, and then finally her hand on me—grasping, stroking, fondling. Handling me with tender, lingering affection until: zappo, zing, mercy, mmm! And then replacing the sheet over me as if nothing had happened when, in fact, everything in the world had happened.

What I find most amazing in recalling these episodes, and once they began there was one per visit until my parents returned, is that Felicity managed to keep a straight face during them. How ludicrous and terribly funny it must have seemed to her, all that heated activity going on with none of it being discussed or even acknowledged. That's what made it seem magic to me at the time, of course. As if it were a third force, connected to but independent of Felicity and me. To encourage and entice this third force, I performed pathetic little maneuvers: arching my hips as I pretended to stretch, faking restlessness so I could toss and turn closer to her chair next to the bed, pinching the sheet between thumb and forefinger so I could, ever so sneakily, pull it down to the top of my underwear. And *something* must have been working, 'cause it happened once per visit.

(I sound terribly coy to call it "it." But I would be inappropriately crude in saying she jacked me off. It wasn't like that at all. Masturbate sounds too dryly medical. To say that Felicity made manual love to me is fairly accurate—but unforgivably cute. I don't know what term to use, but I was sixteen and it was great.)

I took multiple showers to get ready for her. I put on Dad's witch hazel. I watched at the window and then raced to bed when I saw her drive up. I was wildly, body and soul, in love with Felicity.

From my current perspective (fifty years old and inclined toward nostalgia), I would be foolish to conclude that a few weeks of my sixteenth year were the best time of my life. But I conclude exactly that. I had the house to myself. I could sleep late, lie around, think, read, sing. I discouraged visits from friends, telling them I was too sick for company, but I didn't feel sick at all. After a morning alone and before I had a chance to become bored, Felicity would come over, fix lunch, recite some of her story, and then before she left she would relieve some of the pressures of adolescence. I had the afternoon alone, more time to think and dream. One of Mom's friends would make my supper and leave something (a pie, cookies) for me to snack on in the evening. It was great; I wonder if I ever would have tired of that routine. Would it have become tedious after another week or could I have lived like that for another year, ten years, the rest of my life? I don't know, but for the time it did last, it was great.

The window in my bedroom was large; I could open it and sit on the sill, my legs dangling over the side of the house, to watch the storms come in from the west. Wonderful theater, because there's nothing on the prairie to curb atmospheric violence, and the flat land and arching sky make a perfect stage— big enough, wide enough, and unobstructed—for storms that have been building for a thousand miles. Beginning as minor turbulences outside Denver and then moving like an unchecked slide into insanity, these storms turn inward and feed on themselves, picking up innocent currents and temperature variances across the blank flatness of Kansas and Nebraska, northern Missouri and Iowa. With no mountains or large bodies of water to dissuade them, the storms arrive black and terrible onto the Illinois prairie. And I'd sit there on the sill watching them until the rain started, sit there and cheer 'em on, hollering in the wind and screaming at the thunder ("All right!" "Go to it, baby!" "Yeah, *Yeah!*"), excited by it all and unafraid of any of it. I was sixteen, living alone, and in love with a beautiful, older woman; nothing could touch me back then.

On Felicity's last visit, the day before my family's scheduled return, she told me she wouldn't be coming over to my house anymore. I nodded eagerly, meaning that I understood—and meaning that I was glad she wouldn't be there when my family was because I wouldn't know how to act.

"But you can come over and see me anytime you want," Felicity said.

I nodded again, less eagerly this time.

We were standing by my front door, and when I didn't speak, Felicity took in a breath. "Well . . ."

I knew she had to go, but there was something I wanted to say.

"What?" Felicity asked, seeing the prestatement set of my face.

"Uh . . ." I was looking at the door.

"What?" This time she asked it softly, in nothing more than a whisper. So I looked her in the face and delivered a sentence that had been resting and itching in various parts of my brain for two years.

"I love you."

She smiled.

"I want to marry you. When I get out of high school."

She did not remind me she already was married; she did not tell me how stupid I was for saying such a thing. She just put her warm hand to my face and whispered, "Honey Bear, Love Bonnet, Sweet Prince," and a dozen other endearments.

•   •   •

When I was in high school, the last two years of high school, I began smoking and drinking and playing games with girls. I started with cigarettes just because you can strike so many poses with them: let 'em dangle from your lip, hold 'em between your second and third fingers, toss 'em in the air and catch them in your mouth, strike matches on the legs of your dungarees or on your zipper or with your thumbnail, flip the butt out the window of a car speeding through the night so the glowing coals explode like a little bomb on the road. But posing, I picked up a lifelong addiction.

I started drinking because it was something to do at parties and on the fenders of cars parked on lonely roads in the night, on the prairie. And with booze, I could mask shyness and summon bravado. Masking and summoning, I acquired another life-long addiction.

And then the girls. We boys treated them like creatures from another planet, as if their thoughts and feelings bore absolutely no resemblance to our own. All you could do was try something and see what happened. Touch there, do that, say this—and then wait for the reaction. Compare notes with other guys. "Squeeze just above their knee . . . suck on their earlobe

. . . tell 'em you love 'em . . ." All pure behaviorism. I became addicted to those games, too, and now sometimes forget what the object is.

Smoking, drinking, game playing, and the mobility that access to a car gave me left little time for Felicity. Whenever she was sitting out in her royal chair, as I drove by, I'd honk and she'd wave in reply. But I didn't visit her very often, and it didn't happen again until the night of my high-school graduation.

Graduation day, following tradition, fell into five levels: the graduation ceremony at school, gatherings with families and relatives, a big party at a local restaurant, separation into couples for a drive or a movie or whatever, and a regrouping of the males, who gathered together for conversation (unbelievably filthy and ignorant things about sex; sweet, innocent idealism about the future) and Southern Comfort. I got drunk and sick.

Driving home miserable and worried about the reception I'd get from my family, I was struck by an impulse as I approached Felicity's house. I turned into her lane and slid to a stop by the side entrance of that little square house.

Knocking loudly at her door (my heart beating fast and me suddenly wishing I were even drunker), I called for her in a singsong voice: "Felicity! Oh, Felicity!" I thought I was being daring and terribly dramatic. It was past midnight.

The kitchen light came on and the door opened wide. Felicity, backlighted and door-framed, laughed to see me. "Well, well. What do we have here?"

"We have me," I said, grinning crookedly and weaving. "Can I come in?"

She laughed again. "Absolutely, Sweetness-and-Light. Absolutely."

I entered the kitchen and she shut the door behind me. Felicity was wearing a red silk robe and I imagined (how I imagined) that underneath the silk was nothing but Felicity. "That story," I said, sitting down because I'd become abruptly dizzy, "that story you been telling me."

"Yes, Love?" Her face was bright with amusement.

"Well, you know."

"Hmm?"

"You *know*. It sounded like to me that the woman and that boy . . . you know. You made it sound like, you know, they did it."

"It?"

"*It*," I insisted. When Felicity laughed loudly, my face burned. To stop her laughter and to gain control of the situation and to do what I'd come there to do, I quickly stood and put my hands to her breasts: left to right and right to left. I expected her to knock away my hands or maybe to slap me; my face was, in fact, twitching with the anticipation of being hit. But she just stood there and stared, her eyes showing some emotion that at the time I could not identify.

"Oh, Honey Bear," she finally said. "This is just too, too perfect."

Then I threw up. Caught by surprise, I was barely able to release her and turn away in time so I wouldn't actually upchuck right on her. Ever polite, I kept apologizing even as I was vomiting.

"That's okay, that's okay, Doll," Felicity said as she held me—a hand on my forehead and an arm around my shoulders. When I was finished, including even the several dry heaves that conclude such things, Felicity led me to the sink and bathed my face with wonderfully cold water.

"I'm sorry, so sorry," I told her earnestly as she took me into her living room and put me gently, full-length, on her couch. "I'll clean it up. I will. I'll clean up the whole mess."

"Nonsense. That's nothing. It's you we have to take care of." She headed for the kitchen, stopping on the way to say, "And I'll take care of you, Button—I will."

She came back with a bowl of water and a washcloth. I'd eased into a light sleep. "I'm sorry . . . sorry," I said, blinking awake again.

"Hush, Honeycomb. No more talk." We looked at each other a moment and when she could tell I was about to apologize again, she said, "No more talk."

She put her left hand on my forehead and brushed my unruly hair up and away from my face; her right hand unbuttoned my shirt. With her left hand, she soaked the washcloth, squeezed it out, and wiped my eyes; her right hand unfastened my pants. She put the cloth across my hair line and, with the forefinger of her left hand, lightly traced all of my face—oval outline and the features it contained; her right hand pushed down my underwear to expose my private parts to the dark night air that had seeped into and filled the room. As her left hand caressed and cooled my cheek and then my neck, her right hand made hot and languid strokes up and down. I was electrified.

Remaining motionless, even to the point of breathing shallowly, I studied her for some acknowledgment. But Felicity's face was set in the pose of a Madonna, full of grace; she looked at me as I'd seen my mother look at me, when I'd lain in bed with rheumatic fever. Felicity's face was carved by a sculptor bold enough to make those lips so full, that nose so perfectly, vertically straight.

Her left hand, constantly refreshing the cloth that refreshed my achy eyes, worked with the soft competence of a child's nurse. Her right hand, however, was a whore. It squeezed and loosened, jerked and then held tight, stroking up and down the length of me.

I examined what was happening, looking up from her left hand, across that benevolent face, and then down her right arm—but, still, I couldn't figure out how it could be that two so completely different activities were being performed on me. Hoping the magic wouldn't end too soon, I just lay there—participating in the ceremony only to the extent of an occasional and involuntary twitch, clench, swivel of my hips.

Just as matters were moving toward a conclusion, she brought her right hand close to her face and spit in her palm. Such lewdness from so chaste a face. I was astonished—and highly excited.

When she returned the right hand to its position and I felt upon that most tender member the warm wetness of her expectoration, I knew then that my time was near at hand. I thought it only gentlemanly to warn her, but she used a finger (of her left hand) to seal my lips.

Bingo. With whorish efficiency, her right hand squeezed me between spasms and then held tight until all the aftershocks had subsided.

From the pocket of her robe, she took a delicate handkerchief that was woven of a light, translucent white thread and embroidered all around its edge with blue loops. In each corner was a tiny red rose resting on a spray of dark green leaves. She used the handkerchief to wipe me clean, all the spots and trails along my trunk, and then she folded the handkerchief twice and put it back in her robe. I was amazed to see such a thing.

"Felicity."

"Don't say anything, Pretty Brown Eyes."

When she went into her bedroom, I used the opportunity to button my shirt and fasten my trousers. I was upright on the couch by the time she returned, smoking and carrying an ashtray. "Was it good for you, too, Honey?" she asked, sitting cross-legged at my feet.

Painfully ignorant, I answered forthrightly by nodding vigorously. Thank God, Felicity did not laugh. She just sat and smiled and smoked. Such willpower.

"I'm out of high school now," I told her. "You could come with me, to college. Live with me."

"I can't do that, Baby."

"I could go to Chicago and get a job and then we could live there together."

"No. You have to go to college. Prepare yourself. You're going to be a world-beater. People are going to lionize you—remember?"

"I'm going to be a great writer."

"I know you are."

"But you haven't even seen any of my poems or stories or anything."

"You can show them to me anytime, Sweetheart. But I got the kind of faith in you that doesn't require evidence or reasons."

"Come up to college with me and you could teach me how to be a writer."

"No." Felicity rubbed my leg. "You got to go through that by yourself. I'll wait till you get over that particular experience. Remember what I told you. I'm a disciple of delayed gratification. You just keep in mind that someone back here has complete faith in you."

I nodded. I believed her. Eighteen years old and I was absolutely convinced that the world belonged to me, that all I had to do was go out there and collect it. How I managed to squander that much confidence, that great amount of faith she placed in me, I don't know.

When she sat next to me on the couch, I turned to her and said, "I love you."

Felicity smiled and smoothed the hair at the side of my head.

"I'm serious," I insisted.

"I know you are, Baby."

"Will you come and see me off at the train next week?"

"You leaving for college so soon?"

"Yeah. I got a summer job there."

"Okay."

I stood up to leave. Felicity, still on the couch, said, "Did I ever tell you the key advantage to writing, to being a writer?"

"No."

"It's something you can do in the privacy of your own room." Then she laughed and I, not getting the joke, laughed, too—and waved and left.

That next week, standing on the train-station platform and surrounded by family and friends, I didn't see Felicity. I lingered until the conductor called, "All aboard!" My mother started crying, because she thought my reluctance to get on the train was a sign that I was scared to be leaving home. But the only thing I was scared of was missing Felicity.

Finally on the train, looking out the window, and still not seeing her, I felt a sense of loss. There are words for that. Sad. Forlorn. Hollow. I felt exactly the same way several years ago when I started to call Sy Lamont, with whom I used to work. He and I had disagreements about dancing rabbits and glass eyes; after he retired and moved to Florida, I'd call him every six months or so and ask him if he really saw those damn rabbits and did he really hold that glass eye in his hand or was he just kidding me. The last time I started to call him, I remembered— just as I was reaching for the telephone—that he was dead, had died several months before. At first, I was simply irritated and disappointed, as if recalling he was away on vacation and I wouldn't be able to reach him. Then the full realization finally soaked in: He was dead, gone forever.

It wasn't quite that bad when I was eighteen and leaving for college, because back then no one had died on me yet and, as it turned out, I hadn't even been abandoned in farewell by Felicity.

The train pulled slowly and when my car cleared the station, I saw Felicity standing at the side of the station house— standing close to the building so she was seen only by me. She caught my eye, smiled, and brought her hand to her lips. Then she laid her palm flat in front of her mouth, pursed her lips, and blew a kiss to me.

Like sunlight and moonlight and the light from train-station lamps at midnight, blown kisses are able to pass through glass. I know this because my hand was on the train's cold window and when Felicity's kiss reached me, I felt the center of my palm become suddenly warm. I put my hand to my mouth.

As the train took me by her, I spread my fingers and held the palm flat against the window: ready to catch another kiss. Felicity was holding her hand in a similar manner, ready to catch one of mine, but by the time I realized what she was doing, I was too far down the tracks and the angle was all wrong for throwing kisses.

Even with that last kiss missed, I was addicted. To farewell scenes and to Felicity.

GRAVĒDA

The part Felicity told me when I was in high school.

10. Gravēda spends her first morning on the beach hiding in her rock den. She tells herself she should think of important matters: how the reunion managed to go so bad so quickly and why the tribe has halted the journey on the beach and where is Ismo and what's to become of Gravēda herself. But she's unable to concentrate, because her mind keeps racing back to thoughts of Genipur—her mind like a puppy who can't bear to stay away from a guest no matter how sternly the master commands, "Down!" Finally, Gravēda thinks to hell with it and lets her mind romp and lick and jump all over the boy.

That's the problem: He's just a boy. Half my age. Still, he's handsome; his eyes are dark and brooding. And I think he likes me, she muses. Gravēda shakes her head. I'm stupid.

She brushes back her hair and raises her chin. Then Gravēda suddenly drops her head and giggles, putting her hands to her mouth—giggles because now she's wondering what kind of kisser Genipur is.

Oh, she knows she's acting like a fool—acting as no forty-year-old woman should act. But her social development stopped when she was twenty, and the last time she talked to a male she *was* a girl. So perhaps she can be forgiven for sitting there among boulders and hugging herself as she pretends Genipur's arms are around her—and then rubbing her chin on her shoulder and imagining it's him. Talking to herself coyly as, in her mind, he tries to nibble on her earlobes and she whispers encouragement: "No, no, Genipur."

She gets herself so excited that her breathing comes in pants and her lower belly hurts. She closes her eyes and squeezes herself hard. "Yes, yes, Genipur. Sweet, sweet Genipur. That's my special name for you now. I won't tell anybody. Not even my very best girl friend in the world. *Sweet Genipur.*"

She dreads giving up the daydream 'cause she knows when she does that everything will become obvious again—that the journey has made her old and scarred and tough and that he's just a boy.

11. Gravēda, still hidden among the rocks, is startled by a strange voice on the beach. "For saaaaale, for reeeeent, for freeeee," it sings, adding quickly, "Rooms and warrens. Get out quick."

She sneaks a quick peek over the boulders and sees a small, humped figure walking away from her. "For saaaaale, for reeeeent, for freeeee. Rooms and warrens. Get out quick." As it walks, hobbles along unsteadily, the figure rhythmically swings a large bell; but the bell must be clapperless because it makes no noise. The only sound on the beach, other than that made by the sea, is the fading voice, chanting: "For saaaaale, for reeeeent, for freeeee. Rooms and warrens. Get out quick."

From the back, the figure reminds Gravēda of the old priest Eller. But he must have been eighty when the tribe left Gravēda and her Momma twenty years ago. Surely he's dead now, Gravēda thinks. Then, again, the odd voice *is* reminiscent of Eller's, and the figure *is* dressed in tattered, torn, and dirty robes—just as Eller always wore.

It's noon, with the sun over Gravēda's head and traveling the journey today without her; the idea of that makes her uneasy. She stretches and looks up the beach to see Crat limping toward her. A big white bandage is wrapped around his left foot and with each step he seems in danger of toppling over and spilling everything off the large wooden tray he's carrying.

When he gets to the bottom of the boulder pile, he calls pleasantly: "Gravēda!" Almost singing her name. This makes Gravēda wary, and she fingers her sword.

Crat puts the tray on the flat rock and calls again. "Gravēda!"

She climbs down to the sand but stays several feet away

from him. She has an urge to comment again on his ridiculous outfit, the purple robe and bright red sash, but decides to keep her mouth shut.

"I trust you slept well," Crat says politely.

She nods.

"After that unfortunate incident yesterday," he says, nervousness now showing in his voice, "I thought the least I should do was offer you a nice meal to start your first full day on the beach."

She looks around for the bowl that Genipur brought her, but it's gone. The kid must've taken it; Gravēda decides not to mention his visit. She examines the goodies that Crat has brought: golden fried rabbit muscles, a pile of pawpaws and persimmons, steamed white-fleshed fish in broad green leaves, and a large clay jar of water. She takes a big drink right away and although she's not all that hungry, she begins eating 'cause Gravēda has learned from the journey not to pass up food. Tomorrow there might be none and what you eat today is stored in a most convenient and readily accessible form: fat.

After she finishes the fish and rabbit, Gravēda wipes her greasy fingers on her hair. Starting from the center part and working down through the wavelets to her shoulders, she soon has her fingers reasonably clean while the fatty grease puts what she believes to be a glistening edge to her black, black hair. Crat watches all this, standing on his one good foot, with the other leg cocked so the bandaged foot can rest against the leg that's supporting him—looking all the more like a stork in silly plumage. But Gravēda's impressed with his almost perfect balance.

She burps and starts on the pawpaws and persimmons, which are ripe and mushy-good—completely puckerless. She appreciates that and begins to feel bad about snipping off his toe. Gravēda whispers: "Sorry."

"What? I didn't hear you," he says.

But she doesn't feel bad enough to repeat the apology. "Nothing. Forget it."

Gravēda eats self-consciously, aware of Crat's constant stare. He finally takes a breath and says, "I'm sorry, Gravēda, really I am. Sorry about yesterday. I should have realized how troubled you'd be, rejoining the tribe after all that time and seeing the ocean and everything. What was it? Ten years caring for your mother and then ten years catching up with us? A magnificent display of will."

She keeps eating, thinking, Crat's a pretty saintly guy to be saying these nice things and bringing me food when you consider what I did to him. She tries to remember if she already told him what she'd long planned to tell people when they asked about her ten-year journey alone on the trail: *It had its moments. I'll be damned if it didn't have its moments.* She is, in fact, about to say this when Crat begins speaking again.

"I'm going to make everything up to you, Gravēda. I'm going to be your sponsor here on the beach and take care of you. Bring food and teach you about the beach rules and tell you everything that's happened since the tribe got here."

"Good! You can start by telling me where the other travelers are. The older ones. Like Ismo."

Crat nods as if expecting the request. "I'll tell you all that, but I want to do it the right way—giving you a complete background so you understand not only the whats but also the whys."

His pedantic manner irritates her. "Forget the whats and whys. Tell me the wheres. Where's Ismo?"

"For some time he lived in the caves with the other old travelers. You have to understand, many travelers were killed trying to cross the uncrossable ocean, and those who weren't drowned felt so ashamed about the journey being halted that they've holed up in caves and are living like hermits."

"And that's where Ismo is?"

"Not exactly. . . ."

She cuffs him on the ear, knocking Crat off balance so that he falls to the sand. They stare at each other. Gravēda is given to sudden rages that quickly dissipate—a quirk developed in reaction to years of pursuit by ravens. She scans the sky in automatic routine. Now she feels like apologizing to Crat again. Instead, she asks, "You got any ambergrist?"

"At least take a look at these," he says as he stands and hands her a sheet of paperbark. "These are the rules and regulations we live by, now that we're on the beach."

Gravēda uses the paperbark page to wipe pawpaw pulp from her fingers and mouth. When she hands the crumpled mess back to Crat, he smiles but his stomach turns acidy.

"You should be thankful for the ocean," he tells her, "because if it hadn't halted the journey, you wouldn't have caught up with us."

She shrugs. "You got any ambergrist? I sure could use a taste—just for old times' sake."

Crat shakes his head.

"No ambergrist?"

"Its use is prohibited here on the beach. We've found that substances such as ambergrist and distillates interfere with efforts not only to build viable interpersonal relationships but also an individual's personal examination, his self-assessment. . . . Gravēda?"

She has walked away, climbing now among the huge boulders to hide again in her cool rock den. Gravēda always did take inanities as personal affronts.

12. "Damn." Gravēda hits her fist lightly against one of the boulders. She was hoping for a taste of ambergrist, because it has nearly magical abilities to lift the spirits; travelers used it during the journey to take the edge off hunger and fatigue—and even to quiet a baby's tummy. Gravēda was practically raised on the stuff.

Priests always were rabid about the dangers of ambergrist, explaining to their classes of youngsters that if you consume more ambergrist than your body can burn off, the excess will be stored in the muscles of your heart until your heart gets so full of it that the muscles harden into a crystal that can't be broken or etched—unaffected by any element, even time. Then the priests would repeat the legend about the Passionate One, the traveler who once tried to rush ahead of the tribe and meet God on his own. He traveled on nothing but ambergrist and, according to the old story, all that was ever found of him was the crystal mold of his heart resting on a bed of green clover and bearing a hairline crack. The rumor was that priests kept that heart and still carry it as an icon.

"Damn," Gravēda says again, lying back and trying to get comfortable. She never wanted to tempt a crystalliferous heart. "I just wanted a little taste for old times' sake." Then she hears that strange voice again.

"For sale, for rent, for free. Rooms and warrens. Get out quick."

Gravēda gets to her feet and, looking over a boulder, sees the little humped figure walking past the base of her rock pile. "By God, that *is* Eller," she whispers to herself. "But how . . . He must be a hundred years old."

With one hand he swings that silent bell, and in the crook of his other arm he carries a sheaf of papers. "For saaaale, for reeeent, for freee. Rooms and warrens. Get out quick."

You crazy bastard. Gravēda grins. She always liked old Eller 'cause he was so decidedly unpriestly. Dirty in dress, irreverent in manner, he was absolutely derelict in the priestly duties of attending the sick, educating the young, ensuring that the tribe maintained all the old traditions. Mostly what Eller did was sneak off by himself and write poetry. Some of the most god-awful stuff you could imagine: *O what is a traveler but mobile faith*—junk like that.

During evening camps or when the journey was temporarily halted to wait for some woman to give birth to her baby, Gravēda and the other kids would sneak up on Eller and grab away his pages. Then they'd run over to where the rest of the tribe was gathered and would read the poems out loud. Everyone thought it was a gas. For days afterward, kids would go around saying things like, "O what is a rock. O what is a toenail. O what is an Eller but a mighty queer feller."

He would chase them with a stick, but even then Eller was too old and slow to catch anybody.

"I can't believe he's still alive," she whispers, shaking her head.

As the figure makes unsteady progress away from Gravēda's boulder den, she quickly climbs down and sneaks to the side of him. It *is* him!, she says to herself as she gets close enough to see how advanced age has redoubled his congenital ugliness: big, fat liver-lips that hang lethargically open; a stringy head of hair that shows a random pattern of bald spots, as if Eller suffers the mange; bags under his eyes and, in fact, all his flesh so devoid of tone that it just hangs there on facial bone; and the damnedest nose you'd ever hope to see—a huge misshapen strawberry with short, bristly hairs tufting out of its pores.

Gravēda is chuckling as she leans to touch him. "Hello, Strawberry Nose!" she bellows as she jabs him in the ribs.

Eller is so frightened that he throws up his arms, tossing away the bell and the papers. He trips over his feet as he attempts to identify who has accosted him—finally landing clumsily on his butt amid the scattered paperbark sheets.

Gravēda laughs as she hollers at him. "O what is an Eller but a mighty awkward feller!"

He collects some of the pages from the sand, brushes them off, hugs them to his sunken chest. Then he looks up, tosses his head, and says archly, "Gravēda, you bitch."

Which elicits from her belly laughs. "Give us a poem!" she yells.

Looking down at the pages, Eller says, "I'm not into poetry anymore. I'm what you could call your ideal spectator now."

Still laughing, Gravēda says, "Still crazy after all these years, heh, Eller?"

But he's intent on the pages in his hands. "This is not in the script, not in the script at all," he mutters.

"What?"

"How was it?" Eller asks, still looking at the pages. "Twenty years separated from the tribe, then traveling alone to catch up."

"It had its moments. I'll be damned if it didn't have its moments." Gravēda is always pleased to be able to give that response, so often rehearsed over the years.

"I know that!" Eller exclaims. "It's all right here," he says, shaking the pages at her.

"What?"

His face suddenly contorts into a look of wild fright as he shakily points behind Gravēda and then yelps, "Swizzle snake!"

She whirls around, sword lifted and ready. But there's nothing behind her, and when she turns to face Eller again, he's laughing. "It went up your swizzle," he says, "right up your old swizzle."

"You buzzard."

He takes a gnarled stylus from his robe and begins to write furiously. "All here, all right here."

When Gravēda reaches for the pages, Eller jerks them away and points his stylus in a manner that suggests he considers it something of a weapon. "Back off, you gingersnap," he threatens, "or I'll write you up a heart attack. Pop a vessel in your brain and give you a stroke you'll never forget." Then he begins laughing again. "Or never remember—yeah, never remember."

Not knowing what the old man is talking about, Gravēda is unable to fashion a reply. She watches him write awhile and then asks in a whisper, "I bet you have some ambergrist, don't you, old man?"

He nods, continuing to write.

"Crat said it wasn't allowed on the beach. How'd you get it?"

Eller looks up at her. "I do it with mirrors—all done with mirrors. You wouldn't understand. That's not meant to be a reflection on you, however." Then he cackles and cackles.

When he holds a hand to her, Gravēda pulls Eller to his feet. He collects the rest of the pages from the sand and then picks up his bell. "What's wrong with it?" she asks. "How come it doesn't make any sound?"

"None are so blind," he says, shaking a finger at her, "as those who will not hear."

"What?"

Eller turns and hobbles away from her.

"Eller!" She wants to ask him about the ambergrist.

But he doesn't look back. "For saaale, for reeent, for freee.

Rooms and warrens. Get out quick." And Gravēda is left there shaking her head and grinning after him.

13. With Eller gone, Gravēda has nothing to do until the sun sets. Then she has the sun. Sits in the sand, wallows in the sand. Watches the sun set into the sea and wonders how in the hell she got in the position she's in.

Crat interrupts her sunset by bringing more food: rose hips, acorns, dandelions, fish stew, chokecherries, wild onions, honey. Such food. Gravēda is unaccustomed to it, but she eats with relish. Crat also offers a bowl piled high with small eggs, explaining that he's experimenting with the domestication of quail. Gravēda refuses to eat eggs. Anything but eggs.

As she eats, he talks: asking her to give up her sword and knife (which she, of course, refuses to do) and claiming he seeks to disarm her for her own good. She tells him harshly that if he wants to do something for her good, he'd get the tribe to celebrate properly her reunion. All in good time, Crat says, all in good time. Meanwhile, he tells her, she should avoid the company of travelers. Gravēda still doesn't mention Genipur to him.

But it is Genipur who's on her mind all through the night, and it is Sweet Genipur who stands like an apparition in the predawn light of Gravēda's second day on the beach.

He calls to her softly. "It's me. Genipur."

She motions for him to come up to her rock den, and he climbs timorously. "I'm sorry to wake you like this," Genipur says when he sits as far from Gravēda as he can manage in the tight spot between boulders. "This is the only time I can get free to see you. Without anyone else finding out."

She studies his unmarked face. But when she leans close, he leans away. They sit in silence for a moment and then she asks, "Why did you act so frightened when you brought me that bowl of stew? Are you scared of me? You are, aren't you?"

He shrugs.

"Did you think I was going to kill you?"

He shrugs again. "Maybe."

Considering her obligation to the conversation fulfilled, Gravēda sits and stares, waiting for the boy to tell her why he's there. But even as the silence extends itself, she doesn't mind. It's fun having the company. She begins thinking about his eligibility as a husband and suddenly blurts out in a rushed whisper, "Are your parents alive?"

He seems startled by the question but answers directly: "Yes. They're both living in the caves with the other old travelers."

Ah, she nods. Disappointed. He can't be my husband yet. I wonder if he thinks I'm old. She can't figure out any graceful way to ask him.

They sit awhile longer. She nudges his foot with her own, telling herself it was an accident but knowing it wasn't. He moves his feet, smiles tightly, clears his throat. She waits for him to speak, but he doesn't.

Gravēda is about to begin whistling to pass the time when the boy says, "The priests always talk against continuing the journey."

"They don't."

He nods vigorously. "Yes they do. They want to make an adjustment to the journey."

"An adjustment?"

"Yes. So we don't have to go out on the ocean."

"But how can you travel toward the setting sun without crossing that ocean?"

"You can't. But the priests don't want us to sail the ocean. They think the whole tribe will drown."

"And what do you think?" Gravēda considers calling him "Sweet Genipur," but she doesn't want to spook the child.

"I think the ocean can be sailed. A bunch of us already have built boats. We grew up on the beach. Been here since we were kids. I know we can make it. The only reason we haven't left already is that it wouldn't be fair to leave the old travelers in those caves. But as soon as they're, you know, gone . . ."

"Dead?"

"Yeah. Then we're going."

"You're not afraid of the ocean?"

"Naw." He seems to puff a little.

When Gravēda leans to scratch her ankle, she smells saltwater on him. "You do a lot of swimming, do you? Even though it's against the rules?"

"Sure. But I have to do it at night. So the priests won't catch me."

"Why the hell is everyone so afraid of the priests? It sure wasn't that way on the journey."

Genipur bristles. "I'm not afraid of the priests."

Gravēda nods.

"But they might try to stop us even after the old travelers are gone. And some of the others, the ones who helped me build the boats, they're not too sure about the trip. I *am* afraid the priests will talk them out of going. That's why I'm glad you're here. You'll help convince people we should be continuing with the journey. People will listen to you. You're a real traveler."

Gravēda smiles, sits up, brushes back the hair at the sides of her head. Then she elevates her chin just a bit. They seem to have exhausted everything they know to say to each other. Gravēda begins tapping her fingers on rock. But when Genipur stirs as if in preparation to leave, Gravēda quickly asks, "Are there creatures in the ocean?"

"Fish?"

"No. I mean, *creatures*. Things that could make strange sounds."

Genipur opens his mouth as if to say, *Ah*. "You've heard them, too, huh? Like some kind of music, right? It happens about this time every year. Nobody knows what it is. Some of the older travelers used to say it was God out there begging us to continue the journey."

Gravēda gets edgy.

"Things were really strange before the old travelers went to those caves. People were always drowning themselves. They'd hear those sounds and then someone would say it was God and then two or three travelers would jump in the ocean and we'd have to drag them back. Who knows?" he says, resting sweet chin on sweet knee. "Life is crazy. I don't think I'm going to get married, even after my parents are dead and I'm eligible for it. Who wants to bring a child into this world?"

Gravēda is horrified to hear this. "That's blasphemy, kid. I never was much for all the traditions of the creed and everything, but I know the tribe, and each traveler has to do two things. Keep moving toward the setting sun and have a baby. Each couple having one baby until the tribe—"

"I know, I know," Genipur says, disgusted. "Until the tribe is reduced to The One and by that time we will have reached the spot where God is waiting. But that kind of loses its flavor after ten years of no traveling—if you know what I mean. Hell, the reason I want to launch our boats is for the adventure of it mainly. And I don't need to get married and have the baby for that."

Gravēda spits on him. Just a reflex. An expression of the disgust—and disappointment—she feels at hearing his easy denial of the things for which, toward which, she's been traveling during the past ten years. But as soon as she does it, she's sorry. She presses her fists into her legs, damning herself for having such a rash nature.

Genipur, however, isn't appalled; he doesn't even wipe the spittle from his hand. "When you're on the beach long enough," he tells her quietly, "you'll hear a lot of blasphemy."

Gravēda sighs. Look at the boy looking at his feet. He seems so obviously in need of the comfort of her arms that she itches and aches to hug him. Would this sweet child squeal in horror if I were to grab him tightly? She commands herself not to do it, and commanding so, she scoots a tad closer.

Genipur takes a deep breath and blows it out, blows it out along her arm. Sweet torture for one who has for so long been so alone, to feel warm breath in close quarters with the sun not yet up. She wonders if she can get away with pinching him ever so lightly.

Things get kind of shaky here; one of those times when you know something's going to happen. When, in fact, it has begun.

Dark eyes shine in this early light—half moon and half sun, star-dappled light—showing tears.

Genipur nods. Gravēda doesn't know what that means exactly, but the boy nods. And then, perhaps from the embarrassment of tears, he smiles broadly and shows teeth.

That's when dignity and caution and rationality all abandon Gravēda. She becomes a girl again, seeing next to her the one she dreams she'll marry, the one who would have what Genipur now shows: straight and white and even teeth. She puts a hand to her mouth to cover her own misshapen, discolored teeth. I love you, I love you. She closes her eyes and repeats it over and over in her mind, now whispering it past her hand: "I love you, Genipur."

It startles them both. No!, she thinks. I meant to keep it in my head. And it was there because of those dumb girlish dreams about a husband, handsome and young. . . . I didn't mean to say it out loud. *Such an idiot*—first I spit on him and now I declare my love. All because of stupid teeth. Damn, she thinks, why don't I admire more glorious qualities: a noble carriage or derring-do. But teeth? She suddenly remembers Ismo and is all the more ashamed.

And Genipur. Poor, astonished Genipur. He doesn't even realize his smile set this whole thing off, 'cause he's still doing it—smiling wide now from the embarrassment of having this rock troll say she loves him.

Gravēda wonders where the words are to make everything okay again. All she can think of is: "I'm sorry I spit on you."

"It's all right," he says—smiling, smiling, smiling.

And then, as if to offer final proof that she's gone quite mad, Gravēda reaches her hand toward his mouth in wild hope that a fingertip of hers might touch those teeth.

He jerks back just as she brushes his lip. Genipur is shaking his head, trying to say something. "I'm afraid of you," he finally declares. "God help me, but I'm afraid of you, Gravēda." In a great rush, he climbs over boulders to get away.

Gravēda remains sitting, blinking, thinking. She feels a spot of moisture on her fingertip—from when she touched his mouth. Acting quickly now, before the breeze carries that spot away, she puts the finger under her tongue. And sucks. It is there that a drop of Genipur is picked up by her blood and distributed throughout her body; when he reaches her heart, wild palpitations ensue.

She presses her hand on the bone over that heart. "Sweet Genipur. Now I carry you here."

14. Gravēda balls up: knees to chest, arms around legs, hands locked onto wrists—pulling tightly. This is how she hides from the morning's sun. Like some sort of hermit troll in her hermit troll den.

Crat brings jellies and honey and water, which he leaves on the flat rock after calling repeatedly to Gravēda, who does not answer. Toward midday, hunger and thirst encourage her to leave the den, but before she does she hears the angry cawing of a raven, which makes Gravēda burrow even deeper between rocks. Finally she peeks out. A shiny black raven perched on cliff's edge high above her. Another scout looking for her? Why don't they give it up? They should be back in the forests that ring meadows, laying eggs for a new generation of ravens, instead of spending so much effort on stupid revenge. She watches the raven spew caws from deep inside its body, jerking to launch the ugly sounds as if those ugly sounds were spring-loaded. She slips behind rock. She wonders how it happened: that someone who once traveled as magnificently as she—sword and feet ready to stick and squash anything that crawled, hopped, slithered, and scampered within sticking and squashing range—could end up hiding from a bird and too timid to go down and collect food that's been left for her. And that child Genipur is ineligible for marriage and Ismo's off in some cave, crazy or dead. She balls up again: knees to chest, arms around legs, hands locked onto wrists—pulling tightly.

But that sun! By high afternoon it has accumulated enough power to sweat her out of the den. Checking to make sure the raven's gone, Gravēda climbs onto one of the huge boulders high in that jumbled, giant pile of boulders. She takes off her robe and unties the leathers, putting everything in a pile next to her. She lies back, sunning herself like a lizard and warily watching for signs of movement in the sky above and on the beach below; seeing any, she will roll off the boulder and slip among the deep shadows of her den.

"Hell with this." Gravēda dresses, grabs her sword, and climbs down to the sand to eat and drink what Crat left for her. Then she walks along the beach, sweating under the heavy robe and leathers. Crat has told her that there's absolutely no reason for her to be wearing such clothing on the beach, but she remains fully dressed in defiance of this temperate place.

She walks until the sun begins to set, catching her beached and childless again today. She doesn't have to be told that it was during these dusks that the old travelers plunged into the ocean in a mad desire to continue the journey. She feels the urge herself.

But Gravēda defies the urge, defies the sun itself. She takes off her robe and spreads it at her feet. She unties each of her leathers and puts them, and her sword, on the robe.

Now she's naked.

And if any of the young travelers happen along, she thinks, let them note how different my body is from theirs, so slim and smooth and clean. I am heavily muscled and scarred and gnarled, the effects of ten years' hard traveling recorded on my body like a biography.

With her feet, she digs casually but steadily to make something of a pit, wide and deep, in the sand. She sits in that pit, arranging herself to watch the sun, which by now has set itself upon the edge of the sea. Then she starts burying her body, rocking back and forth to work herself deeper into the sand—and scooping handsful of it onto her legs and stomach and breasts until only her arms and head are free.

Now she's beached.

As Gravēda watches the sun fall below the sea's horizontal line, that sun she's followed all her life exercises upon her a draw that is gravitational in nature. It even pulls on her womb, which she can feel stir beneath pounds and pounds of flesh and sand.

When the sun goes below the ocean, light along the beach

becomes indirect and in that light she watches the waves come in and, staring without illusion at those waves, she calculates time. How long will it be before I see Ismo? How long will Sweet Genipur's parents live? When will I have my baby? When will I launch into that ocean?

The regularity of the waves and the effects of the increasing dark hypnotize Gravēda and in this hypnotic state she's given a message, reaches a conclusion that causes her to abandon all calculations of time: Ocean waves count off eternity by ones.

15. It's early in the evening when Crat finds Gravēda in her buried state. They argue, Crat telling Gravēda that burying herself in the sand is just the type of thing that Crat was hoping she wouldn't do. "I thought you were going to take a low profile so you wouldn't upset the other travelers," he says.

Gravēda spits.

"I'm going to have to report this to the council."

Gravēda grits her rotten teeth.

He calls her a desperado; she screams back that he and everyone else in the tribe who refuse to continue the journey are renegades. Then Crat drops a small egg on the sand next to her.

"The quail chick inside is still alive," he says. "Was about to be hatched when the hen abandoned the nest. I brought it here because you're the only one I could think of who'd be capable of eating an unborn creature."

She lunges at Crat, but the sand holds her. The priest stares in fascination, like a man standing just out of the reach of a vicious, but tethered, dog. "Monster," he calls her before he hurries away.

By the time Gravēda has struggled out of the sand, Crat has disappeared in the darkness. Gravēda throws back her head and screeches; the sound rolls out to sea.

She washes herself at ocean's edge, and then returns to her robes and leathers. Gravēda picks up the egg to crush it but when she holds it, she thinks she senses movement inside the fragile shell—as if it were possible to feel such a thing. She cramps.

"Stupid, stupid," she hisses, slapping her naked lower belly. "It's just a goddamn quail." Not knowing what to do next, Gravēda simply stands there to dry in the night breeze.

"Gravēda?"

She knows the voice, the sound of which echoes in her head. Gravēda quickly hides the egg between her breasts, grabs her robe and holds it—modestly, she likes to think—in front of her, and then turns to face Sweet Genipur. "What do you want, boy?"

"Boy?" He's weaving; his mouth hangs open. "Boy?"

"So you've managed to put your hands on some distillate, huh? Bring some for Gravēda, did you? I sure could use it."

"Boy?" he repeats. "I'm a man!"

"Had to get distilled to come see me? Of course. You couldn't face the monster sober, could you?"

"Don't you believe I'm a man?"

"Child," she says softly.

"No," Genipur insists as he loosens the cloth from around his groin and allows the material to fall to the sand. "Man!"

"Nasty boy," she tells him gently as she sits, careful to keep the robe about her.

"I am fully a man," he intones, hands on hips.

So she dares him with whispers: "Come and sit by me, fully a man."

Now, even though drunk, he becomes unsure of himself. He steps near, so close she can smell him like the saltwind from the sea. "Not afraid of me anymore?" she asks.

He bends back from the waist, as if that is an answer.

She looks at it and giggles girlishly. "Oh, sit down and stop brandishing your weapon," Gravēda says, patting the sand next to her. He kneels heavily, landing close; she arranges the robe, holding it tightly in front of her. "Am I really so bad, such a monster, that you have to get distilled just to have the courage to visit me?"

He grins stupidly. "I decided to come make a woman out of you."

Gravēda is caught by a spasm of laughter that makes her choke; she laughs and chokes and laughs some more. Genipur's still grinning, pleased with this confirmation of his charm.

She manages to ask as she laughs, "Tell me, Child, have there been many others you've made women of?"

"You'd be the first."

Which sets her off all the more. Somber Genipur has become a clown. "We'd have to be careful," she teases, " 'cause I'm eligible to have a baby and eligible women can get highly excited. In fact, I'm overdue."

"You'd better watch it then, Baby, 'cause I'm one hell of an exciter."

Gravēda grins. This is fun. Then, to see how deeply asleep his fear of her is, she puts her hand on his naked leg. He doesn't move away. He leans his weight to her hand. Nerves deep in the center of her begin to fire.

He places his face close to hers. Gravēda becomes giddy when she realizes she could, at that moment, reach out with her tongue and lick those porcelain-smooth surfaces of his straight and white teeth. "Do you still think I'm a boy?" he whispers in a challenge.

The answer is so wonderfully obvious that Gravēda could cry. "Yes."

He jerks back angrily. "I'm a man! Can't you see I'm a man?"

With her free hand, the one that's not holding the robe, Gravēda smooths the hair at the back of his head. "Of course." She pulls him close. "I see it now." She rubs his neck. "You're a man." He grins smugly. Such a boy.

But he's a boy fully in control, because when he uses the tip of his tongue to trace a wet track along the top of her nose, strange phenomena occur within Gravēda—as if warm and sticky honey she'd eaten earlier has now somehow spilled from her intestines to spread throughout her lower body: seeking a way to seep out. "Oh, my," she says in deep appreciation.

"You have the most magnificent nose in the world. I've never seen one that's so perfectly straight up and down."

"Really? I hadn't noticed." Of course, coquetry. Gravēda has no shame in these matters.

"Now, let's see what else you got," Genipur says, suddenly pulling away the robe and throwing it behind him before Gravēda can grab it back. She's mortified; the boy shouldn't have done such a thing. Although she never before felt so naked, Gravēda does not attempt to cover herself with her hands. Let the child look. And he does, conducting a thorough examination. She wonders what he thinks of what he sees. Do her heavy breasts shock him?

Gravēda becomes flustered by Genipur's attention and by his proximity. When she finally speaks, she does so meekly—as if apologizing. "I'm inert now. But once, once I was marked by energy."

"You're weird, Gravēda."

The warm and flowing stuff inside her congeals, and she turns to retrieve her robe. But Genipur pushes her back and then raises his hands toward her breasts. He hesitates touching her because he's nervous, because never before in his life has he seen so fully ripe a woman as Gravēda. Genipur is unsure what to do and how, exactly, to do it.

He places his hands gently on her breasts, left to right and right to left; he presses, as if to flatten them. When he does that, the breasts part slightly and something small and dark and wet rolls out. It falls flapping down Gravēda's abdomen to end up on her closed thighs.

Genipur gasps and stares. Whatever that thing is, it's alive. Too drunk to think straight, Genipur is under the impression that somehow he has broken something. He was afraid of this happening.

When Genipur looks at Gravēda, she realizes that now she is in control, and she immediately takes advantage of the situation. "Stand up, boy," she tells him harshly.

Genipur obeys. "I'm sorry," he says. "I'm really sorry. I didn't know. . . . I . . . ." Supplication is all over his face and voice.

"Step close," she commands, and he steps close. When Gravēda places her hands on his upper legs, she can feel those warm legs tremble. She looks up at him: His face is twisted and over his shoulders is a nightful of stars.

Gravēda's Poppa always told her he knew she was special and specially blessed, because when she was a baby she used to reach for the stars. Used to work a hand free of her swaddling and, late at night, would reach up and attempt to touch those twinkling lights in the sky. At least that's what he always told her, that she was special 'cause she used to reach for the stars.

Recalling this makes Gravēda ashamed of what she's doing with the boy. It seems so frivolous to be playing around with Genipur—as if she has betrayed all those years of hard traveling by ending up like this, knelt in the sand with a frightened boy at hand.

But his face is smooth and his teeth are straight and she can see that in some ways he indeed is manly.

So she grabs him suddenly and tightly, causing the child to swoon.

Perhaps it is sacrilege, what she's doing. But she continues doing it with enthusiasm.

Genipur may not be a star but Genipur is what she reaches for now, because unlike the stars, this boy is fully graspable.

"Cheep," says the chick. "*Cheep!*"

16. Tee-hee, tee-hee—shame on me. Nasty Gravēda. Hussy. Rock troll desperado hussy. Playing boom-boom on his zoom-zoom. Chasing swizzle snakes and gnawing belly steaks. Juicy, salty, malty, mmm.

Already accustomed to the self-indulgence of lying in her den well past sunrise, Gravēda stretches and groans and giggles as she recalls the previous evening.

And when she finally rises to look out over boulders, she notices, this morning for the first time, that the ocean is quite beautiful, actually. And today's clouds, look at them: white as Genipur teeth, coming in from that world of water in a well-disciplined formation, miles wide and making gentle and majestic progress across the heraldic blue sky. Was all this such a visual treat, did the air smell so sweet, did gnarled toes curl so tightly to toughened feet *before Genipur*?

She thinks not.

Gravēda wanders around the beach near her den, waiting for Crat to bring her food. But he doesn't show up. Too bad. She was ready to forgive him, ready to forgive the entire world today.

And then she waits up all night for Genipur, but he doesn't come either. No Crat the next day; no Genipur the next night. Gravēda catches crayfish and drinks the last of the water that Crat had left for her. She doesn't even see old Eller. Has the whole tribe left me again?

No, no. Genipur will come again. Tonight—or the next night. As soon as he can get away. Thinking this, believing this, Gravēda's waiting follows a pattern:

During the day, she lies around—resting her head on a boulder, cheek on rock, looking up and down the beach in wild hope of seeing someone. When she notices she's licking the rock, licking it gently with the tip of her tongue as if she has a craving for some rock mineral, she stops doing it immediately. When she flops down among the boulders and rolls over to lollygag in the cool shadows of her den, she sees that interlocking Gs have been scratched all over the rock. She traces them with her finger. But mostly what she does during the day is lament the slow passage of the daylight hours.

Sun! Look at it dawdling across the sky. Something's wrong. Someone should alert the Old Man to this mechanical breakdown in his system: The sun actually stops in midafternoon, hanging there in the sky for years and years. Hurry, hurry. Come on, night! Good, old night. Genipur visits me in the night.

When repairs are made and, finally, the sun eases down, Gravēda thinks about Genipur as she waits for him. She considers ways to possess him and wonders if the sweet child might let her fully explore his teeth with her tongue and fingers. She'd like to examine the differences in the wide teeth at the back, the sharp ones at the side, and the big ones in front. She could compare their various textures. Are they as smooth on their backsides as they are in front? And does his saliva taste different when sucked from his cheeks than it does when lapped from under his tongue? If the boy would just lie back and let me at him, Gravēda thinks, I could find out everything I want to know.

She naps and wakes, naps and wakes throughout the night. Occasionally, Gravēda will run her hands over her face to make it glisten (she hopes it glistens) with skin oils. Then she waits. Slips off her robe and leathers—and waits some more.

Uh-oh. Slow down, night, so long in coming and now so eager to leave. Linger awhile longer to give Genipur *time*. But look at the sky above the cliff.

Oh, look, look: Here comes the sun. Perverse, contrary, cranky old sun, limping across the sky yesterday but speeding into place this morning. Traveling so fast that Sweet Genipur doesn't have *time* to come visit me.

WHEN
I WAS
TWENTY

When I was twenty and had been away to college for two years, I came home in a state of advanced and aggressive obnoxiousness. Is there anything more tiresome and pompous and generally icky than a twenty-year-old halfway through its college education? There is not. (They alone, for example, are responsible for making the reputations of bad writers.) I would rather voluntarily call a life-insurance agent and ask him to drop by the house and look at my portfolio to see if I have adequate protection for my loved ones or even ask a zealot (religious, dietary, jogging) to explain in full detail the benefits of his zealotry or engage in almost any other odious activity than spend time with a college sophomore. And yet I were one.

College was in the East, and although I could have come home during the summer between my freshman and sophomore years, I found jobs and other excuses to stay away a full-blown two years. When I finally did return to the prairie, that reunion marked the first in a long line of reunions (and their accompanying departures and absences) I would manufacture and insert in my life—all because I never got the chance to be a soldier boy or war correspondent who could kiss his sweetheart farewell and then, four years pass, see her on the dock waiting wet for me.

When I finally did arrive home from college, everyone was *so* glad to see me. It was great. Still is. Combine enough time and geography (stay far enough away, long enough) and almost all the little complaints people have against you will be forgotten, and those not forgotten will be forgiven—leaving only the blood grudges to deal with. But back when I was twenty, I hadn't yet accumulated any blood grudges, so I came home to smiles and hugs and celebrations exclusively. It was great.

The way to play these reunions, I learned in later years, is to be humble and laconic. Smile a lot, answer questions cheerfully, keep telling people how great it is to be home again. Be Jimmy Stewarty.

But I played my first reunion just as you'd expect a college sophomore would: I generally paraded myself, half-assed and half-educated, around the prairie. I wore a ratty wool jacket with suede patches on the elbows, wore it in spite of the heat, and when people suggested that I might be more comfortable with it off, I'd say, I'd actually say to them: "Oh, I've become so accustomed to this old thing that I feel absolutely naked without it on."

And those damn pipes. I'd brought three home with me and was always fussing with one of them. When Mom asked me how long I'd been smoking pipes, I said: "Long enough that they seem like trusted old companions now. In the evenings, for example, I prefer this comfortable brier [I'd purchased it six weeks before coming home]. It seems to go with wood fires and wool [this was July in the Midwest, remember—no air conditioning], don't you think? And maybe a slightly aromatic tobacco. You don't mind pipe smoke in the house, do you, Mother?"

She should have stuffed the bowl in my mouth but, being a mother, she just gave me a bewildered look, smiled, and said, "Oh, no, Sonny. It smells kind of nice, really." I was, of course, her son, her baby, her boy; for the next twenty-five years, until her death, I committed offenses more severe and less funny than acting like an ass because of a pipe. But her reaction to my sins (divorces and drinking are examples) always was bewilderment, as if it simply were *curious* that these things happened to her baby, her boy.

Pop, however, was more clear-eyed. He had the old stag's natural wariness of young bucks, and he rolled his eyes and made hurumphing sounds when he heard Mom say my pipe smelled kind of nice. He, of course, still had to smoke his cigars on the front porch. All this delighted me; it was a way of getting back for all those times I had to pick up the cigar butts from around the porch's perimeter.

All throughout that summer, I eagerly shared aphorisms with the common folk. When listening to my father and brother-in-law bitterly discuss the Communist takeover of China, I chinked a lull in the conversation with this: "Whoever battles with monsters had better see that it doesn't turn him into a monster. And if you gaze into an abyss [pause to puff on the old brier], the abyss will gaze back at you." They eyed me suspiciously, as if I'd begun speaking in tongues.

It's a damn shame that I can't recall the exact details of my father's face but can remember precisely how I posed and preened during that summer. And I wonder by what perverse twist of memory is the sound of my mother's voice lost to me (she often sang at my sickbed) while I can clearly hear my reedy voice quoting inappropriate and misunderstood snippets to my astonished family that summer. Is that kind of selective memory my fault? And, if it is, to whom do I apologize?

I gave my brother-in-law an especially hard time. After one of Mom's belly-binding evening meals, the whole family (Mom, Dad, Sis, Brother-In-Law, Infant, and me) was on the front porch. I was sucking on an empty pipe; Dad was smoking a cigar downwind from the rest of us; Mom and Sis were talking about the baby's heat rash; and Brother-In-Law was attempting to engage me in conversation.

"Well, Sonny, what you going to do with yourself?"

I stared the stares of professors, searching for a way down, descending and condescending to answer.

"I mean," my brother-in-law tried again, "what are you studying to be? Where you going to work after college?"

The rest of the family, never so bold or rash as to ask such a direct question of the prince, became quiet and tense in anticipation of my answer.

"Permit me to quote the young Ibsen," I said, suck, suck, sucking. " 'Downward I must break my way till I hear the orestones ring' "—suck, suck—" 'in the deep is peace, peace and desolation from eternity; break me the way, my heavy hammer, to the hidden mystery's heart.' "

I had no idea what that meant in relation to my brother-in-law's straightforward question, but neither did anyone else. My mother and sister nodded in bovine acceptance. My father turned away and looked out over the prairie, as if suddenly struck with an acute attack of senility that tossed him back to some fascinating childhood memory. My brother-in-law, mouth hanging slightly ajar, looked around at the others to determine what his own reaction should be. Because his mouth was agape, a sudden upward rush of bean-and-pork-generated gas came out of his throat in a loud guttural belch. He was terribly embarrassed. When my sister tsked, he said, "Excuse me," in one of the most pitifully soft voices I've ever heard a man use.

In response, ass that I was, I waved my hand to excuse and dismiss him. I could have helped him laugh it off, could have made a joke or something. But I just waved and sort of shook my head as if to say, Well, what do you expect from the bumpkin? I don't know why I've always been so especially mean to him. He eventually inherited my father's businesses, but I didn't want them anyway. And the brother-in-law has over the years tried to strike a friendship with me; he's always treated me cordially. But I continue to insult the man so craftily that he's never quite sure if he's being attacked. I don't know. One of my many recreations, I suppose.

But I got my comeuppance that summer. Kept fooling around until I got in deep trouble with a girl—although, at the time, I didn't realize I was in trouble. One never does, *at the time*, does one?

I was throwing around all those quotes (aphorisms, poems, witticisms), because I was accustomed to the kind of conversations sophomores have while they're at college: using quotes to cover every conceivable situation in life. Why waste limited brain power on an original observation when you can pick up what someone else once said? And you can always find *something*, some quote that applies to good food or warm days or the dangers of sleeping alone.

In any case, I didn't appreciate what a rare and wondrous thing it was to quote a sonnet to a girl who's lived all her life on the prairie. Back then, the closest that a Midwest, hometown girl ever got to romance was when a couple of potato-heavy (and steak-short) young studs fought over her—and she rewarded the winner with her favors, which required tasting the stringy, bloody spit that leaks from recently broken teeth. Quoting poetry is an even more powerful, and sweeter-tasting, form of romance.

Too dumb to understand all this, I played Pretentiousness to a hometown girl's Innocence and she responded with Worship, against which I've always been Helpless. The upshot being that we were married four years after that summer. (Well, the real upshot being that we were divorced six years after we were married, because she was biologically unable to play the hometown girl's Trump; the marriage was, as they say, fruitless.)

We had dated in high school and corresponded during my first two years at college. She claimed in writing that she was saving herself for me; a statement that, I must admit, accumulated a great deal of interest on my part. I came to visit her the second night I was home. We parked on a straight and little-traveled country road. It went something like this:

" 'Shall I compare thee to a summer's day?' "

"What? What'd you say, Sonny?"

I held up my finger. "Just listen."

"Oh. Sure."

" 'Shall I compare thee to a summer's day? Thou art more lovely and more temperate: [Place right hand on her left cheek; press lightly for emphasis.] Rough winds do shake the darling buds of May [Make voice harsh.], And summer's lease hath all too short a date. Sometime too hot the eye of heaven shines [Look up and out the car's windshield; only the sister moon shining—and coolly, too—but continue on anyway.], And often is his gold complexion dimm'd. And every fair from fair sometime declines, By chance, or nature's changing course untrimm'd. [Pause here. Put left hand on her other cheek. Maneuver bodies so they're pressed close. Continue in a trembling voice.] But thy eternal summer shall not fade [Use thumbs to stroke gently near her eyes, smearing makeup and inadvertently creating a slightly ghoulish effect; continue on anyway.], Nor lose possession of that fair thou ow'st. Nor shall Death [breathlessly intone the word] brag thou wander'st in his shade, When in eternal lines to time thou grow'st. [Pause; let left hand sort of ooze on down to right breast—then continue quickly before a protest can be registered.] So long as men can breathe [sigh Cherry Blend breath into her face], or eyes can see [open wide those Baby Browns], So long lives this [kiss her softly and then pull back so she can see Sincerity on the kisser], and this gives life to thee.' "

Then quickly did I wallow myself between her legs and work a hand between our tightly sandwiched bodies.

"Shakespeare?" she inquired, grimacing and occasionally "ooing" because I was pinching us both in my effort to get the hand positioned.

"The Bard," I confirmed somewhat breathlessly as my hand finally arrived at the general location under her skirt—and then found a northwest passage over the top of and under her underwear. But still not home yet.

"Oh," she said in a disappointed voice as she twisted and thrusted in such an odd fashion that I couldn't figure out if she was trying to give herself to me or was attempting to struggle out of my clumsily heavy embrace, "I thought it was Shakespeare."

We continued (I didn't even laugh) like this for some time, silently bumping into each other like two people who have almost collided in a hallway and then are unable to get around each other—both moving together in one direction and then the other, remaining solemn and a bit exasperated in spite of the hilarious nature of the situation. Both of us fearful of breaking the mood (which was one of sweaty desperation, one that begged to be broken), we didn't talk or look at each other as we kept bumping and humping and grinding. She occasionally issued little gasps, but I think those were in reaction to my scratching her.

I thought there was a distinct possibility that we might complete the sex act (a term as romantic as our performances) without ever acknowledging what we were doing. Well, she would say as she afterward smoothed her skirt, it certainly is a warm evening. Yeah, I would reply as I zipped quietly, it certainly is. Say, did we just— But she would quickly interrupt, Not that I'm aware of.

And then, of course, there was always the possibility that we wouldn't complete any sort of act, because for some time I continued groping without success. I knew it was down there someplace, but I didn't know the exact nature of what I was looking for, and the quarters were cramped and we weren't giving each other directions. But then, then I whispered, "I love you," and everything was revealed to me.

.   .   .

When I was twenty, I discovered the lubricity of saying "I love you." That statement slid me into marriage and, in subsequent years of dalliance, into a lot of trouble.

You have to understand. Once I discovered the toniclike effect of those three words, I couldn't resist using them. It seemed cruel, in fact, not to administer something that was so easy for me to administer and so welcomed by those to whom it was administered.

One might think that *now*, in these days of indiscriminate coupling, "I love you" would have reached such a frequent and thoughtless level of use (said casually, along with directions: "I love you; a little higher and watch the teeth, okay?") as to have lost all power to thrill and entice. But I don't think so. Just the opposite seems to be the case: People go to great lengths to avoid saying "I love you." That refusal seems to be the one last refuge of honor among strangers who become technical lovers; they're going to be tough, by God, and not tell anyone "I love you."

Not me. I declare love as soon as the door's locked. And these declarations always have been appreciated, even by the most cynical and hardhearted of women. Maybe not believed, but always appreciated. It's the same when a B-girl sits next to you and you buy her a drink and she says you caught her eye as soon as you walked in the place, your job sounds fascinating ("And so you have to check their records and books to make sure

all the assets and, what'd you call it? those little debit things add
up right, huh?—wow!"), and you truly are a wonderful hunk of
manhood. Just because they're all damn lies doesn't mean you
don't appreciate *hearing* them.

By now, however, I have used the statement so frequently
and indiscriminately that it has lost all its meaning to *me*. And
now, if I really did fall in love, I don't know what I'd say. "I
adore you." "You mean the world to me." "I like you a whole
lot." I don't know. Just about anything except "I love you."

I guess the only time I declared love with sincerity was back
when I was sixteen and told Felicity I loved her.

Her name came up at the kitchen table, a week after I'd
been home from college. Sis was over visiting, and she and Mom
were fixing my lunch; Dad and Brother-In-Law were off somewhere on business.

"You know," I said, sucking reflectively on an empty pipe,
"I think I'll go see Felicity today. I feel bad I haven't seen her
before this." Mom abruptly turned away from the table and
went to fiddle with something on the stove; Sis stared hard and
queerly at the ham she was slicing, as it if had just moved,
had twitched at the touch of her knife. I had no idea what was
going on.

"Felicity still lives there, doesn't she? I've been watching
for her every time I drive by but . . ."

Mom clattered some pans and left the room; Sis came over
and sat next to me. "What the hell's—" I started to ask.

"Shh," she cautioned, looking at the doorway to make sure
Mom was gone. Then to me, conspiratorially: "Felicity's husband, who's in the asylum, you know . . . well, he's been getting
worse and worse."

"And that's what's upsetting Mom?"

"No, wait—I'm telling you. A few months ago, Felicity
came home from one of her visits to her husband. She was in
pretty bad shape. Just sitting out there in that silly chair of hers,
the one she made from the tree stump. She sat there all day
long. Then we were coming out here that night and it was rain-

ing and we saw her still sitting out in that chair. Can you imagine? We thought she had died or something." Sis paused to let me picture Felicity in the rain.

"We came home and got Daddy and then we all took her in that little house, and I helped her get on some dry clothes. She didn't act weird or anything. Just kind of quiet, like she had her mind on other things."

"And Mom feels bad about her?"

"Sonny," Sis said impatiently, "I'm getting to that part. After it happened, Felicity sitting out in the rain in the middle of the night, Dad started going over there to check on her. He began spending a lot of time over there. Doing little fix-up chores, bringing groceries from town—stuff like that."

"Really?"

"Dad said he was just being neighborly."

I snickered.

"This isn't anything to laugh at, Sonny. Mom is really upset."

" 'Cause she thinks Dad and Felicity—"

"Exactly."

"What does he say when Mom asks him about it?"

"Oh, she doesn't. You know them. They'd never talk to each other about something like *that*. Mom tells *me*, though. She tells me all about it. I was thinking maybe you should talk to Dad."

I nodded but knew I never would; what a ridiculous and awkward conversation that would be. "Is he still going over to see her?"

"No. I don't think so. He knows how much it bothers Mom."

I shrugged. The idea of my father and Felicity having an affair was preposterous. I recalled what had happened between Felicity and me that summer when I was sixteen and my family was away on vacation, and then I remembered images of my father's lardy white body, which I'd occasionally and inadvertently seen over the years. I shook my head.

"What?" Sis asked.

"Nothing."

"Anyway," she continued, "don't dare mention *her* name to Mom again. And don't you dare go over there, either. It'd break Mom's heart if you took up with that woman."

"Took up with her?"

"Mm," my sister replied, once again slicing ham.

A few nights later, on the way home from a date, I noticed the lights on at Felicity's house, felt that old impulse to turn into her crooked lane, and did. Seeing her lights and then thinking about her sitting in that little house made me realize how much I missed her. Missed the way she made me feel when she paid the kind of close attention only she could pay. She made me feel like I was on stage, singing, in the spotlight, the recipient of wild ovations. Can you hear it? All that applause, that cheering and stomping—and the more I sing, the more they love it. By comparison, the time I spend with other people, the conversations I have with other people—all that seems like just so much vamping till ready. Seeing lights on at Felicity's house that night made me realize how much I missed her magic.

.   .   .

When I was twenty, I thought forty was old, was when you sort of start to uncrank and settle down and go to church and wait to die. Whatever age you are, I have observed, someone twice your age seems old. When you're four, eight seems incredibly old and worldly. When you're ten, twenty represents that exotic state of adulthood. And when you're twenty, forty seems old—just as when you're forty, eighty seems old. I suppose the opposite is true, too: someone half your age seems incredibly young; I know that, now, twenty-five-year-olds strike me as being childlike.

I'll tell you something else I have observed: The older women I slept with when I was in my thirties (although, come to think of it, our liaisons were marked by a distinct lack of sleep) now are collecting Social Security. The only observation I can make that's ghastlier than that one is this one: By the time the younger women I now sleep with (and we do a lot of that) are old enough to hold a civilized conversation, *I'll* be collecting Social Security.

So as I stood on Felicity's doorstep and waited for her to open up, I thought I would see the face of an old woman.

She opened the door. She was dressed in that red silk robe. She looked just the same as she'd looked when I saw her last—two years ago at the train station. In fact, she was the same woman I first saw in my father's office six years before: Felicity was beautiful, open-petaled and ripe.

"Honey Bear!" She grasped my face in both of her hands and kissed me loudly, wetly. "Come on in, little Honey Bear. I was wondering when you'd be over."

To show her I no longer was the tongue-tied kid who'd last been in her parlor, I attempted to be flippant, provocative, and cruel: "Do you realize that this is the only time in our lives when you'll be twice my age?"

"Ouch!" she exclaimed, pausing and then laughing again. "You know how to wound a woman, don't you, Child?"

She led me through the small kitchen and into the living room that shared the front half of the house with one other room, her bedroom. Under the living room's front window was a large, plain wooden table; books and papers were stacked on it, under it, all around it. I couldn't tell you what color the walls of that room were painted, because every inch of those walls was covered with something: paintings, prints, a couple of old ties, photographs (framed and unframed), some hats, certificates. The eclectic clutter was unlike anything else I'd seen on the prairie; it was more like my room back at college.

When I sat on her couch, my memory was prodded by its nap and I thought of something even more provocative to say, but I censored it. I took out my pipe and began rubbing it over my face, concentrating on the creases by my nose.

"Home from college, huh, Babe?"

"Ah," I said, nodding my head and attempting to contort my twenty-year-old face into a look of sagacity. Meanwhile, I continued rubbing the pipe along my nose.

"What the hell you doing?"

Oh, good—she'd finally noticed. "I smoke a pipe now, you know. And facial oil," I announced pompously, "is the very finest element for preserving the brier used in pipes."

She gave me one quick, astonished look and then burst into wild laughter. I smiled a little, too, but I had sense enough to put away the pipe. "Oh, Butternut," she said, still laughing, "you're an absolute tonic for me—an absolute tonic." She leaned close, so close I felt the heft and warmth of her bosom on my upper arm, and then she kissed me on the cheek. I looked down and saw her cleavage. "Now," she said, pulling back, "what'll we have to drink tonight. I know you college boys—God, how I know you college boys."

I grinned like an idiot and said, in what I hoped to be a worldly manner, "Anything. I drink anything."

"Good, good." She went to a tall cabinet, floor-to-ceiling, that took up almost the entire back wall of the room; it contained the widest array of liquor I've ever seen in a private collection. During the times I drank at Felicity's house, beginning that night and continuing with widely spaced visits for the next twenty-five years, she was able to provide any drink I ever asked for.

"How's about gin on the rocks?" she asked. "With just a splash of quinine to ward off the malaria. I been drinking it for years and ain't had a case of malaria yet. Then I'll brew up some coffee and we'll chase everything with coffee and Amaretto. Our bodies won't know what to do with that combination. It'll make us crazy."

"Good!" I shouted, suddenly gay. "Let's get crazy!"

And we did. I went home that night, roaring. The morning's hangover was the most astounding one I'd ever had, but in an odd way, it made me feel wonderfully world-weary. I cut short the next night's date and was at Felicity's house just after the sun set.

"Tonight, Lovebug," she said, standing in front of the huge liquor chest, "we'll drink . . . uh . . . brandy."

"Delightful! It's been ages."

"Since you had brandy? How long?"

"Twenty years!" I squealed, causing her to laugh like a fool.

Because the brandy lighted an unusually warm fire in my belly, I sipped slowly.

"I thought for sure you'd ask to hear more of Gravēda," she said.

"I've been waiting," I replied quickly. "I been waiting—really."

"Oh, I just bet you have." We were sitting together on the couch. She leaned over and pinched my thigh and, in response, I tried to tickle her ribs and managed in the process to cop a quick feel. "Aaaa!" she screamed. "Copping a feel, copping a feel!" We both laughed.

She pulled away, poured more brandy, and then sat next to me again. "Okay, Blossom." Then she began reciting in that soft Southern accent and, with the tranquilizing effects of brandy and Felicity, I turned dreamy. In fact, she had to shake me a little when she said, later that evening, " 'Bout time for you to hit the road, Hon. Don't want your folks to start worrying about you."

"I'm in college now," I said, standing to get myself fully awake. "They don't worry about me."

"Baloney."

I took a sip of brandy, grimaced, and then declared: "I've taken some courses in literature." I wanted to show off my education, what there was of it.

"Uh-oh."

"What?"

"Nothing."

"*What?*"

"Nothing, nothing. I should have expected this was coming."

I drank some more brandy. "I've thought a lot about this Gravēda story you been telling me."

"You mean the parts you've been awake for."

"Hey, hey—I was awake. Just concentrating." She laughed. "So," I continued, "do you want to hear my observations?"

"No."

She said it flatly and I think she was completely serious, but I laughed and said, "Sure you do. Everyone profits from a little enlightened criticism."

She rolled her eyes. "Keep in mind, Chinch Bug, that Gravēda is a story I made up just for *you*."

"Nonetheless . . ."

"Nonetheless?"

"*Nonetheless*, I think it contains some basic flaws."

"Oh, boy. No, okay—go ahead. I can see you're determined to say it no matter what I want, so go ahead."

"Take the symbolism—"

"Please!"

"Yeah, well, it's rather pitifully obvious, you know. The symbolism, I mean. Gravēda traveling westward across a great land, destroying things that get in her way. The exploration and exploitation ending only when she reaches the sea. Kind of obvious, huh?"

"My, my."

"And that bit about the ravens. So heavy-handed, you know. Obviously you have something you want to say about our treatment of Negroes."

"Goodness. I should've made them pigeons, huh, Pattycake? Just to confuse things a little?"

I laughed and leaned a bit with the effects of brandy. "That's not the point."

"What's the point, then?"

I didn't know. I was simply regurgitating the types of comments I'd heard during those droning literature classes I'd sat through at college. The point, I guess, was to impress Felicity, but it wasn't working out that way.

"In the future," she said dryly, "I'll try to come up with some exotic symbolism. Stuff you won't be able to figure out right away. Anything else?"

Although it was obvious she didn't want to hear anything else, I plunged ahead. "I could talk about the setting or, I should say, the lack of setting. No sense of time or place or history. And how about the cardboard nature of the characters?

Gravēda and Genipur have a certain charm, but that's undoubtedly due to the charm of the characters upon which they're based." I laughed; Felicity didn't. "The rest of the characters are trotted out so Gravēda can have convenient foils."

Felicity, lips pursed, was nodding. "Is that all?"

"I could go on," I said, grinning and slurring my words, "but I don't want to crush you, Honey." I was feeling my apples by then, I was. "I could talk about the symbolism of the caves you keep mentioning and that one character, Ismo, who's supposed to be in the caves and how that applies to your own life, your husband in the hospital and all that."

She held up her hand.

"What?"

"No more, that's what."

"Hell, I didn't think you'd be so damn touchy about this. You sure as—"

"No more. That's it. No more."

"Can't take it, huh, Felicity?"

She wanted to slap me. I could see the impulse originate within her and I could watch her fight it, control it, finally subdue it. A fascinating display. "I think I'll switch to Scotch," she said, getting up and walking to the liquor cabinet. She returned to the couch with a tumbler half full and neat. "I'll tell you a quick little story, only this one won't be very artful. Because it's true."

I wasn't eager to hear any more stories. "It's getting kind of late. . . ."

Felicity took my arm and sat me on the couch. "This won't take long. It's something that happened when I was a little girl, about nine or ten, I guess. When I was growing up in Louisiana, our house was a few blocks from the river and that's where we'd always go to play—down by the river. Some Negro families lived down there. We were pretty good friends with them, in that way Southerners have—their version, our version—of being friends with Negroes. On this one day, this one day I want to tell you about, I was playing with some Negro kids in their yard. My father came along, said hi to us kids, and then went into the house. I didn't think it was unusual 'cause there was an old Mammy who lived there, and we used to buy stuff from her—preserves and jellies and things—and she was a real autocrat who sort of ruled that neighborhood down by the river. If there was any trouble brewing, like if some white boy was fooling around with a Negro girl, Mammy would talk with one of the white men, somebody like my father, and then they'd take care of things. So I didn't think it was too unusual for Daddy to be going into her house.

"But when he came out a few minutes later, he grabbed me by the hand and sort of half dragged me home. He told me I was never to play with any member of that family again and wasn't to go over there again, either. Same went for my brothers. I wondered what happened, what possibly could have happened in that house. Mammy was a huge woman—three hundred pounds and shiny black. I wondered if she had bawled out Daddy like she used to bawl out us kids when she caught us doing something. That didn't seem possible, but what else could it be? Something bad. Everything changed after that day. Daddy used to take us kids, white and black, down to the river where we'd bottom-fish for channel cats and snapping turtles. But no more. Not after that day. He'd go fishing with my brothers and me but not with the neighborhood kids. Never organized any baseball games or anything like he used to—not after the day he went to talk to old Mammy."

Felicity took a big drink of Scotch, held it in her mouth a moment, and then swallowed it with a look of disapproval. "I didn't find out what happened until years later, when I returned home to help raise my brothers after Daddy died and Momma got sick. I met one of the girls from that family; she was about my age, and she told me she was in the house that day, hiding in one of the bedrooms and listening to what was happening. A couple days before all this, Mammy had overheard some of the kids talking about a white man who was being indecent with them. Exposing himself, I guess. When she questioned the kids, they wouldn't tell her anything. So she came up with this plan to call in some of the white men in the neighborhood, the ones who were friendly with all us kids, and ask them about it. Only someone like her could get away with doing that. My friend, the girl who was hiding in the bedroom, said that Mammy asked each man one question. Mammy believed she could tell if someone was lying not by what they answered but by how they answered. She always did that with us kids. Looked into our eyes to see if they 'shine with the truth.'

"My friend said that Mammy asked each man, 'You been poking lilies at my children?' I guess it took a while for my father to figure out what she was getting at but when he realized what was being asked he said, 'I never done anything like that with any child.' Apparently he passed the test. My friend said that before he left the house, my father said to Mammy, 'I suppose you felt it was necessary to ask that question.' He said it real quiet but my friend told me she knew, just from the sound of his voice, that he was mad. And hurt. Like I said before, after that everything changed. I don't mean to suggest that our lives were profoundly altered, but there was a definite change. I think Daddy was even more guarded with his own kids after that."

"Did she, that old Mammy, ever find out who was fooling around with the children?"

"I don't know," Felicity said. "I suppose she did. Her powers to detect lies were awesome. None of us kids could get away with fibbing to her, I know that. Maybe it was one of the other men in the neighborhood or maybe the kids had just been kidding around and Mammy misunderstood them. Hell, I don't know," Felicity said, suddenly angry. "That's not the point. What I'm trying to explain is how someone's entire life can be changed by *words*—a comment, a question. Who knows what dark parts of Daddy's soul were touched by that accusation? Well, it wasn't really an accusation. But I'm convinced it would've been better if that question had not been asked at all.

"And I'm not going to sit here," she said, becoming angrier, "and let you do the same thing to me. You're just fooling around, saying things and . . . and speculating in areas you know nothing about. I'm not going to allow you to hurt me or to say something, inadvertently say something, that's going to get me thinking about things and then make me mad at you and mess up everything between us. If you're going to insist on analyzing this story I been telling you ever since you were an innocent little odorless boy, I'd just as soon end it here. I'm not going to let you stumble on something that . . ."

I got up and walked out. Didn't say good-bye to her, nod, make a comment—*nothing*. Just walked out and went home. I thought it was a dramatic thing to do.

I visited Felicity again a week later. Although neither of us mentioned what had happened, the complexion of our time together had indeed changed, had become strained and guarded. She still recited the Gravēda story, but I didn't comment on it.

When I next stopped at her house, she asked me how things were going with the hometown girl I was seeing. Becoming expansive with gin, I described rather too rawly some of my exploits.

"You'd better be careful, Bunny," Felicity said. "In a small town like this, even a renegade like me knows who's who. That girl'll put you in a little box house with a Plymouth in the driveway and an Electrolux in the closet. She'll arrange that before you know what hit you. I'd rather see you quit college, ship out on a steamer. Go live in Paris. Something. *Anything*."

"Jealous?"

Felicity smiled. "You are insufferable. Is this what college has done to you? The place should be razed. Listen, Puppy, I have nothing against that girl as an individual, but she doesn't strike me as the type who'd be satisfied living with a writer. You two get engaged, and you'll switch majors. End up working for some corporation or maybe come back here and run your Daddy's businesses."

"Speaking of Daddy," I said, making my eyebrows dance luridly.

Then it was Felicity's turn. She walked over to her bedroom, shut the door behind her, and didn't come out. I finished my drink and went home.

There was one more move. I came back the next night and after listening to some more of the Gravēda story, I began teasing Felicity for having introduced a character who was blatantly patterned after my hometown girl.

"You promised me you weren't going to analyze the story anymore," she complained.

"I promised no such thing."

"Listen, Kiddo, you want to get involved with that breeder, it's okay by me."

I walked out on her, and that was it. The game was over for the summer. I didn't talk to Felicity for the next two months, didn't visit her again until the night before my departure for college.

She greeted me at the door with her hands held up near her shoulders, palms facing me. "Mea culpa, mea culpa, mea culpa," she chanted.

"What the hell's that supposed to mean?" I asked, walking past her and going into the living room, where I fixed myself a drink. Rum and Coke; Felicity brought the ice.

"It means," she said, "that it's totally my fault for the way things have gone this summer and I'm totally contrite and totally ashamed of myself." She put her hand on my shoulder. "And I feel like shit 'cause you're going back to college tomorrow and we haven't had the good times, the kind of good times I thought we'd have this summer. I shouldn't have let other things interfere, distract me. All my fault. Guilty as hell. Mea culpa."

I blessed her with what I considered to be the sign of the cross.

"Oh, thank you," she said, batting eyelashes. Then we kissed, and the kiss lingered.

I put my arms around her and we swayed a bit. "See," Felicity whispered in my ear, "isn't this better than arguing?"

I murmured something in the positive.

"And I was hoping to get to know Zachary better this summer, too," Felicity said quietly as we continued to rock.

"Who?"

She eased her hand down the front of my pants.

I sucked in what little gut I had back then and said, "Oh."

"Ah."

"Ah."

We sort of danced, each of us holding on to a favored part of the other, into the dark living room and put ourselves upon the couch. But Zachary also was a stupidly impetuous college sophomore and he made his concluding remarks all along Felicity's wrist and forearm before either of us got fully undressed.

Felicity was a saint about it, offering no complaints or comments. We sat in the dark, holding each other. I had a wonderful opportunity for making my departure sweet: I could have just sat there hugging her, keeping my mouth shut. But I started thinking about what my sister had told me, finding Felicity sitting out in that chair at night, in the rain. "I got something I have to tell you," I said quietly.

"Uh-oh."

"What?"

"You're going to make some sort of declaration, aren't you? Why don't you forego it, Baby? Just think it, but don't say it."

"This is something that needs to be said."

"A dec-*la*-ra-tion."

"I'm serious, Felicity."

"A serious declaration. The worst kind."

I sat back away from her a bit and lighted one of her cigarettes. "I see you're still working on that chair. Carving out legs and armrests. It's getting to look real delicate now. That's good—good that you have something to keep you busy, I mean."

Then she lighted a cigarette—and eyed me.

"You can't live your life through me," I said. "You can't just sit around and wait for me to come visit you. I won't be coming home that often, you know."

Felicity sighed.

"I know I'm being tough on you—but someone has to say it. You got to start living, Felicity, *living*. You can't just vegetate in this little house while your husband's in the hospital and I'm off at college." I took her hand and squeezed. I was prepared for the sobbing to commence, was prepared to accept her back in my arms so I could comfort her. "You got to go out there and make a life for yourself before it's too late." I should've been hit across the snout with a stick.

Felicity spoke quietly, without discernible emotion; I assumed she was holding it all in: "If I say some things to you, will you promise not to get mad and walk out on me? I mean, if I speak real lovingly, will you promise not to get mad?"

I nodded. "Sure." I figured she was going to tell me she couldn't possibly live without me, maybe even try to talk me into not returning to college or into taking her back with me.

"Okay." She inhaled, exhaled, took a bit of tobacco off her lower lip. "People—psychologists, doctors, whatever—believe that for infants, really young infants, the only world that exists is the one they can see with their eyes. You stand in front of the baby and the baby looks at you and you exist. But when you duck down or step out of the room, you no longer exist for that baby. He has no recollection of you, no sense that you're still in existence but simply out of his sight. But at a certain stage in an infant's development, a profound insight occurs to the child: He realizes that things exist even when they're not directly in his sight. That's when a baby learns to cry for Mommy."

"So?"

She put her hand to my neck. "Now, remember. I'm saying this lovingly, so don't get mad. I think you're like a very young infant. The only world that exists for you is the one that's in front of you. When you leave people, you mentally put them in cold storage, in a sort of suspended animation. Then when you return, you expect to be able to pull those people out of cold storage, revive them, and continue with matters exactly as they were before. You haven't developed to the point where you can cry for someone, cry for the loss of someone, because in your mind people don't really exist, aren't really living, when they're apart from you."

I stubbed out my cigarette. "Don't worry. I'm not getting angry. But I still don't see what you're getting at."

"Well." She put her head back. "I'm not sure either, I guess. I know that the only way things will work between us is if I'm the fan and you're the star; you're the worshiped and I'm the worshiper. And you're never going to ask about me or my life or what I do when I'm not with you. But I'm going to tell you some things, just this once. Just so you can keep matters in perspective. I have three college degrees. I was a professor of English in New York. I've had thirty-seven poems published in magazines and reviews. I have a world of friends out in California, where my husband and I used to live before the war, and I write about two letters a day. I receive about two letters a day, on the average. You don't get mentioned, I'm afraid.

"I do love you. But I love you in exact proportion to the amount of time you spend in my life. Making up that Gravēda story and working it in my head so I can recite it for you is one of my diversions, one of my recreations. The 'obvious' symbolism in that story hasn't even occurred to you yet, Doll.

"I want a child. I want my husband to be well. I didn't mind leaving New York because I no longer got a kick from cocaine—literally and figuratively speaking. But now I want to go back there. Or back to San Francisco or back to Louisiana—back somewhere. I want all those things. And if I don't get what I want, it'll be a shame. I've believed in you from the beginning and if you don't turn out the way I think you could, that'll be a shame, too. But, then, life is full of shames like that."

I felt as if I'd been hit soundly across the snout. "In other words, I'm no big deal in your life. Is that what you're saying?"

"No, Kitten—not at all. It's just that I have you, your life and my life, in some sort of perspective, and I don't believe you do. You're like that infant whose world is limited to what's happening right before his eyes. I'm suggesting that you should, just occasionally, think about the world that you're not a part of, that goes on without benefit of your presence.

"Wild elephants are shitting on the plains of Africa. Right now. Think about it, Slim. Right now in the world, someplace in the world, a baby is being born. Right now! This is not just talk. It's really happening. Hundreds of people are screwing right now, right this minute. Thousands of them, maybe tens of thousands of 'em. Ejaculations from Bangkok to Peoria. Whales. Right now whales are diving, surfacing, swimming. All these things are happening right this moment!" She lighted another cigarette, took a few drags, and seemed calmer. "Sometimes I go too much in the other direction. Get to thinking about the whole world so much that I can't concentrate on what's happening right in front of me. Sometimes I figure up the time difference so I can guess what my friends are doing, whether it's time for them to be having breakfast or sleeping or whatever. And then I imagine watching them, like I'm right there with them."

I stood up. "I guess I better get going. Do you think you'll be able to come and see me off at the train tomorrow morning?"

Felicity laughed and held out her hand. I pulled her to her feet. "Oh, Baby Brown Eyes, you are something else. I tell you all this stuff and you want to know if I'll come see you off. You got to be the most self-centered person in existence. No, no— don't get mad. You have the exact attributes a novelist needs."

She walked me to the door. "Well," I said, "will you be there to see me off? I'll sit in the last car."

We kissed deeply. Her full and warm lips were open, her tongue darted and explored, our teeth clicked and our saliva intermingled. All the while, her hands ran up and down the length of me. Then she suddenly pulled away and just stared.

"Well?"

"I don't know if I'll be there or not," Felicity said.

I shrugged and left.

I had no doubts that night or when I got to the train station the next morning. Felicity would come to see me. I was convinced she was, at that moment, waiting at the side of the train station, and I'd spot her when the train pulled out. She'd blow kisses and I'd catch them. So I hugged everyone good-bye, got a seat in the last car, and waited to see Felicity.

But she wasn't there. I couldn't believe it. She wasn't at the side of the station, waiting to throw me kisses as I went by. I felt betrayed. As if the audience, which always before had applauded wildly, just sat in silence this time as I sung, as I sung. As if I had looked down one Sunday morning to find every one of my churches empty. My feelings were hurt. I was pissed.

But at the first intersection beyond town I saw Felicity's big black, grill-grinning Buick. And she was beside it, waving at the train's last car and then throwing kisses when she finally saw me. I waved back, a prince acknowledging his cheering subjects.

And then as I rode straight and parallel tracks out of the prairie, I gloated. Like a fat toad. Full of bugs and terribly satisfied with myself and with life in general.

G R A V Ē D A

The part Felicity told me when I was twenty and home from college.

17. Chest pains awaken Gravēda in the middle of yet another night alone, and these pains worry her almost as much as does the absence of the tribe—gone now almost a week. Why did they leave?, she wonders. Am I that much of a monster? When I traveled with the tribe, I was just like everyone else. She wishes she could stop thinking and sleep, but the piercing hurt right in the middle of her chest keeps her awake and while she's awake she hears those big, sad sounds coming in from the ocean. It's a plaintive wailing that travels so low across the water and comes from such a distance that Gravēda has to cock her head to make sure she's really hearing it, to make sure the sounds aren't simply originating from inside her own head—maybe caused by the chest pain or by her loneliness. Sweet Genipur. Has he left me, too?

And then with the dawn, she curses the sun and Genipur—and herself for being so vulnerable to both of them.

When Gravēda was a girl, traveling with the tribe, no one studied the past, which was considered unknowable and unimportant. Why spend time on the past when it was the future that was set, determined, knowable, and worth knowing? Simple observation revealed what was happening and will happen to the tribe: each couple having one child until the tribe will dwindle to a few, the final two of whom will marry and produce The One, the last and remaining member of the tribe. And by the time The One is born, the tribe's journey toward the setting sun will have reached the spot where God waits—waits to greet The One who will be the final and refined product of faith.

But everything's changed now. For the first time in her life, Gravēda is more sure about the past than she is about the future and now, as never before, the past seems more comforting to her than does the future.

So when the next night on the beach arrives, Gravēda takes her mind back to when she lay between her Momma and Poppa and would see in the dark sky those bewildering, dazzling, twinkling lights that seemed both far and near. She remembers how they drew on her and how she'd reach, tentatively, for them. As she reached, her eyes squinted in instinctual preparation for something that might move rapidly or, even worse in the quiet night, might make a sharp sound.

You have to understand. Back then Gravēda was unsure about the distance of stars—and about the extent of her reach. So perhaps she can be forgiven for the boldness of lifting her arms higher and stretching her fingers and actually expecting to touch one of those lights.

She remembers her Poppa waking and then jabbing her Momma: "Look! Gravēda's reaching for the stars."

Gravēda remembers how her Poppa boasted to other travelers that his daughter reached for the stars at night.

So perhaps now she can be forgiven—being half asleep and half awake, half dreaming and half not—for rolling onto her back in that rock den and reaching for stars after all these years.

18. Gravēda is awakened in midmorning by her own name being called harshly by some woman. Unaccustomed to sleeping late, Gravēda is disoriented.

"Gravēda!"

She sits up and rubs her puffy eyes, her greasy face. Again her name is called, so she stands up and looks down at the beach to see the tribe assembled there—all the young travelers and their priests. Gravēda searches among them, but she doesn't see Ismo or Genipur.

"Come down here, Gravēda!"

I know that woman, Gravēda says to herself. It's Nestus. She was too young to be in Gravēda's group of friends, but Gravēda still remembers her—remembers the blond hair, the oddly erect way she carries herself, the haughtiness in her voice. I wonder what's up. Gravēda waves down to Nestus, who doesn't wave back. "Come down here!" the woman hollers again; to Gravēda, it sounds like a command.

Gravēda climbs down, her sword banging on boulders as she drags it behind her. "Nestus, Nestus," she says, embracing the woman, who stiffens in her arms. Gravēda steps back. "How the hell are you doing, Nestus?"

"Come with me," Nestus says quietly.

Gravēda is thinking that perhaps the tribe is going to give her the reunion ceremony that she should have received when she first showed up on the beach. But Nestus's manner does not suggest a party.

As they approach the tribe, which parts to let them through, Gravēda experiments with compliments she could pay Nestus—to soften up the prude. *You're looking so trim, Nestus.* The truth is she's scrawny; I bet if you rolled her out between giant boulders, Gravēda thinks, you wouldn't get more than a cup of juice. Me? Ha! I'd fill barrels. *Nice tan, Nestus.* Actually, she's had too much sun, which has made her skin look stained rather than tanned; her face is so tough and leathery that I bet I could strop my knife on her cheeks. Gravēda smiles.

"Nice robe, Nestus."

The woman frowns, as if she disapproves of what Gravēda has said. Gravēda shrugs, thinking: Those purple robes and red sashes look stupid anyway.

When they get to water's edge, Nestus turns Gravēda so they're both facing the tribe. Gravēda whispers to her: "You ever get married? Have your baby?"

Nestus answers straightforwardly and without emotion: "Yes. We had a little girl. But both my husband and child were killed in one of the attempts we made to cross the ocean. We were out there for days and finally had to turn back. The boat cracked up on some rocks, and I barely made it to shore myself."

"Oh, I'm sorry, Hon. So you had to become a priest, huh?"

"More than that, Gravēda," she says with a sigh, as if all this explaining is just too, too much the burden. "I'm the president of the council of priests, and I'm the one who decided there should be minimal contact between you and the rest of the tribe. I'm the one who organized the retreat the tribe's been on—a retreat called so we could decide in a collegial manner what we should do about you."

Minimal contact? Retreat? Collegial manner? "What the hell are you talking about?"

Nestus shakes her head and then motions for the tribe to move in a bit closer; Gravēda sticks her sword in the sand so the grip stands comfortingly close to her hand.

Nestus clears her throat and steps away from Gravēda. "Stands before you," Nestus says, talking louder than is necessary for everyone to hear, "the last traveler." She sweeps her arm in Gravēda's direction.

Could this be the opening speech in a welcoming ceremony? Gravēda doesn't think so. Whatever it is, she hopes it doesn't last long, because Gravēda has to pee.

"I assigned her a sponsor," Nestus is saying, "and made sure she was well fed. I wanted her to be isolated until she learned our ways, but now I think that was a mistake. Apparently some of you are fascinated with this woman, have built her up in your own minds as a symbol. I want you to see her for what she is. . . ."

Gravēda is tempted to interrupt Nestus and ask if a break can be called—just long enough for Gravēda to run over to the rocks and pee.

Nestus suddenly calls out Gravēda's name and Gravēda, who hasn't been listening closely, smiles shyly and waves to the tribe.

"What do you think about our investigations into the origin of the tribe?" Nestus asks.

"What?"

"Do you think we came from a larger tribe that still lives somewhere back there—in the east, where we came from?"

Gravēda shrugs; she has no idea what Nestus is talking about.

"And if you propose we continue the journey, how do you suggest we cross the ocean? What design would you use for the boats? How will you store sufficient food and water for the crossing? How far is the other side? *Is* there another side?"

Gravēda crooks her finger, urging Nestus to come close. When she does, Gravēda whispers to her: "I have to pee."

Nestus gives her a look of disgust and then speaks again to the tribe. "Do any of you really think she can lead you? That she has the answers you seek? Who among you will put your lives in the hands of this woman, this unfortunate throwback . . ."

But Gravēda, who's moved into the water to pee, isn't listening. When she's up to her waist in the ocean, she closes her eyes in a bit of concentration that brings relief. Nestus, meanwhile, is telling the young travelers, "Maybe that's what she proposes, to wade across!"

Gravēda stares at them as they laugh and point. I wish I could talk as smoothly as a priest, she thinks, 'cause then I could tell them how I really felt and if they knew that, they'd feel sorry for me. Some of them might even say it out loud: *Poor Gravēda.*

Eller, who sits in the sand at the side of the tribe, doesn't look up from the papers on which he's scribbling furiously.

When Gravēda climbs up on a large rock with a flat top that's an inch or so below the water's surface, Nestus says something that elicits another laugh from the tribe. Gravēda slaps her sword into the water so the blade hits against the submerged rock and sets up a vibration, but this time the swordtalk has little effect—other than creating an agitation in the water, which attracts fish that move like shadows without any noticeable means of locomotion. They swim dangerously close to the blade, angling their bodies and showing Gravēda glimpses of their muddy yellow undersides.

She wonders what other kinds of creatures live in the ocean and what the size is of the ones that make those night sounds, those wails and squeaks and melodious moans? And if she had to swim the ocean, how could she possibly protect herself from underside attacks by shadowy creatures? The idea of drowning doesn't bother her as much as the thought of being out there in the ocean and then feeling a bump caused by something rising up in the dark from the depths—the chance of becoming prey to things Momma never knew to warn her against.

"She can't seem to figure out how to get off that rock," Nestus is saying to the young travelers whose easy affections belong to her.

Gravēda throws back her head, fills her lungs tight and quick, and shrieks so loudly and hideously that Nestus is quieted and the tribe eases back a cautious step or two. When Gravēda wails again, her arms thrashing to make mad patterns in the air, the tribe prepares to retreat.

But then Gravēda sees Genipur walking toward the tribe, and she stops screaming. She stands straight. He'll give 'em hell, my Sweet Genipur will. He'll tell the tribe that Nestus is the one you have to worry about—not me. Nestus with her logic and evidence and investigations, she's the one who'll get the tribe lost. Go ahead, Genipur. You give 'em hell, Lover.

When Nestus notices Genipur, she quickly walks to him and, resting a hand lightly on his shoulder, says something in his ear. He glances out at Gravēda, nods to Nestus, and then takes backward steps until he's part of the crowd.

Gravēda slouches, as if suffering a sudden failure of bone and muscle tone.

"All right, all right," Nestus announces, "it's all over now. You've seen what the last traveler is really like, and we can all return to our duties." The tribe departs, chatting amiably in small groups as if they're reviewing an interesting performance. Even Genipur leaves; only Nestus and Eller remain on the beach watching Gravēda. As she tries to get off the rock, Gravēda slips under the water's surface and comes up struggling and choking. She expects to find Nestus laughing at her but, instead, the woman calls out in a voice that seems sincere, "You okay?"

Gravēda grunts and sputters and waves her sword. "I'll kill you, you bitch. I'll slice you up and down your skinny length." But the wading is slow and by the time Gravēda gets out of the water, Nestus and Eller are gone. Gravēda stands there alone, tired and wet and once again not knowing what to do or where to go.

19. Gravēda begins walking up the beach, trying to reconstruct the old rhythms. It feels good to be walking.

Then she hears Genipur call after her, and those damn chest pains start up again. When he reaches her, Gravēda feels no anger toward him and, in fact, hugs him so tightly that water is squeezed out of her robe to run in warm rivulets down her legs. "Where've you been, Sweet Genipur? Where in God's name have you been? I was so worried. I waited for you every night."

When Gravēda loosens her embrace, Genipur replies, "I had to go down to the caves. Because of my father. He died."

"Oh, Baby. Darlin' Child." She hugs him again and tries not to smile, tries not to think: one down, one to go. Gravēda wonders if his mother is in good health and, if the woman does die soon, will Genipur marry me? She's tempted to ask him.

"Where you going?" Genipur asks.

Gravēda shrugs. "Why didn't you say anything back there? I thought you might stick up for me. That Nestus, she's . . ."

Genipur turns away from her and looks toward the ocean.

"Hmm?" Gravēda asks, nudging him gently.

"Nestus and I have . . . uh . . . we have a special kind of relationship." The boy seems embarrassed.

Gravēda doesn't understand—and then when she does, she can't believe it. "But Nestus has already had her baby. She told me—didn't you know? She can't marry you. She's a priest, damn it!"

"You still don't understand how things work here on the beach."

"What?"

"People can marry more than once. A woman can have more than one baby."

"*What?* You mean like litters—like *dogs?*"

"You know exactly what I'm talking about, Gravēda. You've heard about it happening, even back when the tribe was on the journey. A woman having a second child or a man making babies with two or three different women."

"Scandals."

Genipur shrugs.

"Where the hell does this leave us—*me?* I thought you and I . . . What about that night we spent together?"

"That was a mistake. I was distilled that night."

Gravēda hits him, knocking Genipur instantly to the sand. She's ready to hit him again; she even considers raising her sword.

"That's your answer to everything, isn't it? Nestus was right about you."

Gravēda, sorry now, holds out a hand to help him up. But Genipur slaps it away, gets up, and leaves without saying another word to her.

20. So Gravēda continues walking because in the end, as in the beginning, that's all she can do. She walks that strip of sand, sometimes narrow and sometimes wide, that is bordered on her right by the vast sea and on her left by the steep cliff walls. Random boulders are strewn in between.

Walking is good, each step pounding out complications and grinding down explanations: milling her worries. And with fatigue comes that hazy consciousness that allows her mind to travel. Back to when she was a child, frightened awake by sounds and shapes in the night. Poppa would come and hold her tightly, saying that what she heard or saw was the legless night eagle who reports to God. Legless so he won't land and rest, the night eagle must fly close to make sure Gravēda is okay 'cause she's so special that God has to have a report on her each morning. That's what Poppa told her, that the legless night eagle searched for her among all the fires that all the travelers built for the night.

But the thought of some leglessly deformed, shadowy bird sent by God to check up on her was not comforting. Scared the hell out of Gravēda, in fact. No, it was Poppa's arms, not his stories, that soothed Gravēda in the night.

As she walks along the beach, the sky becomes dark and low, impressing upon the world an anxious anticipation of storms. She walks and dreams, something she's been known to do, of legless night eagles and fishy shadows, fish that fly and eagles that swim.

Then she's awakened, as she walks, by the rain. The first drops that hit her are big and so few in number that she can count them on her shoulders and on her face. But quickly the individual drops merge into a drench rain, and Gravēda wonders if she should look for shelter. Soon, however, she is so wet that the debate is moot and—knowing she can't get any wetter—Gravēda relaxes and continues walking, walking.

She wanders close to the sea, which has become excited at being fed so generously with rain. A heavy wave strikes her legs, erodes the sand under her feet, and causes her to lose her balance and turn her ankle. She curses the ocean with screams that are dampened and made ineffective by the curtains of rainwater through which she continues to walk.

It's no wonder the rain defends the sea, because when those multibillion drops hit the ocean, they diffuse into it, absorb its power, and alter slightly its composition. Like souls entering heaven.

But Gravēda? She has to keep walking alone, so thoroughly soaked that she cannot take on one additional raindrop soul. Each new one pushes another drop off; the rain hitting her shoulders causes the rain at the bottom of her robe to drip. She is a vessel, full to the top.

Still she walks, becoming step-by-step less angry with the ocean, the rain, Genipur's betrayal. Instead, Gravēda begins to feel cold and tired and sorry for herself—as if the rain has leeched from her all the warm passions and left in their place the congealed ones: pity and remorse, pity and remorse.

It's dark now, not from the time of the day but from the effects of the increasing storm. As she trudges through wet and heavy sand, something catches her eye—something so strange and unexpected that Gravēda has to stop and think about it.

She saw a light coming from the face of the cliff to her left. A light that for a moment stood out so brightly from the darkness that it seems to Gravēda the sun must have taken up residence in that solid rock to wait there for a break in the weather.

21. Of course she investigates, because *it could be*. Who knows where the sun goes during a storm? And if not the sun, what's the origin of the light coming from that solid wall cliff over there?

By the time she gets across the beach to a spot directly under the light, it's gone. She searches along the foot of the cliff until she finds a series of ledges and outcroppings that serve as a pathway. She climbs, slips, catches herself, and climbs some more—not knowing the destination of the path because the rain blinds her. Gravēda climbs blind.

But soon she has to rest. The storm has turned terrible, the rain losing its distinction as rain, as drops of water falling through the air. Instead, Gravēda seems to be surrounded by something that is not quite rain, not quite air but is, instead, something in between. And it is through this fully saturated air, this air-blown water, this *rain-air* that Gravēda feels her way up the cliff. Head bowed to protect her face.

Yipes! Nearly falls off the cliff, so startled is she by the light that flashes this time right at her feet. Gravēda takes a moment to compose herself and then she bends tenderly to see if she can find the source.

She feels an opening, an opening to a small round tunnel in the face of the cliff. Knowing instinctively that this is a situation best entered blade-first, Gravēda points her sword into the tunnel and crawls in after it. She wonders if this is where the old travelers live, if Ismo is inside. And what will he look like, and will he remember me?

She's barely out of the rain when she comes to the end of the tunnel, which is blocked by heavy, coarsely woven material.

She understands now: It was this curtain, occasionally blown aside by the storm, that allowed flashes of light to escape into the night. Using the tip of her blade, Gravēda pushes aside the material and squints her eyes until they're accustomed to the bright, bright interior light of a large cave.

The floor is uneven, and the cave's wildly irregular walls lean outward as they travel up to a high ceiling. All over those walls are shelves and ledges, niches and cubbies, which hold thick candles, delicate tapers, glass lanterns, and smoky lamps. All burning brightly.

Mirrors. The cave is full of mirrors. Propped on the ledges, leaned against the walls, stuck in the backs of niches are dozens of mirrors: huge ones and small ones, shards, ovals, squares, and jagged shapes that seem to be the result of accidents. The mirrors and candles cause such a confusion of brilliance that Gravēda can't readily tell what is original light and what is reflection.

She sits there in the mouth of the tunnel and is amazed. Look at it all; along the ledges are dozens and dozens of little knicks and somewhat larger knacks: pieces of cloth, shells, drawings, polished walnuts, locks of hair, and a random bone or two.

Gravēda crawls partially into the cave, keeping partially in the tunnel because the cave is such a strange and scary place. The tremendous heat from what must be a hundred light sources causes steam to rise from her wet robe and skin and hair. As if she is softly, painlessly, on fire. Trying to find a more comfortable position, Gravēda moves her hand and almost upsets an open bowl of flaming liquid.

Then she sees movement inside one of the shallow cubbies. Squinting against the brightness, she's finally able to make it out: Eller is in there! He's no more than six inches tall, but it is indeed Eller.

Gravēda watches in fascination, finally realizing that what she's seeing is only his reflection in a mirror at the back of the cubby. Following a line of sight from there to the left side of the cave, Gravēda finds Eller sitting at a wooden table a few feet off the cave floor. But he's only half his regular size. Sitting there writing on pages stacked high on a most amazing table. A trough has been dug out along three sides of the table, to Eller's right and left and in front of him. And that trough is full of wax, which contains closely spaced and brightly burning wicks.

Then Gravēda realizes that the half-size Eller is a reflection, too. She shakes her head. Sight suffers odd distortions in this cave, distortions caused by an excess of illumination.

Searching around the cave for the original, Gravēda finally sees him on an extremely wide ledge that runs all along one wall—right up there near the ceiling. So intent is he upon his writing that he hasn't noticed her yet. Gravēda smiles.

Moving quietly into the cave, she carefully stands on the uneven floor. She slowly raises her sword—and then bangs it sharply on a shelf of rock. The sound mimics the cave's light: bouncing all around and then filling the oddly shaped interior— even scaring Gravēda a bit. Eller jerks upright and comes off his chair as if bitten. Gravēda laughs and laughs as the sound of her sword continues traveling around dissipating itself.

"I scared you dry that time, didn't I, Nose?"

"Not at all," Eller answers, although he's clearly flustered.

"Hell I didn't."

"I knew you were going to do that," Eller insists. "I just . . . just didn't have it down yet." He begins to straighten the pages that were tossed all over the table when Gravēda frightened him. She admires his unpriestliness: his torn and dirty robe hanging loosely around his neck, hands ink-stained to his wrists, eyes shot through with blood, hair stringy and wild, and a face flushed as if with some excess—exertion or weariness or drink or thought.

When Eller burns his fingers pulling pages out of the hot wax troughs, Gravēda laughs again.

"I will not be ridiculed, laughed at, called names. Not in my very own well-lighted room, I won't."

So she calls him some more names and laughs again—just to get his goat.

"Okay, young woman, I'll just let you get bitten by that swizzle snake coming up behind you."

"Ah, go on. I fell for that one before." But then Gravēda is overtaken by the creepiest of feelings and, glancing behind her, she sees on a waist-high ledge this most hideous creature: About the length and thickness of her forearm, it looks like a hunk of rolled lard with a large and malevolently triangular head; eyeless and sluggish and dirty and doughy white, it undulates toward her. So unlike anything that could possibly be alive. Gravēda would be willing to believe that it's just a hunk of wax, melting wax or maybe enchanted wax—but then its thick body sort of squeezes in, relaxes out, squeezes in. Not breathing as much as *pulsating*—the labored beating of a sluglike heart.

She high-steps it across the cave and presses against the wall under Eller's ledge. "What the hell's that?"

"A swizzle snake."

"No, really. I've never seen anything like that before. What is it?"

"It'd shock you if I told you," Eller says, chuckling. "Nasty stuff."

"Let me come up there with you," Gravēda asks as she nervously tries to find a foothold in the wall. She keeps an eye on the swizzle snake.

"No, no, no. Not allowed, not allowed." Eller looks down. "Stay there. It won't hurt you if you stay there. Here, be a good girl and I'll give you something you've been asking for."

When she glances up to see what he's talking about, Eller disappears from the edge of his ledge. He returns with a small stoneware jar, which he drops to her.

"What?"

"Open and see," he says. "Open and see."

She does. "Ambergrist?"

Eller nods. "Ambergrist."

Gravēda takes a light taste. Ah, ambergrist, indeed. Digging her finger deep into the jar, she gets a large honey-glob of the stuff and pops it in her mouth. At first taste, ambergrist is high, thin, and sour, but as the dark amber syrup flows over her teeth, Gravēda tastes sweeter stuff. And when she moves her cheeks slowly, items of grit catch along her gums and burst with flavors that range from fruit to salt to musk.

She closes her eyes, takes another fingerful, and turns away from Eller—as if tasting ambergrist is an ablution too personal to be seen by someone else.

Another bite, another; the jar is empty. And then, when the *taste* of ambergrist is gone, Gravēda is exhilarated.

She sways. Looks up at Eller. "Haaa. Appreciate it, old man—really do. Been more than ten years since I had any."

He smiles wickedly. "That's all you get, all you get. Don't want a crystal heart, do you?"

Gravēda smiles absently, closes her eyes again, dances in her head and maybe just a little with her body, weaving. "Momma ate ambergrist for years. That business about it collecting in your heart muscles is nonsense."

"And you never heard about the Passionate One's crystal heart?"

Her eyes flutter open. "Mmm." Still smiling. "It was one of Momma's favorite stories."

"Tell me, tell me," Eller begs like an eager child.

"Oh, you know that old story."

"Sure, sure. But I want to get it down again. In more detail. More nicely said this time."

"I don't tell stories very well." Gravēda chuckles to herself about something.

"Just think it, then. That's all you got to do. Just think it."

She nods, her eyes half shutting of their own accord as she goes along with Eller, not knowing what he's trying to prove. Long, long ago—which is the way Momma used to begin the story—a young man in the tribe was so in love with God, so eager to meet up with God, that he convinced himself he could race ahead of the tribe and reach the spot where God waited, where the tribe eventually would end up when it had dwindled from the many to the few to The One. People tried to talk this young man out of so foolish an adventure but he was, well, too passionate to be dissuaded. He figured he could make it to where God waited if he traveled day and night, night and day—without ever stopping to rest. And he figured he could do *that* if he lived on nothing but ambergrist, because ambergrist gives you the impression you can travel forever. So he strapped huge jars of the stuff to his back and took off in a rush for glory. Years and years later, according to the story Momma told, the tribe came across the Passionate One's remains. His body had rotted away, and his bones were scattered where he lay, had lain, had fallen, had stopped. And on a bed of dark green clover was a perfect mold of his heart. Made by an excess of ambergrist, which had collected in his heart and hardened. It had a crack in it, people say, and people say the priests still have the Passionate One's heart, keeping it as an icon.

"Keeping it as an icon," Eller mutters under his breath.

"What?" Gravēda looks up, but Eller isn't there. She gets scared, thinking he's abandoned her to swizzle snakes and God knows what else. She examines the jar and tries to scrape out another taste of ambergrist, just for the protection it offers. "Just an old story, huh, Eller?" she calls, hoping to entice him back.

When he finally returns to his ledge, Eller holds a strange object about the size and shape of two large fists put together. It is indeed an ambercolored crystal—with something inside. Gravēda laughs and wonders if he's going to try to palm this off as the Passionate One's crystal heart.

"The Passionate One's crystal heart," Eller announces.

"Ha!"

"It is!"

"Toss it down and let me see."

He shakes his head wildly.

"Come on. If it's really made out of ambergrist crystal, it won't break even if I drop it."

"Can't. Can't let you see it. I put the ending inside."

"What?"

"The ending."

"What ending?"

Eller laughs madly. "Why, your ending, of course, of course. The ending to your story."

All this becomes too much for Gravēda. Her neck's getting stiff from looking up, so she bends her head and rubs the crick.

"I don't know what you're talking about, Eller. Stories, endings—I just don't understand."

Eller giggles. He's sitting on the ledge now, feet hanging just above Gravēda's reach. On his lap is a pile of pages; in his hand, a stylus; next to him, what he claims to be the crystal heart. "*Your* story."

"My story?"

"Unh-huh," he says, nodding his head in an exaggerated manner. "I wrote the ending first and then stuffed it inside the Passionate One's heart 'cause ambergrist crystal is impervious to all the elements, even time—and that's the kind of protection a good ending needs. I did that, sure. Unh-huh. You got to protect your endings."

"Eller, Eller!" Gravēda shouts, slapping the wall under his feet. "Please talk sense."

He throws back his head and laughs. "Okay—just this once. Beginnings and endings are easy—that makes sense, doesn't it? It's the middles that're tedious, 'cause we got to live in the middles. That's what I'm working on now. Your middle. First the ending, then the beginning, and now the middle. The ending's here." He holds up the crystal heart.

Gravēda shakes her head but smiles. Could the old man really have written a story about me?

"Oh, sure," Eller says quickly. "*Your* story."

Gravēda laughs. "Then let me read it."

"No, no—not yet. But I'll show it to you eventually. Everything except the ending, which I already put in the heart for safekeeping."

"Let me see it, let me see it! You old rascal—let me see it."

"No, no, Nadine!" Eller cackles.

Gravēda manages a foothold on a small rock shelf and boosts herself up to grab for Eller's leg. "I'll write you a nasty fall," he warns. The shelf crumbles and Gravēda falls hard.

She looks up from the floor to see Eller writing madly, muttering to himself: ". . . shelf crumbles and Gravēda falls hard." He glances down and flashes his eyes. "Told you so, told you so," and then returns to his pages, speaking under his breath, "Told you so, told you so."

"You're driving me crazy!" Gravēda shouts.

"A short spin, a jaunt!" Eller shouts back.

Gravēda stands and rubs her tailbone. "You don't know anything that's happened to me, so how can you possibly write my story?"

"I can do *anything* I want," he says petulantly. "I'm a hundred years old and can do anything I want." He sticks out his tongue and then looks at his pages, saying as he writes, ". . . anything I want . . ."

Gravēda's head begins to spin now with the effects of excesses: light, heat, reflections, ambergrist, and Eller's mania. She covers her eyes with both hands. Blinded, she finally can see little trails of rationality and after a moment's rest is able to ask what she considers a reasonable question. "Why are you writing my story?"

"Preservation, preservation. Who knows? Maybe it'll be found in the Twentieth Century and translated—put in a book by some brilliant novelist."

She uncovers her eyes. "What's a novelist?"

"Ha!" he snorts. "That's nothing. What's the Twentieth Century?"

In frustration, Gravēda makes a sound in the back of her throat. "Ahggh."

"Is that 'ahggh' with a g-g-h or 'ahgghh' with a g-g-h-h?"

Then she laughs and laughs, because what else is there to do? "You're crazy as a coot."

"Coot-coot!"

"As a woo-woo bird."

"Woo-woo."

Gravēda laughs all the more. "If you won't let me read about my past," she says, catching breaths, "at least tell me some of the stuff that's going to happen to me in the future." She specifically is interested in hearing what he might say about her chances with Sweet Genipur.

"Woo-woo, heavy." His eyes pop open, comically wide. "Heavy stuff coming up. Blood and battles and real-live murders. Horrible imprisonment. Huge creatures invading the beach from the sea."

Gravēda stops laughing. "Come on, Eller. You're just trying to scare me."

"Write on." He pauses and then begins to shout manically: "Read on! *Live on!* Every word the truth after a fashion. All coming up. Soon to be a major production! Stars galore!"

"Stars? You mean like twinkle, twinkle stars?"

"Twinkle Twinkle, maybe," Eller says in what passes for deadly seriousness. "If she can get a chunk of the gross. Not the net."

"Not the net?"

"Never the net."

"Oh, Eller. I can't take any more of this, I really can't."

"Me either."

"You're crazy."

Then he looks at his pages and writes as he speaks under his breath: "Oh, Eller. I can't take any more of this, I really can't. Me either. You're crazy. Then he looks at his pages and writes . . ."

"*Stop!*" Gravēda screams.

"Stop, bang, underscore," he says, still writing.

"I'm leaving. You want to make me nuts, don't you?"

"Uh . . . no," Eller says, turning thoughtful. "You make a good woman."

Gravēda heads for the tunnel, walking carefully to avoid possible swizzle snakes, open bowls of burning liquid, and God knows what else. "I'm leaving," she repeats.

"Where are you going?"

"Ha! Don't you know?"

"Oh, sure," Eller quickly replies. "I know, I know. Tell me so I can see if *you're* right."

Gravēda bends down to enter the tunnel. Half afraid that Eller will bewitch her into staying, she dares one last look at him. "I'm going to the caves where the old travelers live. To see if Ismo's there."

"I know that, I know that," Eller says, writing furiously. "Just keep climbing up that path outside there and then go along the top of the cliff. If the clouds break and the sunset plays on those caves, why, you'll see things that haven't even been written yet."

In exasperation, Gravēda waves her arm at him and then gets on all fours and crawls into the tunnel, hearing the old man mutter as she goes: "In exasperation, Gravēda waves her arm at him and then gets on all fours and crawls into the tunnel, hearing the old man mutter as she goes . . ."

WHEN I WAS
TWENTY-
FOUR

*W*hen I was twenty-four, I became an adult and assumed I should acquire adult sorts of things—such as a job and a marriage. College took six years because I fooled around, switched majors, and then ended up taking advanced courses in advertising, which was considered a new and exciting field to work in back then. All my life, I had followed programs that other people explained to me, completing one step and then moving to the next, doing what I was told to do. By this method I became a college graduate, a job applicant, and a candidate for matrimonium. After graduation, I played my part in a series of job interviews and then went home to get married. I was a brand-new baby adult.

I hadn't seen my family (grown by then to a Mom, Dad, Sis, Brother-In-Law, Niece, Niece, Infant Nephew) for four years, so to them I still was an unapproachable prince. Not so with my hometown girl. She had visited me several times at college, bringing along as chaperone either her ugly friend or her older sister, the one who didn't get married, stayed at home to take care of the folks, and who had the abject look of an old maid, of unfulfilled sexuality gone to bitter seed, even when she was in high school. These two women, the ugly friend and the older sister, were somewhat the romantics back then and had been convinced that our liaison was going to be legitimized by marriage anyway, so they were cooperative in covering for the hometown girl and me when we stayed together, alone, in my college apartment. It was illicit and therefore a thrill for us all.

College students these days must have to go a bit to arrange an illicit thrill. Certainly, having your high-school sweetheart visit for the weekend can't be much of an event, not when college students routinely are bringing their roommates—of the opposite sex—home with them and then trying to convince the folks that it's hypocritical to sleep apart at home when, in fact, the students are living together on campus.

I know about this not only because I read Dear Abby but also because about a year ago one of my fellow vice-presidents invited me to spend a weekend with him and his family at their beach house. His son was there—home from college with his roomie, a female.

Sunday morning I was coming out of my room when I glanced down the hall and saw the two of them, this boy and girl, in the bathroom. The door was open. He was standing there shaving and the roommate, she was on the pot. Seeing me, they waved—both of them! And then shut the door.

I thought: This is young love? Nineteen-, twenty-year-old love? They acted as if they were two old sisters who had lived together forever. Don't it break your heart? Don't you wonder if they ever experience the bittersweet part of love that makes you miserable, the illicit part that makes your pulse run? I don't know. Somehow, it seemed so much classier, more honorable and Romeo and Juliety, to meet on the sly.

My hometown girl and I would talk for hours, long faces and quiet voices, about how wrong it was for us to be sleeping together before marriage but how we couldn't help it, couldn't help ourselves. (And during these discussions, I'd sit there half thrilled and half ashamed, thinking of Felicity.)

Because the time my hometown girl and I spent alone in my apartment was sin time, we treated it with care. Always indulgent with each other, always on our very best behavior. She secretly wanted to be shown around campus and introduced to my friends; I secretly wanted to stay in bed and romp. So, in the etiquette of the times, I urged her to come with me so I could show her around campus and introduce her to my friends, and she said let's just stay in bed and romp. I won those arguments; I might have been in the foothills of adulthood then, but I didn't say I was particularly bright.

It was during one of those weekends that we decided to become engaged—the same weekend that she stared into my eyes and told me in a flat statement that she'd do almost any-thing for me. We were in bed. After making the statement, she continued to stare, as if I were supposed to be thinking up possi-bilities. Exciting myself into general goofiness, I missed the sig-nificance of that key word: *almost*. I didn't realize what a world that word could cover.

It's like the weather reports you hear these days. Used to be, the weatherman would say it's not going to rain tomorrow and then, if it did, you could conclude the weatherman had made a mistake. Now, however, the weatherperson says there's a fifteen-percent chance of precipitation tomorrow and, if it rains, you can't conclude anything—except that the fifteen-percent chance hit. During our marriage, when the hometown girl re-fused me something I very much wanted, I tried reminding her that she once had said she'd do anything for me. No, she would correct, she had said she'd do almost anything. Oh, yeah—I remembered. The fifteen percent. What could I say? She was right, and we never hung from chandeliers or moved to Australia.

After we were married, I started a job with a mighty corpo-ration and we moved to the suburbs of New York. Bad times. I kept thinking that all of Felicity's predictions were coming true except the one about the hometown girl being a breeder. She was barren and when the stakes of our arguments got high enough, I used that against her, too.

It was during the bad times of this marriage that evil origi-nated in me. Started innocently enough, with a change in the theme of one of my recurring daydreams: I no longer was the one who died in a horrible accident; I no longer imagined *my* funeral, who'd be there and what they'd say. Instead, I began to daydream about my wife's death and how people would treat me at her funeral and what I'd do as a widower man. It got to the point that I used to imagine, when I heard her car leave the garage, that she'd never return from that shopping trip. It got to the point that I'd feel a twinge, a little twinge of disappoint-ment, when hours later I heard the car pull back into the garage.

I didn't realize then that these occasional evil thoughts should be treated like pinpoints of cancer traveling unattached in the blood, to be rejected and expelled as soon as they're detected.

So I held on to mine and played with them. Elaborate daydreams about my wife's death, and then later about how some corporate backstabbing could move me a rung or two up the corporate ladder, about sleazy little sexual escapades I might be able to stage—all of it beginning with that very first twinge of disappointment I felt when I heard my wife's car and knew she had returned safely from a shopping trip.

I wonder if that's the way Hitler got his start. Surely, he didn't conceive full-blown that obscenity that men for a thousand years will link with his name. It must have begun with something relatively small, some first bad thought. When as a boy he walked by a Jewish business and imagined how satisfying it would be if the place were to burn to the ground, or maybe he saw a wealthy Jewish family on the street and secretly wished they'd all get hit by a train.

He cultivated his evil until it became a monument to evil. Mine, being personal and petty, simply destroyed my marriage and then went on to debauch me until, in my early thirties, I became something of a symbol myself. A local one, just at the place I worked—but a symbol all the same.

You have to understand. All this happened to me because I considered my dirty little imaginings to be harmless. They were, after all, just in my head—no one knew about them, no one was being hurt by them. I didn't realize at the time that evil originated that way. I didn't realize that, upon feeling that first twinge of disappointment, I should have dropped to my knees and prayed for protection.

But I don't know. Maybe my marriage would have failed even if I hadn't cultivated those spores. My wife and I suffered disillusionment almost from the beginning, and sometimes I think that all the experimentation and easy living arrangements that kids try these days will make things different for them. If at twenty years of age you can stand there and shave while your lover takes a dump, how can anything possibly disillusion you? Life without disillusionment. It don't seem natural.

In any case, whether it was cultivated evil or broken illusions or that demanding selfishness that was a by-product of my royal airs, the failure of my first marriage was all my fault. Mea culpa, mea culpa, mea-fucking-culpa.

•   •   •

When I was twenty-four, a baby adult home to be married, I was eager to see Felicity. Not only was I becoming wise enough to miss her magic, but I also was curious about all the gossip I'd been hearing. My hometown girl and then my sister couldn't feed me the details quickly enough. Felicity had become a scandal.

Her husband had died and she'd become embroiled in some sort of trouble with the hospital officials; she was suing them or they were suing her, no one seemed to know for sure. There was talk that *she* was going to be committed to some mental hospital. She'd been arrested for shooting a BB gun at cars that went by her house and, of all things, at Boy Scouts who were marching through one of the fields next to her property. She'd been jailed or threatened with jailing. Then she got into a big fight with the lawyers she'd hired to help her out of all these messes, and they were suing her or she was suing them or maybe they were suing each other. No one seemed to know for sure. But everyone knew that she sat out in her carved chair at all hours, drunk and railing against the world. And some people said they'd seen her walking along the road at night, picking up dead animals that she carried back to her house.

"And she's *fat*," Sis told me the first evening I was home. "I don't mean she's just added a few pounds, I mean she's . . ." Sis puffed out her cheeks and held her arms way out from her body. I got the idea: *fat*.

I went over to visit Felicity the very next day. That tree-stump chair no longer looked as if it belonged in royal receiving rooms, in the chamber of some Viking warrior. Spindly legs had been carved out of the once solid base, and the armrests had been cut and planed into fragility. The back of the chair, once magnificently high and thick, had been carved in airy filigree, through which you could see.

I knocked at the door, but she didn't answer. I looked in; the kitchen was a mess. Felicity had never kept her place neat but I could see it had gone beyond clutter, had become filthy. I knocked again and called her name. Then I went around and looked in one of the front windows. I thought I saw movement, someone or something crouching down by one of the chairs, but the place was so dark and in such a shambles that I couldn't tell for sure. I walked around back.

Lord love a duck! Her backyard was a cemetery! Dozens of grave markers lined up in military precision. Most were crosses a foot or two high but some were tablets and a few were odd little monuments of elaborate design. It gave me the creeps, made me anxious about what might be behind me—as if I might turn around and see a monster Felicity advancing on me with a butcher knife or BB gun.

"Felicity!" I called toward the house and then waited for an answer and called again. No reply.

I examined some of the markers. They were wooden, beautifully carved, and all of them painted a dazzling, pristine white. In the middle of the plot was a large and highly embellished cross. Running at angles to the heavy horizontal and vertical bars that made up the central cross were a variety of delicate wooden rods that ended in floral scrolls and fleurs-de-lis. It was an exquisite piece of work, a kind of heraldic trellis. Across the horizontal bar was carved the name "Mother Frances Xavier Cabrini." On the vertical member, just below the intersection, was the figure of a bird, carved in bas-relief.

Next to this was a marker made of a series of interweaving, gentle bentwood arches into which had been carved astragal bands and highly detailed serrations. I bent to examine it but at the same time was afraid to touch anything because the work was so delicate that it seemed a probing finger might break something, chip a serrated tooth, knock over an arch. Strange. Across the tops of two of the larger arches were inscribed the names "Julius Rosenberg" and "Ethel Rosenberg." So strange.

Then I suddenly got this eerie feeling that I should get out of there. So I quickly walked past the rest of the markers, the florid carvings, the crisp geometric designs, and the names inscribed on the crosses and tablets and arches. I recognized some of those names from the news.

Talking with my sister that evening, I was tempted to ask her about the bizarre little cemetery but because Sis hadn't mentioned it to me, I figured the backyard graveyard was one secret Felicity had managed to keep. So I said nothing as I listened to Sis describe in hushed and horrified tones how "the thing" between Dad and Felicity again had become so bad that, at one point, Mom even broached the topic of divorce—not with Dad, of course, but with Sis. I told Sis I didn't believe anything was going on, had ever gone on, between Dad and Felicity and that even if he had visited her a lot, he was just trying to be friendly to a woman who obviously needed a friend. My sister dismissed all that with a shrug and said, "It's all over with now anyway. He hasn't visited her since she got in trouble with the law."

I spent the next day discussing wedding details at a joint conference of the two families. I'd decided to accept the corporation job in New York, and the wedding would be held a week before I was due to report for work. We planned to honeymoon on our way east. Meanwhile, I had the summer—two months until the wedding.

Next day at noon, I went to see Felicity again. She didn't answer my knock, but I heard something—a voice or voices—in the backyard so I went around to investigate.

In the middle of the miniature cemetery sat Felicity, bearlike. She was mumbling, her back to me. If it wasn't for the voice and the shiny black hair, I wouldn't have believed that the hulk sitting there was Felicity. Surrounded by a litter of chewed-up limes, she was carrying on a whispered conversation that she punctuated by waving around a bottle of tequila held by its neck. She was circus-woman fat.

I spoke softly. "Felicity?"

She let out a startled yelp and then, with some difficulty, made a quarter-turn of her fleshy body so she could see me. "Honey Bear! I'll be damned if it ain't Honey Bear hisself! I heard you was coming home." She laughed. "Come sit by me, Dolly Babe."

As I made my way through the grave markers, Felicity took a long drink of tequila and followed it quickly with a bite out of a whole lime. I got a look at her face and realized just how bad off she was. Eyes swollen and red and unfocused. Her skin pasty. No makeup. Drunk.

"Have some tequila, Sweetness." She pulled me to the ground, and I landed hard enough to hurt.

"I think I'll pass," I said tersely.

She laughed, took another drink and bite of lime, and then shuddered. She turned away and I was glad of it. Watching her body tremble was enough; I didn't want to see the expression on her face. I was not prepared for this; even after all the gossip I'd heard, I was not prepared for this. In the years I'd known Felicity, up till then, she seemed never to change: no heavier, no lighter, no older, no perceptible difference in her manner. But sitting there like a drunk grizzly, swaying and shuddering from the effects of tequila, this person seemed so unlike Felicity as not to be her at all. I didn't know what to do. Pretend not to notice the difference in her? Try to cheer her up? Wallow around on the ground with her, commiserating? I didn't know; I wasn't prepared for this.

She hung a lumbering large arm around my neck. "Ever see my cemetery before, Love Button?" I shook my head. "No? Of course not. I forgot. You weren't here. All this happened while you were gone. Well, what you see here is cold, hard, dead evidence that old Felicity's turned crazy. People in town would die to see this." Her head jerked. "I made a funny!" She laughed and coughed and lighted a cigarette.

When I realized my lips were drawn back in an expression of disgust, I forced my face into a blank look.

"I got Mother Cabrini here. And over there I got the Rosenbergs. Did I tell you 'bout the Rosenbergs? Oh, that's just too, too perfect. I shot a couple redwing blackbirds off a power-line and buried them there. Get it?" She started to laugh but got caught in a strangling sort of cough that forced her to spit something foul on the ground. I had to look away.

She offered me the bottle, but I refused it again. We sat awhile. I think she dozed and, as she did, I stared at the flesh of her upper arm, hanging loose and deeply dimpled. Fat women should not wear sleeveless blouses. I wanted to get out of there.

She jerked upright and looked at me. "What?"

"I didn't say anything."

She blinked, looking around. "What?"

I shook my head and we returned to silence. When it seemed that she might fall into a deep sleep and begin snoring, I shook her awake and asked, "What is this place? I mean, I don't—"

"This is my cemetery! I find some little dead animal and I bring it here, give it a name, and bury it. Before they took my guns away, I used to shoot 'em and bring 'em back here."

"*You* shot them?"

"Sure."

I still didn't understand.

"So I can honor them, eulogize them—build monuments to them."

I shook my head. "I still don't—"

"Come on!" she hollered drunkenly. "Don't be so damn stupid. I give names to the anonymous, hallowed resting places to the unconsecrated. Markers to mark where they'll lie for eternity. I write poems for them. I get distilled in their behalf. What dying creature, man or beast, could ask for more?"

I shrugged.

She shoved me roughly. "You wanted me to eat Mother Cabrini, didn't you?"

"What?"

"That mourning dove I shot. You thought I should take her feathers off, cook her up, and eat her, didn't you? Well, hell with that. I don't eat saints like they're so many pieces of chicken or something."

"Maybe we should go inside, huh? I could fix us some coffee."

"Oh, I know what you're thinking. It's a hell of a thing to kill something just so you can glorify it. But why should I be different? When they offered me that flag, I didn't take it. A hell of a time for honor, that's what I told 'em. And you can bet they didn't like that one little bit. Screw 'em." Felicity inhaled deeply off a cigarette that had burned nearly to her lips. "And if I hadn't shot the Rosenbergs off that powerline, which was a golden opportunity nobody could pass up, what would've happened to them? Lived for another season or two and then get caught by some animal. Eaten by a cat and turned into catshit. Or die of starvation and their bones left to rot someplace. *Forgotten.*" She tried to light a new cigarette from the butt but burned herself in the process. "Damn it!" she exclaimed, throwing both cigarettes to the ground. "Of course I kill to glorify. Just like everybody else. Blackbirds and mourning doves and foxes and snakes—I kill *everything.* But out of all the animals who've ever lived and died, how many have had their passing celebrated as have those who lie before you now?" She swung her arm clumsily.

"The monuments," she said, pushing a finger in my chest. "That's what counts. The monuments you leave, you breed. That's what survives you. The memories." She took a heavy drink of tequila and then sort of leaned back, collapsing supine. "God, I'm tired," she said, sighing heavily.

"You do beautiful work. The crosses and other things. Exquisite."

"I'm pretty good at it." Felicity belched softly.

I stood and then debated as to whether—and how—I should help her get up. Finally, I put my hands in her damp underarms and sort of hauled her to her feet. When she wasn't looking, I wiped my hands on my pants.

We were heading for the house when Felicity suddenly stopped and then dragged me to the back of the cemetery. "There's one that I got to show you, absolutely have to show you."

"What?"

"This one!" She was pointing at a thick wooden tablet, on the face of which were carved dozens of tiny crosses. Some of them were in relief, and others stood three-dimensionally in tiny cupolas. I'd never seen so many different kinds of crosses, none of them more than an inch high.

"What's this one?"

She grinned. "Can't tell you. My secret."

"What?"

"It's my secret and I ain't telling, ain't telling," she teased.

To humor her, I knelt and examined the cross-studded tablet. Etched all along the bottom was a row of little aquatic-looking creatures, highly stylized renderings of tadpoles or something like that. "What'd you bury here? Tadpoles?"

"I buried you there."

"Me? What do you mean?"

Felicity laughed. "Can't tell, can't tell. Look at all them crosses. Patriarchal, papal, Greek, Celtic, Maltese, tau." She began dancing in a little circle, singing: "Pommée, botonée. So many kinds of crosses you can carve, you can carve. Pommée, botonée, and tau taus, too."

Then she tripped and fell on one of the markers behind us. As I helped her up again, she was laughing until she turned around and saw what she'd done. "Oh, no!" She gathered up the broken pieces—decidedly feminine stuff: floral scrolls, blossoms, sprays of brittle-thin leaves, threadlike tracery. "This is my Pat Nixon monument. Oh, Lord. I've broken poor old Pat's cross."

"Pat Nixon isn't dead."

"I know that," Felicity said angrily. "The people I name 'em after don't have to be dead. That's not one of *my* rules. Poor old Pat." Felicity was cradling the broken wood.

"Come on. We'll go inside."

"No!" She jerked away from me. "I got to repair this. A mink is buried here, you know that?"

"A mink? Where'd you find a mink around here?"

"Well." She smiled as if maybe this whole thing were a joke after all. "Perhaps, just perhaps, it's really a weasel. But that's not the point. We found it by the road when we went to the river, and its pelt wasn't hardly damaged at all. I buried it a couple of years ago when Nixon went on television to explain that slush fund."

"I don't get it."

"You don't get anything. Didn't you see Pat when he said she doesn't have a mink coat? That all she's got is a respectable Republican cloth coat? Do you remember the expression on her face? My God, that poor woman. All her life she's dreamed of having a mink coat, just like every respectable, brittle, Republican woman dreams. She's been dreaming it ever since she was a respectable, brittle, Republican little girl." Felicity's voice began to break and when she dropped the wood and hunched closer to me, I could smell her.

"Pat wouldn't have been flamboyant with her mink," Felicity continued in a quieter voice. "Oh, no. She wouldn't have drug it across the room like some sort of harlot-starlet. No. She would've taken good care of it and wore it like it was her due, her due as a Republican wife married to a Republican asshole. That's their compensation for marrying Republicans. Mink coats. But, no—*oh, no. He* goes on television and tells the world all she's got is a goddamn cloth coat. He humiliated her. In front of the whole country."

Felicity sobbed and pulled me tight. "And then her dream was gone. He stole it. She knew she wasn't ever going to get a mink coat after that. Oh, Pat, poor Pat! Someday you'll have one if, by God, I got to buy it for you myself. It'll be thick and rich and warm as you ever thought it would be and then when the wind blows you can pull that high collar around your scrawny Republican neck. God bless you, Pat Nixon!"

Felicity was hanging on me so heavily that I had a difficult time keeping us both upright. She was crying and shuddering and coughing; I didn't know what to do.

"My husband's not buried here," she sobbed. "Oh, no— they wouldn't let me bury *him* here. I told 'em to shove that goddamn flag . . ." But she was crying too much to continue.

Felicity grabbed the hair at the sides of my head and

brought me close to her face, so unattractively boozy and blubbery and blowsy. I tried not to make a nasty expression in reaction to her breath.

"You come to take me away, Love?" she asked. "Like you said. Remember? I would've gone with you then if I thought we could've gotten away with it. I'm serious. I lied to you before. About loving you only a little bit. I've always been in love with you. Since I first saw you. And . . . and I just been waiting for you to grow up. A disciple of delayed gratification—I told you that, didn't I?"

"Felicity . . ."

"I love you, Baby. True to God, I love you." But then I guess she saw something in my face, because she suddenly put her head down and when she spoke again, her voice was different. "I'm drunk. So terrible drunk." She looked up. "Will you kiss me? As bad off as I am, will you just do that? Kiss me. Please?"

But when she lifted her weight on tippy-toes, I averted my face and offered only the hollow of my neck. Which she took greedily, crying all the more.

·   ·   ·

When I was twenty-four, I wanted to be tough. I thought it was okay to feel things on the *inside*, to get scarred up from bad women and hard times. To have lived such a rough life and suffered the blues so often that when you looked off into the distance, people could just read all that mileage in your eyes. But I wanted to be tough on the outside, showing to the world only the blank face of Gary Cooper, with the look of Gable and Bogie's offset mouth. I wanted to be an American man, just like all those I'd seen up there on the screen.

And now, at age fifty, I have to tell you I'm pretty good at it. I don't cry and tears don't touch me. My voice doesn't quiver when I fire a man, even one who begs for one more chance, which I don't give. I have a general's courage, not the physical bravery needed for hand-to-hand combat but the administrative balls necessary to commit thousands of men to their deaths when the administrative plan requires it. My exterior, in fact, has become so tough that I'm no longer sure what it protects. I might have hardened all the way to the core.

But it wasn't always that way. Back when I was twenty-four, the crust was thin and what it covered was soft. So I told myself I had to be careful with Felicity, had to remain in emotional control, had to make sure I didn't get involved with her in a way that would mess up my impending marriage. I kept reminding myself that *technically* Felicity and I were not lovers, that we had never engaged in sexual intercourse; it was a thin distinction.

I finally talked her into leaving the backyard and going into her house, where I put her down on the couch in the living room—which was a mess, littered with underclothing that was stained in ways I didn't want to know more about. While she slept, I took a stab at cleaning the kitchen: washing dishes and making neat stacks out of the dirty pots and pans. I didn't like doing it. I wasn't trying to repay her for anything (the night she took care of me when I vomited, for example), because it doesn't bother me that things like that remain one-sided. I was just keeping myself busy while the percolator, which I'd found and cleaned, was bubbling a fresh pot of coffee.

When she finally came into the kitchen, she told me it was an insult to clean up a woman's house for her. "I was just trying to help," I said.

"You help by not noticing the mess. That's the gracious thing to do."

I told her the mess was hard not to notice, and she said if I didn't like it I could leave, and I replied that I might just do that. But then the coffee was ready, and we sat down and drank several cups in silence. When I went to the door, she asked me to come back the next day. I said I would. And I did.

I went over at lunchtime, and Felicity insisted on fixing an omelet for me. Her house was cleaner, and she looked better—wearing a deep-red dress, cinched in a way that displayed what waist she had. She was wearing makeup, too, but there was no disguising the generally ravaged looks. Her skin and the fat under it seemed like sponges that had absorbed great quantities of nicotine and alcohol and were permanently stained.

"So you're feeling better today, huh?" I asked as I ate the omelet with gusto even though it didn't taste very good.

She rolled her eyes and replied in a broad Southern accent: "Ah feel as if Ah have been repeatedly hammered down and pried loose."

"Hangover?"

"You got it, Babe. I'm sorry about yesterday, I really am. You caught me at a bad time."

I nodded, scooted my chair back from the table, and lighted a cigarette. Felicity brought an ashtray and took away my dish, which she rinsed in the sink as she spoke. "I don't know how many times, or for how much time, I'll see you while you're home, but I'm determined to make sure our time together is good. You might not think so, by the way I acted yesterday—but that was a special case. I didn't dream you'd catch me out there. I assumed, if you came over, you'd come over in the evening."

"I'm a big boy now. I can visit you in the daylight."

She sat at the table and took a cigarette from my pack. "What does your future wife think of you visiting me?"

I shrugged. "She doesn't mind."

Felicity laughed.

But as I began visiting Felicity every afternoon, the home-town girl became increasingly upset. When she tried to talk me out of going over there, I told her she wasn't my mother and shouldn't tell me what to do. After that, she didn't comment on my visiting Felicity; all she did was give me a look, a look I've seen a mother give to a child who is misbehaving in church. A look that says: I can't do anything about it now, but just wait till I get you home, Bub—just you wait.

I spent more time with Felicity that summer than I'd ever spent with her before, and she recited more of the Gravēda story than she'd ever recited before. The story took on a new impor-tance, an even stronger bond between us. It replaced conversa-tion when conversation became awkward, and because the story was something we had had in common for ten years, we reminisced about it—about what we called the old times, in the hospital when she crushed blackberries on my lips and in my bedroom that summer when my family was away on vacation and at her house that one time, on her couch. The story was, in fact, like our child and, like a child, it gave us something to talk about, gave us a reason for being together.

Which is ironic when you consider that Felicity predicted that my hometown girl would use children as a means for holding on to me. "You'll either get a divorce," she said, "or you'll have a record number of kids 'cause every time there's some trouble, she'll get preggers." I told Felicity I didn't want to talk about that, and she dropped the subject.

All that summer, in fact, Felicity would do whatever was necessary to make sure our time together was indeed good time, just as she had pledged. She made it clear that she wanted to go to bed with me, but she never came out and asked so I never had to refuse. But I got my excuse all ready anyway: that it wouldn't be right to do something like that in the last few weeks before my wedding. The truth was I was scared of going to bed with Felicity, scared I'd either be repulsed by her fatness or, in spite of the way she looked, would fall in love with her again—would fall in love the way I did when I was fourteen. I had to be careful, because my crust wasn't tough yet.

I waited until the week before my wedding to ask Felicity about all the trouble she'd been in. It was early evening and she was serving whiskey sours. "Which of the many stories do you want to hear, Honey Bear?"

"Any of them. About the BB gun, for example. Did you really shoot at Boy Scouts?"

She laughed. "Yep."

"Why?"

"Well, let me see. All of that was mixed up in the bad times I was having when my husband died. I got in all kinds of trouble with those bureaucrats at the hospital and then, after he died, with the whole damn military in general. I was drinking a lot. And, well, the thing with the BB gun started when I was sitting out in that chair watching those damn cars go speeding by."

"You keep talking," I said, "and I'll fix more drinks."

"You're a joy forever, Doll. What happened was, I got sick and tired of those cars going past at ninety miles an hour. I'd be in the yard, trying to think or trying not to think and then, zoom!—some damn kid would go speeding by, kicking up dust and running over rabbits and cats and dogs and, well, I just got sick of it. So I brought out the BB gun and took to shooting at those cars I thought were traveling at excessively high speeds."

"That's wonderful," I said, laughing.

"Yeah, and I got pretty good at it, too. Figured out how far I'd have to lead a car to make sure I hit it. I was chipping paint jobs and cracking windows to beat the band. The kids would slam on their brakes, jump out to inspect the damage, and then give me the finger. But they never came in my yard."

"Probably 'cause you were holding the BB gun."

"Exactly!"

We both laughed.

"Then," Felicity continued, "the county sheriff came to call with two of his deputies. Like I was some sort of dangerous criminal or something. And they threatened to arrest me, and I told them maybe they should adopt my methods 'cause you'd be surprised how few speeders there were ever since I began using the BB gun. They were not amused."

"And the Boy Scouts?"

"I guess I just was fed up with uniforms in general. My husband, my brothers, those idiots at the funeral, and then the sheriff. And, well, I was in a mood the day those poor kids and their dumb-ass leader came hiking through that field. I'd been drinking and was waiting for speeders. Had the BB gun hidden under a blanket over my lap. And then I saw them, all soldiered up in their uniforms with hatchets and knives on their belts. Their leader was that skinny jerk who has the drugstore over there by the tracks. Never did like him anyway. And he was hollering, 'Eyes front, eyes front,' as they marched past—like the very sight of me was enough to give boys a bad case of unclean thoughts."

"So you just started shooting at them?"

"*Well*. At the druggist, really. And I was so far away that I couldn't possibly have hurt them, but he began screaming how he was going to get the law on me and everything."

"You can't blame the man, Felicity. I mean, really—shooting at Boy Scouts."

"I had my reasons." She grinned. "They were an affront to me. You ever heard that old saying about Boy Scouts? Little boys dressed up like idiots, led by idiots dressed up like little boys."

I laughed.

"But not so funny when they grow up and play the same kind of games as soldiers. Oh, shit—I don't know. One of my brothers was killed in the war and one of them got crippled up. And you know what happened to my husband. I was just in no mood for uniforms that day."

I looked at my watch and was about to tell Felicity I had to go when she said, "I hate it when you check your watch like that."

"Like what?"

"When you sneak a look like that. It reminds me what you have on your mind all the time you're with me. Someplace else to be, someone else to be with."

"Hey, excuse me all to hell. You know what the situation is."

She held up both hands. "You're right, absolutely right. I have no call to say anything. I take it back."

I smiled. "I like it when you give in to me."

"I'll give in to you anytime you want." She leaned close and put her hand to my cheek. "You look so good to me, Honey Bear. Break a woman's heart with those Baby Browns of yours."

I gave her a light kiss but when she moved close for more, I stood up. "I'm late already."

"I understand. I just want you to know. *Anytime*."

I didn't visit her again until the day before my wedding—and then I came over for breakfast because there were all sorts of things I had to do that day. The bachelor's party was scheduled for the evening. Then the wedding in the morning and off for

New York. This was supposed to be the last time I'd see Felicity.

She fixed eggs and bacon and toast and orange juice and then served me and watched me eat. "I feel like I'm on display," I told her.

"It gives me pleasure to look at you, but I'll stop if it's a bother."

"It's okay."

When I got to the coffee-and-cigarette part, Felicity said, "So. Here it is. I knew it'd get here, but I'm still not prepared for it."

"What're you talking about?"

"Your departure."

"Well, this has been a pretty good summer for us, hasn't it?"

"Pretty good."

"And everything's okay with you now? I mean, most of the trouble you were having is in the past, right?"

"Yes—most of it. The Boy Scouts are pressing charges, and I'm suing the hospital."

"You have a lawyer?"

"Oh, sure. The crack legal team of Keegle, Squiggles, and Squeeze."

"Who?"

"The official name is Kleindell, Smith, and Sims—from Springfield. I started calling them Keegle, Squiggles, and Squeeze after I got into some arguments with Mr. Squeeze—Sims—about the way he was handling my case. I withheld their fees, and they threatened to sue me, but we're working it out now."

"I'm sorry. About all your trouble. I really am."

She shrugged. "I brought it all on myself. Everything. I guess I should've left here right after my husband died, and maybe I should have left years before. But now, this place seems like home."

"That shouldn't stop you from leaving. This *is* my home, and I don't have any problems leaving it."

"So I notice."

I checked my watch. "Sorry. But you know how it is."

"Sure. Lots to do the day before your wedding. I hope I haven't complicated things for you."

"Nope."

"I guess with the way everything happened, with my going bonkers and you being away . . . well, I guess I put a lot more importance on what was between us than I should have. I used to dream about you coming back and taking me away from here."

I started to say something.

"No, no. I know it was stupid. I don't hold you accountable for my stupid dreams. Jesus Christ. I'm a fat, alcoholic, forty-four-year-old widow, and you're just a boy, a young man, getting out of college. And about to be married. Can't forget that."

"Felicity . . ."

"No, Darlin', I don't want you to say anything. When you get a little older you won't feel so obligated to say something, to say something nice, when a woman opens up her heart to you like this. I just want you to understand how much this summer has meant to me, how much I appreciate all the time we've had together. I know I'm not pleasant to look at, to be around. And, God, the way I was that day you found me in the backyard—I'm surprised you came back at all. Hell, Honey, I repulse myself."

I didn't say anything, and I even managed to fight back the impulse to look at my watch.

Felicity looked out the window and spoke quietly, almost as if she was reciting: "When I was a little girl, I used to walk barefoot in the mud flats near the river—on those days when it was so hot that I was thankful for the gooey coolness of mud and oblivious of creatures that might live in mud. I remember this one day I saw an old black man sitting on a rock at the river's edge, tying the end of a thick rope around a hunk of rotten meat. When I asked him what he was doing, he said, 'Catching a turtle, little girl.'

"I asked him why he wasn't using a hook, and he said you didn't need one to catch a turtle. 'Catch 'em with stubbornness,' he said. When he got the meat on, he tied a piece of iron to the rope and tossed the whole thing in the river. Said he was going to catch an alligator snapper.

"I thought he was teasing me about some creature that was half turtle, half alligator, and when he pulled the rope out of the water and then tossed it back in again, I asked him if there really was such a thing as an alligator turtle. 'A alligator *snapper*,' he corrected. 'Gets bigger than you. No limit to their size—the more they eat, the bigger they get. And *old?* The earth ain't been around long enough for one of them to die of old age.'

"I kept pestering him with questions, asking if they really ate rotten meat and he said they eat anything. 'Dumpling Child,' he said, 'that mean turtle will just sit down there on the old man's bottom floor and wait for something to swim close to them mighty jaws. And it don't matter what it is that comes close—rotten meat or some little fishy. Whatever it is, *snap!* That's what makes 'em so ugly—all the bad stuff they're willing to eat.'

"'And do they really look like alligators?' I asked him.

"'No,' he said, 'they just look ugly.'

"I was getting bored and about ready to leave when he quietly said, 'There he is.' The rope didn't jerk or splash in the water; it just slowly pulled taut, the old man leaning back against it, standing and then setting his feet for leverage against whatever was pulling on the other end.

"He explained that no matter what happens, the turtle wouldn't turn loose of that rope. 'Cut off his head and he'll still hold on. Won't turn loose till the sun goes down.'

"I watched that rope for what seemed like an hour before I saw the creature break the surface. I hid around the back of the old man while he pulled the turtle across the bank, its giant claws gouging deep and parallel scratches in the mud. When I finally peeked around and got a good look at it, I told the old man to throw it back.

"He just laughed. 'I'll put him in a barrel and feed him chicken guts. A week or so of that and his meat'll be clean enough to eat. Tastes just like chicken.'

"I kept telling him, 'No, no!' I thought something that terrible should never have been brought up from where it lives. You should've seen it, Honey Bear. Nearly five feet long and weighing more than I weighed back then. Its shell, like a humped-up and misshapen rock, was covered with growths, fungus—filthy things. Its jaws held that rope and meat as tight as could be. And the worst part of it all was that face—except you wouldn't call it a face. That *thing*. Its eyes opened wide like they were astonished, and that head so despicably ugly that I thought the Devil must've created it—or maybe God when he was angry about something. More than just hideous, Darlin', that turtle had the look of evil that had metastasized.

"And when I creeped close, the turtle hissed through closed jaws like a devil snake. The old man told me, 'Watch it, Missy. Old Mr. Snapper could rip the long bones right out of your legs.' And I believed him, believed him without a trace of doubt in my heart. In the presence of that monster, I would have believed anything."

Felicity reached across the table and squeezed my thumb. Then she leaned back in her chair. "I would have believed anything except a prophecy, had it been made back then, that I'd one day become something very much like an alligator snapper. Like some kind of human monster version of it."

I stared at my cigarette.

"*Now's* when you're supposed to pop up and disagree with me," Felicity said, laughing. "Tell me that I'm not like an old snapping turtle at all, that I'm still desirable to you."

"You *are*. I—"

"Oh, shut up." She laughed again. "I was just kidding. Listen, you got to get going. I appreciate you coming over here this morning, listening to my motor mouth. One last thing. You're going to kill me for asking you this, but will you stop by tonight? After the bachelor's party."

I made a pained expression. "No can do, Felicity. That thing'll go on to all hours and then I got to sober up in time for the ceremony. It's a morning wedding, you know."

"Yeah, I know. But I don't care how late you come by. Just stop on your way home."

"I can't."

"Come on. *Please*. There's something I want to show you. Something I got just for you."

"Not a wedding present."

She laughed. "Not hardly."

"What then? Show it to me now."

"I can't. It's not something you should show someone in the middle of the morning. You can stop by here for just a minute tonight. That's the great thing about my house being on your way home. Just think, if I'd bought a place on the other side of town, you and I would've never—"

"I'll try. If it's not too late, I'll try to stop for a minute."

"Good." She didn't get up from the table when I went to the door. "And remember, I don't care how late it is. I'll be waiting."

"Okay."

The rest of the day was a blur of details and unlistened-to conversations and dozens of short trips, ferrying in-laws and cheese trays here and there. By the time I left my bachelor's party, it was three in the morning, and I turned into Felicity's lane because of that old impulse and because of a single light that seemed forlorn in that little house, that dark night.

I walked in without knocking. Felicity was reading by candlelight at the kitchen table, in the middle of which was the world's largest bouquet of roses—yellow and red and pink. Maybe a thousand of them, or so it seemed in the soft light—with me so weary and intoxicated. She wore a red caftan and was made up like she was going to a party, her hair perfectly done, wearing pearl earrings, gold chains around her neck. She was flanked by two large candles that burned to see her better. The scene was so overpowering that it had no trouble at all pushing through my thin crust and touching me.

"I left the bedroom light on for you," she said. But we never got to the bedroom. After ten years of courtship, we made love on the kitchen floor. Although I fumbled with her under-clothing, she didn't hurry me or try to do it for me. And I was glad, because Felicity wore wonderful underwear—stuff so deli-cate and intricate and small that the diminutive was absolutely required. I slipped hooklets from eyelets, popped snappettes, and undid buttons that were the same size and of the exact pink-white color of a baby's thumbnail.

I fell asleep and the candles burned out; I awoke to the dark, Felicity touching me all over. "At least I have this," she said—speaking so softly that I wondered if I was supposed to hear.

Although the linoleum, embossed with wild flowers, was cool, my skin stuck to it and pulled when I turned over. "Hmm?" I asked dreamily.

"At least I can hold you tight one last time—before she gets you."

"Is that why you wanted me to come here tonight? So it'd work out like it did in the story?"

She laughed softly.

"That's what you wanted, isn't it? You said you wanted to show me something, but what you really want is for us to be together like Genipur and Gravēda. Isn't that true?"

Felicity fondled me. "What I want, what I want. I want the sun not to come up so it'll be night like this, you and me and Zachary, forever. What I want is to smell behind your ears and in the hollows of your neck. What I really want is for the two of us to breathe together: mouth on mouth, your exhalation taken as my inhalation and then I'll return the breath to you and you'll warm it in your chest and blow it back to me, the two of us breathing back and forth as a unit until no one can tell which is your breath and which is mine, until we have inhaled each other, our lungs have absorbed each other—and when we part we each are a part of each other."

I was smart enough to be quiet for a moment. Then I said, "A poet."

She punched me lightly in the ribs.

"But *I'm* not a writer," I told her. "I tried, but it didn't work out. No passion for what I was writing. It seemed like a game, every time I experimented with writing I had to *pretend* to be feeling something. I kept trying, for you I kept trying. I was tempted to send some of my stuff to you, but now I'm glad I didn't."

"Doesn't matter. I have faith in you and faith isn't based on whatever promise you show or don't show. Faith isn't based on evidence, on informed opinion, predictions of future success. Faith is just there, without doubts or questions or absolutely any reason for being there. Mad faith."

"You're not listening. I don't *want* to be a writer. The only reason I even tried it was because of you, because you planted that idea in my head when I was a kid and had my own fantasies about being a war correspondent. I got a job now—a good job with a big corporation. And that's what I want. Do you believe me? Felicity?" She didn't say anything. "*Felicity.*"

"Darlin', when you say my name, I believe anything you tell me. Claim you visit the moon nightly, and I'll ask if the earth shines, too—and does it shine blue?"

"There's no talking to you."

She was on her side, with her elbow propped so she could rest her head on her hand. Close to me, still rubbing and touching me. "I told you I was a disciple of delayed gratification. See? I've delayed this gratification for years—and now here it is."

Then I noticed that the kitchen windows no longer were as black as they had been. "Oh, Lord."

"What?" she asked.

"My marriage day is about to break. They'll have the posse out after me."

Felicity rested on her back, and I leaned over her. She said: "Perverse, contrary, cranky old sun—huh, Babe?"

"Yeah." With the increasing light, her breasts became starkly visible—surprising in their bareness and size. I held them and squeezed them and hefted them to gauge their weight. Felicity smiled as she watched me.

Silence. Day hurrying: brighter, brighter, birds, brighter.

"Is that a tattoo?" I said it like a child who has just seen magic. "*You have a tattoo?* I never knew that."

She was grinning. "That's what I wanted to show you. I've been waiting for you to notice it. My surprise."

I leaned close. The tattoo was on the inside of her left breast and there was light enough now to see the colors: bright, crystal, and fine. The inch-high heart, exquisitely red, was cracked on the right side—near the point. It rested on a spray of dark green leaves. And baby blue tears, three of them, dripped from the broken heart. It was beautiful.

I looked up at her with all the questions in my eyes.

"I got it for you."

It took me a moment to understand—and then I shook my head, immediately rejecting what she'd said.

"*I did.* A friend of mine from San Francisco came to visit last year. He was on his way to Chicago. He's a really wonderful artist—and he does tattoos. Had his needles and inks with him, so I told him I wanted one for my lover who's always leaving me. I said I wanted a tattoo to show my lover how my heart cries for him."

"No!" I sat up and turned away.

Felicity put a warm hand on my bare back. "What's wrong, Sweetheart?"

The crust. It was gone and I was unprotected and this is not what I needed to see and hear on my wedding morning. I faced her. "You've had that tattoo for years and years. Probably got it for, for your husband when he went off to the war. You've had it for a long time, before you even knew me. You must think I'm an idiot."

"No."

"Well, don't say you got it for me. Even if you're just kidding around, don't say that."

"But I'm not kidding."

I shook my head again. "You didn't get it for me."

She leaned to my ear and whispered. "Yes I did. Because my heart cries for you."

I looked at her.

She nodded.

And then I believed her. Against all logic and evidence and good reason, I believed her. We made love again.

By the time I got home (there met by a highly distressed Family), I was running late for my wedding and had no time to shower—could only shave and then dress in the car on the way to the church where I got married. And now I remember nothing about that ceremony except how it smelled: the old lace and fresh lilacs, an Ivory-scrubbed bride, and the lingering, lingering scent of Felicity.

GRAVĒDA

The part Felicity told me when I was twenty-four and home to be married.

22. Now Gravēda is out of Eller's well-lighted cave and is climbing the path to the top of the cliff. Evaporating cavesweat makes her shiver and shake, but the storm is easing and the rain at last has become regular rain, just drops of water falling through the air. She sees sunlight in the seams between clouds.

Gravēda thinks about what happened in Eller's cave but is unable to make any sense of it. She wonders if Eller really is writing her story and, if he is, can he possibly know everything that's happened to her. Does he know, could she even make him understand, how she felt that day she was picking berries on a hillside and heard Momma scream and Poppa yell? Could Eller describe what Gravēda saw when she got to where Poppa lay dead, Momma lay bleeding, and the bear went lumbering casually away as if unimpressed with what it had done?

Gravēda thinks about all this until she reaches the top of the cliff and begins to walk along its edge. Then her stride lengthens and walking replaces thinking, because walking is better than thinking. When you're walking, you can look in the distance and see a hill and say, That's where I'm heading today. And when you get there, you can turn around and see the place you camped the night before and you can say, That's where I've been.

Not so with thinking; it leads you in circles so that after hours of thinking you either are lost or end up right back where you started. And all you have to show for thinking is head pains.

It was walking—not thinking—that carried Gravēda ten years alone on the trail, and it's walking that brings her to the caves where the old travelers live.

She looks down at the cliff's rock face, which slants into the ocean in four terraced steps. The terraces are pathways that run in front of large holes, the entrances to the travelers' caves.

Gravēda is about to climb down to the first pathway when the setting sun flashes through a rip in the clouds to color her, and the slanting rock below her, in bright yellow light.

The sudden sun draws out the travelers. Four of them step tenderly from caves to pathways, moving like cripples. They wave their skinny arms and slowly lift and lower their feet. These pathetic dances are accompanied by little halfhearted chants, moans and groans and the creaking of stiff old bones.

23. Gravēda waits for crowds of old travelers to pour from their caves onto the pathways, but no more appear. Only those first four, who slowly twirl a time or two more and then quietly step back into the caves—leaving Gravēda alone on top of the cliff, once again vulnerable to thought.

She is about to talk to herself, about to say: What a *blank* sight. But Gravēda doesn't know how to fill that blank, can't think of the word. Where is the word?

Ghastly? Yes, it has an appropriately breathless quality but, then, that specific word is a bit refined—a touch too arch—for Gravēda.

Horrible and terrible have been worn too smooth, too comfortable.

Grisly is dark, is grim—but is not precisely right for them.

Piteous, Hideous & Invidious are technically correct, but they fail to touch the soul. Leave 'em to lawyers, leave 'em to lawyers.

Vexatious? Gee, Gravēda thinks, I don't know.

Execrable sounds like shit.

But then she finds it.

"What a wretched sight," Gravēda says out loud, quietly, to herself.

And that's it, of course. That's it exactly. Distressed in mind; miserable in appearance. *Wretched.*

Having found the word, Gravēda experiences relief. It is the state of wretchedness, as represented by those four old travelers, that Gravēda has been seeking. Of course. To be able to climb down there and settle in one of those caves and become completely, devoutly *wretched*. Cry all day long, and scream in your sleep. Weep out of loss for the past and despair over the future. Hide in the corner of your cave and wallow in your wretchedness. Grow skinny and frail. And never stop crying. The tears come before you realize what it is you're crying for and they come after you've forgotten it, too. So many tears that they trickle out of the caves and keep the face of the rock wet, and in the cool mornings those warm tears raise a fog.

That's what I'll do, Gravēda concludes. Go down there and live as they live. Crying and complaining, mourning. I'll stay in my cave like a hermit crab in his shell. I'll whine and whimper and suffer from shame as if shame is a disease—debilitating, incurable, and wretched.

Gravēda now understands the glory of these old travelers, living like lepers in their caves. They've done the right thing. They've reacted to the loss of hope, the perverted end of the journey, in the correct way. They know exactly what to do. Go into devout mourning. Pursue wretchedness as once the journey, the path to God, was pursued.

Maybe this is hell, Gravēda thinks. And if it is, it wouldn't be unbearable—not when you can treat suffering in a way that makes suffering your eternal vocation and can give yourself over to it completely, practicing wretchedness as Gravēda once practiced walking: totally, constantly, and seemingly without end. Gravēda's constitution could adapt itself to such a hell.

She could become a devoted disciple of despair, dedicate her life to it. Sure. Already her thoughts begin to rarefy as her eyes blur with tears and her throat prepares for the low, moaning wail that forms in the lower back part of her mind. Gravēda is right there on the edge of being wretched.

24. Gravēda climbs down to the first path and enters a cave. She follows a long corridor past empty chambers and comes to steps, which she descends. More hallways and then a large room lighted by oil lamps. Here are the four, sitting in rocking chairs and dozing.

"Mercy!" one exclaims, causing the other three to jerk awake. "Look who's come to see us."

"Gravēda!"

"My daughter told me you'd made it to the beach."

"After all these years, huh, Honey?"

Gravēda nods and walks cautiously into the room. This is not what she expected. Rocking chairs and tables covered with cloth. The four are old women and they seem genuinely pleased to see her. One of them leads her to a chair and another brings her a slice of raisin bread; the other two sit and beam.

"How long's it been, fifteen years?"

"Twenty years," another says.

"No."

"Yes," the old woman insists. "It was my son's thirtieth birthday when we left Gravēda and her mother. I remember it distinctly."

"Twenty years," Gravēda says. "It's been twenty years."

"See! I told you."

"And my daughter told me that your mother, rest her soul, lived for ten years after the tribe left. And you've been traveling for the last ten years all by yourself to get to the beach."

Gravēda nods.

"Goodness," one of the old women says. "Ten years traveling all by yourself. That must have been some trip."

"It had its moments," Gravēda says quietly. "I'll be damned if it didn't have its moments."

The ancient, frail women smile at her; one of them has drifted off to sleep. The other three rock in silence.

"Where are the rest of you?" Gravēda asks.

"The rest of us, Dear?"

"The rest of the travelers who live in these caves."

Three of them titter, waking the fourth.

"We're all there is."

"No," another says. "There's her." The woman points to a doorway.

"Five of us are left, Gravēda. Sarah isn't feeling too well."

"She lost her husband a few days ago."

"Rest his soul."

"But . . ."

"What, Hon?"

"Where's Ismo?"

"Ismo?"

"Mercy, it's been . . . what? Four, five years since he died."

"Rest his soul."

"Five years. I remember because it was right after that when my son decided to become a priest. And he's been a priest five years now. It was five years ago when Ismo died. I remember distinctly. Five years."

Gravēda is confused. "The priests told me—Crat made it sound like Ismo was still alive, that he still lived down here in the caves."

"Oh, no."

"Five years. He's been gone five years. I remember it distinctly."

"Don't be upset, Gravēda. Priests sometimes tell you things, little white lies, for your own good."

"Little white lies! My God—"

"Don't shout, Dear."

One of the women motions toward the doorway. "We don't want to wake her."

Silence. The one nods off to sleep again, and the others wait for Gravēda to say something. "I didn't think things would be like this in the caves."

"Like what?"

She shrugs. "I guess I got the impression that the travelers living here were like, you know, *hermits*. And then when I saw you a few minutes ago, out on the pathways . . ."

They giggle again, hiding their mouths with softly wrinkled hands. "Oh, she caught us."

"Yes."

"You caught us, Dear."

The sleeping one awakens and joins in the giggling even though she doesn't know what it's about. They're like children, like ancient children.

"That used to be a ceremony we had."

"When there were lots of us still living here."

"Back in the old days. We'd go out there on the pathways every day at sunset."

"But it's just our exercise now."

"I thought it'd never stop raining."

"If I don't get out there at least once a day, I really start to stiffen up."

"I have to go," Gravēda says abruptly.

"But you just got here."

"I thought maybe you were coming down here to live with us."

"Yes. My daughter told me that."

She shakes her head; something like panic is beginning to have an effect on Gravēda.

"Those of us who live here are keeping the tribe together, you know."

"My son has said as much, last time he visited. And he's pretty high up now. In the council, you know."

"Sure. When the last of us are dead and gone, the tribe moves. Either out in the ocean or back in the other direction— but the whole thing starts again as soon as we're gone."

"It'd be nice to have you here, Gravēda."

"Plenty of room."

"And nothing bothers you here. The best security possible."

"*You.* Always with the security."

"It's important. No one knows that better than Gravēda. Huh? After what happened to her folks."

"If you came to live here, the tribe would have to stay together for a long time. You're so young."

"A child."

Gravēda stands. "I'm sorry. I have to go. I'm glad I could see you after all these years. I don't even know if I . . . if I remember you. Twenty years. But I have to leave now. I'm sorry. I don't mean to be impolite."

But the women feel they've been wronged. Two of them close their eyes, and the other two look away. The pace of their rocking quickens.

"I'm sorry. Really. Can you tell me. Does one of you have a son named Genipur?"

"His mother is in the other room there. She's the one who lost her husband a few days ago."

"Rest his soul."

"I still say he didn't fall."

"Nonsense. We haven't had a suicide for years."

"Two years ago to be exact. I remember 'cause it was right before my son first got elected to the council. I remember it distinctly."

"In any case, he fell. We all agreed on that."

"You can say whatever you want. I'm just telling you that the man knew these rocks like the back of his hand. But if you want to believe he fell. . . ."

"Don't be hateful."

"Me? I'm not hateful. My heart goes out to that woman. You think maybe I haven't lost a husband myself? How long do any of us have? You think I don't appreciate that? I'm just telling you. The man knew these rocks like the back of his hand."

"He was a good man."

"And you think I'm saying he wasn't?"

Gravēda leaves, and if they notice her departure, they don't say anything. She becomes momentarily lost in the passageways but then gets out on the lowest path, the one closest to the sea. She follows it around until it leads to the beach. Before jumping to the sand, Gravēda turns around and looks back up toward the caves. She shakes her head. Wretchedness, sure—she could have devoted herself to a life of wretchedness. But life in those caves is hell—what hell really is like: niggling disappointment, confusion, and a type of general and free-floating anxiety that is as pervasive and unopposable as a heavy morning's mist.

Gravēda walks along the beach but she no longer knows where she's going. She vows not to return to her rock den, and not to live in some cave someplace. She wonders if she can make peace with Nestus, make love to Genipur. Then she thinks about Ismo, dead five years. How did it happen, and did he call my name when he died? Was my name there among his last words? It's night now.

She walks and walks, and then she stops and looks out to sea.

25. Gravēda jumps in the ocean.

She draws herself into a ball, knees to breasts and hands locked around legs, and just rolls into the surf to let the sea have its way with her.

The ocean casually displays its power by tumbling Gravēda, who chokes on saltwater and coughs and still is determined not to release her arms from around her legs. But she is not committing suicide, not exactly.

A sea creature grabs her roughly, the idea of it made all the more terrifying because she's being grabbed by hands. Imagine: a sea creature with *hands*.

The creature, however, pulls her not to the depths but up to dry sand, and when she opens her eyes she sees that it is Crat who has rescued her. In a sudden rush of gratitude, Gravēda grabs Crat's wounded foot and hugs it to her, inadvertently tripping him.

"Gravēda, *please*." He jerks and pulls until he gets his foot away.

"Help me, Crat. You have to help me. I've been down to those caves. You lied about Ismo. I don't care. But you have to help me. I don't know what to do. I don't know where to go. I can't make any decisions. I don't—"

He puts his hand on her shoulder. "Shh." Then he helps Gravēda stand. "Let's get you by a fire. Then something to eat."

Gravēda nods. Good—let someone else make the decisions about where to go, where to sit, what to do. Gravēda no longer can.

Crat walks her to the cliff. She sits by a rock overhang. When he places Gravēda's sword next to her, she looks at him and says, "I forgot about it. Probably the first time in twenty years I didn't automatically carry my sword with me. And now you're giving it to me. I thought you'd try to take it if you ever got the chance."

"So much you still don't understand. We're not going to force you to give up your weapons or to join the tribe or to do anything. You have to take these actions voluntarily."

Gravēda views him with a new appreciation, this priest she has wounded and insulted and who now has pulled her from the sea. "Crat, I—"

"We'll talk about it after I get you warm and fed. I'll be right back."

Gravēda shivers in the dark until Crat returns with an armload of wood and a closed jar, which he hands to her. "Here, this stew is still hot. You get started on that while I build the fire."

She eats greedily and soon is warmed inside and out. "Crat?"

"Yes?" He sits next to her.

"I want to rejoin the tribe. I want to do what you and Nestus and the rest of you, the council or whatever, want me to do."

"Are you sure, Gravēda?"

"I'm positive. I'll be completely cooperative. I'll even incubate eggs for you. That one hatched, you know."

"Yes. I found the chick. It was dead. Do you want something to drink?"

She'd kill for a swallow or two of distillate but she dares not ask him for that. "Some water would be nice."

Crat is gone for what seems a long time and when he returns with a skinbag of water, Gravēda takes it and drinks heavily. "I just talked with the council," Crat tells her. "All the priests were excited when I told them what you said. They're discussing it now. Nestus is going to bring the entire council down here."

"What'll I have to do?"

"Follow the rules—that's the first thing. Then we'll want to explain to you what we've concluded about the journey. You could be a great help in convincing those young travelers not to attempt to cross the ocean."

"Whatever you say."

"Really? Are you *sure*, Gravēda?"

"I'm positive. I can't take it anymore. I just want to get married and have my baby. Hell, I'll raise it right here on the sand. Maybe this *is* the end of the journey. Maybe we were meant to come just this far."

"Not exactly. That's not exactly the way the council views matters."

"What then?"

"I should wait till Nestus gets here, but I think it'll be okay to tell you the basic things. We have good reason to believe that, years and years ago, our tribe was part of a larger tribe. Somehow we got separated from or left the big tribe or were sent away for some reason. What the council wants to do, wants to convince all the travelers to do, is to go back and see if we can't find that larger tribe. Or some evidence of it. We realize this will take generations and generations, but we think—"

"Whoa. You mean you want the tribe to travel toward the *rising* sun? To go backwards?"

Crat points his finger at her. "Now, listen here, Gravēda. You just got done telling me how you wanted to join us, how cooperative you were going to be. I got the council coming down here and everything. Don't give me any trouble. Okay?"

Now that she is warm and dry and fed and watered, Gravēda feels not quite as contrite as she felt before. But she swallows back her anger, nods, and says, "I'm sorry. Go ahead."

"All right," Crat says with some satisfaction. "The other fundamental conclusion we've reached is that a man and a woman can have more than one child. We have a great deal of evidence to support this. We're convinced now that having one child per couple was something that developed culturally, socially. There is no biological prohibition to multiple offspring."

"What the hell are you talking about? That's nonsense."

"Oh, for God's sake, Gravēda. You're incorrigible."

"Wait a second. The whole idea of the tribe is to keep reducing in number, each generation half the size of the previous one, until the last two travelers—"

"Don't you *dare* quote the creed to me. I taught it for more years than—"

"Well, you sure as hell didn't learn anything from it, did you?"

Crat starts to say something angrily but then stops, takes a breath, and speaks in an even voice. "We now know that travelers can have large families—four or five children—"

"Four or five children? Again with the litters. I should have put all this together before. Tell me: How in the hell are we supposed to produce The One? If the tribe gets larger instead of smaller, how can we end up with The One who's supposed to meet God?" Gravēda glares at Crat; she figures she got him on that one.

"The answer, Dear, is obvious. There never will be a last member of the tribe."

Gravēda stands, sword in hand. "I'm not listening to any more of this crap. I'll organize an expedition and we'll continue the journey right across that ocean. I'll take along anybody who wants to come. The rest of you be damned."

"Too late, Gravēda. The young travelers already are having large families. Priests are marrying. People who've been married before are remarrying. The ocean can't be crossed. We tried it for years, and not a single person made it. As soon as those old travelers in the caves are dead, the tribe is returning to where we came from. To our heritage. You can't stop progress once it's started. And it has started."

Gravēda shakes her head. "I sure as hell wouldn't want to be responsible for keeping God waiting out there someplace, waiting for The One to show up while the tribe is heading in the opposite direction—and getting bigger along the way."

Crat laughs. "You're stupid. God may be an exquisite and useful concept, but do you really think He's sitting across the ocean someplace? I mean, you think He's actually sitting on a rock and waiting for one of us to show up, don't you? Of course you do. Stupid. Incredibly stupid."

"Don't talk to me like that, priest. If I'm stupid, what do you call yourself? You're performing an abortion on The One— killing that child before he's even born. How did you priests manage to screw up something that was so simple and straight-forward?"

In exasperation, Crat waves his arm at Gravēda. He walks away a few steps and then turns to her. "It's all a matter of logic."

"A scandal of logic," she tells him.

"I don't have to put up with this. None of us does. The council has been working on a special little place for you and as soon as I tell them how you've changed your mind, that you're not going to join us after all—well, you'll be behind bars before morning."

"Behind bars?"

Crat turns and walks without saying anything else. Gravēda rushes to him and, in a quick rage, demands: "What are you talking about? Behind bars—what do you mean by that?"

"Out of my way, slut."

Gravēda hits him on the side of the head with the flat of her sword, and the old man goes down hard.

26. Gravēda hates that word—and the way some men can make it sound, like a flat hand slapping against thick mud. *Slut.*

"Get up, Crat." She nudges his shoulder with her foot. "Crat?" There's something about the stillness with which he lies. Gravēda bends down. "Well, I'll be damned." Crat is dead. "The bastard must've had a heart attack."

As Gravēda stands there and tries to figure out what all this means and what she should do about it, twelve bobbing torches approach her.

"Gravēda?"

Good Lord, she thinks—embarrassed to be caught there with a dead body like this. "Nestus. Hi there. Look what's happened. Poor old Crat has up and died from a heart attack."

Nestus and the priests with her crowd around the body. After a quick examination and some whispering, Nestus comes up to Gravēda. "He's got a big gash on the side of his head."

"Must have hit something when he fell?" Gravēda ventures.

Nestus shakes her head.

"Well, he and I had some words. I might have bumped him a little. I mean, just a nudge. I sort of nudged him with my sword. But not enough to kill him, if that's what you're thinking."

"Now you've done it, Gravēda."

"I haven't done anything. He died of a heart attack."

"You killed him."

"No."

Nestus nods.

"I don't give a damn what you think," Gravēda says, gripping her sword. "From what Crat told me, you priests got your thinking so messed up I couldn't tell you anything anyway."

Nestus stares at Gravēda, and Gravēda stares back. Then Nestus seems to relax her posture a bit, and her stern look lightens. "You murdered Crat. Please don't insult me all the more by repeating those lies. You murdered him. I think we could take you into custody, all of us priests. But I'm sure you'd manage to kill a couple more of us in the process. So, for the sake of preventing any additional deaths, I'm willing to offer you a deal."

"I don't need a deal from you."

"Sure you do. You apparently couldn't tolerate staying down in those caves with the old travelers. We sent Crat out looking for you and he gets killed. When the rest of the tribe finds out about this, they won't tolerate *you*. What're you going to do? What's to become of you?"

Graveda shrugs.

"Here's what I propose," Nestus says. "We'll bury Crat and tell people he did indeed die of a heart attack. We'll encourage the travelers to welcome you into the tribe; we won't talk against you."

"And?"

"And in return, you give me your sword."

"No. I'd be naked without it."

"Listen to me, Graveda. If you rejoin the tribe, you might be able to take up with one of the young men. Get married and have your baby. I know that some of them are fascinated by you, consider you extremely exotic."

Graveda becomes flustered; she's vulnerable to that kind of talk.

"But if you don't give me the sword," Nestus continues, "everyone is going to avoid you. We'll make sure of that. You'll be an outcast. Even more than you are now."

"So I surrender the sword, no one finds out about Crat, and you priests do what you can to make sure the other travelers accept me. Right?"

"Right."

Graveda considers. "You give me your word on that?"

"I give you my word."

"Okay." She hands the sword to Nestus, who walks back among the other priests and says something to several of them.

They rush Graveda, grabbing her arms and legs as ropes are brought out and put around her. Graveda does not resist; she is too astonished to resist. "But you gave me your word!"

Nestus shrugs.

"How could you lie like that?"

"Lies, truth—such nebulous concepts."

"You bitch."

"Uh, uh. No, no. Mustn't ever talk to me like that again. I own you now. You're just not very bright, you know that, Graveda? You simply have misunderstood how things work around here."

But the priests have misunderstood, too. And they have

misgauged, have misgauged such things as the power of rage and the strength of ropes.

27. Gravēda's arms strike like striking snakes and her hands, like the jaws of snakes, clamp around the necks of two priests who've been holding her. They gag and struggle. A priest at her feet pulls a rope tight in an attempt to trip her, but Gravēda remains standing and when Nestus advances with the sword held over her head, Gravēda lunges for her.

Nestus hesitates a moment before swinging the sword and that moment is all Gravēda needs to get her sword back. With it in hand, she hesitates not at all; two quick blows and two priests become instant amputees.

"Grab her!" Nestus screams. "Get those ropes around her!"

They're finally able to trip Gravēda, but not before she manages to sever a leg. As she rolls around in the sand with priests on top of her, Gravēda's face is rubbed in blood. It stings her eyes. The close and unholy odor excites her into a full and possessive lust-rage. She can taste blood now, salty and nasty blood.

Making low and demoniacal sounds, she tosses the priests off her and gets to her knees. She suddenly is hit in the back of the head with one of the staffs that priests carry and this stuns her so that they're able to tie ropes tightly around her legs.

She grabs and manages to pull a priest close to her. She bites rapidly and viciously at his forehead, like a dog trying to reach marrow. He screams so pitifully that the other priests drop the ropes and pull him away.

Half standing, half crouching, still tied around with ropes, Gravēda swings her sword wildly at anything that moves within the sword's reach. A hand, fingers, another arm, ears, half a foot—priests are separated from various parts of their bodies.

"Pile 'em up!" she yells. "Stack 'em, stack 'em!"

Only the constant urgings from Nestus, her grabbing priests by their necks and repeatedly throwing them back into the fray, keeps the battle going. Gravēda is being hit with the staffs and eventually she drops to one knee, that knee falling on a priest's face so that his head's pushed into the sand and his front teeth break.

Again, she's rolling in the blood and stabbing at priests, cutting them and gutting them. Soon, pints and pints of blood are being absorbed into the sand, and here and there lie little piles of intestines and scatterings of major organs with wild designs that, although perfectly adapted for internal purposes, appear to be oddly jerry-built now that they're lying on the sand or protruding from the wounds of priests who bravely but stupidly attempt to stuff everything back in place. All around are ungodly sounds, people doing their best to express profound injury.

When her sword catches up in a rib cage, two priests are able to wrestle it away from her. Gravēda grabs an amputated leg and hits her assailants with meaty thwaps!—breaking this one's neck, slapping that one silly.

But reserves have been called up and soon Gravēda is completely encircled in ropes and subdued. She screams terrible epithets at them.

"Take her up to the cell!" Nestus shouts over Gravēda's voice. "Quick! Before the whole tribe is out here. Get the wounded up the beach! Come on, come on! Move!"

As four priests carry her across the sand, the moaning and shrieking of wounded priests fade; Gravēda misses the music.

She herself has become silent, allowing the priests to carry her up a steep path and then across rocky terrain. She figures they're going to take her to some secluded place and kill her.

28. But they don't.

Just before dawn, Gravēda is carried into a large cave and put against the back wall, left bound as the priests work furiously to anchor in place a set of bars that block off the part of the cave where Gravēda lies.

In torchlight, she watches them. The bars are green saplings about the thickness of Gravēda's upper arm; the vertical and horizontal members are set a foot apart and tied at their intersections with thick leather bands to create a cagewall of square windows, each one a foot on all sides.

The cave is large, a roughly triangular shaft that goes straight back in solid rock for a hundred feet or so. The floor is flat, and the walls tilt inward to meet in a peak about forty feet up.

The entrance to the cave is a small, domed doorway covered by a heavy slab of wood. Ventilation is poor; the fumes and smoke of a dozen torches, implanted along the inward-slanting walls, collect at the top of the triangle.

By the time the priests have anchored the cagewall, which has been shaped to fit the cave exactly (top and bottom; side to side), Gravēda has struggled out of the ropes. She looks around her cell, which takes up the back third of the cave. There's a small compartment off to one side and when she sits in it, the priests standing at the bars can't see her. In the floor of this tiny room is a hole, a foot and a half across and perfectly round. It's a sewer hole, leading to the outside.

Gravēda is too hurt and tired to attempt an escape, but escape and revenge are on her mind as she leans against the rock wall and rests.

Hours and hours pass. Maybe the next day has come and gone and it's night again—Gravēda doesn't know. Sometimes she sleeps and sometimes she falls into unconsciousness.

"Gravēda!"

She opens her eyes wide and listens carefully.

"Gravēda! Come around where I can see you."

It's Nestus; Gravēda doesn't move.

"Okay, stay back there. I don't care. What I've got to say is short and to the point. You're going to remain here until the tribe is ready to move. If you try to get through these bars, I've instructed the guards here to kill you. When the last of the old travelers is dead and the tribe begins the return journey, then we'll leave and you can find a way to escape. If you're still alive. I don't know if that'll be a month from now or a year. But if you even get close to these bars between now and then, we'll blind you or kill you or do whatever it takes. Don't have any doubts about that, Gravēda. You are wretched—a monster who's unfit for life outside this cave. I hope to God you die here."

Gravēda is so sore and stiff that it takes her several moments and great effort simply to stand. She walks tenderly around the corner of her little room. Nestus is by the cagewall; on either side of her are priests holding sharpened staffs.

Gravēda thinks she might be able to knock down the cagewall by rushing the bars and throwing herself against them. She checks out how they're anchored, with wooden braces and large rocks. She wonders if the leathers she wears will protect her from the priests long enough to get the cagewall down.

"Don't try it," Nestus warns. "These priests were out there on the beach and they know what you're capable of. You get close enough and they'll kill you—I guarantee you."

"Give me your word on it?" Gravēda asks.

Nestus doesn't acknowledge that. "Here's where you'll remain until I can get the tribe away from you. Including Genipur. *Ah.* Didn't know I knew about that, did you? He belongs to me, Gravēda."

"I'll kill you, Nestus. Slit open your belly so when you try to run away, you'll trip over your own guts."

She shakes her head. "I've instructed the guards not to talk to you or even to talk to each other while they're in here. Except for your own, my voice is the last you'll hear. This is it, Gravēda."

After Nestus leaves, Gravēda returns to the side room. As she tests her bruises with careful fingers and checks for things that might be broken, she hears stoneware being slid on the rock floor. Then she smells hot soup; a skinbag of water is thrown to the back of the cave.

They're feeding and watering me like some kind of goddamn animal, she thinks. Worse than that. As if I were the monster they've been calling me all along. She decides not to eat or drink anything, not even to go out where they can see her. Soon everything's quiet and Gravēda just sits and waits.

Tee-dee, tee-dee, tee-dum. And in this tedium, the cave fills with a silence as thick and suffocating as water. The kind of pervasive silence in which she can hear her own heartbeat in her ear and can imagine, as the quiet continues unbroken, the sound of nearby heartbeats.

29. Because the smoky torches barely hold back the dark, everything in the cave is gray and poorly defined. It's enough to make Gravēda believe that her eyes are dimming. She notices this, too: In the half-light life of the cave, she's lost the ability to mark time.

She's sure time passes, but she doesn't know how much. Gravēda watches for signs of time from the two holes that link the cave to the outside: the small doorway in the front and the sewer hole in the back. When the doorway is uncovered (so her food can be brought in, her guards changed), sometimes light shows and sometimes it doesn't. She tries to keep track of this but becomes confused. The door opens and light shows; time passes; the door opens again and light shows again. But Gravēda can't figure out if the successive displays of light are from successive days or if the light is the morning light, the afternoon light of the same day. Sometimes the sewer hole shows light and sometimes it's dark, but Gravēda is unable to keep track of that, either.

The guards are no help; they don't speak to her and only occasionally do they break the rule about not speaking to one another. Nestus visits infrequently. She just stands at the bars and stares at Gravēda.

Eventually, Gravēda begins eating again. Nothing else to do in the cave but eat—good food, rich food, more food than Gravēda ever ate on the journey. Fried rabbit and baked fish, served in steaming leaves. Berries and nuts and a variety of veggies. Hard little tart grapes; mushy large and pregnant pears. Red apples and blueberries. Lotsa honey. And always the stew, bowls and bowls of that good and hot stew she first tasted that first day on the beach. How long ago was that? Gravēda doesn't know.

Every day (and maybe every night—maybe on the hour; who knows?) the guards lay out a course along Gravēda's side of the cagewall, and now she considers it her duty to make her way through it, bite by bite, until she finishes everything. Then another course is set and she starts again. Perhaps this is Nestus's plan, to keep her drugged with food.

Walking is what Gravēda did during the journey and eating is what she does during her imprisonment. Ten years of walking got her to the beach, and now she wonders where she'll be if she eats tenaciously for the next decade.

She's taken off her leathers and put them on the floor in the side room; she wears only her robe, using the leathers as a pallet to protect her from rock scrapes as she sleeps. But there's another reason she removed her leathers: They don't fit anymore.

Gravēda occasionally toys with the idea of trying to knock down the cagewall, but the guards are always alert and they appear to be absolutely capable of using those long, thick, sharpened sticks to blind her, to kill her if that becomes necessary. And besides, Gravēda feels inadequate without her sword.

Just to hear her own voice, she sometimes threatens Nestus. "Did I tell you how I was going to slit open your belly and loop that blood-wet gut around your scrawny neck? Huh? Bitch!" But Nestus listens calmly and then walks away, saying nothing. And Gravēda goes to the back of the cave and sits and rocks on her haunches and pretends she's waiting for something, for someone.

·   ·   ·

She wonders if soon the guards might have to install a relay to toss food priest-to-priest in a continuous flow, from the beach where it's all prepared to her: the ultimate consumer. That's how mighty an eater she's become, as mighty an eater as once she was a walker. Now she marks progress not in miles but in gross poundage.

Her robe has become terribly tight, and when she's sitting in the hidden area she pulls the robe to her armpits so her fat can hang free. She sits there and wonders if soon she'll have to go naked. She looks down.

Opening eyes wide to see details in this dim light, Gravēda

examines her corporation. Above the belly mass that sort of spills over the top of her thighs are breasts that have become lipid-holding tanks, bulging with surpluses. She separates these humdingers and sees three distinct rolls of fat: The first, just under her breasts, is a modest ridge; the second is thicker than her arm and continues halfway around her back; the third roll is so large that it hangs and Gravēda can, whenever she has a mind to, grab ahold and flop it up and down. Feeling under her belly, she finds that her thighs are pressed together so tightly as to form a seal between them, running from just above her knees all the way up. When she withdraws her hand from that heavily humid area, she notices that her fingers are slick with grease and sweat.

Gravēda has become a thumper.

·   ·   ·

Then one day (or one night—Gravēda has no way of knowing) Nestus comes into the cave and is greeted boisterously by the guards. They congratulate her and say things that make her laugh, that actually make *Nestus* laugh. When Gravēda comes out from her little side room, the priests become instantly silent, with the guards raising their sharpened staffs and pointing them at her. Gravēda goes back to the hidden area. She knows what is going on. Nestus and Genipur have announced their intentions to get married, or maybe he and Nestus already are married and she's pregnant.

Gravēda tries to convince herself that she's wrong, that the guards were congratulating Nestus for something else. But Gravēda gets those piercing pains in the middle of her chest again, and she can't help but believing that Genipur is lost to her. Then, everything changes.

Gravēda stays back in her hidden area almost all the time, no longer rushing to the cagewall when she hears her food courses being laid out. Now she waits until the torches are low, flickering and needing to be replaced, before ambling to the bars so she can gather up an armload of food and bring it back to the private compartment, where she eats in dark solitude.

She puts her tattered robe on the pallet of leathers, and Gravēda goes naked now. The guards report this to Nestus, who waits by the cagewall to see the naked Gravēda. But nothing is said.

Eventually, Gravēda discovers a way to escape. She closes her eyes and sits motionless for hours—or days or weeks, she doesn't know. But it is in this state, eyes closed and cave silent and corporeal mass quiet, that Gravēda's mind is freed. And once free, it immediately races outside.

The colors! The first thing she notices is the colors. Sky blues and grass greens and oceans that reflect her eyes. Clouds are *white*. Day is bright! And all the details, branches and rocks and leaves, are in blade-sharp focus. It's wonderful. Gravēda races along, races along—and occasionally climbs high for the sake of panoramas.

As her mind travels, Gravēda wonders if there's a chance it won't ever come back to this cave, this lump of flesh. The prospect is so enticing that she urges her mind on: Run away, run away.

But always those chest pains jerk her back, frighten her awake in the cave, and weight her mind with a general listlessness that discourages travel.

Then she tries another kind of journey. Eyes closed, sitting motionless for hours or days, Gravēda embarks on an internal trip. Searching among organs under acres of skin, she is relentless until finally she finds the source of her pain. Gravēda discovers she has a Genipur infection.

And she remembers how she got it, too. Genipur first infected her when she touched to the underside of her tongue that spot of moisture from his lip, introducing him to her bloodstream. And then there were all those opportunities for reinfection during that night they spent together.

The disease was benign until Genipur and Gravēda were separated; then, bitter at the prospect of living alone and forever in fat old Gravēda, the Genipur spore grew into wiggling silver creatures that now inflict pain whenever they remember him, when she thinks of him, at the mention of his name.

Gravēda has heartworms. They burrow. They snip perfectly round holes of pain throughout what she'd always believed was a tough and fibrous organ. They pierce her.

Gravēda knows, even without conducting an internal investigation, she knows: Her infection can be cured only by proximity, by placing Genipur close to her, constantly.

·   ·   ·

But Gravēda receives no Genipur remedies, just food. She gets fatter. Unspecified amounts of time go by.

If someone were to tell Gravēda she's been in the cave for six weeks, she'd believe him. But, just as willingly, she'd believe she's been in the cave for six months—or a year, or even more.

She considers the possibility that she's been in that little cell for decades, that she's become an old woman. And if the priests who guard her are still young, perhaps it's because they are the children of her original guards.

She closes her eyes and sleeps for an hour or a day.

When she awakens, it's dark but, then, it's always dark when she's awake. Gravēda tries to sleep some more, tries to do a little traveling, but none of it works out. As a diversion, she uses her tongue to play with one of her bad teeth, and the jolting pain—teasing it, seeing how bad she can make it and then waiting until the pain eases into various levels of lesser aches—occupies her for a while, an hour or an afternoon. She doesn't know. But eventually she becomes bored with pain.

Then, for purposes of entertainment, she begins slapping her body. It doesn't matter where: her side, her thigh—her whopper belly. The slaps' concussions set up in her fat a series of wave motions that travel the length of her, rippling off the extremities. This is pretty good fun, she thinks.

The seemingly limitless growth of her body fascinates Gravēda, and she wonders if she could use it as a basic standard of measurement—to gauge time, for example. She could estimate the length of her imprisonment by *weight*—figuring it at, oh, a pound a day.

How long have I been here?

Slap, slap.

At least a couple long hundredweights, I'd say.

And how much longer will I be imprisoned?

Slap, slap-slap.

Ooo. I got tons, friends, tons and tons to go.

Gravēda speculates that perhaps her size, her weight, her galloping girth will someday free her from the cave. She sits there and imagines it. Imagines getting too large for the hidden side room—so large that the edges of her fat peek into view of the guards—and then getting larger still. She can imagine getting so big that she'll fill up the whole cell and eventually will have to lie with her exit over the sewer hole and her swollen head next to the cagewall so she can keep her mouth open and can direct the priests to continue to shovel it in, shovel it in! And they'll comply, unwittingly helping her to escape by pumping up her leviathan size until it piles against the cagewall and then breaks through the bars so that she spills out and fills the entire cave. And then the priests will have to feed her from the outside and she'll grow and grow until she applies such irresistible pressure to the rock that she cleaves this very mountain and finally is able to stand in the middle of the mountain's split-open heart: a colossus who squashes priests on her way across the beach, wading the goddamn ocean, to the setting sun—to a place where God sits on a boulder and waits for the one with enough faith to finish the trip.

Then Gravēda laughs.

The guards look anxiously toward the shadows at the back of the cave; they nervously finger their spears.

Gravēda laughs again. She thinks it's funny to imagine that a wedge of fat can break a mountain. She slaps around, slaps around her gullible flesh.

After a certain amount of time passes, Gravēda hears some familiar commotion at the cagewall and then smells a fresh course of food being laid out for her. She salivates heavily; her cavernous stomach squishes and whines, gurgles and splashes.

She grabs at the rock wall to get the necessary leverage to move that bulk to a standing position. Not very mobile anymore, Gravēda puffs and pants from the exertion required to transport her great and magnificent baggage of flesh even the most modest of distances.

She carefully lumbers around the corner from her side room. Accustomed to the guards' stoic reaction upon seeing once again her grand nudity, Gravēda usually doesn't even look at them. But this time she does; she happens to glance up at the four silent ones who stand at the cagewall, their spears resting lightly on the horizontal bars and the spears' sharpened points in her cell, pointing at her.

"Genipur! Dear God, Sweet Genipur!"

The guards glance at each other, raise their spears, ease the sharpened ends a little farther into Gravēda's cell.

They've put Sweet Genipur on guard duty! But Gravēda blinks, takes a step closer, and realizes he's not Genipur at all. It's just a new guard. A kid. A young priest who resembles Genipur, but who doesn't have Genipur's chocolate eyes. Remembering those eyes—dark chocolate, bitter chocolate, big round dollop kisses of chocolate—Gravēda presses a fist to the fat between her breasts. It hurts—damn, it hurts—when they bite like that.

Gravēda comes a little closer to the bars, the closest she's been since they put her in there. He's a nice-looking boy but so scared; the tip of his spear trembles. Still outside the reach of that sharp wooden point, Gravēda takes another step toward the boy because it gives her pleasure to look at him.

The guards on either side of the young priest whisper to him.

"Steady, David."

"Hold your ground, boy."

He's shaking all over now—like a puppy, he's shaking. And when Gravēda takes one more step, the young priest jabs wildly at her. Although Gravēda is out of range and safe from his pointed stick, she's still startled by his rage, his mad fear of her—by the viciousness with which this boy is trying to stab her, blind her, kill her. He makes hard consonant sounds as he thrusts repeatedly.

What?, she wonders. Is he just trying to show the older

guards that he can man the monster wall as well as any of them? Or does he really hate me that much? A bone-deep hate arising from origins that neither he nor I understand.

The guard closest to him rests a hand on the boy's shoulder, a signal that the kid need not keep jabbing at Gravēda. Somewhat embarrassed but still hot, the child pulls back and assumes the same stance as the other three: fingering thick sticks in nervous anticipation. But he continues to stare at Gravēda, and she continues to stare at him.

As she watches his eyes, she realizes he's examining her body. So Gravēda looks down and sees that her skin is waxy with dried grease and she sees that grass, which the guards have been throwing into her cell as bedding, sticks to her fat along with bits of food, a gnawed rabbit bone or two, some dirt, a few pebbles—a variety of junk trapped in her rolls of fat. She brushes herself off and then thinks: To hell with it.

Gravēda raises her arms. "Look, look!" Let 'em look, let 'em survey the hills and valleys, the rounded ridges and tight crevices of my body. I must look nude to the extreme.

Gravēda, her arms still over her head, turns slowly around. She has made peace with her bulk, has come to accept this majestic substantialness as her own. See how she can entertain them:

Facing the guards again, Gravēda pushes a finger two knuckles deep into her navel. The guards can only speculate as to whether that fingertip touches bottom; it does not. The boy has begun to tremble again, and Gravēda has begun to hate him for doing so. When she uses both hands to pull back on her hanging stomach so she can examine genitalia, this—finally—is too much for the kid. He curses her and begins again that wild jabbing.

Gravēda laughs. "Can't take it, huh, kid? Ha!" Holding her arms wide from her sides to make herself appear even more menacing, Gravēda bounces from foot to foot like some sort of monstrous puppet as she purses her lips into an exaggerated O: "Oooo, Oooo, Oooo," she says—or moans or wails or whatever you'd call what she does. Hell, she thinks, this is loads more fun than making toothaches or slapping fat.

But as Gravēda dances around, dances around, she happens to catch the boy's eye and it seems he's about to cry. Although the other guards are concerned for the young man and would like to comfort him and tell him everything will be okay, they dare not leave their positions along the bars. He finally gives up on the jabbing and just stands there trying not to cry out loud.

Gravēda decides it's up to her to hold him. Crazy, but she suddenly stops fooling around, stands for a moment to catch her breath, and then takes another step closer to the boy. As she makes that step, she raises one arm—reaching her hand toward the young priest. It is a gesture that says she is sorry, that she is sorry and now would like to touch him and maybe hold him and do the best she can to make everything okay again.

As soon as Gravēda is within range, the boy grits his teeth and grips his staff with both hands and makes one heroic thrust. Even in his panic, he has managed to strike quickly and hard. The sharp wood point hits not where the boy was aiming, the center of Gravēda's chest, but just to the right of that. The spear is stopped by a rib, but not before Gravēda's left breast is pierced all the way through.

When the boy jerks back his wooden staff, everyone takes a moment to stare at the bleeding wound. Then a guard says, "I'm going to get Nestus," and Gravēda covers the gash and walks unsteadily, almost staggering, back to the little side room where she can faint away with no one seeing her.

30. The blood in that massive body must be measured in gallons, because it seems that quarts leak down the front of Gravēda—and still she lives. She doesn't dare move her hand away from that hole on the inside of her left breast; even when she goes into shock, and from there to a coma, her hand continues to press against that breast wound.

Gravēda lies sick for days; when she recovers, she's been transformed.

Bugs have been crawling on and around Gravēda ever since she was put in her cell, but while she was unconscious they infested her. Most of them were benign, keeping her clean by exploring her mountain of flesh for scraps of food that had fallen on the slopes, carrying away flakes of dead skin, eating the waxy grease that encased her. But the ants, they were different.

They swarmed over the dried lake of blood, and when they finished it off, they began on her flesh. Even in her coma, Gravēda reacted to the pinpricks of a thousand, ten thousand, pincer jaws; she unconsciously brushed them away from her face, kept them off her eyes and away from her nose.

But they had the run of the rest of her, eating away at a flesh boulder that, were it actually rock, would be measured in true tons. The ants consumed pinches of her, here and there, and they raised crop after crop of welts on the prairies and high plains of her skin. But you had to laugh at their stupidity.

Call in the reds and the blacks and the cousin termites. Marshal your forces until you're uncountable and, *still*, you won't reduce her in significance. Dumb-ass ants! Do saltwater drinkers dream of draining the ocean? Can dirt eaters ever hope to consume the earth and then float in space? So why do you try? There's more of her than your entire bug species can collectively imagine.

And yet they continued to pursue the instinctual goal of reducing Gravēda to multibillion pellets of antshit. Talk about your blind faith.

Through bulk alone Gravēda did, of course, finally defeat them, but the little bastards didn't give her a victor's due. They didn't form their battalions into ranks to pass in review. They didn't even wave their little antennas good-bye.

They just left. As far as the ants were concerned, Gravēda no longer existed as soon as the last of them removed his back leg from her calloused foot. That's how it ended: One moment she was infested, and the next moment she wasn't.

As the transformation continued, Gravēda burned with an infection-caused fever that gave her the constant shakes and prompted her mind to overheated visions that she remembered even after she got well again, that she couldn't forget no matter how hard she tried.

Nestus called repeatedly from the cagewall, telling Gravēda that a priest was there to treat her with medicines and ointments. There was no answer. The guards wanted to lower the bars so they could go back to see if she was alive, but Nestus wouldn't allow it. They threw skinbags of water to the edge of that little room so that if Gravēda was alive but unable to walk, she'd at least have something to drink. And they continued to call her name.

But even after she awoke and surreptitiously pulled a bag of water to her, she didn't answer them. Gravēda drank as if her insides had puckered dry, and she assumed that what she was hearing—her name spoken with concern—was part of those crazy dreams she'd been having.

Then she just sat. Sat and looked without seeing anything in particular. Her eyes, like wet marbles embedded in the lardy flesh of a face misshapen by excesses of flesh, recorded images that were flat and unreal. She'd lost her perspective.

Her hearing became dull, perhaps because of the dams of wax that had hardened in her ears. Her taste had become all but worn out by the great poundage of food she'd eaten, and her smell was jaded by the rancidness around her, by the rancidness that was her. Gravēda's sense of touch had been blunted by the fatty deposits that were stuffed under the skin of her fingertips.

In this deprivation of senses, Gravēda sat motionless and lost the control she had over the decision to move or not to move. Was she sitting quietly in reaction to what she'd been through, or was she truly *unable* to move? If she wanted to raise her arm, could she? Did she want to, would she ever want to?

All the questions became moot when she stopped asking them, having finally lost even the ability to ask questions. In one last, heroic effort, she tried to stop the transformation: She pushed her tongue against a rotten tooth; she worked it viciously back and forth in its rotten socket. The pain should have jarred her awake, but it simply dissipated into a mere aching discomfort and then into nothing except dull and uninspired sensations.

When she reached that painless, motionless, thoughtless state, the transformation was assured. It was then that she took to caterwauling.

Between those cries that chilled the hearts of priests, Gravēda slipped into stasis. Her blood moved sluggishly, she breathed only occasionally, and the line between sleep and wakefulness—between consciousness and unconsciousness—blurred. Finally, she became completely silent, having achieved reptilian composure.

Gravēda remained as immobile as the rock against which she leaned, and moss crept from that rock to her shoulder and then down one side of her bulk, carpeting it with fuzziness. Spiders cast silk tethers from the wall behind her to her matted hair; so still was she that those webs might as well have been spun from iron. Because Gravēda did not move.

That was the transformation: into something humpbacked, moss-covered, immobile, stupid, ugly, evil, stubborn—and waiting.

She didn't realize she was waiting until what she was waiting for appeared. The monster who was Gravēda heard movement in the sewer hole and turned to it, the motion of her head so slow as to be undetectable. Her eyes became wide and intent.

Even in the shadows of the cave she could tell the hair was blond and the skin was smooth, but the monster responded to nothing but the movement: something wiggling its way to within her grasp. She tilted forward, slowly forward from her sitting position, and leaned down toward the back of that head.

Her fat and powerful hands, moving as if through molasses, assumed flanking positions next to the ears. With a monster's instinct, she knew what was going to happen; in her monster mind, it already had happened: grabbing those smooth cheeks and hooking her dirty fingers under that distinct jawline, and then holding with an unbreakable grip, a vice so tight that no sound would come from the head she was grasping. Then she would move her feet onto the shoulders that were just then struggling up the hole, into her den. Still holding on to the head and with her feet on the shoulders, the monster simply would stand up and place irresistible forces in opposition: the weight of her body against the strength of her grip. The bone and tissue that connect head to body would give way.

As soon as she closed her hands on that head, the sequence would be unstoppable. The Gravēda monster would end up holding a decapitated head, perhaps with a length of spinal cord attached.

A fish had swum within range of the jaws of an alligator snapper, and nothing in the world can save such a fish.

Except that this particular fish, at the last available moment, whispers in an urgent and frightened and familiar voice: "*Gravēda?*"

31. The hands pause. Something about that voice fires off a memory—and then another and another, until Gravēda's head is exploding with remembrances of how he looked and felt and tasted. She eases away from him. Genipur.

"Gravēda?"

Her heartbeat quickens, breaths come in short and closely spaced gasps, systems long dormant begin to pump again. Of course she remembers Genipur.

"Gravēda? Are you in here, Gravēda?" He starts to climb up out of the hole.

"No!" she says hoarsely.

"Gravēda. It's me—Genipur."

She leans her head against the rock. Oh, I know it's you, Doll—Sweetness, Honeylick. The identity I'm not sure of is my own.

He's about to lift himself out of the hole, and Gravēda tells him again: "No!"

"What's the matter?"

"Go away."

"Gravēda, what's wrong?"

How does she tell him that, until just a moment ago, she was a monster?

"I have to talk to you," he says plaintively. "It's about to happen. The move. I have to talk to you about it."

"No."

"I *have* to." Genipur, who now sits on the edge of the hole with his legs dangling in it, searches the dark for her. His eyes already have moved over her shadowed form, rejecting it as too large to be Gravēda.

"Genipur," she says, excited to hear herself say his name but also frightened that he might reach out and brush up against her fat leg, which is within his reach. "Come back later. In a month or so."

"A month! You don't understand. It's happening right now."

"In a couple weeks then."

"No! Now. I have to talk to you right now." His hands begin to feel along the floor of the cave.

Panicky, Gravēda quickly says, "Tomorrow. Just give me till then. I promise everything will be okay by tomorrow. Come back then."

"But—"

"Something's happening with me, too, and I need . . . and I need a day or so to . . . to make things right."

"All right," he says, working himself back into the hole. "I'll be back tomorrow night."

"Or the next day."

"No," he declares, disappearing down the hole. "Tomorrow."

3 2. Gravēda sits there just awhile longer, to savor these last moments of reptilian composure. Then she's up, bones creaking, muscles protesting, silken threads breaking. She looks down at herself and is ashamed, so she rummages through the filth on the floor until she finds the remains of her robe, which she holds to cover the front of her as she walks around from that little side room.

I need soap and something to scour with—horsetail stems. And water, lots and lots of hot water. Gravēda intends to tell this to her guards, to beg them for soap and water, to shame them into filling her request by showing them the wound on the inside of her left breast—if that becomes necessary. The wound still hurts, and Gravēda can touch it only tenderly.

No one is at the cagewall, no one is in the cave. "Hello? Hello!" No answer. I could get out of here, she thinks—I could push down these bars and be free. But now, of course, Gravēda doesn't want to leave the cave, because she doesn't know what would happen if she were to go down to the beach. Maybe she wouldn't be able to find Genipur or wouldn't be able to go off alone with him. No. Gravēda wants to stay in the cave at least until Genipur comes back and they can be alone in that little side room. It's not freedom Gravēda needs at this moment; it's soap and water so she can get clean enough to play whoopee with Genipur.

"Guards! Priests! Nestus!" But no one answers. She hangs on the bars and hollers until her throat hurts. "Someone! Please! I need hot water and soap and horsetail stems. I want to be clean again! Please! I'm innocent. Innocent! Crat died of a heart attack. A bad ticker. And the others, the others—well, that was self-defense. Please! Someone!"

But there is no one. Gravēda begins to clean up the cave as best she can, pushing everything down the sewer hole—the un-eaten and rotting food, the filthy old bedding, empty skinbags. When she finishes all that, she becomes panicky with thoughts of time: How will she know when tomorrow night has arrived? How much time already has passed since Genipur left? Hours? Half a day—or more? Gravēda screams again for the guards, but the guards aren't there. She goes back to the little room and uses rocks to rub off the moss from her skin.

"Gravēda! I got you clean in the next chapter! Did you hear me, Gravēda?"

Holding the robe in front of her, Gravēda peeks around the corner. Eller is standing by the bars, and six buckets of steaming water are on her side of the cagewall. She comes out to see him. "How . . . how'd you do this?" Gravēda is willing to believe in magic.

"I also got a clean robe for you. Plenty of soap and stuff."

"But how—"

"Oh, I heard you hollering and I got some priests to bring this water up before they left. Everyone's going, you know."

"How could I possibly know?"

Eller laughs. "I can get anything I want. I'm a hundred years old and I can get anything I want. Pinch girls on the butt, and they don't slap me. Hell, pinch boys on the butt. Anything I want. So I tell some priests to bring up hot water and soap and horsetail stems and a clean robe, and they do it. Take time out from their departure to do it. I can get—"

"Eller! How much do you know of what's happened to me, of what's been going on in here?"

His eyes widen. He's taken offense at Gravēda's question. "I know everything," he says indignantly.

"No you don't. There's been a lot of stuff you didn't—"

Eller waves his hands. "Enough, enough." Then he pushes through the bars several cakes of lye soap, handsful of Bouncing Bet leaves, and whole bunches of horsetail stems. "Go ahead," he insists. "Get started. No—wait. Let me see what they did to you."

Gravēda is momentarily confused and then she realizes what he's asking to see. She demurely lowers the top of the robe. Eller grimaces, shakes his head, and then says, "Well, that's a bit of nasty business, isn't it? You go on and clean up now."

"Can you tell me what's happening on the beach?"

"After you get clean. I'll be back."

"What time is it?"

"Right now? High afternoon. Why?"

So, Gravēda thinks, he doesn't know everything after all. "Could you come back at dusk? I'd like to be told when the evening is starting. You can't be sure here in the cave—whether it's night or day."

"Okay." Eller waddles out.

Gravēda immediately starts cleaning. She puts several cakes of soap, some crushed Bouncing Bet leaves, and ashes in one of the buckets of hot water and then splashes this cleaning mixture around the cave. She begins scrubbing down the walls, using horsetail stems as scouring pads. She uses two more buckets of water to clean the floor—and then flushes all the debris down the sewer hole. It was a stinking mess but at least now it's stinking outside the cave.

Finally, the only thing in the cave that's not clean is what was the nastiest thing in the place to start with. Gravēda uses the last three buckets of hot water on herself.

33. She starts with her hair. It's so tangly and matted and dirty that at first the lye soap and juice of the Bouncing Bet won't lather, but Gravēda continues washing and rinsing, washing and rinsing until suds appear and begin to have an effect on the grease. She pulls out the tangles, scrubs the sores on her scalp, and eventually, when she rubs her fingertips down her hair, she can hear it squeak. That seems like a signal, a first peep of innocence. Gravēda styles her hair, starting at the center part and running her hands through the thick and clean hair until it remembers the old shape.

She washes her face, then her ears and neck. Then she washes them again. She uses a twig to clean out her ears, and she squeezes and picks at the sores and blemishes on her neck. Then she washes everything one more time. Her face feels drawn, tight with cleanliness.

Gravēda stands over the sewer hole and begins to wash everything else. Under her arms, little things are growing. Don't ask. She scrubs them off. She washes her breasts, careful around the wound. She uses horsetail stems to rub away the prickly bumps between her breasts, and then she plucks the hairs from around her nipples.

Using a piece of the old robe, which she's tied to a stick, Gravēda cleans her back the best she can. Washing between the rolls of fat around her stomach, she finds sand and leaves and little round stones. She continues washing and rinsing, washing and rinsing. If those are little creatures in her navel, she dispossesses them. The less said about the discoveries she makes while cleaning her middle section, the better. But when she finishes with that, Gravēda repeatedly washes her hands—trying to clean from them the very idea of what they've just had to do. (When she stares at her hands, moving them around in the air and putting their fingers through paces, those hands seem to take on the personality of mindless but dutiful servants who're willing to do anything for her. Good hands.)

Then, finally, Gravēda is clean. Itchy, chafed, stinging in a thousand places—but clean. It feels good, even the parts that hurt. More than just clean, Gravēda feels purified.

She goes out to the cagewall to fetch the tall grass Eller has had delivered for fresh bedding. When she returns to the side room, Gravēda hears something in the hole and immediately becomes giddy as she makes sweet assumptions: It's Genipur; I bet Eller forgot to tell me dusk had arrived and now Genipur is here.

But when she looks down the hole, all she sees is a black and fluttering *shape*. Recognizing the silky sounds of feathers struggling against themselves, Gravēda shouts: "Damn, *damn* ravens!" She figures they must have found her by the scent of all that filth, all her debris, she's been flushing out into the world.

The sewer hole is too small for the bird to spread out his wings and fly, and it's too vertical for him to climb—so he just sort of flutters amidhole. Gravēda dumps a bucket of dirty water on him, and then puts her head in the hole to watch how he bounces and skitters off the rock, the steep incline, below the hole.

"If you were back in your tree humping," she screams after him, "you'd have ten new generations by now!" Damn birds.

Gravēda brushes off the inside of the hole; this is where Genipur is going to be in a little while. She wonders how he could possibly fit through there. Is there that much of a difference between us, am I that much bigger than Genipur?

Here comes the raven, wings spread and probably broken, painfully hopping and hugging his way up the rock toward her again. She shakes her head. How long, damn it? If I could, I'd lay those frigging eggs myself.

When the bird gets within range, Gravēda dumps another bucket of dirty water on him, causing the raven to tumble ass over beak for several yards down the slope. Then he manages to hold on to a small ledge, where he shakes and spreads his feathers—aghast. He can't get to her but he can't leave her alone, so the raven just perches there, his beak wide open but silent. In his mind, he's cawing loudly. In his mind, that stupid bird actually is cawing.

Gravēda puts her face to the hole and shouts, "Leave me alone!" The bird's response is to crouch, as if he's about to fly off that ledge. But something in his birdbrain tells him it ain't going to work, not with wet feathers and broken wings, so the raven just crouches there to wait for a launch signal that's never going to come.

When Gravēda realizes she's sweating, she curses the bird again. Then she goes to the bars, puts on her fresh new clean robe, and gathers up in her arms a special present Eller left for her: dandelions, primrose, violets. Back in the little room, she spreads these wild flowers over the grass and then she lies down. Tries to strike poses. She figures she won't look too bad if the light's low, which it always is.

She checks the sewer hole one more time. Almost dark now; why hasn't Eller come to tell me that? The raven, nothing more than a darker shadow among dark shadows, is dead. Gravēda thinks: Good, the night's off to a wonderful start.

Back on the flowers, she takes off her robe. She nibbles some violets in hope they'll improve her breath. Then Gravēda decides it would be better to have her robe on, but a few minutes later she takes it off again. She lies and waits, lies and waits. Nervous and fluttery, and sometimes smiling with no apparent reason for doing so.

But Genipur doesn't come; he doesn't come.

34. And then he comes.

Although Gravēda has been doing nothing but waiting and watching for him and thought she was prepared for his appearance, he pops up so quickly that she loses her breath. A little gasp—to get the breath back—and then she lets it out again.

"Gravēda?"

But she doesn't answer right away. So long alone, so long apart from him, how can I possibly prepare now for his touch, for the warmth of him close, for the young male smell of him that even at this moment reaches softly across open space so that I can breathe him in, breathe him out?

"Gravēda!" The whisper is sharp this time.

Her eyes are accustomed to the dark, and Gravēda wants to sit there and watch him awhile longer.

The boy struggles up through the hole until he's sitting in the cave, searching for her but not yet detecting Gravēda's open-mouth breathing: Genipur in, Genipur out.

"Over here, Lovelock," she finally says.

He waits a moment until he has his bearings and then jumps up and is upon Gravēda with wild enthusiasm.

It's more than she could possibly have hoped for, and Gravēda squeals with delight.

As his body feels the great cushion she's become, as his hands explore her dimensions, he says, "Gravēda, you . . . you're . . ." Then he pauses, censored by a boy's mother-taught politeness.

"Substantial?" Gravēda offers.

Her hands are on his cheeks when his head nods and his lips widen into a smile. Then she kisses him and his mouth opens gently, his breath warm and all over her face. (If you're going to take me, Lord, take me now. It won't get any better.) She's full of anticipation, and anticipation is everything.

They hug tightly and she calls him Lovebug, pulling off his robe a bit too eagerly. This breaks the mood, and Genipur leans away from her. "We have to talk."

Gravēda, wide-eyed to get as much of his nudity from the low light as she possibly can, speaks like some sort of savage: "You talk; me play."

"Wait!" He resists her pull. "Some things I have to say." Genipur sits up, straight as pride.

But Gravēda has to remain fully supine because if she sits,

her fat will bunch in great rolls. So she lies there watching and waiting for those Butterlips to speak.

Genipur takes a lot of time thinking about how to phrase what he's going to say. The child is so deliberate. He idly feels around in the grass bed and then asks, "Flowers?" as he holds several of them to his face for a better look.

"A nice touch, don't you think?"

"Mmm." His mind on other matters.

"Mmm," Gravēda mimics, her hand on his thigh and traveling north.

"I can't come to you under false pretenses," he finally declares.

"You can come to me under any pretense—as long as you come to me."

He shakes his head. "No. I have to tell you. My mother is the only old traveler left alive. And she's sick—bad sick. But the tribe has left anyway, because Nestus saw an opportunity she couldn't pass up."

"You're an opportunity *I* can't pass up."

"Listen to me, Gravēda."

"I'm listening." But she's exploring more than she's listening, and Gravēda can tell that Genipur's interest in her explorations is stiffening.

"Something very strange happened on the beach, and I'll tell you all about that later. What I wanted to say now is that Nestus used the excitement, fears or whatever, she used them to convince the tribe to begin the return journey. And now the only ones left are me, my mother, and Eller."

"And me."

"And you—of course."

"Well, that's good news, Honeybun. We can care for your mother until she doesn't need our care anymore and then you and I can launch out in one of your boats."

Genipur shakes his head and starts to speak again, but Gravēda maneuvers his hands onto her breasts—left on right, right on left—and Genipur responds with enthusiastic and rough manipulations. "Wow!"

Gravēda's eyes roll, she grimaces, and she helps the young Nipple Tightener to mount up. He quickly falls into place between her legs. They begin moving together with what one might call a natural inclination.

Breathing heavily, Genipur says, "Your appearance on the beach might have changed everything, but we thought you were dead—or had abandoned the tribe. It wasn't until a couple days ago that Nestus told me she had you locked up someplace. I wanted to take the boats out. I was even going to do it all by myself. I'm a traditionalist. . . ."

Moving her hips, Gravēda thinks: Scoot over a tad, Royal Jelly, and you'll be a lover.

"But I have to tell you. I lost my faith in the whole project. If it weren't for my mother being unable to travel, I would have been with Nestus right now. I didn't know where you were. I didn't know what to do."

Be quiet, concentrate, move up just a little, and you'll know exactly what to do, Love Piston. It'll come naturally, Gravēda wants to tell him. But the angle is all wrong, and Genipur suddenly slides off the side of Gravēda and clears his throat.

"What?" she asks, put out.

"Okay. I have to say it. As soon as my mother passes on, I'm going to catch up with the tribe and marry Nestus."

Gravēda, still lying flat, accepts the news calmly. Maybe she thinks she'll be able to talk him out of marrying Nestus or maybe, after all that time alone in the cave, she believes that having him right there with her at this moment is enough. She pulls him close and whispers something nasty in his ear.

"Oh, God, you make me crazy," he says. "No one has ever done the things you've done to me." When he grabs her breasts again, Gravēda winces and holds his wrists. "Did I hurt you that time?" Genipur asks.

"It hurt before, too."

"I'm sorry. I didn't mean to be so rough."

"It's not you, Sugar."

"What then?"

Gravēda says nothing, just waits until Genipur's hand finds

the scarring wound on the inside of her left breast. "Dear Lord! What happened?"

She strokes the hair at the side of his head and then plays with his earlobe. "I missed you so much that my heart broke and sort of spilled down the front of me."

"Huh?"

She kisses him.

"They stabbed you, didn't they, Gravēda?"

She says nothing.

"Oh, God, I bet you've suffered in here. And look at me, out there fooling around on the beach, abandoning the journey, agreeing to marry Nestus. I'm not worthy of you, Gravēda."

Sure you are, Succotash. She hauls him aboard, and they lie there a moment. Genipur whispers, "I love your nose. I love your faith. I'm sorry things didn't work out for us." On his chest he feels her breast wound. "And to think how you've suffered!" And then his hips begin to grind, as if to bring her retroactive relief. "You know what the problem is?"

Yeah, she thinks—you're still about three inches too high.

"People who've lost their faith can't tolerate someone like you, someone who has kept her faith." He thrusts repeatedly.

Gravēda wants to tell him that the only thing special about her is that she's been kept locked up, but she's no longer able to participate in the conversation. Her mind is on other matters. Now, if this Sweet Dummy would just move down. . . . . Wait. Ah. *Maybe*.

"On the beach," he pants, pumps, "I celebrated you."

Shush, Blossom.

"And I searched for you, found you, so I could get you out of here—set you free!"

One good move, Sassafras, and you'll set me free all right.

"When I thought you were dead or off on another journey by yourself, I told stories celebrating you and I called you Fidelity."

She grabs his shoulders and pushes him down.

"Faith, Fidelity—those are the names I gave you."

Okay, now over to the right.

"And . . . and at least I'll do this for you. Set you free. Even if I have abandoned the journey, at least I'll do that. At least I'll . . ."

No, no, Bunny! You're taking a coital interest in what happens to be nothing more than a sweat-slickened roll of fat. How embarrassing. If you'd just move a little to the . . .

"Uh!"

That's him. Home at last.

"Uh. Uh-uh!"

Oh, Gravēda thinks, such an articulate rascal.

"Uh-uh-uh-uh!"

Talking volumes.

"Oh, wow, uh-uh!"

What a way with words. Gravēda feels compelled to answer him: "Ooo! Ooo!"

And in this way they become the perfect couple.

"Uh, uh! Ah. Wow! Oh-uh."

"Ooo, ooo. Yes. Ooo!"

Because they've learned to exchange their views and really communicate, *share*, their opinions on matters of mutual interest.

"Uh-uh-uh, oh, ah, No!"

"Ooo, ah, Yes, Yes!"

Skin friction and air temperature combine to produce such a sweat that Genipur's chassis slips and slides and threatens a dismount until Gravēda grasps his winglike shoulder blades and holds on; Genipur responds by grabbing her ears. They're set now—and Genipur gallops.

"Gravēda! Oh, Gravēda! It's dusk. You wanted me to tell you when it's dusk and now it is. Or, actually, it's past dusk. I got busy with some . . ."

Gravēda grits and clenches. *Eller!*—not now, you silly son of a bitch, *not now.*

"Is that Eller?" Genipur asks in midstride.

"No one," she insists. "It's no one. I didn't hear a thing."

"Gravēda! Are you back there? I wanted to tell you what I was working on."

Eller, you senile idiot. . . .

"Gravēda! I'm about to complete the denouement of your entire story and . . ."

"The what?" Genipur asks, slowing to a trot.

"Nothing—ignore him," Gravēda insists, moving beneath Genipur so that the boy responds, canters.

"Such a climax you're going to have!" Eller yells from the cagewall, causing Gravēda to laugh out loud.

Genipur raises up on his hands. "What's so damn funny? What the hell's going on here?"

Gravēda is desperate that the moment not be ruined, lost. "I didn't laugh. I just . . . just got carried away. Because of what you're doing, the effect it's having on me." Upon her face she puts a look of pain, biting her lip. Gravēda knows they're suckers for that.

Genipur wants so much to believe her that he just goes ahead and does.

"Well, anyway," Eller says from the bars. "It's dusk—or it was dusk. I got to get back to work. Catch you later, Gravēda!"

She bites her lip harder to keep from laughing again.

"Okay, baby," Genipur reassures her. "Okay."

Gravēda nods wildly, choking a bit on the repressed laughter—all of which Genipur interprets as yet another, higher, less cultivated plateau of female passion. "Okay, baby, *okay*!" He's saying it as a warning. Then he spurs to the line, hoping to finish before the poor woman faints dead away.

There.

He tightens.

She tightens.

He says, "No."

She says, "Yes."

He makes a sound deep in his throat and whispers something that sounds like "Morty." Gravēda guesses it was a childhood friend of his. Then she quickly tells him how wonderful he was, how no man ever has made love to a woman as he's just made love to her. She feels him relax. Fragile—they're all so fragile.

She tightens all the more. Ah, keegles; ah, squiggles—and, *there*, squeeze.

The excitement seems to have left Genipur (who suddenly is exhausted and vulnerable to sleep) and has entered and taken exclusive residence in Gravēda, who feels like chatting.

But, she thinks, this is good, too—this silence, this easy rhythm of his approaching sleep. Genipur withdraws from her with each beat of his heart.

Later, he rolls off and cuddles into the side of her, awakening just enough to say, "I loved it. What we did. I loved it."

"Me, too," Gravēda lies, petting him as he quickly and easily slips back to sleep. What she really loved was the *idea* of it, but you can't tell such a thing to a boy.

3 5. Too bad sleep isn't a more potent potion. If it were, Gravēda would run her hands through Genipur's hair and then pat it back in place. She'd put his arms and legs through full articulations just to watch how they moved. She'd manipulate him roughly, softly—every whichway. She'd fool around. Heft him in his flaccid state. No—that's an ugly way to say it. Gravēda would heft him in his placid state. She wants to lick around his mouth, clean his face, nuzzle deeply, and nibble at will.

But sleep is so tenuous that Gravēda has to make do with a visual examination: checking the soft beard, the velvety folds of his inner ear, and settling on eyes that even though they are closed, set deep and shaded dark, are powerful enough to hold and carry Gravēda.

She silently declares his chest and tummy to be precious. The hairs encircling his nipples swirl clockwise, as if engaged in a sedentary chase, around and around. At this point, she's tempted to kiss, but she does not.

The pattern of the hair on his trunk reminds Gravēda of some landscape she might have seen from a hill: a small pond, a spring-fed pool, of hair high on the crest of his chest, and from that flows a straight and narrow stream feeding into a large and round lake down below—the lake of hair that covers his abdomen. In the middle of this lake is an inverted island, a hole, an unpretentious hole, a cute hole. This hole also tempts the tip of Gravēda's tongue.

God! Old Man! Just one thing I want from you now: *time*—time enough before I die to memorize this Genipur geography, time enough to know every hair by its position and heading. So I can identify—tummy quadrant 4-E; north by northeast; hello, hair!—each one.

She rests on her side, staying close to him.

Don't take me now, Lord. Genipur smells of the sea, and of me, and there are whole stretches of him I've barely begun to explore.

Gravēda is in love. Her love is like a phenomenon in nature (like lightning and thunder and rain): distinct and identifiable. Gravēda can't explain any of this, just as she can't explain lightning and thunder and rain, what makes them or where they come from, but she knows what she sees and hears and feels. She knows when she's out in a storm, when she's wet. And Gravēda knows when she's in love.

There it is: in reclined peace, asleep, a curled angel in repose. Gravēda's love. She would follow him onto the sea, *into* the sea. Take care of him and never change her mind, never leave him behind. You have to understand. Gravēda is a sucker for love.

And so she takes him in her arms and holds him tightly, because it might be for the last time. After this, *she* gets him.

WHEN
I WAS
THIRTY

*W*hen I was thirty, I was like a foundling who had been reared by a family of magicians and then grew up and went out into the unenchanted world. I'd become disillusioned and missed the old magic; I wanted to come home to see if it was still there, to see if I could get it back into my life.

This grown-up foundling (whom I was like when I was thirty) once had lived where rabbits routinely are pulled from hats, gold coins drop readily from behind earlobes, and incantations are said more frequently than grace. But when the foundling still was a child, before he went out into the magicless world, he was unappreciative: A doddering uncle producing glowing crystal pyramids from seemingly empty hands impressed the child no more, no less, profoundly than an early evening sky impresses you. The child wasn't moved to tears by his grandmother's ability to make an untouched violin play a gypsy's soul, but then you don't weep for whippoorwills who cry in the night. And when the child's sorcerer father, accidentally hitting his thumb while hanging a favorite amulet on the wall, issued an oath that called forth airscreams and skyfires, the child was no more awestruck than any child is so struck by natural thunder and lightning and the terrible force of a full-grown man's full-blown anger.

After the foundling grew to be a man (as I grew to be a man), he left his enchanted home for the real world where, alas, rabbits are not routinely pulled from hats, gold coins do not readily drop from behind earlobes, and incantations are said much less frequently than grace. When the tediousness of the real world made the man's center increasingly hollow, he began to doubt his memory: Was it really, actually, truly magic—what I had at home? On an impulse, then, the man would return to see if the magic was still there, to see if he could get it back into his life.

This is how it was with me, with me and Felicity. Not until I was away from her for six years, until I was thirty and in trouble, did I realize how little I had appreciated her magic. Having her as a neighbor, having grown up with her so close to me, having become so effortlessly intimate with her, I suppose I just assumed that such women were relatively commonplace—that eventually I'd meet other women whose laughter was like water at a rolling boil, who had crying hearts tattooed on their bosoms, who had husbands in insane asylums, who were authentic eccentrics, who'd make shameless love to me on linoleum embossed with wild flowers—who'd place in me their unquestioning, mad faith. Because I'd grown up with it, I guess I assumed it wasn't so rare to have someone tell you a story that lasted for years and years.

Then I got divorced and turned thirty. I was smart enough to see what you indeed can see when you reach thirty: what the rest of your life will be like. I was not going to ship out on a steamer; I was never going to live in an exotic place; I was not going to be celebrated. I was going to become a minor success in the corporate world; I was already on my way.

When I realized all this, I was angry for not having listened more closely—especially in the earlier years—to the story Felicity had told me, was telling me. Alone in the evenings, alone in a bar, I would try to reconstruct the entire Gravēda story and then discover I'd forgotten so much of it—side actions, minor characters. I'd have to make up things myself to bridge these gaps. I began wondering how it would turn out, and I experimented with my own endings. For the first time, I appreciated how rare it was—this thing Felicity had done and was doing. I realized it was the most amazing thing that had ever happened to me and was ever likely to happen to me. Even as I became tougher and my crust thickened right down to my core, I remained sentimental about Felicity. Although I busied myself with women who had charms, women who could perform amazing tricks, none of that is magic.

So, as my crusted-over center became increasingly hollow, I, too, thought more and more about the old magic and I, too, wondered if my memory was accurate. Eventually, I gave in to the impulse and went to visit Felicity. You know. To see if rabbits really are routinely pulled from hats, if gold coins actually do drop readily from behind earlobes, and if incantations truly are said more frequently than grace.

.   .   .

When I was thirty, obeying an elaborate impulse that I kept alive with pep talks and a constant half-buzz, I flew to Chicago, arranged a long-term lease on a car, drove unannounced to my hometown, and began living with Felicity. It was a crazy thing to do. I was thinking I'd stay there only a few days, and then maybe the two of us would go off someplace or I'd just leave. I guess I wasn't thinking at all. I was reacting—to living alone for the first time in my life (no family, no roommate, no wife). Alone in a cruddy little apartment with rented furniture because, in a pique, I had told her lawyers she could have the goddamn house and everything else, too. (In subsequent divorces, I have kept my piques under control—not that it's done me much good.) I also was reacting to fear, because I was thirty and had caught a look at the rest of my life.

Living with Felicity, I managed against all guilt and coincidence to avoid—except for one instance—my family. People were gossiping about the mystery man who was at Felicity's house, but at the time no one knew it was me. I had changed in six years—put on weight and grown my first beard—and I was careful to avoid people, to stay out of the front yard. Felicity and I did our dining and drinking in.

But at some later point, it became generally known that I had sneaked thieflike onto the prairie to live in sin with a neighbor lady. This created a scandal that, according to my sister, put our father in an early grave. But she was wrong. Not about the grave being early but about *why* it was early. My father didn't die of embarrassment.

"I told you so, I told you so!" That's how Felicity greeted me when I presented myself on her doorstep that summer. *I told you so* and a big kiss.

"Nobody likes a smart-ass," I said, entering the familiar kitchen.

"I told you so, I told you so!" she continued, singing and dancing around in a way that made me want to laugh.

I tried to be serious. "A divorce is a sad, a tragic thing. Absolutely pathetic. People use it as a weapon—"

"I told you so, I told—"

"Bitch."

Then we both laughed like a couple of fools.

"So bad news does indeed travel fast, huh?"

"Oh, Honey Bear, we probably knew about your divorce before you did."

"You're probably right."

She sat next to me. "What you need is a drink."

"You're probably right."

I watched her closely as she brought in the gin, tonic water, and ice in a silver bucket. Felicity was Felicity again, having lost all that extra weight, eyes clear again, and her manner so bouncy and gay that you'd be tempted to call her girlish. But she was a fifty-year-old woman. Distinctive-looking, a full and well-ripened figure, bold features—but clearly fifty. Her whiskey, cigarette-smoky voice and the deep lines that formed successive parentheses at the corners of her mouth and that radiated from the outside of her eyes across her temples testified to that. She was marked by time in a way that a younger woman simply can't be.

When I asked Felicity if I could stay with her, she brushed aside the request as being unnecessary—as if she'd already assumed I'd be coming home that summer to live with her. As if she had been waiting for me.

We talked and drank gin there at her kitchen table, becoming intimate again: laughing and gossiping, indulging in reminiscence, and then lapsing into a comfortable silence during which we stared at each other with the same thought on our minds. I had to unpack the car in the morning because we were in bed before dark, fumbling and stumbling and making love with the tumbling intensity of hungry puppies who at long last are being fed—given as much food as their pink puppy mouths can gulp and shove into their round puppy bellies.

We had Bloody Marys with breakfast.

"You're going to give me the habit," I told her.

"I doubt it."

I finished my eggs. "Well, let's have another, then."

The suggestion made her happy. "Do you have any idea how hard it is to find a good drinking partner here on the prairie?"

"Slim pickings, huh?"

"You betcha."

"I'm kind of surprised you haven't left. I mean, I'm glad you still live here so I can come see you, even if it is years between our visits. But you always talked about going back to one of the places where you used to live. It's funny how we've traded places—me in New York and you here." I paused. "I was afraid you wouldn't be here."

Felicity spoke as she cleaned off the table. "I *have* traveled some in the last couple years. To San Francisco once. I stayed in a cottage by the ocean. I visited some of my professor friends around the country. But everything's changed. The old places aren't the old places anymore, and neither are the old friends. By default, this has become home."

"I'm glad. For me, I'm glad. Even though you always have been rotten to me."

"Rotten to you!" She pinched my arm.

When I grabbed her ass, she squealed and slapped my hand. "Sure you were mean to me," I said. "There you were, a woman of the world. And me? A kid, a mere child. And you put all that stuff off on me. About how I was so self-centered, not thinking about the rest of the world or even aware that an outside world existed. Remember? Wild elephants are right at this moment shitting on the plains of Africa. Remember?"

Felicity laughed. "I'm a bad girl. How can I ever make it all up to you?"

I scooted back my chair and unzipped my pants—just to shock her and make her laugh again.

"You scamp!" She lunged for my crotch, and as I fought to keep her hands out of my pants so I could zip up again, we both fell to the floor. "Like a warrior's sword!" she shouted as we giggled and rolled under the edge of the table. "Don't unsheathe it unless you intend to use it!"

"Ow! You're hurting me!"

"Sissy!" We were bumping our heads on table legs; I had one hand over my crotch and was using the other to pinch her wherever I could; she finally maneuvered me up against the wall. "And once you take it out, don't put it back until it's been blooded." She whispered that in a way that made me crazy.

We were resting against each other, panting and at a standoff—with all four hands heavily into my groin. "But I didn't take it out," I protested.

Felicity was unusually strong and against my best efforts was able to snake her hand into my fly. "*Well*," she said, as if she'd just been proven right on some disputed point.

All the fight went out of me as I watched the top of her head descend along my trunk and rest between my legs. "Goodness gracious," I whispered.

"Mmm," she responded.

After dinner that evening, we sat at the edge of her backyard graveyard and drank planter's punch. We both complained about the heat and finally, after I was more than half distilled, she convinced me that we should sleep outside that night. When she brought the blankets and pillows, I said, "It's spooky out here. Probably animal spirits and everything. Are you sure this is a good idea?"

Felicity made growling sounds in the back of her throat and wouldn't stop until I threatened to return to the house and sit up all night with the lights on.

I awoke sometime in the middle of the night; Felicity was standing. "What's wrong?" I asked.

"Nothing. Just admiring the night. How light it is, how many different sounds you can hear. People talk about nights being dark and quiet but that's true only when you're inside."

"When are you going to tell me the next part of Gravēda?"

"Tomorrow. I'll start it tomorrow."

"Am I going to find out what's in the Passionate One's glass heart?"

"So you remember, huh? You'll find out in due course."

"You told me you buried me under that tablet over there, the one with all the little crosses. What'd you mean by that?"

"I'll tell you sometime, but not right now."

"And are you going to tell me the truth about your tattoo, too?"

"Tattoo, too, tattoo, too—you sound like a choochoo. Full of questions tonight, aren't you, Hugabunny?"

"Let's get naked."

"Oh, okay."

As soon as we undressed, Felicity pushed me back flat and began stroking and tracing and examining me—from toes to temples and all the inches in between. "You like this old thirty-year-old body, don't you?" I asked her.

"Mmm. But I liked it when it was fourteen years old, too. Maybe that's why I fell in love with you. 'Cause you were fourteen. I think I told you I helped raise my three younger brothers after my mother got sick. Daddy was dead and the boys were eleven, thirteen, and fifteen when I returned home. What a household that was. Smelled like a musk factory. Those boys sneaking around bathrooms and bedrooms. My, what puberty puts a boy through. I had to keep my underwear under lock and key."

I laughed.

"Think that's funny, huh?"

"You're funny."

"It's inevitable and I don't regret it or anything, but it's kind of sad the way boys have to grow up. Not funny—*sad*. I remember my brothers, when they still were little boys—they were so white and clean and unmarked. Like a pristine landscape. Smelled so sweet, even when they were dirty and sweating. The hair on their belly and thighs . . ." Felicity was drawing her fingers languidly across my belly and down my thighs. ". . . Was so light and soft that you could hardly see it. Innocent little genitals." She grasped mine, no longer innocent.

"And they all had beautiful voices. Did solos at church that would break your heart. Then the pollution started. That damn chemical factory—"

"Ouch! Watch it with the chemical factory, huh?"

"Dumping crap into their clean streams and the streams carrying it everywhere so that they started sweating out chemicals, stinking up the house. I used to threaten to take 'em out in the yard and hose 'em down. Stinking even after they just stepped out of the tub. Rut.

"And their hair turning dark and coarse. So poisoned with those hormone chemicals that the hair would twist and curl around itself like it was in some sort of death throe. Everything getting big and brown. Sweet voices thickening and cracking. The whole landscape turning rough and brambly. A shame, you know?"

I poked her in the ribs. "Why didn't you just castrate the little buggers?"

"The thought crossed my mind, Buster Brown," Felicity said, squeezing my testicles and making me yelp. "I *know* that boys have to grow up. God knows I appreciate a good man. I'm just saying that the loss of innocence is kind of sad. Little boys who once could sit on their big sister's lap and tell me all their secrets and cry 'cause their pet rabbit died and then they were turned into, polluted into, snickering adolescents who saw a dirty joke in everything. And then into men who turned the whole goddamn world into a dirty joke."

"Sounds like you could be a man hater."

"Don't be ridiculous. My problem is that I love men too much. And they'll always break your heart."

I snickered.

"You bastard. You would've turned out just like my brothers if you'd been their age. Go off to war. Couldn't wait. One killed, another crippled up. All three of them dead now." Felicity turned over, putting her back to me. "I guess you reminded me of my brothers back when I first met you. They were all in the army then."

I rolled close, my arms around her so my hands could work the front of her. She responded, arching her butt into me and squirming as she muttered something mean about "*men*."

We stayed off booze the next day because Felicity had this theory that if, once every three days, you didn't drink for at least twenty-four hours, you'd never become an alcoholic. She was full of pseudoscientific theories.

"Move away from that television," she told me one afternoon.

"Why?" I was lying on the floor, too lazy to move.

"Those tubes give off rays that'll make you sterile."

"Oh, Felicity, you're so full of shit."

When she came down to give me trouble, she saw that I had stood three cigarette butts, just the filters with a little bit of ash on top, on the floor next to me. "What's this?"

"I put the ashes in that napkin but I was too tired to get an ashtray so I just balanced the cigarettes on their filters and let 'em go out. Didn't you ever do that?"

"Well, I'll be damned," Felicity said, genuinely surprised. "That's got to be the height of something. I mean, when you can't even get up to put your cigarette out."

I yawned. "Hell, that's nothing. When I was in college I used to go into what we called a deep-laze. For a whole day or maybe more, I wouldn't move. Just lie there in bed or on the floor. Twenty-four hours, thirty hours—not moving at all. Drifting in and out of sleep. Hating it when I had to get up and go to the bathroom. God, it was great. Like hibernation."

"A deep-laze, huh?"

"Yeah. Wonderful way to escape."

She stretched out next to me on the floor; I still hadn't moved. "You know what I used to do?"

"What?"

"Pigouts."

"You mean when you eat a lot at one sitting?"

"Oh, more than that, Honey Bear. My pigouts would last

for days. I'd go through a dozen packages of Hostess cupcakes, a pound of cashews, and quarts of ice cream. The more I'd eat, the hungrier I got. Not in my stomach but in my mouth. I'd get cravings and always be running to the store for something. Ate two of those long, thin jars of Spanish olives on the way back from town one afternoon."

We lay there for a couple of minutes, absently watching television but both of us thinking. "Felicity?"

"I'm way ahead of you, Sweetmeat."

"Do you think it's possible? Do you really think we could go on a combination deep-laze pigout?"

"It'd be the first time in the history of mankind that such a thing was ever attempted."

"I'm willing to try."

"Me, too."

We discussed the rules for an hour or so, and then she went to the store and brought back four bags of junk food. We lay in front of the television and ate until we fell asleep deep in the night, awakening to make our way to the bathroom through the packaging and bottles that were spread in a semicircle around us: Oreo bags, Snicker packages, 7-Up and root beer and Dr Pepper containers, and uncountable wrappings from Reese's Peanut Butter Cups—the small ones, which she kept in the refrigerator.

In the morning, I complained about her frequent trips to the kitchen, saying that we were in danger of breaking the deep-laze, but Felicity argued that we had to have a constant supply of food or lose our pigout status. "This is a combination, re-member? A deep-laze pigout."

"Right you are. Bring it on."

Throughout that second day, we dozed in front of the tele-vision and ate Slim Jims, French burnt peanuts, and bananas with peanut butter on them. We drank beer and grapefruit juice. I'd ask her to light my cigarettes and then push in on my chest to get them going; she claimed that all the work made her too tired to light cigarettes for herself, so I let her smoke the second halves of mine.

When she brought in the last of the Hershey bars, Felicity asked: "Did you know that chocolate soothes a broken heart?"

"No," I said, taking off the wrappers and rolling them into tiny balls, which I tossed on the floor.

"When someone breaks your heart, little silver wiggly things are released into your bloodstream. They're what make you sad and itchy and weepy. So you eat some chocolate and it spreads out through your blood like some kind of calming sludge that immobilizes the silver wiggly things and then you feel better. You're still downhearted but you don't feel quite as miserable."

"Sounds reasonable to me."

"Sure. That's why although it's nice to bring your sweetheart a box of chocolates, when you really *need* to give chocolate is when you leave someone."

"I'll remember that."

She poked me in the arm.

"That kind of violent movement will disqualify you from a laze-out."

"Oh, shut up."

We slept and then celebrated the twenty-four-hour mark of our deep-laze pigout by eating two bags of thick pretzels on which we spread cream cheese. A couple bottles of root beer and then we rested again.

Felicity said she had a craving for Fudgicles but I wouldn't let her drive into town to buy some. She called the store.

"Well, if he's not working today," she said into the phone, "*you* bring them out. I know, but . . . what? It might not seem like an emergency to you but it sure is to me. Bring 'em out after the store closes. Come on, Dave. For old times' sake. Yeah. Of course. Just leave the box on the porch. After six-thirty. Okay. Thanks."

Two boxes of twelve Fudgicles each were delivered. "These are the only things that cool me off on hot days like this," Felicity said.

I ate ten of them, and Felicity had finished the other fourteen by the time we were settling in for the night. "How can anybody eat fourteen Fudgicles?" I asked.

"I wish I had just one more," she said, flipping the last stick onto the floor.

The deep-laze pigout ended anticlimactically at ten the next morning. Felicity and I had made ourselves sick; we groaned and belched dangerously as we cleaned the living room and then went in to take our showers. "Should we call the wire services?" Felicity asked as she dried my hair with a fluffy white towel. "The world's first deep-laze pigout and we managed to survive, what?—more than forty hours."

"Forty-one hours to be exact. But no publicity, please. I did it for the art."

"Me, too. What do you want to do now?"

"Take a nap."

"And I'll fix us a snack."

Then we both laughed like a couple of fools.

During that entire summer, I think our conversations took somber turns exactly twice. Once during the night we got loaded on Gibsons and Felicity told me she was going to take me to San Francisco, because that's where, as a young woman, she fell in love with love and now she wants to be there with the *person* she loves. She said I could write my novel out there. I flared up, saying that the business about writing a novel was her idea, not mine, and that I didn't want to do it and would never do it because my life was controlled by a huge, misshapen, wart-covered toad that sits at the center of me. "And it's lethargic and it's careful and it hates anything frivolous, so for chrissake don't talk to me anymore about falling in love with love or going to San Francisco or writing novels or anything else like that!" I was too drunk to remember how she responded, but I know I didn't tell her anything more about the toad because I know I wasn't *that* drunk.

The only other serious conversation I can recall began when Felicity told me that space exploration was mankind's glory, and I responded by trying to impress her with how concerned I was about what was happening on earth—sit-ins down South, the gassing of Caryl Chessman. She finally said: "Enough. I don't want to think about any of that stuff. I think about it enough, too much, when you're not here. As long as I got you, I want to pretend that right now there are no wild elephants shitting on the plains of Africa."

We spent afternoons in her parlor, letting the room grow dark with the day as she recited Gravēda for me. She stopped the recitations at a point that seemed to me to be the end of the story, but she said it wasn't, that there was more coming, and that she'd tell it to me later. But she didn't recite any more of Gravēda that summer. Instead, she began reading out loud for me: *Lolita, Breakfast at Tiffany's, Grenadine Etching*. We slept odd hours, awakening each other with impromptu requests. We accompanied records with our lip-synced performances; she was Patsy Cline and I got to be Frank Sinatra. We ran around the house in our underwear. I gave her baths. She trimmed my beard and toenails.

But mostly what we did that summer was fuck. All the time, all the ways. We played Gladiator and Slave Girl, Master and Mutt, Undertaker and Corpse—and all those other games that no one but Felicity ever has played with me. Button, button, who's got the button? Do you have any idea how many places you can hide a button on the human body? We played it where you had to find the button without using your hands.

My penis grew three-quarters of an inch that summer. It really did. Felicity kept a running measurement marked on the bedstead—the way some parents keep track of a child's height. Maybe she fudged; I don't know.

"If you get any bigger, Lovesalot," she told me after one measurement, "you're going to split me in two. You make me sore in ways I didn't think possible. A constant love-ache. I don't know if this will disgust you or not, but sometimes I walk into a room and see you standing there and I get wet just by the sight of you. I've been going around about half ready ever since you got here. In the shower I do things with the soap I haven't done since I was a teen-ager. Find myself rubbing up against the backs of chairs, too. When I sit next to you, my legs automatically splay and I have to remember to put them back together. I don't know. Maybe it's the heat. But I feel like I'm in chronic estrus."

With Felicity, I was massive.

And when we weren't making love, we were laughing. Laughing until we had to struggle for breath, hold ourselves tight to stop it from hurting, slap our legs, pound the table—and then end up wiping our eyes with the backs of our hands and saying those damn, damn, damns.

In other words, I returned to Felicity and found the old magic still there. Indeed, indeed, indeed: Rabbits routinely were pulled from hats, gold coins dropped readily from behind earlobes, and incantations were said much more frequently than grace.

· · ·

When I was thirty, I was a businessman—and a good one, too. Nothing fazed me. I didn't really care about what I was doing, about much of anything, and that's exactly the kind of aloof attitude that helped me land big accounts, win major promotions. We businessmen don't like underdogs; we're impressed with top dogs whose attitudes are cool and slightly disdainful.

I did what was necessary. Loyal to whoever was in command at the time. Laugh at bad jokes, at bigoted jokes. Take short fat bald men out on the town, show them around, act as if their visits were the highpoints of my life. I can squeeze a handshake so tightly that little beads of sincerity seem to pop from my skin. Give you eye contact until your eyeballs burn. And when a bunch of us go out drinking and whoring until the predawn, we all show up for work an hour early the next morning. Nothing fazes us. We're businessmen.

I didn't tell any of this to Felicity, of course. I lied to her. Letting her believe I had quit my job when, in fact, I was off on six weeks' leave of absence. Everyone at work had agreed that after the divorce and then honchoing a sales campaign that landed me an assistant vice-president's slot, I needed a rest. I spent the first week in my cruddy apartment and then, following that extended impulse, went to the Midwest to stay the remaining five weeks with Felicity.

But I was such a coward that the morning of the day of my departure arrived and I still hadn't told her I was leaving. I stood at the stove heating water for tea as my mind cooked up various lies I might use. I just needed something to get me out of there, because once back in New York I'd be safe. Felicity and I never wrote or called each other.

I lighted a cigarette and smoked it down while the water boiled. Felicity had this theory that you should use water as soon as it starts to steam, because boiling causes water to lose oxygen and that makes it flat and tasteless. She got that out of a Robert Ruark novel, and she didn't want to hear any of my explanations to the contrary. "It took me a lifetime to accumulate all my little quirks and beliefs and theories," she once told me. "Don't try disabusing me of them at this late date. Just do what I say, Love Nodule. Turn off the water before it boils."

I lighted another cigarette, cooked up more lies, put loose tea in a cup, and allowed the water to continue bubbling away precious oxygen.

Felicity was out back of the fields getting blackberries for our breakfast. She left early to pick them with the dew still on, and she had threatened to bring them back and squish them on my lips as she had done when I was fourteen—and then place berries all over my anatomy so she could go snuffling for them.

The possibilities interested me, but I shook off the temptation.

None of the lies I came up with was any good. I had a secret—something that had happened when Felicity was out of the house one day—but I didn't know if I should use it. Or how I could use it.

A week before this departure day, Felicity couldn't get her car started so she took my rented one into town on a booze run. I was reading in the living room when I heard the kitchen door open. I went in there to help her with the boxes and saw my father standing just inside the doorway. I guess he'd noticed that the mystery man's car was gone, and Dad had sneaked up to the house in hope of finding Felicity alone.

I don't know who was the more surprised. I suppose he was, because at least I knew he was in the area. I wonder what he thought, seeing me there when I was supposed to be a thousand miles away. I guess we both were thinking that neither one of us had any business being at Felicity's house. I already was preparing my defense: At least I'm divorced, Dad. The only thing I've done wrong is sneak into town without telling anyone I was here. What's your story?

But a defense wasn't necessary. We just stood there and stared, our expressions reflected in each other's faces. If one of us had laughed, had even cracked a smile, I think things would have worked out all right. Maybe he would have said, mum's the word—and I would have winked and that would've been that. But we didn't smile or speak. The problem was that neither of us knew who the outraged party was supposed to be, who the injured party was supposed to be—or if either of us should have been outraged *or* injured. Not being able to figure that out stymied us.

Still, I think he was tempted to break the stalemate. Maybe he was about to point to the front of my shirt and then when I looked down, he would flip his finger up to hit my nose—just as he used to do when I was a kid. But when Dad suddenly got a funny look on his face, I knew that neither of us was going to be able to say or do anything to erase the awkwardness.

Dad ended it by kind of sliding backward out the door. I went to the window and watched him cut through a field to get to where he had hidden his car. I remember the look on his face just before he left; he'd figured out that *he* was the injured party, being played for a fool by a woman—and by his own son. It was pathetic. Made me appreciate even more the value of a hard and thick crust; at least I don't ever have to worry about a broken heart putting *me* in an early grave.

I smoked another cigarette and boiled more air out of the water for a second cup of tea. I wasn't above using that incident with my father to facilitate my departure, but I didn't know *how* to use it. Maybe I could tell Felicity I'd been thinking about it for the past week and had slowly become outraged—and now was so damn mad I couldn't bear to stay with her another minute.

No. I wasn't going to say anything to Felicity about my father; I'd have to come up with something else.

When I'd told Felicity how upset I was about hitting thirty, she'd said she felt the same way about fifty. Back in New York I'd just started dating a twenty-year-old college student. (But dating doesn't seem the right word for it—seeing her, taking up with her, screwing her? Whatever.) I thought about her as I stood in the kitchen that day of my departure. Twenty, thirty, fifty. They each have their good points but, good golly, a twenty-year-old co-ed is a wonder to behold. That one who was waiting for me back in New York would become my second wife.

I kept looking out the back window, past wooden grave markers and across flat prairie—watching for Felicity. And then: shit. I nervously lighted a cigarette from the one still burning in my hand. *Shit.* Felicity was coming, and I still hadn't thought of a good-sounding lie. I watched her approach, swinging a silver bucket in rhythm with her stride. And she was singing.

You made me love you—I didn't want to do it, I didn't want to do it . . .

I had no way of knowing if that's what she was singing, but that's the way I've chosen to remember it.

Felicity looked happy. I thought at the time that someone should record her on film, swinging and singing on her way to the house that morning, because she seemed to be expressing the quintessential statement on happiness. Which made things worse for me.

Until the fat old toad blinked its bored eyes and hissed a bad-breath message: *Get on with it, asshole.*

I knew what he meant. I put six Hershey bars, which I'd been squirreling away for the last week or so, on the kitchen table and walked quickly to the car. I'd already loaded my suitcases.

I sat there a moment—until I could see her in the rearview mirror. God, if she didn't look happy; not twenty years old, but happy just the same. I started the car and pulled away.

Good thing that old toad was in control, because I might have stopped when I looked in the mirror again and saw Felicity's expression. Still smiling widely but now looking a little confused, or bemused. As if she were saying to herself: "Now where's my Honey Bear going in such a hurry this early morning?" And maybe, someplace in her mind or more probably in her heart, already knowing the answer to that question.

Drive on, urged the ugly toad—and I did, slowing just a little for one last look at what was left of that once-magnificent tree-trunk chair. It was nothing more than a stool, and it'd be gone by the time I came back. Sure, I was planning to return. All you have to do, when making the kind of departure I was making, is to let an extremely long absence go by before attempting your next reunion. I'm something of an expert on these matters.

Driving to Chicago, I attempted pathetic defenses of myself: Felicity and I both knew that our time together had to have a conclusion, so why not make the departure as quick and unexpected as possible so that all the tears come *afterward* and not while we're together? Or: I was too sentimental; I couldn't bear saying good-bye to her. Or: I was afraid of making a last-minute commitment to her—one I knew I couldn't keep.

But the truth is this: No matter how wonderful magic is, no matter how much you miss it when it's gone and regret not appreciating it when you had it, once you do get that magic back in your life and it's there every day, then it becomes commonplace all over again. Even the magic of a woman who routinely pulls rabbits from hats, makes gold coins drop readily from behind earlobes, and says incantations more frequently than grace.

G R A V Ē D A

The part Felicity told me when I was thirty and living with her.

36. Genipur awakens in Gravēda's arms, being held tightly by her—which is the way she thinks he always should awaken. Outside it's become day but the cave remains dark and close, which is the way Gravēda prefers matters where Genipur is involved.

"I got to go," he says, attempting to pull away.

She holds tightly.

"I told you. My mother is *dying*. I shouldn't have been away from her as long as this."

Gravēda holds tightly.

"I have to be there. I don't want her to die alone."

Gravēda releases him; she understands the value of having someone with you when you're dying, having someone hold you close at that important point in your life when you're dying. "Will you come back soon?" she asks.

"I won't have to. You're going to get out of here."

"How?"

He laughs. "You'll see. I brought you a present."

"A present? What? Where is it?"

"I couldn't carry it in here with me, but I'll toss it through the hole after I leave. *And* Eller told me that one of the guards left you a present, too. A young priest who was guarding you, I guess. Eller said it's under a tarp by the cave's entrance."

"All these presents!" She is giddy. "Is it my birthday or something?"

Genipur laughs again. "You come down to the beach after you get out. Eller will show you where my mother and I are staying. I really have to go now. You be careful on the beach. A lot of ravens down there."

"I will." They kiss; Gravēda makes it linger.

"*I have to go.*"

She nods and releases him reluctantly. A moment after Genipur has wiggled through the sewer hole, something large is tossed up into the cave, landing clanging on the rock. Gravēda immediately picks it up and immediately is comforted by its hard, cold weight. Always dangerous, now she is armed and dangerous.

37. She takes her sword to the cagewall, picks a likely spot waist-high, and begins to hack at the crisscrossed saplings—cutting at an angle and then straight, at an angle and then straight so that chips fly and progress through the wood is rapid.

After Gravēda has created a large exit in the cagewall and has struggled through it, she leans on her sword and rests. Now she seems hypersensitive to sensations—sounds and smells and everything that touches her: the cold handshake of her sword and the threaded texture of her new robe against her skin. In such intimate contact with the world, Gravēda becomes doubtful about the whole idea of freedom. As a diversion, she walks to the corner of the cave near the covered door and throws back a tarp to see what present the young priest left for her.

"Well, I'll be damned," she says, examining the three large stoneware jugs she has uncovered. Pulling a corncob from the top of one, she sniffs and smiles. With so much distillate so close at hand, Gravēda now knows exactly what to do.

She drinks and thinks, thinks and drinks. She decides to face the outside world as the outside world sometimes simply must be faced: in a highly distilled state. By the time Gravēda pulls back the heavy wooden slab from the doorway, the world has become nearly as dark as her cave. But she doesn't mind. Sitting near the entrance, Gravēda suddenly realizes that all the confusion she's faced since she rejoined the tribe isn't really that confusing, and the impossibility of crossing the ocean doesn't seem that impossible, and maybe Genipur will marry her after all. Gravēda knows how to practice the art of distilling life's complications.

She thinks about killing Nestus and, weighing sword in

hand, imagines how it'd feel to slit open the woman's belly. And if Nestus, bleeding and jerking in a panic, lifted her arms to Gravēda, what would Gravēda do? She decides she'd accept Nestus in her arms—because the bond is strong between murderer and murdered, the one compelled to ask for forgiveness and the other able to grant it. No closer bond than that between sinner and the object of sin, between the guilty and the guilt.

Holding an empty jug tightly to her breasts, Gravēda imagines it is Nestus burrowing into her like a weary but determined child who does not want, who desperately does not want, to be abandoned to sleep.

Then Gravēda tosses the jug against a nearby rock; the stoneware breaks into three large pieces. "No!" she hollers. "You're not pinning this one on me." She stands and shakes her head in an effort to throw off the guilt of the murder she's just committed in her mind. Then she laughs. "Wishing it don't make me responsible for it. No, sir. If wishes were dishes, we'd have place settings for all."

She goes inside for another jug and then stumbles around the rocky terrain outside the cave. "Not pinning *this* one on me," she mumbles as she heads for the cliff so she can see the ocean. "Like when Momma died, trying to stick me with her death just 'cause I was dreaming about it all the time. Can't hold me responsible for what I dream."

Gravēda laughs at herself for falling. She gets up, senses the ocean, and lurches toward it. "Long time since I been like this," she says to herself. "Got to get distilled and sure do dread it. *Doo-dah, doo-dah.*"

Resting and taking several quick hits from the jug, Gravēda begins to sing. "*All my troubles are edgeless now.*" She thinks that maybe tiny night birds are falling off their limbs with envy—and laughs at the idea of it.

"*Nestus is a good old gal; ran up on my sword somehow. Had to bury her deep; pray the Lord her soul to keep. Now she's unlinked and traveling free; me and Genipur's going to sea. Yo-ho-ho.*"

Bracing herself against boulders and scrub trees to keep upright, Gravēda begins talking as she used to talk to the graves she found when she was traveling alone. "Momma turned into a hateful old woman, crippled up and leaving me to do all the cooking and cleaning. I'd have to bathe her and everything. When I got to her private parts, she'd start whining and I'd tell her, 'But, Momma, we got to keep you clean.' I was mean to Momma. Let the disgust show on my face. Punishing compassion—that's what I gave her. Then traveled alone through hard times, losing all my refinements." She pauses to catch her breath. "I got stories that'd break your heart."

Now she's at the cliff and seeing in the moonlight that strip of beach and those waves that break white in the night, Gravēda is reminded of the day when she first saw the ocean. How long ago, she does not know.

Gravēda suddenly is seized by a highly distilled form of melancholia. Dangerously close to the cliff's edge, she begins to sing a song of grief. It has no words, only sounds that are mournful and wailing; changing pitch from high and sliding to low, her song slopes to the sea and is carried for miles across oceantop.

And after Gravēda sings everything she knows about the downhearted blues, the sea echoes the song back to her. They duet sorrow. Ain't life a bitch? And love's fickle, too. A man'll always break your heart. Her partner out there sings more elegantly than she, and Gravēda wonders who distills the sea.

And then, in the predawn light, Gravēda sees a huge, dark shape rise from the ocean, close to the beach. Too impossibly big to be alive, and yet it moves: rising to the surface, receding, rising and moving even closer to the beach.

It must be grief, she concludes. The embodiment of grief—its perceptible, incarnate incorporation. Grief is a distinct and readily identifiable phenomenon, occurring in nature as does thunder and rain and lightning and love. Even more than that: Grief swims the sea.

3 8. Gravēda wakes up at the back of the cave, in the little side room that is close and smoky and so familiarly hers.

Oh, misery. Blind in one eye and can't see out of the other. The inside of her mouth is spitlessly astringent. Head pain so bad that she actually searches for the heavy, rusty iron wedge that someone must have pounded into her forebrain. "I'll never drink again."

Then she becomes panicky. What's she doing in the cave? How'd she get here? The last she remembers she was . . . what? Drinking out among the rocks. What really happened last night? Gravēda recalls something about singing at the edge of the cliff and seeing a monster in the water—but she concludes that part must have been a nightmare.

But did I also dream up the part about getting free? If I walk around the corner of this little room, will I see the guards standing there at the cagewall—like always?

When she stirs, she moves against her sword, and knowing it's there makes her feel a little better. She stands, dizzy and still half distilled. "Ohhh." She holds her head. Gravēda feels as if she's been repeatedly hammered down and pried loose.

Moaning and guiding herself with a hand along the wall, she leaves the side compartment and makes her way gingerly to the cagewall. With some difficulty, she gets through the hole in the bars. Then she walks out of the cave and into the day.

She sees and feels what she's not seen or felt in all the time she's been in that cave, months or years. Almost sober and standing in the sunlight, Gravēda notices that the rocks actually shine: grays and browns and off-whites that excite her. So incredibly bright out; Gravēda had forgotten about that. Bushes and grasses around the cave are ecstatically green. And would you look at that sky: blues that could break God's heart.

She inhales deeply, air so pure that it seems to disinfect her lungs. She wonders where that air's been, traveling ten thousand miles over the ocean; she wonders what it has blown across. And does the air she now breathes still carry traces of exotica from across that sea?

All of this requires exclamation. Light. Color. Air. But, as you can see, there's no bang left in Gravēda. She's too worried about what happened, and what didn't happen, last night. Is it possible that Nestus actually did show up and that Gravēda killed her? Gravēda checks her sword for signs of blood, seeing none. Whew. She shakes her head. Misery, misery. "I'll never, ever drink again."

She walks carefully toward the beach, keeping her head down because it hurts to look up. She finds a path and with some effort manages to climb down to the sand. When Gravēda raises her head to get her bearings, she sees something on the beach that causes her to stop breathing momentarily.

"I'll be damned," she whispers to herself. Some kind of creature, some kind of miracle. Something so large and unbelievable that Gravēda wouldn't argue if someone told her that God Himself had washed ashore during the night.

39. The closer she gets, the more Gravēda is impressed with the size of this particular miracle. She stops several yards away, wondering if it's alive. As if to provide an answer, the miracle-creature lifts its huge tail, which is the only part of the thing that's still in the water, and drops one horizontal fluke with a thud that indeed hits the beach like the fist of God. The concussion shakes Gravēda's belly fat in a casual display of incredible power.

Some kind of fish. It's so obviously foundered, trapped and immobile on the sand, that Gravēda is not afraid—not too afraid. She steps up to the middle of the creature and places her hand gently upon it. She didn't expect it to feel like this. She didn't know what to expect, but not this: Its slick black skin actually is soft, seemingly sensitive. Under what environmental arrangement could an animal of this magnitude exist with such vulnerably soft skin?

Heading toward that giant's tail, Gravēda walks off the fish's length. A real whopper, easily fifty feet long. And who could even guess how much this much meat weighs? A ton a foot? Fifty tons?

Gravēda enters the surf to give wide berth to the tail flukes, which rise and fall rhythmically: left, right, left, right. This is done gently now, as if the thing is biding time, holding back, doing a monster-miracle's version of drumming fingertips.

Although its thickness is twice Gravēda's height, this fish—this creature, this miracle, this grief—does not appear to be fat; it tapers gently from massive head to graceful tail.

The wrinkles and skin folds on the creature's back are blistering red in the sun; at her feet, Gravēda notices pink bubbles in the sand. She realizes now what should have been obvious all along: The miracle is dying.

Gravēda comes up the other side, stepping back to get an overall perspective. That squared-off head makes up a third of the fish's length. She slowly approaches the huge, flat forehead.

The creature, which is rolled over halfway on its side, has an oddly narrow jaw that carries a thousand scars, gashes, white streaks, and missing chunks. Makes you wonder what else is out there in that ocean, things capable of putting their marks on something as impressive as this miracle.

Its mouth is white, shiny white and absolutely unstained. As if this thing feeds exclusively on deep-sea versions of cotton bolls and lily bells. Its pearly teeth have a gentle inward curve to them.

In all her travels, Gravēda never has seen a miracle, and she's deeply impressed with this one. When she hears a whooshing of air, she bends close to that chaste mouth—but detects no fishy breath.

At the side of its head, Gravēda sees an eye. But something's not right; this is no fish's eye. When she looks at it closely, Gravēda becomes terribly shaken and tells herself, tries to make herself believe, that the thing she's staring at is no eye at all—that it's just some sort of eyelike growth. A polyp, maybe.

The polyp blinks! Gravēda steps back. The eye follows her. Dark, dark brown eye—shading toward purple. Like a miracle's version of Sweet Genipur's eyes. Gravēda moves farther away.

Can there be anything more frightening than to look into the eye of an animal, what you assume to be some sort of animal, and detect in that eye the look of intelligence?

As the eye continues to follow her, dark eye on blue eyes,

Gravēda gets the chills. She's half prepared for the creature to initiate a quiet conversation in Gravēda's own language.

(Imagine the thoughts that could originate in a head that size—tons and tons of thought. Gravēda whispers under her breath: *Maybe it is God.*)

And then, when the creature quite without warning squeaks and whistles and begins a series of excited clickings, Gravēda goes into a panic. She suddenly decides she simply must get the thing back in the water. She rushes up to it and pushes, but those fifty tons do not, of course, budge. They do not even acknowledge the power Gravēda is applying to them. She steps back to rest.

But when the Godlike fish starts mewling and clicking again, Gravēda begins pushing again—stupidly pushing against the creature's sunburned head. This time it responds, turning more on its side and slapping its tail flukes in what seems to be an effort to move its bulk even higher up on the sand—as if the creature now is afraid Gravēda might actually move it back out to sea.

From a hole in the top of its head, sweet damp air blows across Gravēda's face, brushing back her hair. And finally she gives up. Gravēda returns to the eye—sits there and watches it.

By the time the sun reaches midday, the miracle can barely move its tail: raising it weakly and letting it fall in the wet sand with the lightest of crashes. It mewls as softly as a kitten, and that's enough to make Gravēda cry.

"What?" she asks, placing a hand near the purple eye, which twitches in response. "What do you want?"

The eye stares back intently. "No!" Gravēda shakes her head. "You're not pinning this one on me, either. I'm not responsible. This is some kind of accident or something—your being beached like this." The eye implores. "No! My singing didn't tempt you up here—No!"

But when Gravēda detects what she thinks is supplication in that eye, when it seems that she can see through that eye to a gentle intelligence that is trapped in those tons and tons of dying flesh—well, it just rips her up. "The only thing big enough to comfort you is the ocean," Gravēda says as she crazily attempts to hug the creature—resting her cheek on its slick smooth black skin and digging her feet into the sand so that she can use all her strength and weight to suggest, at least to suggest, the comforting pressure of the sea.

And it is like this, Gravēda leaning as heavily as she can with her arms outspread against the blistering flesh, that the miracle at some point expires.

40. "For saaale, for reeent, for freee! Rooms and warrens. Get out quick! For saaale, for reeent, for freee! Rooms and warrens. Get out quick!"

The ancient Eller is walking along the base of the cliff that walls the beach; he moves slowly, waddling crookedly as he chants and soundlessly swings his clapperless bell. Gravēda runs to him.

"Do you see it, do you see it!" she hollers as she reaches him, almost knocking the both of them to the sand. "That thing, that creature. Have you seen it?"

Eller's rheumy eyes, a hundred years old, are bored as they look toward the creature at surf's edge—and then back to Gravēda. "I don't miss anything," he says. "Not even something that size."

"What is it? Some kind of miracle or something? I bet it was sent by God, huh? It couldn't *be* God, could it? I think it's grief, all our grief put into a creature like that and then sent out in the ocean."

"A fish."

"What?"

"It's a fish. A big fish."

"No!" Gravēda insists. "Not a fish. If you looked at its eyes, you'd know that. It has *intelligence*."

"Okay, okay," Eller says, sighing. "A big *smart* fish."

"Eller, *please*. For once, please don't talk crazy. I have to know what's going on. Kept in the cave all that time and then I get out and the tribe's gone and now this, this . . ."

"Fish."

"Eller! It's not a fish. Some kind of signal or message. An omen or something."

"A fish."

"Eller! *Damn you.*"

"All right, all right. I'll explain everything in a straightforward way. But it won't be much fun. Sit down."

"I don't want to sit down."

He shrugs. "Well, I'm going to. I have to. A hundred years old, you know."

"Come on, come on."

"Patience, child—patience." With some difficulty, Eller carefully sits on a boulder that long ago fell from the cliff into the sand. "That's the *second* fish, uh, creature that's come ashore. The first one beached itself a few days ago, and the tribe reacted about the same way you're reacting. Nestus took full advantage of the situation. Told everyone that the ocean is full of monsters like that and then asked who was willing to take a boat out among such monsters. No one was, of course. So she said it was a perfect time to begin the return journey."

"The backward journey."

"Whatever. It didn't take much convincing. Everyone was so afraid of the big fish that the whole damn tribe packed up and was gone in a day or two. Only one old traveler left alive anyway."

"Genipur's mother."

"Hey! Who's telling this story?"

"You are. Go on."

"Okay. The only old traveler still alive is Genipur's mother. So he agreed to stay with her and then try to catch up with the tribe later. Sound familiar?"

Gravēda nods.

"And I'm sticking around 'cause of you and 'cause I'm a hundred years old and that vintage doesn't travel well." Eller laughs.

Gravēda looks at the dead miracle. "They shouldn't have been afraid of it. You can tell it's gentle, wouldn't hurt anybody."

"Yeah, but you know Nestus. A real politician. Able to capitalize on these natural phenomena."

"What're we going to do?"

"The first fish is three hundred and thirty-three yards down the beach, that way." Eller points. "And it's already beyond ripeness. Lord—get downwind of it and you'll become a real believer. The carcass actually exploded. Filled up with gas in all this heat and went off like a giant balloon. Innards everywhere—pieces of heart hanging on the rocks and everything. You know all those ravens that were on the beach?"

Gravēda shakes her head.

Eller corrects himself. "Of course not. You were in the cave. Anyway, we had a lot of ravens that were pestering everyone, but now those birds are all down there feeding off that first fish. When they finish it, if they ever can finish it, they'll probably come up here. So what I'm going to do is get as far away from the stench and birds as I possibly can."

"You going to stay with Genipur and his mother?"

"Yeah—except by now it might be only Genipur who's camped up the beach. His mother was in the final stages of dying when I saw her last."

"Can I go with you? To see Genipur?"

"Of course. I walked down this way looking for you—so I could take you to him."

"He asked for me?" She was hoping.

"Maybe."

"What do you mean by that? If he said something about me, I want to hear it."

"I'll tell you along the way." Before they begin walking, Eller turns for one last look at the dead creature. "Pathetic, ain't it? Like a beached—"

"I don't want to wait," Gravēda interrupts. "If he told you how he feels about me, I want to hear it now. Is he going to catch up with Nestus and marry her after his mother dies, or isn't he?"

Eller walks carefully, in silence—as if he's heard none of what Gravēda has said.

"Please, Eller," she begs as they walk.

He says nothing.

Convinced that Eller will speak only in his own sweet time, Gravēda tries to think about the miracle's sad death, hoping that she can distract herself from thoughts of Genipur. But it doesn't work. "Eller . . ."

"Okay, okay. I'm not sure he'd want me to tell you this, and that's why I've been reluctant to mention it. But Genipur loves you."

"He told you that?"

"And he doesn't want to marry Nestus," Eller continues, ignoring Gravēda's question. "He wants to marry you and take you out on the ocean with him."

"Genipur said all this?"

"In fact, he adores you. Worships you. Is one of your biggest fans. He can't live without you. He dreams of you nightly."

"Genipur told all these things to you? Did he?"

"He wants you to have his baby. He desires nothing more out of life than being in your arms. Your face haunts him."

"Wait a second, old man. How much of this are you making up and how much of it comes from Genipur? Is *any* of this true?"

He looks at her, as if her questions have been inappropriate. "If you believe it's true, then it is. All you have to do is believe. Didn't you know that?"

"What does Genipur think about me? Just answer that simple question."

"He thinks the world of you. Wants to live out his life with you. Hopes the two of you grow old together."

"And he said these things to you?"

"Don't you believe them? Don't you believe Genipur loves you?"

Gravēda is trying to believe it. "Whether I do or not doesn't matter. I want to know what *he* thinks."

"Whether you believe it or not is all that matters," Eller insists.

"But he's never told me he loves me or wants to marry me

or anything. All he's ever said is that he intends to marry Nestus."

"That's why it's so important that you believe otherwise. That you believe he loves *you* and wants to marry *you*."

"Does he?"

"His heart belongs to you. Your love carries him through the day, helps him make it through the night. He thinks that life without you wouldn't be worth living."

She sighs. Why can't he give me a straight answer? But as they continue to walk, Gravēda attempts to follow Eller's advice: believing Genipur loves her—so that he will. And yet when she searches for evidence of his love, something he might have said or done as a declaration of love, she finds none.

They walk until it's dark and by the time they see a large campfire, Gravēda has managed to pull it off: to hold in her mind a contradiction, that Genipur loves her and that Genipur doesn't love her.

Such a thing is possible, of course: to make one part of your mind believe something you very much want to believe even as another area in your mind, the part that knows better, says it ain't so, it ain't so.

There's Genipur now, standing by the fire and looking into it. When he sees Gravēda and waves to her, one part of her mind begins to have doubts about the side of the contradiction it holds. She can make out his fire-lighted face, his dark eyes, his white and smiling teeth; in response to all this, the part of her mind that knows better simply capitulates.

41. "Hello, Genipur," Gravēda says, thinking *Sweet Genipur* but not saying it out loud, because she doesn't want to embarrass the boy in front of his mother, lying there on a makeshift bed by the fire with her mouth and eyes open wide in the bewildered look of one who is dying.

"Hello, Gravēda," he replies, whispering in deference to that mother.

Eller kneels next to the old woman, checks her eyes, and

then puts his face close to her mouth as if to smell her exhalations. He looks up. "You two kids go on and sleep in the woods tonight. You have a lot to talk about. I'll watch her." Gravēda is surprised to hear how reasonable and calm Eller sounds.

Genipur begins to protest but the ancient priest raises one thin, stained hand. "No, no—you two go on. Your mother will make it through the night."

"Are you sure?"

Eller is rankled. "Of course I'm sure."

Then all three of them look at the old woman's face, but it registers no awareness that she—her life and death—is being discussed.

Genipur touches Gravēda's shoulder. "Okay?"

She feels like jumping up and down and hollering, Yes, yes, yes! But Gravēda controls herself—just nods her consent and then the two of them climb up a cliff path to see if they can find a patch of grass that'll give relief from the irritating sand that crunches between your teeth no matter how careful you are about your mouth, a patch of woods that'll shut out the surf's constant, maddeningly repetitive breath.

"That was nice of old Eller," Genipur says on the way. "I told him earlier that I'd like to get off the beach for a while. That I needed a break. It was nice of him to insist that we get away for the night."

Gravēda takes Genipur's hand. She thinks Eller is an absolute saint.

After getting to the top of the cliff and crossing a rocky patch, they are walking on grass and within a few minutes more are approaching a dark wall of trees.

"Do you mind if we stay out here on the meadow?" Gravēda asks. She never did like sleeping in the forest—too many shapes and shadows.

"No—this is fine," Genipur says, dropping to the ground and stretching out in the short grass, yawning luxuriously as he does.

"Sleepy-time Boy?"

He nods. She gets down next to him and hugs him and kisses him. Then Genipur and Gravēda make love. They make lots of love, and by the time they're finished, night is at its deepest. Then they lie apart, naked on sweet grass with Gravēda's robe over them, and each wonders what's on the other's mind.

"I'm not going after the tribe," Genipur says with the finality of someone who's been practicing a statement in his head.

"Good!"

"But it means I'm betraying Nestus. I promised I'd catch up with the tribe as soon as my mother died. Now I'm breaking my word."

"Nestus broke hers often enough."

"Gravēda." Genipur's voice shows exasperation. "Please don't talk against her. I feel bad enough already."

Gravēda feels bad, too. "I'm sorry. I won't do it again." In fact, she feels guilty as hell, but Gravēda wouldn't dare tell Genipur how she used to plan Nestus's death—dream of it and hope for it. How she would have done anything to get Genipur back in her arms.

Now that he's there, Gravēda wonders how much responsibility she owes. If Nestus suffers a broken heart, could a joint indictment be brought against Genipur and Gravēda? She wishes she could bad-mouth the woman and make Nestus seem as if she deserves a broken heart. But as it is, Gravēda must manage alone that full measure of guilt—like having gas, terribly poisonous and burning gas that you're unable to belch up or pass or complain about.

"Why did you decide not to go after the tribe?" she asks, hoping for sweet mint words from the boy.

"I don't know. Whenever I was with Nestus and she explained the return journey and how reasonable and logical it was for the tribe to multiply and become a respectable and mature group, I thought all that made a lot of sense. But then when I was alone, just sitting around thinking or looking out at the ocean, I'd get this feeling and I knew, just knew, that I'd have to try it. Try to cross the water to see what's on the other side. I could never explain that to her, because I couldn't come up with any logical reasons for what *I* wanted to do."

Gravēda wonders if he now is going to ask her to accompany him on the journey—the real journey, the one that's headed in the right direction. She wonders if he's going to say: I love you. But Genipur says nothing more and soon his breathing is regular. Gravēda doesn't mind so much; being with him is important and good, whether he's awake or asleep. And now she believes he loves her.

She looks around and although the night still is deep, Gravēda can see the trees and the stars and how the off-white clouds streak and patch the sky. It's noisy, too—leaves in the wind, limbs squeaking where they rub, night bugs, bass frogs, and way in the distance, two or three hills over, prancing foxes bark. This isn't night, not real night. Not like it was in the cave where you couldn't see or hear anything. That was night. This light and noisy place out here in the meadow is just a slightly less bright version of day.

A songbird sings part of its routine—a short trill, silence, a few more quick notes, and then the bird doesn't sing again.

Odd, Gravēda thinks. That was no night bird. Not even a mockingbird, which occasionally must practice its imitations at night so they're accurately performed the next day. No—the bird that just sang was a bluebird or a wild canary or perhaps a parakeet. Some kind of songbird that flourishes in the sunlight, one of those delicate things you don't often see because they like to light and sing on the green bud-tips at the very ends of those limbs at the very tops of trees.

Gravēda wonders what would make such a bird sing in the middle of the night, even a relatively light and noisy night. Do songbirds dream, dreaming it is dawn and time to sing? Or dreaming of bugs and berries it has eaten? Dreaming of spring and remembering how soft and exciting it must feel to feel that warm down of another songbird, mounting or being mounted? Or maybe it was eagerness that made the bird sing, eager for the sun.

Ah, but ain't that a point Gravēda could argue with song-birds? She lies back and watches the stars and then turns over and reaches for Genipur.

And when she awakens, all kinds of birds are singing. It is dawn, and birds don't consider the sun to be perverse, contrary, or cranky in the least. In fact: They appreciate its grinding regularity.

42. For the next three days, Genipur, Gravēda, and Eller camp on the beach and care for Genipur's mother as they wait for her to die. Although she seems to get worse each day, weaker and even less aware, the old woman simply won't let go.

Finally, Genipur leaves the camp and goes to his boat, which he and Gravēda have pulled down to the beach. He checks provisions, sails, mast, and hull; when he's not working, he sits and stares at the simple boat he and his friends spent a year building. He sleeps on board.

Eller, meanwhile, spends most of his time writing, so it's been left to Gravēda to care for Genipur's mother, and Gravēda doesn't like that. She's had enough experience with mothers who refuse to die.

Gravēda complains to Eller, saying he should find some way out of this mess. "Marry me and Genipur now," she suggests, "and then we can ship out and you can stay here until she dies."

"I guess not!" Eller says, indignant.

One afternoon, Gravēda changes the old woman's soiled bedding and then tells Eller: "That's it. I'm going to the boat and stay with Genipur. You take care of her or you figure out what to do with her—it's up to you now."

"What?" he asks, looking up from his pages.

"She's yours now," Gravēda says, walking away. "Write her off, hold a pillow over her face—*something*. I've spent too much of my life waiting for someone to die, and I'm not going to do it anymore. You have no idea what that's like."

"Are you . . . What do you . . . Hey!" Eller calls, sputtering and muttering and mad. Gravēda dismisses him with a wave and then is gone.

•　　　•　　　•

"*I* don't know anything about waiting for death?" Eller finally manages to say. "*Me?* The world's leading, acknowledged, and renowned authority on death is being told by a child, a child less than half my age, that I don't know about death? That's ridiculous. That's . . . She'll be dead by morning!" Eller finally yells—but there's no one to hear him except for Genipur's mother and you can't be sure she hears, or listens to, anything.

After fixing some hot water and honey to soothe his throat, Eller takes a taste of ambergrist to energize himself for what he plans to do—which is to talk the woman into dying. Such, he believes, are his powers of persuasion, especially when the topic is one with which he's so terribly intimate.

He sits next to the old woman's bed and places his head on her pillow so that his mouth is next to her ear. "I love you," he whispers, getting as a reaction only a slight focusing of eyes that have for days gone unfocused.

"In spite of your pug nose, lidded eyes, and witch's chin with bristly black whiskers. In spite of your sparse hair that lets your pink skull show. In spite of the fact that you breathe through an open mouth. In spite of everything, when I looked into your eyes I fell so deeply in love that I wanted to jump in bed with you and smother your skeleton teeth with a series of wet-fat smooches."

Eller drinks some honey-water and takes a quick hit of ambergrist. Then he resumes his position by the bed and whispers to Genipur's mother: "You are wise, now, to be wary—to hold disbelief high to your eye." Eller is convinced that the woman is listening closely to everything he says.

He leans so close to her ear that when he speaks she is tickled by his breath and his moving lips. "Your eyes put me close to what I've come to worship: Death. Chilly thrills waved up my back when I realized that Death had taken up in you a complete residency, and I examined you more often than the practice of medicine required, because your body parts are touched by Death and I fondled them as artifacts—in the way that lovers will toy with a ring, a scarf, or something that holds a lover's scent."

Another bite of ambergrist followed by a long draw from a nearby bottle of distillate, and Eller becomes well and tightly cranked.

"But *you*, you show no appreciation. Instead of being flattered by Death's keen interest, you spurn its attention—keep it waiting at the altar! Foolish woman! You reject the greatest force in existence, and for what? For *life*? Puny life? Life is nothing but a twitch in time. It'll break your heart. Life just visits you, but Death will take you home forever. Life is a mean-spirited lover who promises you the mountains in the summer and ribbons on your birthday and who tells you everything will be okay in the morning and who, in all these things and ten thousand more, *lies*.

"Death never lies. It'll never leave you. Death is an unending profundity."

Eller pauses until his breathing regulates itself. "When your son was a child, did you hold him naked from his bath and horrify yourself with thoughts of his death? Simple woman! He was born all but dead. All of us were—just an inch of time separating birth from Death. But when that inch passes, Death will accept us in a state grander and longer-lasting than the forces of time and creation and easily more gloriful than that weakling, life.

"And you can have all that for yourself—right now. Be like me. Stop worrying and learn to love Death. It's ignored me for these past one hundred years, but Death is courting you right now. Stop profaning it by fearing it. Let loose of that little twit of life!"

Eller is panting now. "It's not too late, you know. Death's charity is unbounded; it'll still accept you. You can make the marriage work. Stop struggling. Surrender to the eternal force that'll never, ever abandon you. Do it! Do it!"

Eller is so exhausted that he has to stop and rest, closing his eyes as he speaks softly now, almost in his sleep now: "The truth is known to me, woman. It is tucked back into dorsal brain where it resides as a nuclear chip that powers me and all I do."

It's night, and Eller's voice trails in the dark. He sleeps. He dreams of holding Genipur's mother to the light of the campfire in an effort to candle her, to see if he can find Death among her organs. He dreams that his arguments have convinced her and that she has asked him to prepare her for the wedding ceremony. So he dreams of bathing her gently, patting her dry, rubbing ointment onto her cracked elbows and knees, brushing her teeth, and dressing her in flannel and terry that have been warmed by the fire. In his dreams he tells her stories of light creatures who live on sunshine, of magic clowns who take little girls to magic lands where no one cries or dies and the candy you eat is more nutritional than peas.

Genipur's mother, meanwhile, falls to a languorous drift in which she speaks for the first time in days, saying outlandish things about her baby and her husband; once she even calls for "Daddy!" In the end, she rots—a victim not of Eller's arguments or dreams but of her own internal rusts and smuts.

•   •   •

Next morning, Eller is brusquely awakened by Genipur, who is hollering at him. "You were supposed to come and get me so I could be with her! She wasn't supposed to die alone. You fell asleep and let her die alone!"

Eller begins to cry himself. He's on his knees, hitting at his own chest and pulling on his robe; he's wailing.

"Stupid priest!" Genipur cries.

Gravēda puts her arm around Genipur's shoulder. "It's okay, Baby. Your mother didn't die alone. Eller was with her. Even if he was asleep, he was with her. You saw. His head was right there on the pillow with hers."

"He's a stupid priest," Genipur says bitterly.

And Eller seems to agree, still hitting himself and repeatedly sobbing, "Stupid, stupid, stupid." But if Gravēda and Genipur think that Eller is angry with himself for failing to notify them of the old woman's impending death, they are wrong. What disturbs Eller is the missed opportunity, his failure to get a final and close look at Death. He wanted to be awake and peeping into the woman's eyes at the moment that Death consummated the marriage. He wanted to say good-bye. No, not good-bye. Adieu. Auf Wiedersehen.

Genipur, who now is calm, begins to tell Gravēda what has to be done. He's going to wrap his mother's body in cerements and then carry her to the meadow where he and Gravēda slept several nights ago. That's where he's decided to bury his mother.

Overhearing all this, Eller becomes more agitated. "Cerements? Don't dress the bride in cerements! A bride doesn't wear cerements. Let's lay her out in . . . in angel-wing chiffon over white organza. A gown featuring cameo neckline, three layers of capped sleeves, and a chapel-length train."

Gravēda has to restrain Genipur, who's prepared to throttle the old man. "Don't let him get to you," she tells Genipur. "He's crazy. He doesn't know what he's saying."

"We'll make the bride's upper torso replete with cymbidium orchids and nosegays of lilies. Genipur can be the ring bearer. Gravēda, do you have a robe in the Niobe design? I'll dress in Chantilly lace and sing 'O Perfect Love.'"

Gravēda steps close to him. "That's enough. You're upsetting Genipur and being disrespectful to his mother."

"She never looked lovelier," Eller continues. "Crinkly lace over wrinkly face."

"Listen!" Gravēda shouts, loudly enough that Eller shuts up. "You have three options. You can be quiet. Or you can leave and go on with your craziness someplace else, where we can't see you or hear you. Or I can hit you upside your head with my sword. What'll it be?"

Eller rubs his chin. "Number two!" he suddenly exclaims, and then pauses as if waiting to see if that's the correct answer.

"Okay, fine," Gravēda tells him. "Then get the hell out of here."

Eller leaves, talking to himself. "They should be celebrating, not crying. Joy to the world, the bride is dead! I should have pulled her from that bed and flopped her around camp just to get them in the spirit of the event. Everybody dance!" He shouts back at Gravēda and Genipur: "Everybody dance!"

．　　　．　　　．

Genipur carries his mother up the cliff, across the rocks, and to the meadow. Gravēda, bringing the shovel, trails him by a few steps, and Eller follows along at a distance.

The old priest sits at the edge of the forest and watches the boy dig a deep hole. Gravēda has gone back to camp and returned with two stoneware jars of distillate, which will be placed on the woman's grave as a sign that Genipur's mother represents faith that has been at least partially distilled. A staff, its sharpened end pointing toward the setting sun, will mark the grave.

"They don't understand," Eller mutters. "That woman is beginning something, not ending it. She's ready to bud." He shouts down to them: "She will flower for eternity!"

But as he watches the scene on the meadow below him, Eller begins to smile. He thinks that perhaps Gravēda and Genipur do understand what he's been trying to tell them. They are, after all, planting the woman on a hillside with southern exposure and good drainage.

"*Hmm.*"

43. On the morning following the funeral, everyone forgives everyone for everything. There's no time for grudges: Genipur and Gravēda are to be married in the afternoon and then launch their boat at sunset.

Gravēda is gay all morning long, but then Eller tells her and Genipur: "You two realize, don't you, that you're the last two travelers on the journey. That means your child will be the last in the line of travelers whom God started on this holy journey. Your child is the final distillation of faith. Your child will be The One."

Although it should have been obvious to the both of them,

Genipur and Gravēda are suddenly sobered to think that their child actually will meet God. The idea of it distracts them, and they go through the ceremony in something of a daze.

But now there's work to be done. The boat is dragged to surf's edge, and Eller returns from the campsite with several jars of distillate and one large crock of ambergrist. Wedding presents, he tells them. "One more thing," he says, waddling back to camp.

As the day moves quickly toward dusk, Genipur becomes concerned that the strongest portion of the ebbing current will be lost before they're able to launch the boat. "Where is that man?" he asks angrily.

And when Eller finally does return, carrying a leather-bound stack of pages, he sits in the sand next to the boat, turns to the back of the pages, and begins writing.

"Come on, come on," Genipur urges.

"Come on, come on, Genipur urges," Eller mutters as he writes.

Gravēda knows exactly where all this is heading. "I got an idea," she tells Eller. "You write it and then we'll do it exactly the way you've written it."

The old man looks up at her. "The whole launching? Exactly the way I say?"

"Yes."

Genipur asks, "What the hell's going on here?"

"I'll explain it to you later," Gravēda says.

Eller writes for a while longer and then hands the pages to Gravēda. "Okay," he says. "It's all here. Your whole story. The journey, the beach, the cave, the launching—everything. You can read it on the way." From under his stained robe he carefully withdraws a hollow crystal object roughly the size and shape of a human heart. "And in here is the ending to your story. It tells what happens on the voyage, what happens to your child—The End. Take special care of this, but don't ever try to look at the ending. Agreed?"

Gravēda nods. "I don't suppose you can tell me if it'll be a boy or a girl."

Eller laughs. "No can do, no can do."

"Will someone please explain what the two of you are talking about?" Genipur asks.

Gravēda pats his arm. "Later, Hon." Then she whispers to him: "Let's just humor the old guy until we can get this boat launched, okay?"

Genipur sighs and takes a position at the boat's stern, where the other two soon join him. "Start pushing," Genipur instructs.

Straining against the weight of the boat, Gravēda leans close to Eller and asks him softly, "At least tell me how this voyage will turn out. I mean, do we get to the other side? Is this going to be a rough journey or what?"

Eller, whose efforts in the launching are largely ceremonial, grins and says, "Oh, it'll have its moments. I'll be damned if it won't have its moments."

Gravēda laughs.

When the boat is afloat, she and Genipur get in amidship and set the oars. Eller, up to his waist in the water, holds on to the gunwale and speaks softly to Gravēda. "Scared?"

"Scared of nothing," she says nervously, "if you discount God."

Eller nods, as if he understands. Then he wades back to shore, and Gravēda and Genipur work the oars to get beyond the surf. They head into the sunset, sitting apart.

"No!" Eller hollers from the beach. "No, no! Arm in arm! You got it wrong. *Arm in arm!*"

Although both the light and his eyesight are in decline, Eller thinks he sees them cuddle close. They head into the sunset, arm in arm.

Eller nods. "Yeah. That's it." When he no longer can see the boat, he returns to camp and rigs up a torch, which he lights and carries high as he walks up the beach. In his other hand is the large bell. He swings it and chants: "For saaale, for reeent, for freee! Rooms and warrens—get out quick!" Eller has put the clapper back in the bell but now, of course, there's no one to hear.

WHEN I WAS
THIRTY-
THREE

*W*hen I was thirty-three, everything got out of that locked box I keep in the back room. I didn't realize what was happening until after I'd lost control and the slime was crawling over me, even out where people could see. That might have been the worst part: everyone finding out about the kind of stuff I did in the privacy of my own mind.

I'd always thought it was okay to have evil playthings: those idle daydreams about people getting hurt and killed and cancer, the nasty little acts I imagined myself capable of performing, all the evil thoughts I'd ever toyed with. As long as I kept everything in a locked box and didn't act on it or even tell anyone I had it, I didn't see anything wrong or dangerous about owning evil. In fact, I got a kick out of it. I could go to the back room when no one was around, unlock the box, and take everything out and play with it. Sometimes I'd even shock myself with the kind of stuff I had, how much of it there was, and how big some of it had become. And for the longest time, I was able to lock up my evil pets when I finished fooling around with them—and then leave the room and go out front where I met and talked with people who didn't have an inkling about what I'd been up to.

At the end of my second marriage (it lasted less than three years), I first started having trouble with things getting out. I'd be talking and drinking with someone (a colleague, a client— some guy I'd met in some bar) when suddenly there'd appear a piece of slime—my slime—between us. Next day, I'd make any apologies that were necessary, check that the nastiness was back where it was supposed to be, and admonish myself to be more careful in the future—never to let something like that happen again. But it did, and with increasing frequency. I started doing things that can't be covered by apologies, stuff for which I'll never be forgiven.

I tried my best to hurt people, telling them what other people thought of them and were saying about them, doing that not as an exercise in reckless honesty but just to be mean. I became an embarrassment to myself, finding myself in the office at odd hours of the night with various items of clothing missing or mysteriously torn. What do you say to the receptionist who wakes you at eight A.M. and you're there on the couch in the waiting area with no shoes or socks, coat or tie? Forget the explanation, what *expression* do you hold on your face while waiting for the elevator and people you have to work with are walking by in all their armor, the silky skirts and high heels and the business suits and thick-soled black wing tips, and you might as well be naked and they're staring at you?

I was arrested for drunk driving. I got my nose broken in a fistfight. I woke up with women whose names and faces and the circumstances of our introductions I could not recall—and once with a man. He had flabby breasts. At first, I thought he was an ugly old woman. I didn't know what to say to him. He had hair growing out of his ears.

There's more—more and worse—but I can't bear to tell it. A colleague, trying to console me during that bad time, said, "Years from now, you'll laugh at all this." Well, it's years from then, and I'm still not laughing.

The whole world was going crazy. Beatings and killings and brave Freedom Riding in the South, the Berlin Wall, testing nuclear bombs again, the Russian missiles in Cuba, and Marilyn Monroe committed suicide. But I can trace my troubles during this time to one specific package of craziness: my second wife.

I met her after an evening lecture at the college she attended. I was thirty; she was twenty. I was divorced; she was crazy. We had enough of those combinations (my boredom with life, her full-bore passions) to make our time together zany, and I guess that's what we each needed that winter we went together: some zaniness.

The crazy way she loved me and concentrated her fierce life-energy on me was reminiscent of Felicity, so I married the college student and she promptly dropped out of school to give me everything she had. For the first year, it was great. We worked each other into lathering fevers. We kept our dampers wide open.

Then I ran out of things to ask her to do for me. I was ready to delay at least some of my gratifications. But she was built for speed, not distance—and she was going through our lives at a dead run with her eyes closed.

Ultimately, she became tedious and embarrassing. My second wife had no natural class, no sense of personal dignity. When we argued at a restaurant, she overturned a table. When a business associate of mine said something about letting the South solve its own racial problems, my wife (who'd left the beginning civil rights movement to devote herself to me) threw a drink in his face and demanded that we leave the party. I stayed. When we flew to Hawaii for a vacation, she crowded into the toilet with me at thirty thousand feet above Denver and, giggling, tried her damnedest to engage in intercourse while the stewardess banged on the door.

I relate these incidents rather too easily, as if they're parts of a comic monologue. But there was nothing funny about any of it, no laughs when we finally came out of that airplane toilet and had to face the stewardess and the stares of all those passengers, half-turned in their seats to get a look at us. No yucks during the four hours we were detained at the airport while various law-enforcement agencies ran checks on us. None of the stuff she put us through was exciting or funny—not even in retrospect. The incidents were embarrassing when they happened and tedious to deal with afterward. Just like the entire marriage, just like her—tedious and embarrassing.

As I tried to shake loose, she held on all the more tightly. She came into town at lunchtime and searched restaurants for me. She read my mail. She bought strange outfits and rubber devices. She told me she did whatever she did because of mad love. I was not charmed; I just wanted to be left alone.

To protect myself from the serrated edges of this marriage, I drank heavily. But she wouldn't even let me do that by myself, so we drank together and our spats escalated into brawls. We got to know police officers by their first names. Lawyers, private detectives, and psychiatrists became involved in the most intimate details of our lives. Unlike my first marriage, which sort of dissolved, the second one exploded. But no mea culpa on this one. The woman was crazy.

For some reason, however, I managed to keep all the lids on fairly tightly until after the divorce was final. It was after everything was over and I was living alone again that I became careless about locking the box, that I discovered my slime was getting out everywhere. I was thirty-three when the blackouts started and I began having morning bedmates to whom I had to introduce myself. I acquired a distaste for individuals who were straight, seemingly happy with their lives, and who didn't drink or who could hold their liquor. I sought the company of people who were of a low degree, and I tried to convert my marginal friends to debauchery. To say that misery loves company isn't saying the half of it; misery is downright evangelical.

I committed a form of repeatable suicide by engaging in binges of psychotic, deranged drinking that would spill from afternoon to night to the next day and then be followed by a series of horrors: the horror of waking and not knowing where you are, followed by the horror of not remembering where you'd been or what you'd done, followed by the lingering horror of remembering gradually some of the scenes from the binge. This kind of drinking accomplishes much of what suicide accomplishes—repudiating and obliterating your life and delivering you to a blank oblivion that is a relief from a certain kind of life—but drinking does not saddle you with that permanent side effect of a successful suicide. People kill themselves (the impulse has been with me so long now that I consider it a familiar of mine) not because they want death but because they want that flash of release from life; they want to establish a profound demarcation that puts their miserable lives on one side and themselves on the other. You can, however, kill yourself only once; the wonderfully utilitarian advantage of mad-drunk binges is that although they put you over that profound line, the next morning you wake up back on this side of it. So you can do it again next week—or tomorrow. Repeatable suicide.

In the middle of all my troubles with booze and slime and the divorce-related bankruptcy, I was given a choice by my corporate superiors: I could quit (when you're a vice-president—and I was one of the youngest in the company—they call it resigning), or I could put everything back in the box from where it had crawled, be a good boy, and then maybe I could keep my job.

I wanted to quit. I wanted to run away. But I had no portable trade or skill, and I knew I couldn't move to an obscure village by the sea and be a corporate executive, which was the only thing I knew how to be. And having betrayed Felicity by leaving her the way I did, I couldn't run home to her, either.

So I tied leather thongs around my testicles and gave the loose ends to everyone I worked with. Whether or not my colleagues jerked me around (or how hard or how frequently they pulled on me) was up to them; I had no rights or defenses.

To make sure my leashes were jerked as infrequently and gently as possible, I accepted all the dirty jobs that no one else wanted and I became efficient at handling the dirt. Like a malevolent Statue of Liberty, I stood in front of my department and cried with silent lips: Give me your tired, your unpromotables, the wretched embezzlers; send me your pregnant secretaries and lovestruck administrative assistants; I lift my lamp beside farewell parties, showing employees the gate, the way out, the door. I became a bastard, the office shark. I was Lobo Businessman.

But what I didn't realize at the time was that none of this was necessary. I didn't have to do dirty work; I didn't have to do anything. Just being there, being the most highly debauched person in the place, was enough to ensure my continued employment. They wouldn't dream of getting rid of me. I was the guy with no feet.

I was ashamed at having no shoes until I met a man with no feet. Felicity once told me that it was a sucker's philosophy, a way of keeping people in their places. She said the better attitude to have would be one that goes like this: I was happy to have shoes until I met a man with hand-tooled boots.

But sucker philosophy or not, it was the philosophy that guaranteed my employment. They kept me around because I had worse problems than they did. Their indiscretions seemed less serious when compared to mine. Their wives seemed lighter burdens when weighed against mine. And none of the bastards I worked with had a drinking problem, *if you compared theirs to mine.*

I was a tonic for everyone, because I made *everyone* feel superior: from the clerks who whispered in my wake as I came stumbling back from lunch to my colleagues who sat with me during the endless series of meetings by which corporate America does its business. If people had chest colds, I was dying of lung cancer. If their children were born with cleft palates, mine were blind and suffering from Down's syndrome. Men lamented their small peters only until they found out that mine was shot off in the war.

People could say anything they wanted about me. If I forgot my place and tried to stand up for myself, they knew where to find the loose ends of those leather thongs. Everyone in the world was white, except me. I was nigger through and through.

Make them feel good? Shit. When people saw me come hobbling in on my ankle stubs, their shoeless feet absolutely danced for joy.

•   •   •

When I was thirty-three, I came home to bury my father. He had died of a heart attack; sixty-four years old. The last I saw him was at Felicity's kitchen door, the look of betrayal reflected in his face. When I try, in dreams and drunks, to recall the specific and special characteristics of his face that day, I get it mixed up with the faces of employees and lovers and wives who've gotten the word from me and then responded with that look. Or I dream that he's out there in the darkened audience with the rest of them, and I'm on stage screaming, "You're fired," or "It's over," or screaming nothing at all.

On the flight to Chicago, I made four resolutions: to stay sober while I was home, to say something at my father's casket, to cry at his grave, and to avoid at all costs visiting Felicity. In keeping these resolutions, my record was perfect. Which is to say *consistent*. In other words, I didn't keep a single one of them.

The thing I've discovered about sobriety is that when you engage in it nothing happens.

You go to lunch with someone. You chat, order food, drink ice tea. You fill the silences, look around, the food comes, you eat it. You have coffee afterward. You pay the tab and go back to the office. Nothing happens. You don't get so loud that the maître d' has to ask you ever so politely to leave the place, again. You don't become so mawkish that you tell your lunch partner how much you like and admire him, or how much you love and desire her. You don't decide to make an afternoon of it. You walk out of the restaurant the same person who walked in, unchanged by the luncheon experience. *Nothing happens.*

Or you go to a cocktail party and drink only ginger ale. You walk in and out of the various conversational knots, laughing when you're supposed to and using the time when other people are talking to think up what you're going to say when it's your turn. You compliment the hostess on her dress, her decor, her guacamole dip. And then at a respectable hour, you insist against all polite protest that you simply must leave. As much as you hate to. Because the party was such a delight. Nothing happens. You don't tell crudely inappropriate stories that make at least one person look at you with disgust, to which you respond: "Asshole!" You don't knock the guacamole dip on the white shag carpet. You don't run your hand up between the hostess's legs when she leans to offer a tidbit to the person sitting across from you. You don't have arguments with people who insist you're in no shape to drive home. You're not the last guest at the party. Next day, you don't have to send flowers and notes of apology. *Nothing happens.*

Or you go to your father's wake. You sip coffee with the mourners. You hug your mother when she remembers something that brings on another crying spell. You agree with your sister that you should have come home more often and, yes, you feel sorry now but now it's too late. When everyone leaves, you help with the dishes. Nothing happens.

Contrast that with how much happened on the second day of mourning, when I mixed vodka and orange juice half-and-half in a quart bottle that I hid in the back of the refrigerator. While everyone else drank cocoa and coffee and discussed the next day's funeral details, I drew heavily on my quart bottle and became silent and sullen. When someone asked me if I was okay, I took the opportunity to tell members of the local business community, who had dropped in to pay their respects, what my old man thought of them, what they probably thought of him—and then I delivered something of a lecture on hypocrisy in our time. Later, I gently told Mom that she should have let Dad smoke cigars in the house—and ain't *she* sorry now. And when Sis tried to quiet me, I observed that except for her delivering the world's only eight-pound, twelve-ounce premature baby, she had little reason to act superior to me. My brother-in-law finally escorted me to bed, with me telling him along the way that in his heart he probably was glad that my father kicked off 'cause now he owned the whole business himself. I was resisting him (it wasn't my bedtime), but the choke hold he used was, in my opinion, unnecessarily rough. I've been shown the door by experts, and I know the difference between a hold that's just tight enough to restrain me and one that contains extra pressure, applied as punishment. People take advantage of drunks. They'll knock you around and tell important things to you and then count on your not remembering any of it in the morning. And you don't.

The second and third resolutions, about saying something at my father's coffin and weeping at his grave, didn't work out either. I *thought* of things to say while staring at him in his satiny, pickled, and peaceful repose: I'll miss you, Dad; I never really minded picking up your cigar butts, in spite of all my protests at the time; we should have talked more; I'm sorry; I love you. But I would have felt awkward in speaking them out loud; I didn't know how they'd be taken by Mom and the other people there; I was afraid I might sound false.

Then, as I stood looking at him, I realized that nothing had changed between us. Just like when he was alive: I'd be with him and thinking of things to say but, for some reason or another, would tell him nothing that was on my mind. That's what happened when we startled each other in Felicity's kitchen. Lots of stuff going on in my head but none of it coming out of my mouth.

I considered this a great revelation. Nothing had changed between my father and me even though he was dead. I wanted to tell someone, announce to the mourners that Dad and I hadn't let death change our relationship one bit. But considering how I'd acted the previous day, I figured I had no right to say anything that might be considered controversial.

At his grave, I tried to cry for Mom's sake. I was the only one of the main characters who was dry-eyed; she, Sis, and Brother-In-Law were all but sobbing. I screwed up my face, but nothing came of it.

"You're a cold fish, Sonny," my sister said as I put suitcases in my rented car three days later.

I nodded.

"How many times have you sneaked away to see Felicity while you've been home?"

I shook my head.

"Are you going to come home and visit Mom like you should, or are you going to let the same thing happen with her that happened with Dad? Wait until it's too late and then claim you're sorry about it."

I shrugged.

Just like at the office. I'd made scum of myself, allowing all my slime to crawl out and get on me and the people around me. I couldn't defend myself against my sister's words or my mother's looks, because scum ain't got no right to talk back. Scum has to lie there and say nothing when decent people come stepping.

The fourth resolution, about not visiting Felicity, gave way to an old impulse. I'd left my mother's house, was approaching Felicity's lane, and as I was telling myself not to turn in, not to turn in, I turned in. The royal Viking chair was gone from the front yard; only the ground-level stump was left, and on it was an iron pot full of plastic flowers.

I parked in the back of the house, so no one could see my rented car from the road. The grave markers were gone, too, and I wondered if the bodies had been moved.

I shouldn't have stopped. Things might have worked out all right if I'd come home expressly to see Felicity. But three years wasn't long enough to cover what I'd done to her, not with my showing up just because I was in the area anyway, because I had to be there for my father's funeral. I knew all that.

But I did stop at her house. I needed someone to bend down to the floor where I lay and say, "Hey, Scum, you're not so bad." Someone to make me laugh. To hold me. Help drain away all that hate. I needed Felicity.

.　　　.　　　.

When I was thirty-three, I was full of hate. Hated being the butt of everyone's joke. Tired of eating alone in the kitchen, while the rest of the world was laughing it up in the well-lighted dining room. I hated being the guy with no feet. But at my office and then at my home, I couldn't say anything. When Mom and Sis asked about my wife and I told them that we'd been divorced, their faces expressed what I seriously thought one of the two (probably Sis) might actually say: "Well, what'd you expect from scum?" And I couldn't have said a damn thing in reply.

I was full of hate that I was unable to vent. It had backed up on me and soaked me through and through, soaked me so thoroughly that a finger pressed to my cheek might have caused sour hate to weep from my pores.

Felicity didn't speak to me. She just stepped back from the door so I could come in. She'd been crying, that was obvious, but in general she looked the same as she had when I left her—not *quite* three years before.

We stood there awhile, and then I sat at the kitchen table. She stared out the back window. I knew she was going to wait until I made the first move.

"He's gone, Felicity." I think that's what my mother first said to me when I arrived home: "He's gone, Sonny." I remember it sounding rather poignant, coming from Mom. From me, it was profane. I was sorry I said it; I wished I could have taken it back.

Felicity, still looking out the window, asked, "Why'd you leave me like that? Without saying anything. Making me wonder for almost three years now if I had done something to hurt you, to make you run away like you did. Why'd you do it?"

The question was not rhetorical, but I was unprepared to answer it. I thought we were going to talk about my father a little and then sort of ease into the whole topic of why I had abandoned her.

Felicity turned around and stared at me. She did indeed want an answer. I shrugged. That's when she said, "You're cold-blooded."

Here we go again, I thought. She's going to put me through the same thing they put me through at the office, the same damn thing I'd just gone through at home. My backed-up hate overflowed; I wasn't going to take it anymore. Not from Felicity, I wasn't.

"Well?" she asked.

"Well, that seems to be the general consensus."

"What does?"

"That I'm a cold-blooded bastard." I shrugged again.

She bit her lower lip. "When I think of all the faith I put in you, that investment of faith—"

"I'm not Genipur," I snapped. "I told you that before. I never was Genipur."

"You son of a bitch." She began crying—from anger. "You're not even close."

I smiled, snakelike. "This is the way you talk to a boy who's just lost his father?"

"You rotten son of a bitch. You *ignorant*, rotten son of a bitch."

"Hey, hey. I'm not ignorant about you and my father—if that's what you mean. Did I tell you that when I was staying with you, he showed up once?" I gave her a quizzical look; it felt good to be mean to someone. "I don't know if I mentioned that to you or not. That he showed up while you were out of the house and I was here alone."

Her eyes were big; she was trying to decide if she should believe me or not. And when she finally figured out that it was true, Felicity grabbed the nearest thing to her—the tea-kettle—and threw it at me. She missed, but I was splashed with warm and well-oxygenated water. I stood up and brushed my pants and shirt.

"Why didn't you tell me?" she hollered. "You stupid bastard!" White-foam spittle collected at the corners of her mouth.

But that didn't bother me. When people I'm dealing with become agitated, I crank down tightly—keeping myself as controlled as possible. It drives them all the more hysterical, which makes me even calmer. Like a snake that is patiently, efficiently swallowing a wildly kicking rabbit.

"*You rotten—*"

"Felicity," I calmly interrupted her, as if barely able to hold off a yawn, "your illicit affair with my father was not something I thought appropriate to mention while you and I were living together."

She sat in one of the kitchen chairs, slumping and talking to herself as much as to me. "He never came to see me after that summer, and I never knew why. First you leaving me for no reason and then him not coming around anymore. I couldn't figure it out. What had I done? I wondered what was wrong with me, why I was being punished like that."

"Thank God you had the decency not to show up at the funeral. Can you imagine the effect your presence would have had on my mother, the woman you've betrayed all these years?"

Felicity was astonished; she stared at me and shook her head. "You're heartless," she said softly. The kicking had stopped.

I shrugged.

"Why'd you come here?" she asked. "Just so you could hurt me some more? As if you haven't done enough. What? You figured since you were in town you might as well take the opportunity to come over and stab me one more time?"

I shrugged.

"Oh, I love that gesture. It fits you perfectly."

I shrugged again and then stood, ready to leave.

"Now he's going. Done as much damage as he can, so now it's time to leave, huh? Well, believe me, I want you out of here, too. Just one request before you go. Tell me why you left like you did that summer. Please. Just to satisfy my curiosity."

I was tempted to tell her the truth. That I had been on a leave of absence and when the time came for me to go back to work, I simply didn't have the courage to explain I was going back to my office in New York—not after I'd been letting her believe, all the time we were together, that I'd left the business world. That I had left it for her.

But then I thought: No, you don't want to blunder into using the truth; it's too powerful to use willy-nilly, without proper consideration.

So I toyed with the idea of saying something romantic, telling her I knew what we had going that summer would have a conclusion but that I couldn't bear to face the conclusion, to suffer through a farewell, so I departed abruptly, without saying anything.

No. Shit. She'd see through that.

Then I realized how alive I was feeling, how much it had helped me to be mean to Felicity. My backed-up hate was flowing freely. That's what she meant to me: The only person in the world who was eligible for my anger and hate and frustration. So, finally, I decided I'd answer her question by being frivolous and cruel.

"The reason I left, Felicity, is because the Gravēda story was finished. Oh, I know—you said there was more to come, but

I didn't believe you. Gravēda and Genipur had sailed away, and I knew the story was over. Why should I stick around after that? It was The End."

Felicity came over and put her hand on my shoulder, making me flinch. "No, no—nothing to worry about," she said. "I just want you to sit down and listen to something."

I didn't like the sound of her voice, which was cold and calm. Like mine: "I really have to be going. Got to drive all the way to Chicago, you know." But when she pushed hard on my shoulders, I sat.

"You can't leave just yet. Why, I've just discovered what made you abandon me, and I want to rectify matters. There *is* more to the story."

"Really? Oh, well—my mistake," I said brightly.

Felicity brushed her eyes with the backs of her hands and sat next to me. "I'll tell you the end of the story, the real end. Then you can leave for good."

So she was trying to play snake with me, huh? With *me*, the supreme snake. "Gee, I'd love to hear it, but . . ." I checked my watch. "No time. I'll catch you next trip home."

"This'll only take a minute. Remember when Eller gave Gravēda the crystal heart and told her that the end of her story was inside? Well, that's the part you haven't heard yet. What Eller wrote and put inside the heart."

"Son of a gun. There really was more. Darn."

Felicity smiled. "Sure. Want to hear it?"

I smiled. "No. Just not that curious anymore."

"Oh, come on. Only take a few minutes. It'll give you something else to make fun of."

I consulted my watch again. "Okay. But make it quick."

"It'll be quick, all right."

"Fine. Go to it."

She recited for half an hour or so, but this one was different—not like the old recitations. I never figured out if Felicity worked through the Gravēda story in her mind before telling it to me, or if she had written the story and committed it to memory, or what. But those old recitations were smooth and beautifully spoken. Not this one. As she sat there at the table and told me the ending, she stumbled and hesitated and repeated herself—as if she were grasping for things to say and didn't know what was coming next. Not like old times at all.

When she finished, she stared provocatively at me. I realized how innocent she really was, thinking that a bitter and unhappy ending was enough to crush me.

I intended to disappoint her. "A sad ending, huh? Well, there's a lot of that going around these days."

Felicity was taken aback, not knowing what to do next.

I, however, was on a roll. "Have to hit the road now, Felicity. Don't want to miss my plane and be late getting in to New York. That would upset my wife." I figured Felicity hadn't heard about the divorce yet, so I could get away with making the point: "She's only twenty-three, you know. A woman in her twenties—*mercy*. Every time I see her naked, stepping out of the shower or something like that, it makes me want to beat my head against the table. Lord. I should've brought her here and introduced you two to each other, but a young woman like that doesn't want to attend a funeral. They're too alive at that age to be bothered with death. Alive and hot—but you can remember those times, can't you?"

Felicity went around to the side of the table and picked the teakettle from the floor. She put it back on the stove. "So is that it? You want to play games, see who can be the cruelest?"

I shrugged and went to the door.

"Wait," she said, "I'll play. But let's really pull out all the stops. So far, we've just been dancing around. A lot crueler things can be said than have been said so far."

"I don't know what you're talking about."

"You don't? Let me see if I can explain. Your father, for instance. He knew how to treat a woman. Do you know what that means?"

"I don't care what it means."

"You probably think it's something sexual, that's the depth

of your understanding. You have no idea what a woman really means when she says that about a man: He knows how to treat a woman."

"Don't fuck with me, Felicity. Not on something like being cruel. I wrote the book."

"You did? That's a laugh. Okay, if you're such an expert, go ahead and give me your best shot."

"Not interested." I opened the door.

"Wait. I'm not done yet. Remember when I told you that you were *so big*"—she opened her eyes in mock surprise—"that I was afraid you might split me in half? Remember me saying that to you? And how you *believed* it? I should tell you that it's just one of the things a woman will say to an inept lover. To make him feel better about himself and his inadequacies. But now that we're being painfully honest with each other—"

"None of this is bothering me, Felicity." I lighted a cigarette and took a step outside. "I think it's kind of pathetic, to tell you the truth."

She came to the door, holding it open as she spoke. "You wouldn't know the truth if you found it in your pants some morning, Stubby."

I laughed.

"Do you remember I told you that you were making me sore? 'So sore I can hardly walk.'" She laughed. "Just another one of those things I tell clumsy lovers. Except that most of 'em are bright enough to see through it. Not you, though. Oh, no—not you. You took all those little lies to heart. You let 'em puff you up like a toad."

I shrugged and blew out smoke. "That your best shot? You done now?"

"I was laughing at you the whole time you were with me, Nubbin."

I sighed dramatically. "So you were laughing at me. Glad to be of service. Now you're boring the shit out of me." I turned and walked back toward my car.

"And this!" she shouted—shouted so loudly and emotionally that I was suckered into turning around to face her. I wish I hadn't. Felicity had opened the top of her blouse and even from where I was, several feet away, I could see the tattoo. In the sunlight, it seemed brighter, more brilliant than it ever had before. The green leaves, red heart, three dancing blue tears. Because of the game she and I were playing, I tried to act unimpressed. But I was impressed.

"I never got this for you," she said, her voice strained. "I got this for a real man!"

I hadn't seen it coming. Not that. I wanted to brush it off, wanted to say to her: So what, I knew it all along. But I couldn't force that lie out of my suddenly constricted throat. Felicity had reached me. Because, god damn it, I had believed her when she told me that she got the tattoo for me—that she got it because her heart cried for *me*. Against all logic and evidence, *I had believed her.*

I don't know what my face was showing, but Felicity's was full of regret. I think she was about to apologize, maybe even reverse herself and say that she was telling the truth the first time: The tattoo was mine.

But before she could speak, I cleared my throat to make sure it'd work and then said, said as coldly as I could: "All you ever were to me, Felicity, was a convenient piece of ass."

She slumped in the doorway, shaking her head and saying with a trace of panic in her voice, "No. No, Baby. *No.*"

I took a last drag off my cigarette and flipped it in a high arch. "So long, slut." I said it with such terrible effectiveness, making the word sound like a flat hand slapping against thick mud, that I thought it deserved to be repeated. "*Slut.*"

Then I left, Felicity whimpering so authentically that you'd think I'd hit her with a stick. I got in the car and when I drove past her, she reached out with one hand and a prolonged cry of grief and pain. Like something from the Old World.

GRAVĒDA

The part Felicity told me when I was thirty-three and home to bury my father.

44. After Genipur and Gravēda sail arm in arm into the sunset, they put out a sea anchor and nestle among water barrels and supply bundles for a fulfilling evening on the ocean. Fat chance. Their wedding night is stormy; Gravēda gets sick and, fearing she's about to be tossed overboard, locks herself in the forward hold; Genipur stays up until dawn, bailing and cursing.

By noon of the next day, the storm is over, the water is flat, and the newlyweds seem to be smack dab in the middle of the ocean. When Gravēda tells Genipur this is the first time she's been out of land's sight, he responds with a nervous smile. His first time, too—he suddenly realizes.

For a week more, they sail and see nothing but the sea. And then a week after that. The sun, shining on them directly and reflecting off the water onto them, seems little pleased that they've taken up its course again. Hot. Stays hot. The food runs low, the sweetwater even lower.

Gravēda's only joy has been watching ravens crash into the ocean. They began following the boat its second day out to sea, and some of them were bold enough to land on the mast—or the prow, if Genipur and Gravēda were back toward the stern. She attacked them crazily, stepping on supplies and whipping her sword around in ways that threatened to cut the sails loose, to decapitate the bewildered Genipur. He tried to subdue her, asking again why the ravens have it in for her; she refused to answer; they argued. Genipur threatened to look it up in the story Eller had given them, pages bound in leather, and Gravēda told him to go ahead but don't pester her. She couldn't be bothered while she was on raven watch. But as they sailed farther and farther from land, Gravēda realized that the ravens were flying beyond their range. Some of them turned back reluctantly, too tired to caw, and others were so weary that they landed right next to her, even though that was the death of them. And then the ravens simply began to crash into the ocean.

"Look at 'em, look at 'em!" Gravēda shouts as the feathery black forms lose altitude near the boat and then land in the water, as if the birds expect the ocean to support them. They flop around, floating for a moment with their beaks open wide in exhaustion and their startled eyes on Gravēda—holding her accountable for this, too. Then they sort of spread out on the water's surface, black flotsam all around Genipur and Gravēda's boat.

"Sail on, little sailor," she tells him. "I hope the whole flock tries to follow us." Another one crashes, to the starboard. "Atta way, sucker!" Gravēda laughs; she thinks this is great fun.

But then the ravens are gone and soon after that, so is the last of the sweetwater. A squall, quick and violent as a sneeze, provides three days' worth of rationed water but when that is gone, tongues thicken and panic creeps.

Gravēda and Genipur are thinking the same thing: Turn back, turn back. But neither wants to be the first to say it, and as long as it goes unsaid, they don't act upon it.

Sailing on, not speaking because they are weak and because what either could say, neither wants to hear. Past the point now where the hardiest of the early travelers ever reached; they, too, were frightened and thirsty and convinced that the world of water is endless. And always in those boats and rafts launched by the travelers when they first came to the beach, there was at least one who said what was on everyone's mind: Turn back, turn back. And so they did, many of them dying before they reached the beach again and none of them going beyond the point that Gravēda and Genipur now have passed, silent and frightened and dying but daring not to say, Turn back—at least not saying it out loud.

Looking up at the white sky and half delirious with thirst, Gravēda sees or thinks she sees a bird resting—perhaps even nesting—on top of the mast. Even if it is a dream, she has to act out her part: wielding the big oar clumsily and managing to hit the huge bird only because it is even clumsier. But this is no raven— two, three, four times the size of a raven. And this bird is white. Gravēda bludgeons it anyway, eager for the relief its warm blood might provide. Too weak to subdue the large creature, Gravēda watches as it flops overboard. The bird tries repeatedly and without success to get airborne. Its wings are broken. Serves you right, Gravēda wants to say, but the only thing that gets past her swollen tongue and cracked lips is a thin and breathy grunt. Then she closes her eyes and leans back against Genipur, who does not respond and who, Gravēda thinks, probably already is dead.

The next thing she remembers is heaven—or what she assumes to be heaven. What else would feel like this, like cool sweetwater splashed on her face by Genipur's laughing, almost dancing, spirit?

"Two springs," he tells her. "Just a short walk and already I've found two springs. And a bee tree. We'll have honey!"

"Honey?" she mutters, sitting up to drink greedily from the skinbag that Genipur holds to her lips.

"What?" he asks.

"Huh?" she responds, confused.

"It's an island," he says. "A big, big island. And the rabbits, did I tell you about the rabbits? They must've never seen a man before, because they're so tame you can walk right up and grab them."

"Rabbits? Sweet, juicy, plump rabbits?"

"Yes! Would you like one for dinner?"

Gravēda is out of the boat and gathering rabbits before Genipur can get a fire going.

They stay on that island two months, until they are strong again and have restocked their boat. Then one dusk, without even discussing it, they push the boat away from the rocks and head again for the setting sun. The rabbits, who've known no enemies on that island except for their own cycles of over-population and starvation, gather at the edge of the underbrush to watch Genipur and Gravēda sail away. The rabbits can't quite figure it out, although now their manner bears traces of a nervous wariness that was never there before.

Gravēda and Genipur find other islands, some of them barren but most providing sweetwater, fresh fruit, and trusting little mammals that are highly edible. The newlyweds seldom run out of supplies before reaching each successive island, and they figure this is the way it's supposed to be—God providing for them. They watch for signs that they're getting nearer to where He waits, if not for them, for their offspring: The One. But the quality of the islands doesn't seem to change, the water no sweeter, the fruit no fresher, and the little edible mammals no more trusting than before.

"Let's make our baby," Gravēda tells Genipur one afternoon when they are swimming for recreation near their boat, the last island barely out of sight and the next one just now marring the horizon.

"What've we been doing all these weeks, months—whatever it's been?" Genipur asks. "Supposedly, I've been capable of impregnating you ever since my mother died and we were married."

"Yes, but we haven't really been trying. We've been fooling around, for the fun of it. Let's get serious."

"How do we do that?"

It's the question she was waiting for.

The ocean is especially flat and especially warm; Gravēda and Genipur are especially naked. She floats high in the water, relative to Genipur. "Come here," Gravēda whispers, smiling as if she knows precisely what to do.

When Genipur is close, Gravēda uses her legs to lift him and lock him tightly to her. In fact, he sort of clambers aboard. They float there, they soak there, and that's how The One came to be conceived: on the open sea with the warm saltwater mixing in with everything and perhaps even helping to transport Genipur's contribution.

Gravēda takes to pregnancy as though it were the natural state for her to be in, and all through that pregnancy, she and Genipur wait for signs: that God is near, that God has acknowledged the impending birth of The One, *something*. But the only unusual development is Gravēda's increasing appreciation for being in the sea, which relieves the effects that gravity has on the growing mass at the center of her.

"It's time," she tells Genipur peacefully one afternoon. This is not something she's going to rush through in a panic, not after a lifetime of preparing for it.

"We can go back to land," he offers. Just that morning, they left an island and no other is in sight to the front of them.

Gravēda shakes her head. "There's only one place for this child to be born," she says, undressing and then holding on to Genipur's shoulder as she carefully climbs over the side of the boat.

"Are you sure?" When Gravēda nods and motions for Genipur to join her, he's relieved. So glad she knows what she's doing, and all he has to do is follow directions.

Following directions then, Genipur treads water and holds Gravēda's ankles high and apart. With easy backstrokes of her arms, she keeps her upper half afloat. And that's how The One came to be born: slipping easily from one embryonic pool to another.

"Maybe this is where God's going to meet up with our boy," Genipur speculates when, three days after the birth of their son, they land on an almost perfectly round island with rolling hills of wood and meadow, as if a chunk of land they came from (near where Genipur's mother was buried, for example) has been put out to sea.

"I don't think that's the way it works," Gravēda says softly so she doesn't disturb The One at her breast. "I don't think this guy gets to meet God until after you and I are dead and gone."

"Says who?" Genipur demands angrily. He doesn't like the idea of not being in on the action.

But Gravēda just shrugs; it seems that all the argument in her has been pacified.

They end up staying on that almost perfectly round island five years, telling themselves that they're doing it for the child's sake, that it would be a tragedy if the string of islands they've been following were to run out and the boy had to suffer as they suffered in the beginning of the voyage—that you can't take those kind of chances when you're responsible for The One who's actually, really going to meet God.

But the truth is that Genipur and Gravēda are tired of sailing; the best parts of the trip have been those times, weeks and months, they spent on various islands.

Eventually, however, they do what they must: Genipur rebuilds the boat, and they launch out again—sailing for years and years. They linger at each island that offers, in even the most marginal of ways, the prospect of being the kind of place God might stay. They camp for a year on an island that boasts, steaming and spitting, a live volcano, but nothing comes of it.

And The One (which is what they call their son, who is a teen-ager) doesn't like that island. By now he's been on the sea more than on land, and the trees and rocks and lack of a clear panorama frighten him. Who knows what's hiding behind all those things, over that next hill, on the other side of the volcano? The One feels safer on the ocean, where he can stand up in the boat, turn completely around, and no matter where he looks, can see all the way to the horizon. The idea that scary things might be *below* never occurs to him.

He constantly pesters his parents for more stories about the original journey, the twenty years his mother was separated from the tribe, and everything that happened on the beach. Gravēda finally digs out the leather-bound pages that Eller wrote and tells her son to read for himself; neither she nor Genipur have read the story thoroughly. They used to glance through it, but they were unable to make sense of what Eller had written.

To The One, however, Eller's story is clear and magical. "Did all these things really happen?" he asks Gravēda.

"Like what?"

He reads her a long section, and she laughs. "No. Mercy, no. That never happened, not like he's saying it did."

The One pulls his father aside one night while they're camping on a beach. The boy reads what Eller says happened between Genipur and Gravēda when they were in her cave.

"What?" Genipur asks, leaning over his son so he can see the pages. "Nothing like that happened. I don't think it's such a good idea for you to be reading Eller's story—at least not parts like that."

Genipur tells Gravēda that she should take the pages away from the boy, but when their son refuses to give up the story, neither parent forces the matter. They indulge their child; what else can you do when you're rearing The One who will meet God?

Then one day Genipur gets eaten up by a shark. And it happens just that abruptly.

He is in the water, checking on a leak near the bow, when he yelps. Gravēda asks what's wrong, and he says something bumped him, something under the water bumped him hard and now he thinks his leg is bleeding. "Well, get out of there," Gravēda advises, but her advice comes too late. Genipur is gone as quickly as the last duckling in a row, its soft leathery webbed foot snapped tight by fifty pounds of submerged turtle, which pulls the little fluff ball, the ounce or two of duckling meat, under the water so fast that there's no opportunity for protest.

That's it. No more Genipur, not even little parts of him bobbing to the surface to horrify Gravēda and The One. Genipur is gone so suddenly that it seems he never was there in the water to start with.

Gravēda uselessly slaps at that water with her sword, as if to wound the ocean itself. She insists upon staying in the area for the rest of the day, that night, and most of the next day, telling her son strange speculations about underwater caves and air pockets and the chance ("Just a slim one, but a chance just the same") that Genipur still is alive.

When finally they sail on, she no longer is able to hold off the reality: Sweet Genipur is dead and gone. It makes her a bit crazy.

Gravēda and The One stay for several months on the next island. Hoping to lift and reinforce her spirits, The One asks Gravēda about something in Eller's story—one of the early parts about how mighty Gravēda had mastered walking, allowing nothing to stop, deter, detour her.

But Gravēda angrily brushes away his attention: "Didn't I tell you? A thousand times I've told you. That stuff in there isn't true. It's a pack of lies written by a crazy old man. Lies! You hear me? Lies, all lies!"

They sail on, Gravēda wondering if perhaps Genipur's death was the first sign from God—that He is eager to get the parents out of the way so He can at long last meet The One. Eagerness wouldn't seem to be an attribute of God but, still, Gravēda eyes her son with a new wariness.

The One, now a young man, also is contemplating the various aspects, the possible confirmations, of his divinity. He recalls how he discovered he was The One, how his parents let him figure that out on his own. They repeatedly told him the creed, how the tribe was destined to continue traveling toward the setting sun, no one getting married until both his parents were dead, and then each couple producing only one child, so that the tribe would dwindle, each generation half the size of the preceding one, until finally there would be sixteen, who produced eight, who produced four, who produced two, and those two would have a child who would be The One, the final product of the tribe—a representation of distilled faith and The One who would meet God. That's why the tribe was created: to distill faith into its purest form and then deliver that faith to God, who was out there somewhere waiting for it.

When the boy finally realized that all the travelers who went on the return journey with Nestus didn't count and that his parents, Gravēda and Genipur, truly were the last two authentic travelers, he knew then that he must be The One.

It was a shock, concluding that he was The One who would meet God, and for years he didn't mention it to his parents, thinking they might laugh at him—maybe even punish him, as unprecedented as that would be—for arriving at such a grandiose and sacrilegious conclusion.

But when he finally did mention it to Genipur and Gravēda—beginning hesitantly and then continuing in a rush of questions and explanations—their faces told him he was right even before they had a chance to say anything.

"But why didn't you tell me?" he asked. "Why'd you let me go through all this worry?"

"We didn't want to alarm you," Genipur said.

"How would you have felt," Gravēda asked, "if we came up to you one day and said, 'Oh, by the way, someday you're going to meet God face-to-face'? We decided it'd be better to give you just the background information."

And then Genipur added: "We knew you'd be ready to handle the *conclusion* when you were old enough to figure it out for yourself. This had to come about naturally, in its own time."

As The One gets older, he sometimes doubts the creed. If he's going to meet God, The One wonders, why doesn't he feel special; why is it that he occasionally thinks evil thoughts, does nasty things at night, and hates like hell his destiny—at least the part that means he'll never be married, never lie with a woman? Would the product of distilled faith have lustful thoughts about his own mother?

But as a man, now traveling alone with a mother who's too old and bitter to elicit lust, The One reads and rereads Eller's story. It seems so magically true that The One decides he'll meet God after all. What will God look like? Will there be a ceremony of some sort? How will God use the distilled faith that The One is delivering to Him? And are these questions answered on the pages Eller stuffed into that crystal heart?

"Let's break it open and see what happens," the man says to his mother.

"No," Gravēda answers. "You know the deal. I don't care how often you read that story Eller gave us, but you are not going to break the Passionate One's crystal heart—never."

"But if Eller's story is a pack of lies, like you always say, then what's in the heart probably is a lie, too—so what does it matter if we take a peek at it?"

"No. No!"

"But why not?"

"No, no, no!"

Even though Gravēda realizes she has turned out to be exactly like her mother (bitter about the events of her life, especially the premature death of her husband, and taking it all out on her child), she can't seem to do anything about it. That's a terrible helplessness, watching your child look at you with the same contempt you held for your own parents and seeing all sides of it (why your parents did what they did, why you hated them for it, and why your child hates you for being the same way) except for the side that would explain why you're unable to break the cycle.

Then one day Gravēda dies. She'd been sick for weeks, the victim of one of her many experiments in the edibility of new animals she came across. Eat it first and see if it disagrees with you later, that was her motto.

She'd picked a slimy-looking green frog off a tree limb and, to her son's disgust, immediately fried it on a stick and ate it with great relish. The next day she was deathly ill.

"It was the frog, Momma," The One said, putting hot compresses on her tender old belly.

"I think it was that great relish you concocted," Gravēda replied, thinking: The boy's trying to kill me so he can hurry up and meet God.

"It contained nothing but natural ingredients."

Don't be an ass, she thinks—but dares not say such a thing to someone who's going to meet God.

Gravēda is given close care by her son, held tightly by him when she dies, and then buried deep on the western slope of an island. At the head of her grave, he puts a large stake that is sharpened at one end—the end facing the setting sun. Then he brews several jugs of coconut distillate and places those on the grave. These are statements: that his mother was headed in the right direction and that when she died she represented faith at least partially distilled.

The One stays on the island for several years, waiting for

God to show up. Then he builds a new boat and launches out for the next island, figuring God will be there—and if not there, on the *next* one, or surely on the one after that.

Then The One becomes old, spending more time on land than on the sea, because sailing is hard work and he is tired. No sign of God, and the man isn't even tempted to break open the crystal heart and read the ending, because now he fears the worst and doesn't want those fears confirmed.

Then one day he drowns. And that's the end.

He'd almost drowned a couple of months before, when his boat was becalmed and he had to tie a rope around his waist and get out and swim, laboriously pulling the boat out of those doldrums.

The ocean was his medium, the place where he was conceived and born, and he never feared it until that day he nearly drowned. What scared and angered him most, however, was the idea that his life could have ended so *accidentally*.

He knew he was going to die, because he was old and tired and had become tender. His mind had to work his body in the same way a master works his old and favorite draft horse: with cajolements and affectionate threats and other efforts at convincing the ancient animal to do the work it once did prancingly.

The man was able to accept that, to live with the close prospect of death. But it really pissed him off that he could die accidentally, just slip below the ocean in the middle of a windless day, gone without witnesses or exclamations. No God, no nothing.

To ensure that some sort of record was left, The One carefully wrapped the leather-bound pages of Eller's story and buried them (along with the crystal heart, which needed no special preservation) on the next island he came to after that day he almost drowned.

In his heart of hearts, the man still believed he'd meet God. He wasn't thinking about meeting Him in heaven, which is where *anyone* can meet God. No. The whole idea of being The

One was to see and talk with God, to deliver yourself and your distilled faith to God, while you still were alive.

Even after the man buried Eller's story and Eller's unread ending, he was convinced he'd meet God before he died. "It'll probably be *right before* I die," he concluded. "In that last instant of life."

But he was wrong. Ha-ha. One day, out in the ocean and not in sight of land, he achingly climbed over the side of his boat to cool off in the water. He got a cramp, was unable to swim, and drowned—just like that. No witnesses, no exclamations, no God. And that's the end.

His body fell to the bottom of the sea and what wasn't eaten by little fishies just rotted away. The end, the end, the end.

WHEN I WAS
THIRTY-
FIVE

When I was thirty-five, I moved into New York City from the suburbs where I'd lived with my wives ever since coming east eleven years before. I finally decided to move into the city when I realized the only interesting scenes I ever saw in the suburbs were those of men walking their dogs and then standing there and holding the leashes and looking off into the distance while the dogs shit. These scenes became too painful for me to watch any longer; in my entire life, I've never seen anything more undignified than a full-grown man waiting for and being leashed to a dog that's trying to shit. Man was not meant to end up in such a position, and I couldn't bear watching it any longer.

I suppose men are leashed to shitting dogs in the city, too, but at least the city offers a variety of other scenes. When still living in the suburbs, I would wait for my train by having a drink in a Grand Central Station bar so I could look out the window and watch the dramas. Men walked by, and on their faces were stricken expressions; I wondered what had just happened to them. Had they just been fired, which is another form of repeatable death? Or women walked by with smiles on their faces, and I wondered if they'd just been laid, or proposed to, or promoted, or what. I would sit there and watch a series of middle-aged men and slightly younger women come into the station as couples; at some predetermined point, they would hug and kiss and then part sadly. The same couples, night after night. The men, going home to families (wives and kids and dogs who needed to shit) in the suburbs, seemed not quite as sad as did the women, who had to turn around and leave the station so they could walk slowly to their empty apartments.

I thought if I lived *in* the city, I'd eventually figure out who was in charge of all this, who directed the scenes. One morning when new telephone books were being delivered, I saw a shaky drunk lifting Yellow Pages from the back of a truck, and I wondered who awoke him early that morning and made sure he got to where he was supposed to go. I thought for sure someone was in control of all the thousands of scenes you can see when you walk through the city, someone coordinating the flow of cabs and cops, the placement of sawhorses around open manholes, the stationing of bag ladies and pretzel vendors and hot-watch hustlers on their respective corners, and the assigning of creeps to their subway trains. And who meets those creeps when they get home after the evening rush hour? Who listens to their confessions ("I was a bad boy today; when they rubbed up against me, it got hard and I put my hand down there and . . ."); absolves them so they can be sent on their way early enough the next morning to catch that rush hour, too?

I moved into the city to get answers to these questions, but I have subsequently discovered that no one is in control. There is no director. The stage is vast and we all have the most minor of parts, making up our lines as we go or just walking on, and it is a mistake to call this art, although some people do. I once did.

Sy Lamont helped me find the first apartment I had in the city. It was in the building where he and his mother lived; after he retired, they moved to Florida.

Sy, also an employee in the corporation, spent about half his time out in the field, checking on our regional offices to make sure they were implementing our corporate plans correctly. As part of my punishment for being a bad boy who let his slime get loose, I was assigned to travel with Sy "to get some field experience." We were on the road together for almost three months.

Sy wore too much jewelry and he dressed brashly, in colors too bright and styles too trendy for my corporate tastes. He had a slight build and tiny feet. He was almost completely bald. Although Sy sometimes acted queerly, morose and moody and making comments that were too caustic to be shrugged off by regional-office executives who resented us home-office types in the first place, most of the time he was friendly and ready with jokes and able to make people laugh.

After we were on the road together for a month or so, a

hotel in Detroit didn't have a room for me even though I had guaranteed one for late arrival. While the hotel management searched the city for a room, Sy and I were put in the bar and given complimentary drinks. But after an hour, when a room still hadn't been found for me, Sy asked the front desk if his room had twin beds (it did) and then suggested that I stay with him for the night. I did.

After the obligatory cracks about two men staying together, we turned off the lights and went to bed. Sy spoke in the dark: "It's a shame the way people treat each other."

Wary that he was going to start asking me about the trouble I'd been in (something bad enough to get me sent out into the field with him), I just grunted and acted as if I were half asleep.

"When I was a boy," he continued after a moment, "the kids in my neighborhood tormented this old woman who had two apple trees in her backyard. We'd wreck her fence and steal apples, steal 'em just so we could throw them on her roof late at night."

I still didn't say anything.

"Rumor was she had a glass eye, and everybody told stories about how she was a witch and if she ever caught you, she'd try to get you to drink her potions that would make your fingernails curl and twist like corkscrews or would make your hair fall out or something. I can't remember all the stories. The kids in the neighborhood, me included, made life hell for her. People can be so cruel."

I was thinking: You're telling me, Buddy. Then I got the idea that Sy was working himself up to say something about the way I'd been treated around the office—perhaps to defend me or to apologize on behalf of everyone else. The possibility of someone sticking up for me made my throat feel funny, as if it were going into the pre-cry stages. I remembered how that felt from when I was a kid.

"Then one afternoon she caught me," Sy said.

The old lady with the glass eye caught him? When Sy didn't continue, I had to ask. "What happened?"

"Hmm? Oh. Well, I'd been in her yard throwing apples over the fence to some friends and she sneaked up and got me by the wrist before I could get out of there. I thought she was going to put me in the oven or something."

Again, he became silent, and I wondered if he was falling asleep. "What did she do?"

"She was as nice as she could be. Gave me apple pie and ice cream. All she wanted to know was why all the kids were so mean to her. Was it something she had done or what? I didn't have any answers. We didn't have any reason for tormenting her. She was just someone to pick on. It seems like every neighborhood has someone like that. You know what I mean?"

Of course I knew what he meant. I was the old lady of the office, the one everybody picked on. *Sy understood.* I was ready to go over to his bed and give him a big hug, because it'd been a long time since anyone had been this nice to me.

"I stayed with that old lady all afternoon. She told me about her childhood, and she explained how her eye was put out. In a train wreck when she was a young woman. Then she asked me if I'd like to see it, just so I'd know that it wasn't such a terrible thing."

"What? Her glass eye?"

"Yeah. I was scared, but once she took it out and handed it to me, I was fascinated. There in my hand, that glass eye didn't seem so horrible. I told her that if the rest of the kids knew she was so nice, they wouldn't steal her apples anymore. I couldn't wait to tell them I'd actually held a glass eye in my hand. The old lady said that if I brought my friends to her house, she'd bake us some cookies and would show everybody her false eye."

Sy was quiet for a moment and although I wanted to know how things turned out with the old lady, I didn't think it was a good idea to try to speak just then.

"So I left her house and as I walked away, I turned around and asked her if she was sure it was okay for me to bring my friends there—so they could see everything I'd seen. And she came out on the porch and said . . ."

"Yeah?"

When Sy next spoke, his voice was in cackling mimicry of an old lady's—a witch's—voice: "Okay, Honey, I'll keep an eye out for you."

I didn't think it was funny, to be betrayed like that. And apparently neither did Sy, because instead of laughing, he was silent. In fact, neither one of us spoke another word that night; we just lay awake and hoped for sleep.

Everything was different after that. I put a distance between Sy and me, and he accepted it. I didn't criticize him for what he'd done, and he didn't apologize. We just never mentioned it.

On our way back to New York, the road trip finally over and the two of us in the Red Carpet Club at O'Hare for an hour's layover, we became friendly again. I knew I wouldn't be working with him anymore and figured I might as well try to end the whole experience on a positive note. I got to talking about growing up on the prairie, telling him about how I used to go rabbit hunting and the kind of gun I had and how well my dogs worked the rabbits.

"There was a big park by our house," Sy said, "and back in those days there were lots of rabbits in the park. I used to sleep out there in the summer when it was hot in my room, and one night about midnight, I saw thirty-five rabbits dancing."

I gave him one quick astonished look and then laughed. "Oh, brother."

"What?"

"You're setting me up for another one of your jokes, only this one is so obvious that even I'm not dumb enough to fall for it."

"What're you talking about?" He seemed genuinely confused.

"Oh, come on, Sy. Just tell me the punch line and get it over with."

He shrugged and picked up a magazine.

"Go on," I said. "I'll bite. Why were these rabbits dancing?"

"I don't know. They'd move back and forth at the edge of the park, moving like fish in a school or a flock of birds—back and forth in perfect coordination. Every once in a while, they'd stop and feed, and then they'd go back to dancing."

"Thirty-five rabbits, huh?"

"Yes. I counted 'em. I was hiding in some bushes, and I counted them. I couldn't believe it myself."

"Sy?"

"What?"

"Tell me the joke."

He smiled. "There is no joke. I really saw those rabbits dancing. Listen, if I was making this up, I could make it sound a lot more interesting than I have. You know. 'Ten thousand I saw at a glance, toss their heads in lively dance.' "

I didn't know what he was referring to.

"The only value this story has is that it's true, it really happened."

He was so sincere that I had to fight against believing him. "Right. Now. What happened with those dancing rabbits, Sy?" I asked in a smarmy voice.

He laughed. "*Nothing*. Well, there was the dog."

"Ah. *The dog*. Of course. And what happened with the dog, Sy?"

"You turd. I ain't telling you anything more. Let's go. They should be boarding our plane by now."

"Hey, hey, Sy Baby. You've invested all this time and effort in your little story here, and I want to hear the punch line."

He seemed exasperated. "There is no punch line. Okay. The dog came up and stopped there to watch the rabbits, just like I was doing. I thought maybe the rabbits were dancing as some sort of defense thing—you know, to confuse dogs so they wouldn't attack. But if that's why they were dancing back and forth, it didn't work. The dog went right down there and grabbed one of 'em."

"And the moral of the story is . . ."

"No moral. The dog just grabbed one of the rabbits and trotted away, the rabbit squealing to beat the band. The amazing thing was that the other rabbits just kept up their dancing, running back and forth at the edge of the park like they were crazy or something."

"All of which means . . ."

Sy stood, took his briefcase from the floor, and started for the door. "Hey," I called. "Just 'cause I caught on to you and figured out this was a joke is no reason for you to get mad."

"I'm not mad. It's just that all of this is going nowhere. Why continue it?"

As we walked to our gate, I asked: "So nothing else happened, huh? 'Ten thousand you saw at a glance, toss their heads in lively dance.' And then you went home and slept the rest of the night in your own room, right?"

"Actually, there were only thirty-four. The dog, you know. After I saw how they ignored that dog, I figured I could walk right down in the middle of those rabbits and maybe they'd let me pet them, or I could lie down in the grass and they'd run back and forth right over the top of me."

"And?"

"And I was wrong. As soon as I stepped out from the bushes where I was hiding, the rabbits took off."

"And then you heard your mother calling you for breakfast and realized the whole thing was a dream."

"No. Then I went down there and saw where the rabbits had been feeding on clover. I saw pellets, and I saw tufts of fur where the dog had taken that one rabbit. It wasn't a dream. It really happened. I went to that same spot night after night, but I never saw another rabbit. At least I didn't see any dancing, dancing in the moonlight the way those thirty-five did. Their fur showing different shades as they went back and forth."

Once on the plane, I said, "For the final time, Sy. What's the punch line to that rabbit story?"

He looked at me and said straightly, "For the final time, there is no punch line. It was an amazing thing I once saw, and I thought I'd tell you about it. That's all."

A few years after that, Sy retired and moved to Florida with his mother. He called me one New Year's Eve; he was drunk and there was a party in the background. "I just wanted to tell you," he hollered over the noise, "that you got the wrong idea about that stuff I told you. About the old lady with the glass eye—it was true. The only reason I made a joke out of it at the end was because I think something was happening in that room, something that both of us would have regretted. But you were right about the rabbits. That was just a joke and the only reason I didn't tell you the punch line was 'cause I didn't want to give you the satisfaction of having caught on to it."

We talked about old times for a few minutes and then I said I had to hang up 'cause I was late for the party I was going to that night. I believed him about the dancing rabbits being a tall tale, but I still wasn't convinced the story about the old lady was true.

The whole episode nagged my mind so much that I called him a few months later and asked him if there really was an old lady with a glass eye, and did she really live in his neighborhood and once show him the eye—let him hold it in his hand?

He said it was a joke, a joke he had pulled on a lot of people. "But the rabbits," Sy said, "the rabbits I really saw. Thirty-five of 'em—until the dog came along."

"You're full of shit."

"That could be, but I saw those rabbits."

We talked several more times after that, Sy always changing his story so that sometimes I was convinced that nothing he had told me was true and other times I thought that maybe there really was an old lady with a glass eye or that maybe Sy did see dancing rabbits at midnight. Then he died, and now I don't know what to think.

I'll never forgive Sy. Sometimes in life you get swept up with events or you become thoughtless, and you hurt people without knowing why you did it or how, exactly, it happened. But there's no excuse for being mean with the stories you tell, 'cause you can make the stories come out any way you want. I'll never forgive him for doing what he did to me.

WHEN I WAS
FORTY-
FIVE

*T*ears are a lot like erections in that when you have to force them, they come across limply and hardly seem worth the effort, but when they arrive of their own accord without your having prompted them or even thought about them, then they are wonderful gifts—full and honest—that you give to yourself.

The tears I shed at my mother's funeral made me feel good about myself, which is quite an accomplishment when you consider how rotten I felt after my sister called to announce the news that Mom had died. I'd been useless as a son, visiting Mom only sporadically all throughout my adult life and not having seen her for the twelve years before her death. I would call her every week or so, and I made sure that wives or secretaries sent flowers and gifts on all the appropriate dates, but even I know that kind of thing doesn't count for much.

I came home all set to launch myself into another bout of self-loathing, but then I cried. Not faking it, either—authentic weeping. I wanted to turn to the other mourners, point all my fingers at my face, and say, "Look it, look it! Real tears."

The tears I shed at my mother's funeral made me feel as virtuous as a boy.

·   ·   ·

I stayed in a motel while I was home, because I couldn't bear sleeping at my family's house. Sis and her husband had moved in there a year before, when it became clear that Mom couldn't keep up the place by herself, and then right before she died, they sold their other house. I was tempted to ask my brother-in-law how it feels to keep profiting from death, but I no longer wanted to torment him and already had decided to be on my best behavior during this visit home.

Well, maybe not my *best* behavior. I did get sort of drunk

(but not real drunk) one afternoon and tell bawdy stories within the earshot of children and then sing "I Did It My Way" at the top of my voice while pissing over the porch railing, with the family right there inside the house and the sun barely set on the still-lighted prairie. This was after the funeral; my gift of tears had made me so happy.

The grandnieces and grandnephews thought I was a gas and were fascinated that their relationship to me was one of blood. They had never seen me before, and when I first greeted them, I made a fool of myself by saying: Well, there's little so-and-so . . . and what's-her-name . . . and over there is who's-it . . .

But the names I was using were the names of my nieces and nephews, who had grown up, got married, and were the parents of these kids. All of which I knew, of course; it's just that I temporarily forgot that the children you haven't seen for twelve years will, through mathematics alone, no longer be children. I didn't even do a good job of connecting the right grandniece and grandnephew with the right original niece and nephew, because the one I'd called so-and-so really was what's-her-name's son, and the one I'd called what's-her-name was so-and-so's daughter—and so on. Confused the hell out of me. After that, I stuck to pronouns and pointed a lot.

Now that I'm fifty, I wish I had children. (And I would've, if I could've had them the way I had nephews and nieces: someone else taking care of them so I could visit every few years, every decade or so, and play the Good Time Charlie.) Sometimes I think that maybe, just maybe, one or two of the lovers I've lost track of over the years were impregnated by me and went ahead and had my babies without ever telling anyone I was the father.

I don't really believe any such thing has happened, but I fantasize about it. Felicity is the one who made me want to link up with the ever-branching river that connects everything that lives, leading from the single point of creation, diverging and looping into ten thousand tributaries—wheat and whales and all living things—as it heads for the end of life or eternity, whichever comes first. She always made it sound so wonderful that now I want my role in the whole drama to be a lasting part. I want to add my contribution to the river and send it downstream to the delta, wherever and whenever that might be; I don't want to end up a little offshoot that concludes with me.

I am, therefore, prepared to make this extraordinary offer: If you know yourself to be a child of mine and if you are over twenty-one and solvent, you may contact me through the publisher of this book, and I will consent to meet with you. Please note: I do not want you to come live with me or even stay the night, but I am curious to see how you turned out. How I did. Exactly what it is I'm sending downriver.

.   .   .

"Your wives afraid of funerals or something?"

That's my sister, beginning her nightly probe for information. Actually, I didn't mind her inquiries too much—something to break the monotony of the evening, the three of us there at the house (Brother-In-Law is reading the paper, and the various nieces and nephews and subnieces and subnephews are at their own houses) and it's not yet time for me to return to the motel for the night.

"I don't know what you mean," I said, knowing exactly what she meant.

"Your second wife didn't come to Dad's funeral and now—"

"You know very well I already was divorced when Dad died."

"Maybe. What's the story with this one, who no one around here has ever met, I might add."

"Maybe? What the hell do you mean, *maybe*?"

"I don't remember when you got your second divorce."

"Oh, Sis, come on. This is Sonny you're talking to. You got all those dates memorized. You're an information bank when it comes to divorces and marriages and affairs—"

"*Maybe.*" She was smiling; she liked it when I teased her. "So where's this Number Three? Why didn't she come with you?"

"Well, Sis, you got me."

"Huh?"

"You know."

"Another divorce, Sonny?" She tsked.

"Yep."

"When?"

"Okay, get ready to program all this. I married her when I was . . . let's see . . . thirty . . ."

"Thirty-nine. We didn't get an invitation."

"It was a civil ceremony. Quite civil, actually. Yes—thirty-nine, about six years after my second divorce. And we got divorced last year, meaning that the marriage had a five-year run."

"Better than the second one but still not matching the record you set the first time out."

"Oh, Sis. Don't make fun of my broken marriages."

"Speaking of your first wife . . ."

"Who's speaking of her?"

Ignoring me, Sis continued: ". . . I thought it was rather nice of her to come back home for Mom's funeral. I saw the way she was looking at you. I think there's still something there."

I laughed. "There's a lot there. About two-twenty, I'd say." My first wife had become fat, which perversely delighted me—like discovering that an investment you lost money on became even worse after you cut your losses and got out.

"Listen, Sonny, she's not a bad catch, you know . . ."

"If it's gross tonnage you're after."

". . . now that she's a widow and has considerable property, from what I hear. And a good profession . . ."

"*A dental hygienist?*"

". . . all of which is stuff you should be thinking about, especially if you handle money the same way you handle marriages. A widow with a nest egg could do you some good."

When I managed to stop laughing, I told my sister, "A nest egg that I laid, I might remind you."

"Nonsense. She got her money from the dentist."

"And if she hadn't soaked me for what little I had when I was thirty, she would never have been able to go to school to learn how to become a dental hygienist, and she would never have gotten a job in that guy's office, never would have married him, and never would've become his rich widow. So there. I did everything except give the guy his heart attack."

Sis was laughing in spite of herself, so I continued. "And don't you think I know how she seduced the guy in the first place? Don't forget he was married when my innocent ex-wife began working for him."

"Nothing went on between them until after his divorce."

"Are you shitting me? I know what happened, I just know it. He was cleaning her teeth after-hours, one of the benefits of the job, huh? They probably both had a little shot of laughing gas and then started giggling when he *accidentally* brushed his hands over her breasts. And then he says, 'My friends don't understand how I can spend all day looking in people's mouths.' And she says, 'Oh, Doctor, I think what you do is so exciting and demanding.' And he says, 'You can call me . . .' What was his name?"

"Ralph," my sister said, laughing again.

"Ralph. 'You can call me Ralph.' And then she lets the tip of her tongue brush against his fingers and pulls the dental floss seductively between her two front teeth . . ."

"Stop it, Sonny!"

". . . and then starts sucking on one of his probes."

My sister squealed, which caused her husband to lower his newspaper to find out what the hell was going on. "You got a dirty mind," Sis told me, wiping her eyes.

And then a strange thing happened. I nearly said, *I love you, Sis.* It almost popped out, just like that. I guess because I felt so good joking around with her, teasing her as I did when we were kids, being at peace with her—even if it was only for that one evening.

"So what happened between you and your third wife?"

"Back on that, huh?"

"Yeah—what was it?"

"I don't know. I think we just got bored."

Brother-In-Law abruptly raised the newspaper back in front

of his face. I guess he didn't realize boredom was grounds for divorce and, hearing that it was, he wanted to hide his face before it could reflect his thoughts.

·   ·   ·

I don't know why, exactly, my third marriage failed. It didn't dissolve (like my first one) or explode (like the second one), and my third wife and I seemed to feel the same about each other on the day we got divorced as we did on our wedding day. I don't know. Maybe we got divorced because the marriage was too much like a pleasant but extended bout of sobriety: Nothing happened. We would sit there in our nice big house (actually, her nice big house; I still was tapped out from my previous marriages), and I would read and she would read. When I got to the end of a chapter, I'd tell her something about my day at the office, and when she decided to take a break, she'd tell me something about her day at the office. She'd drink wine and eat cheese; I'd drink Gibsons and eat salted nuts. I'd occasionally get up to pee; she'd occasionally get up to pee. At some point, I'd go to bed and at some other, usually later, point she'd join me there. It wasn't as bleak as I've just made it sound, because we had good times together. She introduced me to skiing; I introduced her to bar crawling. (Although she didn't drink to excess, she didn't criticize me for doing so; when I became abusive, she'd make sure I had cab money and then simply leave and go home.) But after getting back from Vail or when returning from all those interesting neighborhood bars we discovered together, we'd eventually end up back in that house of hers—reading and snacking and drinking and peeing.

Or maybe we got divorced because the sex in our marriage never seemed to work. I dominated my first wife, with her following my directions explicitly ("Move your legs apart, hold that foot in the air, put your fingers in your mouth, close your left eye, breathe heavily, lift that, grab this . . .") until we got to where the line was drawn and she said, "No—not that." It worked the opposite way in my second marriage, with that wife in control of our sex life, suggesting activities that I thought were physically improbable and that are against the law in several Southern states. She brought to bed a variety of paraphernalia that I could never get the hang of; I had to make it clear to her that there were some things I simply would not do. But in both the first and second marriages, sex worked. The intellectual foundations might have been weak, but down there in the dank cellars there were some hot times. My third wife and I, however, were heavily into equality. We were reasonable about sex, talking things over and deciding how we might best go about fulfilling each other's. We were polite. It didn't work.

Or maybe we got divorced because no one ever warned me how dangerously unstructured the second half of life is. In the first half, you simply follow a series of programs that lead step-by-step to conclusions: school, courtship and marriage, a job and a climb up the corporate ladder. But when you're forty and have gotten as far as you're ever going to go, you suddenly realize that you're no longer working toward specific goals—graduation or a vice-presidency or a nice house or whatever. There you are with another twenty or so years of work left in you and maybe ten or fifteen years of life left after that, and there's no program to follow when, before, there *always* was a program to follow. So maybe I got divorced a third time because that gave me something specific to do, a goal to work toward and finally reach.

Shit. None of these explanations strikes me as being true. What my third divorce actually proves is that the reasons I gave for the first divorce (disillusionment) and the second one (craziness) are wrong. My marriages failed because I constructed them to fail. If I didn't get what I wanted, I left in anger; if I got what I wanted, I left in boredom. I'm great at courtship but lousy at marriage. Gravēda was right: Getting there is *more* than half the fun.

•   •   •

I decided to see Felicity the day before I was scheduled to return to New York, and it was an easy decision to make because I knew the value of a twelve-year absence. Doesn't matter how awful the departure was, give me twelve years' worth of absence and I can make any reunion work.

As tedious as I might be on a daily basis, twelve years' absence makes me a celebrity. I starred at my mother's funeral. ('Twas me they hadn't seen for more than a decade and 'twas me they stared at during the services, wanting to see if I was fatter or skinnier, looked a lot older or about the same, was drunk or sober.) In those evenings following the funeral, I was able to joke and laugh with my sister, even though she had been thoroughly disgusted with me the last time I saw her. My nieces and nephews (primary and secondary) considered me to be someone special—not some old fart they had to be nice to because of an obscure blood relationship. Twelve years is a lifetime; hell, you can kill someone and, depending on your social status and method of murder, twelve years will earn you freedom—that's how powerful such an amount of time is.

So it was with a great deal of confidence that I knocked on Felicity's door. I knew that she'd greet me with smiles, hugs, kisses, and exclamations.

"Honey Bear! I've been waiting for you to show up." Smiling, she kissed me on the cheek and neck. "Got everything set up in the backyard. G and T's are the only thing to drink on a day like this. I'll be out in a second."

(What? You thought maybe I was going to be wrong, that she was going to slam the door in my face? I keep telling you I'm an expert in these matters.)

"Sounds good to me," I said, "but very little if any T in my G—okay?"

She laughed. "You got it, Love Bonnet. I do adore a good drinking partner."

I left her in the kitchen and went to the backyard, where two lawn chairs flanked a small, round, white enamel table. Everything faced the setting sun. Felicity came out carrying a tray, on which were a bottle of Tanqueray gin, two bottles of Schweppes tonic water, a silver bucket full of clear, square ice cubes, a stoneware bowl of quartered limes, and two tall and heavy glasses. Felicity knew how to make an event out of drinking.

She put the tray on the table and said, "I'm sorry about your mother. She was a good woman. I don't know if anyone told you or not, but she and I got to know each other pretty well in the last few years. We went to church together."

"No—I didn't know that. Hmm. I'll be damned."

"So will I," Felicity said softly.

She made the drinks and then sat in the other chair. She toasted the sun, and I said it was clever of her to have this whole thing situated out there in the yard and facing the setting sun. She said she'd had it all arranged every afternoon since I'd arrived in town and was just waiting for me to show up. As she handed me a second drink, she asked: "You're shocked at how old I look, aren't you?"

"No! Hell, no. You look great."

"Oh, I love your lies, Snapdragon."

"I'm serious. I been waiting for these preliminaries to get over with, all the drinking and toasting, so I could get you in bed again."

She laughed. "Love them lies, loved 'em ever since you started giving 'em to me."

"I'm not lying. I swear to you, I am not lying."

I was lying. Felicity was shockingly old, her face heavily wrinkled and her mouth having that sunken look that often accompanies a new and not especially well-fitting set of false teeth. Her breasts sagged into a low-slung bosom that rested just above mid-trunk; her shoulders had become rounded and a bit humped; she'd shrunk, too—bent over and looking too much like a little old lady. Such a radical change that even I was impressed by what twelve years had done to her. Her laugh was something of a cackle, and when she kissed me at the door, the only thing that stirred within me was a memory of heavily perfumed aunts and the way they'd greet me at family picnics.

I'd had several drinks and was watching her light a cigarette, inhale deeply, and blow the smoke out of her mouth and nose simultaneously—and that seemed to flatter her, the way she smoked in such an unauntly manner. Felicity still could use a cigarette to make herself appear Bette Davisy.

We drank gin as the sun declined. She kept asking me if I thought of her as a little old lady, and I insisted I didn't. "When I was a young woman," she told me, "a man I was going around with once said that I was so vibrant and alive that it seemed I was getting ninety minutes of life out of every hour. I was proud of that back then. Never thought of the consequences. You know. Living life at time-and-a-half like that. Makes me almost a hundred now instead of sixty-five."

I held her hand across the little white table. "You don't look a day over ninety." She stuck out her tongue.

"So what've you been doing with yourself?" I asked.

"Same old stuff," she replied with a heavy sigh. "Orgies, drugs, rock and roll."

That tickled me and, because I was in mid-sip, made me choke. My distress caused Felicity to giggle and then she started coughing on cigarette smoke, and we ended up laughing and wheezing like a couple of silly asthmatics.

I told her she was a stitch; she said I was a tonic.

We sipped gin, watched sun. I asked her to tell me all her secrets and she said she would. "Which ones do you want to hear, Honey Bear?"

"Oh, I don't know. Start somewhere. There's so many."

"Well, my secret life during the last five or six years has been traveling. Saw friends in California and down in Louisiana."

"But never returned to New York, huh?"

She paused. "Uh, actually, *yes*. Been back there a couple times."

"You have! And never looked me up, never came over to see me?"

"That's not part of it, my showing up on *your* doorstep. It would've gone all bad—you know that."

I started to argue the point, but she held up her hand. Then we both became quiet and looked at the big old red sun, which had touched the horizon. It was like staring at a minute hand: If you're patient enough, you actually can detect movement.

"Write any more poetry?"

"Hmm?"

I wondered if she was going deaf, too. "I said, Have you had any poems published lately? You never let me read any of your poetry, you realize that?"

"You never asked. Besides, the best thing I ever came up with in my whole life is the story I gave you." She toasted me with her glass. "I don't write poetry—no more, I don't."

"Why?"

"Well, I don't know. I've been sick off and on for the last year or so. It's drained my energy. Being sick is what's made me look so old."

"Sick? What's wrong?"

"You don't want to hear the details. That's all we old women talk about—the details of our illnesses. I got friends in town now, you know. Most of them through the church. I guess advancing age has defanged me. They don't hide away their sons and husbands anymore."

"Their mistake, huh? Now. Tell me about your health."

"Why? You intend to examine me or something?"

"A quick pelvic might not be a bad idea."

She laughed. "You always did have a nasty turn of mind."

"Are you going to tell me or not?"

"I am not. You think I want you, of all people, to hear the details of my plumbing problems? Suffice it to say that being sick is what made me old. I was doing pretty good until they put me in the hospital."

"The hospital?"

"Yeah, yeah—just for tests. But by the time I got over it, everything had caught up with me—all those extra half hours, from the ninety minutes I'd been cramming into every hour, from all that time-and-a-half living I've done. It caught up with me. I woke up one morning, and I was *old*."

"Happens to the best of us."

"Ain't it the truth? Ain't it just the truth, Lover?"

When the sun was gone, Felicity lighted citronella candles to discourage bugs. She asked me if I wanted to know more secrets, such as the one about my father. I said I did.

"Your father and I got together for comfort and company. That's all. Or that was most of it. Just comfort and company. I promised to tell you everything, so I'll go into details if you want me to."

"Details aren't necessary."

She nodded. "You're a good boy."

And then we were drunk, and Felicity told me that what she had buried under the marker with all the little crosses on it was the handkerchief she'd used when I stopped by her house the night after I was graduated from high school. The one she used to clean my belly. As I lay on her couch.

"You remember, don't you?"

"Remember? Are you kidding? I could describe that handkerchief thread by delicate thread. What you did to me that night, it was the strangest thing I'd ever seen. With one hand you were patting my forehead and with the other you were—"

"Don't be nasty."

"But what you were doing *was* nasty. That's what made it so wonderful. And then afterward, using that handkerchief to wipe me off—*and then you put it in your pocket.* I couldn't believe it."

She was grinning. "I took down the crosses and markers because they were becoming too much of an obsession. But all those creatures are still buried out here, and I figure this ground still is hallowed. Too much distillate and prayers and poems and tears in this dirt for it not to be holy. And that handkerchief, with your little spermies on it, that's still buried in the corner over there."

I laughed.

"I buried them in complete seriousness," she insisted excitedly. "Didn't I ever tell you my theory on this? How perfectly appropriate the whole thing is? You know, women having that one egg cell a month, the biggest cell in the body, and it plumps up a thick red blood nest and sits there and waits and waits—stolid and calm and waiting. Just like a woman. Always waiting. Can't go out and get pregnant on its own but has to sit there and wait for someone to come calling."

"I get it, I get it."

"Ha! You get nothing. You don't get what happens when nothing happens—when no one comes visiting and the egg cell gets so upset, catches such a bad case of the blues, that it bleeds all down your leg."

"Oh, Felicity!"

"Yeah—and then *next month* you think it learns its lesson? It does not. Same damn thing. Gets its nest all ready, sits up there and waits, no one shows up, and then—pow!—the blues all over again. We never learn. A man'll always break your heart."

"Break your eggs."

"Don't be nasty."

"Me? Me nasty? What about—"

"And *men*? Ha! Perfect. All them little spermies, the smallest cells in the body, and they get all whipped up, crashing ahead, burning with hormonal insistence. They don't think about anyone but themselves. Millions and millions of selfish little bastards."

"You're sure this theory is grounded in scientific fact?"

"Millions of little half–basketball players and half-musicians and half-redheads and little half-girls and half-boys and little half-mathematicians who already need glasses. Each one of them so goddamn dumb that it'd bring tears to your eyes, the way they believe they have a chance at life. And what happens to them?"

"Oh, Felicity, I—"

"What happens to them is that we attack them like they're the goddamn plague or something. Catch them in rubber traps, kill 'em with chemicals, shoot 'em all over Naugahyde seatcovers. I know the kinds of things you guys do. Wipe yourself off with napkins from the local drive-in and then throw those little spermies, screaming, out the window of a speeding car! I know, I know. Shoot them into places where they got no business being, up and down both ends of the alimentary canal. Flushing them! Ninety-three percent of all spermies in the United States are flushed down toilets. Sewer systems alive with sperm! Female sewer workers have to wear plastic panties so they don't get preggers on the job. Did you know that in New York City sewers the spermies grow to the size of carp and they're all white 'cause they don't ever get to see the sun?"

"Stop, stop!"

And finally she had to stop, because our laughter had become debilitating, making us wipe our eyes with the backs of our hands as we again said those damn, damn, damns.

"And that's why I buried your little contribution out here in the yard."

"I still don't understand, but I'm not sure I want to."

"Because, Honey. Because I wanted at least one group of spermies to get the proper and respectful treatment the little bastards deserve. God knows most of them go down fighting, wiggling and swimming, with nary a kind word. It's well documented that the last words most spermies hear come from some whining broad: 'You didn't get any *on* me, did you?' "

"If you make me start laughing again, I swear I'll have a heart attack."

"So I gave yours a proper service. Saluted 'em—offered a little *atta boy* nod of my head. Who knows the geniuses, the cripples, the artists, the short men, the women with big feet, the boys with spaniel puppy brown eyes—who knows what I buried out there?"

"Yeah." I searched in the silver bucket, but the ice was gone. "Hmm."

Felicity began gathering up all the stuff. I blew out the candles and took the tray from her. On the way into the house, I said, "You may have ruined forever certain aspects of sex for me."

"What?"

"Well, some sweet young thing'll be performing an act of oral love and I'll start thinking about everything you've said and it'll make me laugh and she'll ask, 'What's wrong?' and—"

"No," Felicity interrupted, "she'll ask, 'Agghhaht's rhongg?' "

I was laughing again. "Yeah, and I'll say, 'Don't *chew* the little buggers, for God's sake!' And that'll be the last I ever see of her."

"Good."

When we got to the steps, Felicity stumbled back against me and spoke conspiratorially, in a whisper: "If you hold it real tight in your hand, you can feel them wiggling against your fingers—like teeny-tiny tadpoles."

"Oh, Felicity."

·   ·   ·

We lurched around in the kitchen making dinner, spilling things, acting silly. I don't even remember what we ate, but I think it was something out of a can. Felicity is a lousy cook.

But she makes great coffee, the kind of coffee I like: bitter, bitter black, so the aftertaste doesn't leave your mouth from one sip to the next. She brought the coffee into the living room, where we sat quietly—both of us tired and slowly approaching sobriety.

"Ah, this is the life," I declared, slapping my stomach. "I wonder what the poor people are doing tonight?"

"You happy?"

"Yes."

The room's only light came from two candles, which were kind to her. She sat next to me on the couch. "That's all it takes to make you happy, huh? Food and booze and relaxation?"

I didn't want to tell her how I'd talked away all my dreams, that I discovered too late you should keep dreams to yourself so they can energize you. I've spent too much time in bars, talking about dreams with cronies, and talk is powerful therapy, able to defuse fears and make the mysteries of life common and easy to handle—all of which is great if you're dealing with something you want to get rid of. But talk also humbles things that should remain sacred. (Will efforts to understand the Holocaust make it seem less profoundly evil?) I talked the life out of my dreams, and talked about my failures until they lost their sting, too. I talked until I became comfortable with everything in my life. The advantage to all this was that my slime became so weak and uninteresting (because I talked about it so much) that I was easily able to lock it away for good. The lasting disadvantage to all my talk is that now when I dream of glory, I dream in the past tense.

"Well?" she asked. "No ambitions?"

"Nope," I answered quickly. "And I happen to think that the death of ambition is a wonderful development. I feel as if some lifelong enemy of mine has died. The enemy might have been good for me, forcing me to do things right at the limit of my abilities, but all that gets tiring and when he finally died, I could relax." Lies come easily to me.

"Sad," Felicity said.

"I don't think so. Everything about getting older has been great. Sex, for example, isn't the irritant it used to be. I can rise to the occasion but, for me, it's no longer much of an occasion. All the pressure's off. Life is easy now."

"It's not going to stay that way."

"No?"

"No. When you reach a certain age, you get a new enemy and a new set of pressures begins."

"What?"

"Mortality. Dying loses all its theoretical properties."

"I suppose. And then you start having regrets?"

"That's part of it."

"What're yours?" I asked.

"Oh, I don't know. A lot of them. I always wanted to be around at the turn of the century, to see the passing of a millennium, but prospects look dim right now. Hell, I used to think my savings and the little bit I got coming in from some old investments would last me until 2000, but now I don't know. I'd hate to have to live on just that Navy pension. I'm not going to see the end of the century. I'd have to live to be ninety, and when you consider the time-and-a-half involved—well, I don't think I'll make it."

"Sure you will. You think anything interesting will happen in 2000?"

She shrugged. "You know all those preprinted forms that leave a space for the year? Like checks. They've got a nineteen printed on them with a space after it for you to put in the last two digits. All my life I've seen those: nineteen-dash-dash. I just wanted to be around when they change those nineteens to twenties. I think about that a lot. Do you suppose I'm getting senile?"

I shook my head. "Someone has to worry about that kind of stuff, about wild elephants who right at this moment are shitting on the plains of Africa."

She laughed softly. "You remember all the things I told you. I never thought you would."

"I remember."

"There's one secret you haven't asked me about today. Do you know what it is?"

I hoped she wouldn't mention the tattoo, because I wasn't ready to hear that particular secret.

"You didn't ask me about the ending of the Gravēda story," she said.

I was confused. "You already told me the ending. You can't give a different ending now, that wouldn't be cricket."

"Don't tell me what I can or can't do with my story."

"*My* story. You gave it to me."

"Okay, *your* story. Don't tell me what I can or can't do with your story. And besides, I'm not going to change the ending. I'm just going to add on to it. What I told you when I last saw you wasn't the whole ending—there's more."

"But you said, 'The end, the end, the end.' I remember *that*."

"Oh, shush. You should know there's always a little more left after you say, The End. You've had love affairs and marriages, haven't you? Saying *the end* doesn't mean the thing's finished yet. Now, do you want to hear the complete ending?"

"I do, I do."

She went into the kitchen and returned with a large cardboard box. The way she was carrying it and looking into it—so carefully and lovingly—made me think the box contained puppies or something equally, as regrettably, cute.

She put the box at my feet. I looked. There was a hammer and, next to it, something made out of glass.

"The Passionate One's crystal heart," Felicity told me.

I picked it up and faced one of the candles. Felicity apparently had taken a large, dark amber jar and had heated it, probably using a small propane torch. The jar had been formed and folded into something that was vaguely—and only vaguely—heartshaped. There was a hole in the top. The object appeared to be the result of some sort of craft project (intending to turn a jar into a lamp or perhaps an ashtray) gone berserk. Inside were folded sheets of paper.

I didn't want to make any smart-aleck comments, because I didn't know how serious she was about this.

"Well, go ahead," Felicity said. "Break it open so you can read the full ending."

"Okeydoke." I picked up the hammer, feeling as if a doddering aunt were insisting that I try on the atrocious shirt she'd just given me as a birthday present.

I hit the jar-heart timidly, but that barely cracked it. "Tough old heart," I said, closing my eyes and lifting the hammer to smack the glass as hard as I dared.

It shattered. Felicity screamed.

Thinking that a piece of glass had hit her in the face, I dropped the hammer into the box and grabbed her arm. "*Felicity!* Are you okay? What happened?"

"You broke my heart!" She was laughing. "You broke my heart!"

"You bitch. You damn near scared me to death. I thought a piece of glass—"

"You broke my heart!" she shouted, still laughing. "I been waiting years to pull that one."

"A cheap joke, Felicity—real cheap."

"You broke my heart," she said again, terribly delighted with herself.

I reached into the box and lifted out the pages, shaking them free of glass shards. Thirty or so pages of heavily curlicued calligraphy, just as you might expect Eller to write. I read it to myself while Felicity brought in more coffee.

Most of the story simply was a smoother version of the recitation Felicity performed twelve years before, when I was home for my father's funeral. The new stuff was on the last few pages.

It was appalling. The ending read like one of those religious tracts that are handed out on street corners. Lots of stuff about Ultimate Truths and Man's Destiny and the Nature of Man—all appropriately capitalized.

The gist of which was this: After The One died, his body dissolved into billions and multibillions of irreducible grains of faith, which spread throughout the sea. Eventually, those grains of faith—being evaporated up out of the ocean and then falling down again as rain—were distributed all over the world.

God used one of the grains to impregnate the Virgin Mary. The irreducibly pure grain of faith joined with her human egg cell to become one unit that split into two, each of which divided to make four, and those made eight, and those made sixteen—continuing until a child was created. "A child who is the concept of God, born to a virgin, fathered by faith," according to the new, improved ending.

The other grains of faith, I gathered, stayed in the water—available for consumption by men and women.

Then the story quickly slipped into some sort of manifest destiny for space exploration. There was stuff in there about the nature of man being so mean-spirited that he's forced to keep moving on, exploring, conquering—looking for glory or trying to escape persecution. Meanwhile, God supplies this faith (it's in the water!) that comforts man along the way.

As I read, I became increasingly embarrassed for Felicity. This new ending was unlike any other part of the story, and I knew she was going to ask me what I thought about it. I decided I wouldn't tell her the truth, that the new conclusion was leaden and that the only part of it I liked was the last three paragraphs:

"So Man's Destiny is to continue exploring outward and ever outward, seeking profit or glory or escape. Always comforted by Faith, Man in a thousand (or million or billion) years eventually will reach the edge of the expanding universe and, from there, will leap into the arms of God—Who will catch him and ask: 'How was the trip?' Because although God knows the answer, He loves a good story.

"And Man will reply: 'It had its moments. I'll be damned if it didn't have its moments.'

"And then God and Man will laugh like a couple of fools."

. . .

"What do you think?"

"I think it's great! Really. This new ending makes me feel better about the entire story. The way God and man meet—everything. Great, just great."

She stared at me a moment and then spoke in a flat and even voice: "You lying sack of shit." Felicity took the pages away from me.

"What! What?"

"I could tell by your face what your opinion of the ending was, the way you kept scrunching up your nose—like you were suffering indigestion or something."

I shrugged. "What do you want from me?"

"The truth. Thirty-one years of telling you that story and now I want the truth about it."

"Loved the story, hated the ending."

"You did, huh?"

"Do you want the truth or not? 'Cause the truth is that your new ending reads like some sort of quasi-religious manifesto."

"What do *you* think man's destiny is?"

"Jesus Christ, how am I supposed to know. I flunked philosophy one-o-one."

"Be serious."

"I am serious. I don't know. Isn't man's destiny supposed to be to recreate Eden?"

"I figured you'd say something like that. Be relaxed and well fed, huh? Don't you realize that man's mean nature is all part of the plan? Our nature is the stick that prods us out of our comfortable burrows and makes us keep exploring—'cause we're greedy or we're trying to escape other people's cruelty. Give me one example from history when exploration was undertaken for selfless, benevolent reasons."

"I flunked history, too."

"Is everything in the world a joke to you? Nothing you take seriously?"

"Sleep. Sleep I take seriously."

"*Ass*. I'm trying to explain the balanced nature of the whole arrangement. How evil launches us and faith comforts us along the way, and how that combination will take us to the edge of existence, where we really will meet God."

"And He'll ask how the trip was?"

"Yes! And by that time we'll be smart enough to give the right answer: 'It had its moments. I'll be damned if it didn't have its moments.' "

I was tired, and sobriety had greeted me with the usual salutations: a headache and nasty tastes in my mouth. "Well, Dear, my answer is that I'm going to my motel room. This evening has turned out precisely like the new ending turned out to be: tedious." I stood.

Felicity's manner abruptly changed. She grabbed my arm and pulled me down to the couch. "Not this time," she said, her voice mean. "You're not walking out on me this time."

"Don't tell me what I'm going to do or not going to do."

"No!" she hollered. "Tonight isn't going to turn out like this. I'm not going to let you ruin it."

"Come on, Felicity, give me a break."

"All my life I've been thinking about these things, that stuff I wrote in the ending there. You can't just dismiss it by saying it's tedious—and then walk out on me. I'm talking about important things."

"I never thought you'd get like this. You remind me of those old farmers who sat in the front pew in church when I was a kid. All their lives they drank and cursed and cheated and whored around, and then when they got old and could see the end in sight, they suddenly got religion."

"That's a terrible thing for you to say. You don't understand what I'm trying to tell you, Baby. How your entire life can be bought and paid for by a single, important accomplishment. Some creation that outweighs all the bad stuff in your life. That's what I've been trying to get across to you—for years and years, I've been trying. The trip isn't what's important. It's the arrival there. The *there*."

"I don't have any *there*. I don't have anything that pays for my life."

Her voice was suddenly enthusiastic. "But you *can* have. There's still time. If you believe in what—"

"Come off it, Felicity. The stuff you're talking about doesn't happen in real life."

"Yes it does!"

"Shit. What the hell did you ever create?"

She gave me a surprised look and then spoke softly. "You. I created you, molded you, influenced you to make you what you are right now."

I shrugged.

"Please don't shrug like that."

"Felicity."

"What?"

"Don't you realize that in all the years since I got out of college, you and I have seen each other on exactly four occasions—only four different times during those years. When I came home to get married, when I stayed with you that summer, after my dad's funeral, and now. *Four visits* in—what?—in almost thirty years. You can't claim creation, you can't claim a profound influence—not on the basis of what we did together while I was a kid plus four subsequent visits."

She rushed to her desk in the corner of the room, got something from one of the drawers, and came back to where I was standing. "See anything familiar here?" she asked.

I flipped through the stack of telephone bills she had handed me and didn't understand what she was getting at until I noticed—on several different bills—my home telephone numbers. I was confused. Felicity had never talked to me on the telephone.

"About once every other month or so," she said, "I call you. Usually in the evening but sometimes during the day on weekends. I don't say anything. I just listen to your voice and wait for you to hang up."

"I don't—"

"Just so I can hear you. Just so I can hear your voice. So I can listen to the way you answer—the way you say your name, the way you hesitate a moment like you've forgotten your name and then say it in such a no-nonsense manner—almost like a challenge. You never say hello; you just pause and then state your name. Jesus Christ, do you see how I've categorized and memorized all this? Sometimes making that call to you was the highpoint of my entire month. I had to stop myself from doing it too often 'cause I didn't want you to think someone was harassing you and . . . well . . . damn, ain't it pathetic? Ain't this just the most pathetic thing you've ever heard in your entire life? An old woman getting her thrills by calling long-distance just to hear a man's voice—a man she's been with only four different times in almost thirty years." She laughed. "I never thought I'd tell anyone this, certainly never thought I'd tell you. But, Honey Bear. When I talk about the influence we've had on each other, I know what I'm talking about."

Something way beneath my crust stirred; I stood and held Felicity as tightly as I could.

"I don't want to stay alone tonight—not tonight," she said softly.

"I'll sleep with you. May I sleep with you?"

She nodded.

"One thing I want to know, Felicity. Which one are you

going to be this time? The moaner, the screamer, or the lower-lip biter."

"Like always, Darlin'. I'll be whatever you want me to be."

•   •   •

Did we have sex that night? Is it sex when you roll around naked, giving outrageously silly pet names to body parts, groaning dramatically when toenails put lovers' gashes in lovers' legs and when elbows accidentally smack chins? Is it sex when you hold out a part of your body for display and make fun of it, as a child might make fun of a parent on whom that child still depends for life—and the other person laughs with you, and feels just as bad about it as you do? Were we engaging in sex when we mocked the argument she and I had twelve years before, with her sarcastically praising my size and my prowess, to which I always replied: "I believe you, I believe you"? If sex includes any of that, then we had it. But mostly what we had was a good time between old friends. For me, sex often has been slicker and hotter than it was that night, but never better—never funnier. When she took out her teeth, I thought I'd have kittens.

•   •   •

I awoke to the smell of breakfast (and to a variety of other, subtler but more lingering scents). As soon as I came into the kitchen and sat at the table, she put a plate in front of me. On it was an appetizing arrangement of bacon, three over-easy eggs, toast, a sprig of parsley, and an orange slice that had been twisted just like they do it at the Ritz.

Unfortunately, the eggs were runny, the bacon burnt, and the toast cold.

"Jesus, you're a lousy cook," I said lightheartedly.

"Screw you," she replied, her back to me as she worked at the stove, frying—and probably overcooking—potatoes.

"I love it when little old ladies cuss. Makes you seem so cute."

She dropped the skillet on the burner. I looked at her and she looked at me. "Ah-ha," she said, smiling. "You thought that last little comment of yours made me mad, didn't you? Not to worry, Sugar. No more complaints from me. I realize that you didn't earn my love by being a nice guy, so you sure as hell won't lose it by being a bastard. In fact, I admire you for being the meanest, toughest, most selfish son of a bitch who ever walked."

"Why thank you."

"You're my Alexander the Great and Napoleon and Wellington and U. S. Grant all rolled up into one. You probably have your private moments of regret, too, but next day, you're capable of being as bloody awful as ever. You do what you think you have to, and screw everybody else. No one touches you, huh, Babe?"

"Right you are. I seriously don't know whether to take all that as a compliment or not."

She sat across from me. "I seriously don't know whether I meant it as one or not."

When Felicity got up to pour more coffee, her robe parted and I saw the crying heart tattoo. Its colors seemed less brilliant than they had been in the past, in my memory of them. Perhaps graying skin had muted the contrast.

As she poured the coffee, I cleared my throat and said, "All right. Now I've got the courage to ask about one last secret."

Felicity looked to where I was staring. "Ah-ha. Did I really get this tattoo for you? Right?"

I nodded. "What's the answer?"

"You sure you want to know?"

"Yep."

"I'm not going to lie to you."

"I can take it. The meanest son of a bitch who ever lived, remember?"

"Lots of possibilities here. When I first said I got it for you, maybe I was just trying to make you feel good about yourself."

"I know."

"And then when I told you I *didn't* get it for you, maybe I said that 'cause we were having an argument and I wanted to hurt you."

"I know."

"But now I have no reason to tell you anything but the truth."

"I know, *I know.* So tell me. Wait! Let's get one thing clear. I want the literal truth. None of this crap that you got it years before you met me because you knew that *someday* you'd fall in love with a boy like me, and the tattoo was done in *anticipation* of your heart crying for me. No complicated shit like that, okay?"

"Okay. The answer will be straightforward. The tattoo was done for you or it was done for someone else—years before I met you. One or the other."

"Right. Which was it?"

"And an old woman who's worried about heaven and hell surely won't lie at this stage in the game."

"Yeah, yeah. Tell me before I wet my pants."

"What do you want the answer to be?"

"You know. Come on."

"All right. The crying heart tattoo on my left breast was put there for . . ."

She paused, her face showing nothing. My mind held even money on what the answer might be. I came within a hair of telling her not to say anything, of shouting: No—this is one secret I don't want to know! But I hesitated long enough for her to finish the sentence.

". . . you."

I started to make a joke out of it: I believe you, I believe you! But I didn't have the heart to do that. I took her hand and said, "I wish this could be an endless affair."

"Me, too."

She walked me to the car, and we stood there holding each other. "Now that I've finally finished my story, will you tell me one?" She kept her head on my shoulder as she spoke, because she didn't want me looking—at that close distance and in that harsh morning light—at her time-and-a-half face.

"Me? I'm not good at stories."

"You don't know any story I might like to hear?"

I hugged her more tightly. "Yeah, I guess I do."

"Good. You think about it and then start next time you visit. Recite a little more each time you come home, just like I did for you. Who knows, maybe it'll keep me going—help me finish out this millennium after all."

"Okay."

"What's it going to be about?" she asked, her breath and voice on my neck.

"My story? Oh, it's going to be about this young boy who meets this woman and . . . uh . . . she's twenty years his senior, and they have what turns out to be a lifelong love affair."

"How was it?"

"The love affair? It was wonderful."

"No, no, Darlin'. Listen more carefully. I'm asking you about this love affair. Now, *how was it?*"

As we stood there, I wondered what a disinterested observer would make of us: mother and son, older sister and younger brother, lover and lover? Or does it matter what disinterested observers make of us?

"It had its moments," I said. "I'll be damned if it didn't have its moments."

Neither of us laughed. We just continued holding tightly to each other, swaying to an old tune we both knew.

—THE END—

*T*here's always a little bit left after you say,
The End.

Because I'm a businessman and not a novelist, I am compelled to tie up loose ends. That last visit with Felicity went on for two more days. As we stood there by my rented car, she began talking about the river, and I asked if she would like to drive over and stay in a cabin on stilts, and she wanted to know if I could spare the time, and I said, Sure. We spent the weekend by the river. I promised I'd come home the following Christmas and tell her my story. But then in November of that year, I got a call from a college student (she used to work part-time in our office) who invited me to go on a skiing trip, Dutch treat, over the Christmas holidays, and I said, Sure—then never made it home again to see Felicity.

I began writing this book within days of her death so that I could feel something, so that I (in spite of all my sins, black and numerous enough to fill a tree) could do what few people ever do—pay homage to the felicity in my life.

Which leaves only this final secret to tell: At the edge of my left breast there now is a permanent, inch-high, brilliantly red heart. It lies on a spray of dark green leaves, and near the heart's point is a delicate crack, from which leak three dancing blue tears. You have to understand. My heart cries for her.